AN EVIL EMPIRE
BEYOND THE MIND

The Machine spoke to the slaver in its own sonorous voice: "You will clone an army of Ruiz Aws, and go forth to rule the worlds. Who could stand before you?"

Ruiz Aw felt like a powerless insect, caught in some thick amber nightmare. The mindfire pulsed through him, hot and thick, frustrating his attempts to think.

The slaver Corean stopped before him, her splinter gun raised cautiously. "How sweet," she said in a voice that trembled with joy. She reached up and stroked his cheek with a cold metal gauntlet.

Ruiz felt a tiny cold sting as the tendril withdrew from his brain. Just before it broke free, he heard a voice speak with the power of a god. "Slay," it said, and the order boomed along his nerves and muscles.

He launched himself, moving in a red merciless dream. . . .

THE ORPHEUS MACHINE

RAY ALDRIDGE

BANTAM BOOKS
NEW YORK • TORONTO • LONDON • SYDNEY • AUCKLAND

THE ORPHEUS MACHINE
A BANTAM SPECTRA BOOK / SEPTEMBER 1992

ISBN 0-553-29119-X

Published simultaneously in the United States and Canada

Bantam Books are published by Bantam Books, a division of Bantam Doubleday Dell Publishing Group, Inc. Its trademark, consisting of the words "Bantam Books" and the portrayal of a rooster, is Registered in U.S. Patent and Trademark Office and in other countries. Marca Registrada. Bantam Books, 666 Fifth Avenue, New York, New York 10103.

PRINTED IN THE UNITED STATES OF AMERICA

RAD   0 9 8 7 6 5 4 3 2 1

He slew the sweet singer
That our souls might continue to make
Their imperfect music.

—Inscription on a memorial plaque
in Deepheart of SeaStack, on Sook.

THE ORPHEUS MACHINE

CHAPTER 1

B Y the sixth day of the voyage, Ruiz Aw had become friendly with the second mate of the *Loracca*, the ancient barge that had carried him away from his enemies in SeaStack. Gunderd was a short wiry man with bad teeth. He complained frequently and imaginatively about the decrepitude of the *Loracca*, the incompetence of her crew, the lucklessness of her captain: "Four ships sunk under him already. He's a young man yet. Makes me constantly uneasy."

Gunderd affected a costume of gaudy rags and a clanking assortment of gold chains. When Ruiz asked him if he feared falling overboard with so much ballast around his neck, Gunderd replied cheerfully that he couldn't swim anyway. "Best to get it over with quick," he explained. "It's not the dying I fear, so much . . . it's the long slow falling away from the light. Into the cold dark."

"I see," said Ruiz Aw politely, though he found Gunderd's attitude eccentric.

Gunderd gave him a green grin. "Not everyone is such a

philosopher, I admit. You yourself I perceive to be an optimistic flounderer. Am I right?"

Ruiz nodded, amused. They stood together at the rail of the topmost deck of the *Loracca,* just abaft the wheelhouse. They looked out over a blue-black sea, glassy calm. The sky was the color of tarnished brass, clear but for a line of dark clouds to the north. The closest land was far below the southern horizon; the captain had plotted his course to take them well outside a bank of off-lying reefs.

Inside the wheelhouse, the captain hunched over his navigation module and loudly cursed the fate that had laden his vessel with almost two thousand dedicants of the Immolator Mystery, for delivery to the cannibal Blades of Namp. Gunderd apparently regarded the captain as a figure of fun; he winked and flapped his lips in silent mockery of the captain's invective.

A click and whine announced the production of a weather chart from one of the *Loracca*'s predictive synthesizers—and abruptly the captain fell silent.

The Immolators swarmed the broad deck below, reading from sacred tracts, singing discordant songs, beating each other with small ceremonial flails—all of them frantic with suicidal religious mania. Gunderd watched them and made his tiny black eyes wide with melodramatic astonishment. "Though you claim optimism, still you wear the robe of Immolation—surely a more serious impediment to survival than my chains, not so?"

Ruiz smiled, but made no response. Gunderd liked to tease him about his disguise, but his speculations as to Ruiz's real identity and purposes seemed unmalicious.

From long careful habit, Ruiz refused to gratify Gunderd's curiosity.

Ruiz had become acquainted with the second mate at a nightly kanterip game that met in whatever nook of the vessel the captain seemed unlikely to inspect that evening. He and Gunderd were the only players who won consistently—though Gunderd won a good deal more than Ruiz, who cheated just enough to stay a little ahead. One night, a drunken stoker had taken offense at Gunderd's more blatant manipulation of the cards and had attempted to gut the second mate with a cargo hook. Ruiz had tapped the stoker's skull with a handy piece of dunnage.

Thereafter Gunderd took Ruiz under his wing, finding slightly better accommodations for Ruiz and his group of refugees, providing them an extra water ration, and occasionally bringing them food from the crew's mess—food which, though just as plain as the passengers' diet, was pleasantly free of insect life.

Gunderd accepted Ruiz's taciturnity without visible resentment. "Ah . . . you're full of secrets. I look at you and rejoice in my own simplicity." Again his little black eyes glittered.

Ruiz clapped him on the shoulder. "Everyone has secrets—even you, paragon of simplicity though you may be." He turned away and went to the ladder.

Gunderd laughed. "Perhaps, perhaps. So, do you return to your odd crew? I must say, they seem even less like Immolators than you do . . . though the woman has a certain darkness about her. A beauty, no doubt about *that*, but fey. You should be cautious."

The cheer seemed to go out of the bright day. "As you say," said Ruiz, and went below.

He made his way through the thronging Immolators, shaking off those who attempted to drag him into their rituals. Most of them accepted his refusal without annoyance, except for one large red-faced man with a nail-studded flail, whose frothing devotion forced Ruiz to dodge away nimbly.

Eventually he reached his quarters, which consisted of a livestock stall on the second deck. An organic reek attested to the identity of former passengers, but the walls of the stall gave some privacy, and a usually reliable breeze blew through the crevices.

Inside, his fellow refugees waited. Molnekh sat atop their baggage in a vigilant pose, holding a steel club ready. The cadaverously thin conjuror had adapted to the rigors of voyaging better than the other Pharaohans; he looked no closer to death than he usually did.

Molnekh laid down the club, which he had acquired

from an unwary Immolator. "What news, Ruiz Aw?" he asked brightly.

"Yes, what news?" rumbled Dolmaero, the stout Pharaohan Guildmaster. His broad face was pale and sweaty; he still suffered from seasickness and had lost weight since their departure from SeaStack. "Do we approach our destination? I almost think the cannibals would be better than this terrible instability." He rose with some difficulty and rubbed at his back.

"Not yet," said Ruiz. "Don't be so anxious to meet the cannibals." He worried about Dolmaero, whose health seemed precarious. Over the weeks they had spent together since their escape from Corean the slaver, he had grown quite fond of the Guildmaster.

The third Pharaohan sat in a dark corner and said nothing. Ruiz smiled at Nisa tentatively, but her expression was distant.

Ruiz turned away. The change in Nisa tormented him. Not long before, they had been lovers, and she had given him the sweetest moments in his long life. Now they seemed to be two unhappy strangers, thrown together by ruinous mischance.

In SeaStack, Nisa and the others had been recaptured by Corean. Ruiz had been unable to prevent this, but Nisa apparently believed that he was in some way responsible for what had happened to her. Since he had rescued the Pharaohans from a slaver's dungeon, Nisa had asked him nothing about the events in SeaStack, and he had been afraid to attempt an explanation, for fear she would refuse to listen. Since they had embarked on the *Loracca*, she spoke only when necessary. She left her corner only rarely and her beauty had grown even more haggard. It cut at his heart to see her so, which was the reason he wandered the barge, looking for card games and other distractions.

Ruiz lay down on a straw pallet in the corner farthest from Nisa's and used a packsack for his pillow. The spicy resinous scent of its contents overcame the barnyard smell of the stall, for which Ruiz was grateful. Before departing SeaStack, Ruiz had arranged a two-level disguise. On the surface, they were four Immolators, driven by religious lunacy to donate their temporal bodies to the Blades of Namp. However, when they arrived on the burning beaches of Namp, Ruiz was prepared to assume a new identity, that of courier from one of the pirate Lords of SeaStack, who sold the Blades their sacramental drug.

Since the rites of the Blades involved getting high and roasting people on spits, Ruiz wasn't entirely eager to arrive at their destination. Still, that arrival would get them that much closer to the moment when they could leave this brutal world, forever.

He closed his eyes and hoped for a few hours of undisturbed rest.

NISA FELT NO urge to sleep. Since boarding the barge, she had slept poorly, despite her deepening exhaustion. Nothing in her previous life on the desert world of Pharaoh had prepared her for this hideous wasteland of water. It was so *unnatural.* The ocean struck her as some sort of vast malevolent being, its greasy skin forever heaving and twitching, as though it would shrug them off if it could.

The accommodations were far from ideal. Once she had been a princess, the favored daughter of the king. Now she slept on the floor of a stable reeking of manure and vomit.

On the few occasions she had fallen into an uneasy slumber, she had dreamed unpleasant dreams. The slaver Corean, the slayer Remint, the pirate Yubere—all these dire faces circulated through her nightmares in a slow ominous pavane.

She felt abandoned and alone. Ruiz Aw, whom she had once loved and trusted with her life, had permitted terrible things to happen to her. And now he ignored her, except for an occasional knowing smile. He seemed full of a brittle insincere courtesy.

Presently he would allow some new torment, and she didn't think she could stand it.

RUIZ WOKE WITH a sense of wrongness. The stall was dark, and the motion of the barge had worsened.

He sat up and rubbed at his eyes. The wind's sound had risen to an evil shriek; clearly the weather had deteriorated badly during his nap.

"What's wrong?" asked Dolmaero, who huddled against the hull, eyes wide. "What's happening now?"

"It's just some wind," Ruiz said, getting up. A sudden lurch threw him toward Nisa's corner. He caught his balance easily, but not before she raised her arms in a defensive gesture, her face abruptly fearful.

He wanted to kneel down beside her and try to convince her that he was the same Ruiz Aw she had trusted before. But she turned her head away and looked at the bulkhead with ostentatious fixity.

Despair nibbled at him, for reasons he could not quite understand. After all, this disengagement—though painful at the moment—would in the end be the best thing for her. What had he expected, if they survived and managed to escape from this terrible world? Had he really been naive enough to believe that Nisa, a slave, a primitive from a low-tech client planet, would somehow adapt to the complicated life of the pangalac worlds? Would she have a realistic chance to be happy, with Ruiz Aw? Or he with her? Absurd, absurd.

He shook his head and turned away. "I'll go on deck and see what's happening," he said. "Meanwhile, there's probably nothing to worry about. We've been lucky with the weather, so far. . . ."

RUIZ MADE HIS way up through a mob of panicky Immolators. He reflected that human beings could be very strange. All these men and women claimed to be going eagerly to the abattoirs of the Blades; still, they feared drowning. It seemed to Ruiz that drowning was not an unattractive death, in comparison to most of the varieties of death to be found on Sook.

On the top deck the motion was very bad, and Ruiz clung tightly to the rail as he looked out over the dark gray waters. The wind had veered and was blowing strongly off the land; his lips were already gritty with dust from the deserts of Namp. Twilight was approaching, and he found it difficult to judge the height of the waves, but the wind was beginning to blow the foam into long white streaks.

The *Loracca* was making heavy going of it, taking the swell on her high quarter, twisting in the troughs, her hull groaning with the strain.

Ruiz frowned and wiped at his eyes. The *Loracca* plunged along, spray drifting up from each shuddering impact with the sea. He wondered how much strength remained in the old barge's bones. Presumably her owners had been desperate for a cargo, to have accepted the Immolator charter—not a promising thought. Her engines beat steadily, at the moment, but he worried about what would happen if she lost steerageway and lay at the mercy of the waves.

He began to feel a certain degree of pessimism. The sky had an unhealthy bruised look, and conditions had worsened noticeably since his arrival on deck.

A familiar anger began to grow in him; once again Ruiz Aw found himself at the mercy of events beyond his control.

He could see Gunderd in the brightly lit wheelhouse— but the second mate seemed very busy, moving between the course computer and the chart readouts, his usually cheerful face drawn with fatigue.

Ruiz considered going forward; perhaps Gunderd would have encouraging news. However, the captain had posted two armed deckhands by the wheelhouse door, apparently taking precautions against interference by hysterical Immolators. One of them saw Ruiz watching, and made a shooing gesture with his nerve lash.

Ruiz hunched down into his now-damp Immolator robe and went below, where he made reassuring noises at the others and tried not to think of what might happen if the storm continued to worsen.

THE BARGE'S MOTION grew increasingly violent as the night wore on. Dolmaero again became sick, but was considerate enough to crawl outside before attempting to empty his already dry stomach.

Ruiz asked Molnekh to go with him. "Don't let him hang over the rail; we'll lose him for sure."

Molnekh nodded cheerfully; of all the Pharaohans, he seemed the most adaptable.

The sound of retching diminished, washed away by the shriek of the wind.

Ruiz realized, with both anxiety and a small degree of hopeful anticipation, that he and Nisa were alone together. Perhaps now might be a good time to try to find out what was wrong—why she was so distant.

"How do you feel?" he asked.

"Not good." Her voice was flat; she did not look up.

She seemed uninterested in conversation, but Ruiz gathered his determination. They might all sink to the bottom of the sea tonight; this could be his last chance to try to set things right. He moved a little closer to her, so that he wouldn't have to shout over the wind, and settled down with his back braced against the bulkhead. "You've never told me what happened to you in SeaStack," he said.

"You never asked," she said.

He was heartened by the small anger he heard in her voice. Anger seemed far better than indifference. "May I ask now?"

She looked at him, eyes wary. "All right. What do you want to know?"

"What happened after you were taken from the pen?"

She drew a deep breath. "The slayer Remint . . . you know of him?"

"Oh yes," he said, suppressing a shudder. "I know of him—but he's dead, I think."

"Really?" She almost smiled. "I wouldn't have thought anything could kill him. . . . Anyway, after he took us from the pen, he chained us and delivered us to Corean." She fidgeted, her hands knotting together in her lap. "She put me in a machine and asked me questions. Somehow, I couldn't refuse to answer; it was as if my tongue belonged to her. I had to tell her everything."

Ruiz identified the emotion she felt: It was guilt. "Oh

no, Nisa—you did nothing wrong. It's very difficult to lie to a brainpeeler—it takes a lot of practice. Special training."

"Oh? Can you do it?"

"I have . . . in the past. What happened then?"

She shrugged. "Very little. Remint put us back on his boat and took us to another place. We waited there until you came for us."

"Were you badly treated?"

"I was alone in the cell. There was nothing in the cell but a bed and a toilet." Her beautiful mouth trembled. "I was alone."

"I'm sorry," Ruiz said. "I came as soon as I could."

"Did you?" Her voice was full of ugly suspicion again.

"Yes, of course. What do you mean?"

She didn't answer for a time. Finally she turned away and said, almost casually, "Remint told us that you had sold us . . . and then tried to buy your safety by telling Corean where we were."

"Oh, no. No."

"Did he lie?"

"Yes." Ruiz shook his head wearily; small wonder she seemed distrustful and cold. "I had nothing to do with your capture; it was just bad luck."

"Really?" Her voice had a sudden lightness.

"Really. If I'd betrayed you to Corean, why would I have returned for you?"

"I couldn't understand that," she said. "But I've seen so many things I couldn't understand, since I left Pharaoh."

He smiled. After a moment she smiled, too, and though it was a small uneasy smile, he felt better than he had in many days. A particularly violent roll threw her against his shoulder. She didn't immediately pull away, and for a time he was able to enjoy the warmth where they touched.

"So," she said. "What *did* happen to you, after you left us?"

"It's a long story."

She glanced about the dark livestock stall. "I suppose I could spare a few minutes."

"Well, then . . ." He told her about asking help from Publius the monster maker, who had betrayed Ruiz at every opportunity, who had plotted to reign over SeaStack, who had been mortally wounded by Remint the slayer . . . Publius, who had died on the third day of the voyage.

The price of Publius's help had been an assault on the fortress of Alonzo Yubere, who controlled an enclave of Gencha minddivers.

Ruiz told her of returning to the pen where he had left her and the others—and finding them gone.

Her eyes grew a little softer.

"I learned that Remint had taken you. He set a trap for me at a fabularium," he said. "He caught me, too. Effortlessly. But for blind luck, I'd still be entertaining Corean."

"But you got away."

"Yes. I followed Remint back to Publius's laboratories, and ambushed him when he was wounded and off his guard. He almost killed me anyway . . . the man wasn't human. Any other time, he'd have bested me easily." Ruiz shivered. Remembering the slayer, his present situation seemed less threatening.

"And then?"

"I forced Publius to keep his bargain, which was to provide us this escape from SeaStack. Something was going on in the city, something that had the pirate Lords in a frenzy . . . and this barge was the only way out."

He fell silent, remembering the events of the past several weeks. He couldn't shake off a feeling that his life had passed beyond his control, running faster and faster down invisible rails.

"A lot happened, didn't it?" Nisa said, finally, and he could hear that she wasn't entirely convinced. But at least she was speaking to him, which seemed a vast improvement.

He might have attempted further conversation, but just then Molnekh and Dolmaero returned, soaking wet. Dolmaero's normally ruddy face was gray, and his lips had a bluish cast. He leaned heavily on Molnekh, and collapsed on his pallet, breathing with apparent difficulty.

Ruiz knelt beside him and loosened the lacings of his robe. Dolmaero looked up at him, eyes dull with misery. "I suppose I'll die soon, Ruiz Aw. Though at the moment, I'm more afraid of the possibility that I will continue to live."

Ruiz was very worried about the Guildmaster, but he made himself smile. "That's the common reaction to seasickness, but it's rarely a fatal condition."

"Oh, no," said Dolmaero faintly, and closed his eyes.

Ruiz covered the Guildmaster with bedding he had collected over the past few days from Immolators who had prematurely consummated their rites. "Rest for a while," he said. "You'll feel better for it."

Thereafter everyone was quiet. The *Loracca* rolled and plunged, and the wind rose to such a pitch that it almost drowned out the screams of the Immolators.

COREAN HEICLARO, LATE of the Blacktear Pens and once a rich slaver, hid in a dank steel room deep under the surface waters of SeaStack. She stared moodily into a broken piece of mirror, pushing back sweaty tendrils of dark hair. She barely recognized her expensive face; her beauty had suffered during the days she had spent hiding from the pirate Lords, who in their self-destructive hysteria had turned SeaStack into a battlefield.

Blood enriched the canals and lagoons, and the predatory margars were growing fat on the bodies that fell from the heights above.

At least she was alive. And she could take comfort in her fantasies—all of which involved Ruiz Aw and a versatile cast of sharp things, of red-hot things, of barbed things.

At the moment she was alone but for her Mocrassar bondwarrior. The huge insectoid stood silent and still in the farthest corner of her refuge, awaiting her instructions. The Moc was her greatest remaining asset, until such time as she could return safely to the Blacktear Pens. As long as it obeyed her, she was reasonably safe.

Her other asset, an ancient cyborged pirate named Marmo, was away. With any luck, he had posted a query for the Pharaohan slaves Ruiz Aw had stolen from her. The query would go out over the datastream to all the slave markets of Sook.

Sooner or later, Ruiz would sell them. Then she would find him. Then she could begin balancing their accounts.

Time drained away sluggishly, but finally Marmo returned.

"So?" she said impatiently.

He settled into the driest corner of the room, his chassis dull with a fine patina of brown corrosion. "I found a live datalink, though I was almost ambushed there by a gang of starving terrace farmers. . . . Anyway, your order is in the datastream, for good or ill." His voice was devoid of resentment, but Corean knew him well.

"It's for the good," she said firmly—though in the deepest part of her mind, doubts bred. "I'll find him eventually."

Marmo made his voice even colder. "And then what? What will you buy him with? How will you fetch him?"

She opened her mouth to speak an angry impotent curse, but then, as if from the damp musty air, an idea came to her.

"Good questions," she said, smiling brightly.

Marmo seemed to shrink, becoming a lump of worn metal and ancient flesh. "I will not like this, will I?" he asked, in another voice, almost a whisper.

JUST BEFORE MIDNIGHT, Ruiz woke from a light doze. Something had changed. After a moment's confusion, he realized that he could no longer feel the *Loracca*'s engines through the alloy deck of the stall.

The motion had altered into a slow long roll, reaching a dangerous degree of heel at the end of each roll.

The others were awake, though Dolmaero looked little better than he had before.

Molnekh ventured to speak. "I know nothing about boats, Ruiz, but should this be happening?"

"Probably not," said Ruiz. "But there's nothing we can do." He reflected that the *Loracca* carried only two lifeboats, just enough for the crew; perhaps he should look into the situation. He rose wearily, holding on to the stall's divider. "Wait here; I'll have another look. But be ready to come running, if it starts to look bad."

He made his way down to the main deck and clung to a companionway railing on the lee side. The barge was lying broadside to the waves, rolling her scuppers under as the swell passed beneath her. Each time green water roared over the bulwark, a number of Immolators were washed away. Their white robes were indistinguishable from the welter of foam that streaked the toppling faces of the waves.

Ruiz judged that the old barge was coming apart. Ominous grinding sounds came up through a nearby ventilator shaft, and the deck plating was starting to buckle. It seemed only a matter of time before she broke her back.

As if to confirm his judgment, he saw two crew members station themselves unobtrusively near the starboard boat's davits. Ruiz felt certain that they carried weapons beneath their foul-weather suits; apparently they were waiting for the rest of the crew to arrive before standing to the lifeboat's falls.

Ruiz fought his way back through the crowds of panicked Immolators; several times he was forced to kick away men and women who clutched at him, babbling prayers.

When he reached the stall, he saw with relief that the others were ready to go, even Dolmaero—though the Guildmaster seemed very unsteady.

"Take off your robes," Ruiz directed. Under the white robes they all wore brown shipsuits—not too different from the crew's haphazard uniform. Ruiz retrieved a small plastic splinter gun from a place of concealment—the only long-range weapon he had dared to smuggle past the barge's security detectors.

"We'll have to leave most of the dope," he said regretfully. But he swung one small satchel over his shoulder—perhaps it would be well to carry some form of trade goods.

Then he led the way down to the main deck. Molnekh and Nisa supported Dolmaero between them, and they only fell twice.

He made them wait in the shelter of a companionway

while he crept out into the storm. To his great relief, he saw that the lifeboat still hung from its davits. The two crew members waited, their white faces swiveling back and forth inside the hoods of their jackets, as though they could not understand what was delaying the rest of the crew.

Ruiz hefted the splinter gun. It contained a minimum charge; he would have to spend its power frugally.

For some reason he felt a dangerous reluctance to act. The two had done him no harm. Perhaps he'd even played a few friendly hands of kanterip with them. But they stood between him and survival; what real choice did he have?

Ruiz sighed. He steadied his wrist against a pipe. He waited for the pause that came at the end of a roll, and then he put a splinter through both unsuspecting heads.

They dropped unnoticed in the chaos that filled the deck. Ruiz sprang forward and reached the bodies before they could roll to the rail. The two had been armed only with nerve whips, which were useless to Ruiz, but he stripped off their foul-weather gear. He waited for the rail to lift again, and then boosted the bodies over into the sea.

Under the companionway, he thrust the smaller man's garments at Molnekh. "Put these on." He donned the other set, then explained his plan. "Molnekh and I will pretend to be guards; Dolmaero and Nisa will board the boat and look like early-arriving crew. When the next group shows up, we'll take them with us. I'm no sailor; we'll need their expertise."

"Will we live through this?" asked Nisa.

He felt oddly cheerful, as if he had returned to familiar, comfortable terrain. "Why not?"

CHAPTER 2

FIVE crew came running down the side deck only a
moment after Nisa and Dolmaero had gotten settled on the center seat of the lifeboat and wrapped a
disguising square of canvas around them. "What shall I
do?" whispered Molnekh.

"Nothing, until I tell you." Ruiz held the splinter gun
ready under his oilskins.

Of the five, Ruiz identified only the second mate
Gunderd, who steadied the gunwale of the boat while his
people boarded, then swung himself in. "Come on," he
shrieked. "She's going." Apparently he didn't recognize
Ruiz in the wild darkness.

Ruiz shrugged and climbed in, giving Molnekh a hand
up.

Gunderd immediately went to the aft fall and uncleated
the line; he gestured at Ruiz to take the forward fall.
"When I give the word, lower away smartly," he called.

One of the crew, a wide-eyed boy, protested. "What
about the captain and the rest of the port watch?"

"Too late for them, boy—they're on the wet side of the

number two collision bulkhead. Might be too late for us.
Jeric, you get the motor turning." Gunderd looked at Ruiz.
"Ready?"

Ruiz nodded, pulling his hood forward around his face
as if to block out the spray, which now blew hard enough to
hurt.

Gunderd waited until the barge had rolled her rail under, so that the boat was as far outboard as possible.
"Lower away!"

Ruiz let the fall run, and the lifeboat dropped into the
sea with a jarring crash. Gunderd and Ruiz jerked the
shackles loose and the boat churned away from the crushing steel wall of the barge's hull.

"Good job, Jeric," said Gunderd to the crewman at the
tiller, who was a tall rawboned man with a scarred face.
"Head her off; try to move with the crests—but watch out
for cross seas."

"Aye," said Jeric, without noticeable enthusiasm or
alarm.

Ruiz looked back. The *Loracca* was already receding
into the darkness, her lights dimming. He could no longer
hear the screams of the Immolators, and it struck him that
the screaming of the wind was a far cleaner sound, easier
on the ears.

The lifeboat's motion was very quick, but she rode the
waves buoyantly and little solid water came aboard. They
seemed for the moment to be as safe as they could hope to
be. He pulled his foul-weather gear tight and settled down
beside Molnekh.

GUNDERD DIDN'T DISCOVER their identities until dawn
painted the wave tops red.

The storm had moderated slightly by then, and the
waves were no longer as steep. Gunderd rose from his seat
and braced himself against the radio mast for a look
around the horizon. When his eyes passed over Ruiz Aw,
he jerked in astonishment. "You're not Drinsle," he
shouted, and drew a nerve lash from his jacket.

"No," admitted Ruiz. He produced the splinter gun, and then pushed back his hood. "Be calm," he said.

Gunderd's mouth dropped open. "Ruiz Aw? Is that you? Where are your Immolator robes?" Another thought struck him. "More to the point, where are Drinsle and Modoc?"

Ruiz shrugged, and glanced aside at the rumbling seas.

Gunderd sat down abruptly, the weight of his amazement apparently too heavy to support. Ruiz held the splinter gun steady. "I'll have to ask you to throw your lash overboard, Gunderd."

Gunderd did not immediately respond. "Ruiz Aw. How strange. Are you a pirate, then, and are these your fellow buccaneers?"

Ruiz gestured sharply with his gun. "Pitch the lash, Gunderd. Now."

"Yes, whatever you say, Ruiz." Gunderd threw the lash away as if it had grown too hot to hold.

Ruiz was distracted by the face of the seaman Jeric, who watched from his post at the tiller. Jeric's eyes were incandescent with sudden hatred; had one of the dead crewmen been his special friend? Ruiz decided to disarm *Loracca*'s survivors.

"Molnekh," he said, "search them carefully—and stay out of my line of fire. Keep their knives; all the other dangerous stuff goes overboard."

Molnekh moved nimbly aft, and in a moment his clever conjuror's fingers had picked them clean. Several lashes, a brass knuckleduster, and an antique iron cestus splashed into the sea. From Einduix the cook, Molnekh took a small flute of some silvery metal, decorated with delicate carvings. He held it up questioningly.

"Let me see," said Ruiz. Molnekh tossed it to him, and Ruiz examined it. It seemed harmless, unequipped with hidden weaponry. The carvings appeared to be of bosomy mermaids with lasciviously arch expressions. Ruiz tossed it back to the cook, who gave him a smile of gratitude.

Molnekh came back with a handful of clasp knives.

Ruiz considered how best to deal with the crew. If they were to survive, they would need each other, and besides, he'd have to sleep sometime. "I mean you no harm. I'm sorry about the others, but there was no time for discussion."

Gunderd rubbed his salt-sore eyes wearily. "Nor was there any need for you to kill them. The lifeboat is only half-full; I would have given you and your people places."

"I appreciate that, Gunderd—but I didn't know this would be your boat. The captain might have arrived first. I wasn't sure I could count on his generosity."

"I see your point," said Gunderd. "Well, what will you do with us?"

"Nothing dire. When we reach land, we'll go our separate ways."

"Oh. When we reach land." Gunderd looked sourly amused and said no more.

As the light grew, Ruiz examined the others. He didn't know the boy, and didn't remember Jeric; perhaps the seaman didn't play cards. The fourth oilskin-clad shape was a woman with heavy shoulders and a coarse jowly face, who at the moment seemed to have sunk into a blank-eyed trance. He didn't remember her name, but she had attended several of the kanterip games as a kibitzer. The last survivor was the ship's cook, a tiny shriveled man with burnt-orange skin and a long white pigtail. His name was Einduix; he spoke a language no one in the crew understood. If Einduix knew a word of the pangalac trade language, he found it convenient not to admit to the fact.

Einduix had been a frequent focus of Gunderd's complaints about the *Loracca*.

Ruiz sighed. The lifeboat held an unpromising company. On the other hand, their prospects were indisputably better than those of the other folk who had traveled on the *Loracca* and were now probably drifting down through lightless waters, transformed into fish food.

The wind was definitely moderating now; Ruiz no longer had to shout to be heard. It should soon be possible to steer a course back toward land. "Gunderd," he said. "Come sit with me and tell me what you plan now."

Gunderd shrugged and crawled forward to sit on the thwart beside Ruiz. "It would seem you're in command,

Ruiz." He nodded at the splinter gun. "What is your wish?"

Ruiz slipped the gun into his belt. "No, no. I was merely taking precautions against rash impulses. You're in charge. Now, where will we go?" Ruiz glanced out over the sea, which was still lumpy. A big swell was running, so that the boat rose and fell in great stomach-dropping swoops, but it no longer seemed dangerous. "Will we head directly back toward land?"

Gunderd laughed hoarsely. "Not a good idea, unless you truly are Immolators. We're well east of the Namp frontier. Without *Loracca* and her ruptors, we'd be nothing but groceries to the Blades."

"Where, then?"

"Well . . ." Gunderd rubbed his whiskery chin thoughtfully, "Difficulties beset us in all directions. For one thing, the *Loracca*'s owners were improvident beyond reason. The boat's fuel cell is old and weak; shortly it will cease to supply power."

"What about the radio?" asked the boy.

Gunderd gave him a pitying look. "This is Sook. Who could we call? . . . Where was I? Oh, yes. There's an emergency sailing rig, but I fear the boat will prove unhandy. To return to SeaStack against the prevailing winds and currents . . . impossible."

"And so?" Ruiz fought the return of a familiar pessimism.

"I see two possibilities. We could continue east, until we pass beyond the Namp domain. That course has perils in plenty. Margar hunters frequent these waters, and if they catch us they'll sell us to the first Namp galley they meet—though they might keep the women. Onshore gales blow often, and might beach us in Namp. And once beyond Namp, the shore is desolate and uninhabited for almost a thousand kilometers, except for Castle Delt." Gunderd made a curious gesture with his forefinger and thumb, which Ruiz took to be a charm against any bad luck that might be attracted by the mention of the notorious Castle, which trained mercenaries, assassins, and enforcers for SeedCorp.

Ruiz shook his head. "And if we survive all that?"

"Well, eventually you come to a market town at the mouth of the Soaam River, where transport south can be had."

"What about the other possibility?"

"We could sail northeast. With a bit of luck, we'll reach the Dayerak Archipelago in two days. You know anything about the islands?"

"Some," said Ruiz in a somber tone.

Gunderd nodded. "I see you do. So, the islands have their perils, too. And even if we manage to reach a freehold before pirates or cannibals or cultists take us, we might have to wait for a long time before safe transport could be arranged. Where, by the way, were you hoping to end up?"

"Off Sook," said Ruiz.

Gunderd raised his bushy eyebrows. "Oh? Well, good luck."

"Thank you," said Ruiz. "Which course do you recommend, then?"

"Neither beckons irresistibly. But I suppose the islands offer the best chance—though it's a slim one, I'm afraid."

"I agree," said Ruiz.

Gunderd gave Jeric the order. The lifeboat swung off and began to quarter the swell.

As the wind dropped, the boat started to roll violently in the leftover slop. Dolmaero was seasick again, clinging to the gunwale.

Ruiz settled himself beside Nisa, where he could keep an eye on the crew members in the back of the boat. Once again he found that her nearness brought him a warm uncomplicated pleasure. "How are you?" he asked.

"A little better," she answered. "And you?"

"I'm fine." And in fact he found himself in remarkably good spirits, considering the situation.

She nodded, unsmiling. He realized that she still hadn't forgiven him for his unwilling neglect in SeaStack. He resigned himself to patience; why did he expect her to instantly put aside all the unpleasant events of their time together? Corean's catchboat, the Blacktear Pens, the dungeons of SeaStack—these were hardly romantic locales. He had long before promised her that they would escape from this terrible world—and here they were, further than ever from that goal.

A silence ensued, during which the sun began to glimmer through thin spots in the overcast. "At least the weather's improving," she said.

"Yes."

She looked around the lifeboat and sniffed. "But I find the situation confusing. Sometimes we flit along in miraculous flying machines, with engines that make scarcely a sound. Now we wallow about in this crude and dangerous device. It seems inconsistent."

"It is," Ruiz said. "Inconsistency is the norm on most worlds. Pharaoh is different, because the habitable area is so small. But Sook is large and circumstances vary. Some people on Sook flake their knives from stone and wear animal skins. Others control technologies I've never heard of."

"It still seems strange," she said. "Can you tell me where we're going?"

"To some offshore islands." He might have preferred to leave it at that, but she pointedly looked away, as if she didn't expect further explanation. "The Dayeraks."

"And what is an 'island'?"

"A small area of dry land, surrounded by water."

"Does it toss about like a boat?" She spoke warily, as if she thought he found her ignorance amusing.

"Oh no. Most islands are firmly anchored to the seabed. Some are quite large, others no more than rocks that barely break the surface."

"These Dayeraks . . . what are they like? Your friend didn't seem too enthusiastic."

"No," he admitted. "Dangerous people live on some of the islands."

She sniffed. "Is there anywhere on this terrible world where there are no dangerous people?"

"Probably not," he said. "Probably not."

•   •   •

COREAN FLOATED IN Yubere's silver and gold bathtub, enjoying the steaming fragrant water . . . and her successful occupation of his stronghold. Yubere's troops had been almost pathetically eager to accept her leadership. She had simply presented herself at his security gate, as if she had every right to enter. They had quickly succumbed to her presence and her assurance.

The fact that Yubere had welcomed her into the fortress on her last visit, had freely allowed her the use of his brother Remint, had treated her as an important ally . . . all these things disposed Yubere's people to seize joyfully upon her advent, to regard her as their salvation. They had been particularly impressed by her Mocrassar bondwarrior —of a higher lineage than Yubere's Moc, a creature which Ruiz Aw had apparently killed in the course of assassinating Yubere. They seemed to see a hopeful omen in her Moc's superiority.

Yubere had evidently believed himself immortal and had made no attempt to select an heir. Indeed, he had gone to great pains to discourage any initiative among his henchmen.

"Paranoia is its own reward," she said, turning on her side. With her fingertip she traced the black opal butterflies set into the backrest of the tub.

"What?" asked Marmo, who for once watched her, instead of playing his endless processor games.

"Nothing," she said, and slid her hands up her torso, enjoying her own beautiful flesh. Did the old cyborg still hide a remnant of sensuality somewhere deep under the metal? She laughed and submerged herself up to her chin.

"You appear to be cheerful enough," said Marmo. "Why is that? The situation still seems dangerous to me."

"You worry too much, Marmo. Your rumor-mongering campaign has succeeded brilliantly. The pirates look everywhere for their great treasure—especially in each other's pockets. They settle old scores, they spy on each other, they bay after Ruiz Aw. No one suspects us, or at least no one suspects us more than they suspect everyone else."

"It can't last," said Marmo dourly.

She laughed again, and thereafter ignored him.

AT MIDMORNING GUNDERD distributed a meal from the boat's emergency stores: dried fish, starchy biscuits, fruit-flavored glucose tablets. "We won't dry or starve . . . for a while, anyway," he said. "The boat was stocked for twenty—and the watermaker works well enough."

They ate in silence—except for Dolmaero, who gave his share to Molnekh. The crew woman now seemed catatonic.

When Ruiz had finished, he decided to make a diplomatic gesture. "Gunderd, perhaps we should become better acquainted with each other. Will you introduce your people?"

Both groups looked at him as though he had succumbed to some incomprehensible insanity. But finally Gunderd smiled crookedly. "If you like, Ruiz. Well . . . this member of the vegetable kingdom is Marlena, our purser," he said, patting the woman on the arm. "She was making her last run before retirement—and she's been sure that we would meet with some disaster since the hour we sailed from SeaStack. Of course, she felt the same way on every voyage, but since this was to be her last trip, her various dreads seemed more pitiable than usual. Irony indeed."

Gunderd waved his hand at the boy. "And this is Svin, paragon among cabin boys, nephew of our late captain—and general layabout. He knows nothing of any importance whatever, and is quite proud of the fact."

Svin smiled uncertainly.

"Einduix the cook needs no introduction, except to say that we are fortunate to have no cooking facilities aboard —else our chances of survival would be considerably lessened."

Einduix, hearing his name, executed a jerky bow, pigtail bouncing.

"Finally, Jeric, able-bodied seaman and one of the few competent crew on the lost *Loracca*. Also your deadliest enemy, at the moment. His lover Modoc was one of those you gave to the sea."

From his post at the tiller, Jeric watched Ruiz with small hot eyes, teeth bared in a strange grimace.

Ruiz considered apologizing, then rejected the impulse. Jeric would receive such an apology with the contempt it deserved, and Ruiz would gain nothing useful.

"We're all pleased to meet you," said Ruiz brightly. "With such a crew, we're sure to survive." His words sounded somewhat hollow and rather foolish, even to himself, but he went on, attempting to inject sincerity into his voice. "So. I'll introduce my friends."

He gestured at Molnekh. "This is Molnekh, a master conjuror of Pharaoh, where the best magicians in all the worlds are bred. Later he'll perform some amazing sleights, to help us pass the time."

Molnekh bowed theatrically and showed his cadaverous grin.

"And this is Dolmaero, Guildmaster of Pharaoh, an able man in all respects: trustworthy, intelligent, courageous. Though he's presently indisposed, we can rely on him for sage advice."

Dolmaero raised himself from the rail and made a feeble gesture of greeting.

Ruiz touched Nisa's shoulder. "And this is Nisa, a princess of Pharaoh." He almost added, *and my beloved*—but he restrained himself. She nodded distantly and looked back out at the sea, as if she expected to find something of interest in that tossing gray waste.

Gunderd's bushy eyebrows twitched quizzically. "And yourself, Ruiz Aw? What is your specialty?"

Ruiz shrugged. "You know my name. I'm something of a generalist; I've tried several trades and achieved no great distinction in any of them."

Gunderd looked dubious, and the Pharaohans looked surprised. But at first no one seemed willing to contradict Ruiz's assessment of himself.

But then Nisa tossed her head and spoke. "Ruiz Aw is much too modest. And I've grown tired of listening to him tell lies, though he does it wonderfully well. He's a notable enforcer and slayer; he's killed more people than he can count, loved more women than he can remember, lived more years than he's willing to admit. Recently he slew the mightiest man in SeaStack. . . . Remint was this latest victim's name."

Mouths fell open and eyes grew wide. Gunderd seemed especially affected; he wore the expression of a man who, playing with what he had supposed to be a harmless garden snake, has just been told that it is actually a deadly viper. "I had no idea," he said slowly. "Are you sure? Remint has a potent reputation, to say the least."

Ruiz shifted uncomfortably, surprised by Nisa's testimonial. He would have preferred to maintain a lower profile. "She exaggerates a bit. Remint may be dead, but I didn't see his corpse. In any case, I've retired from my former profession."

Gunderd looked unconvinced. "Tell that to Modoc and Drinsle."

Ruiz found it difficult to defend his actions. The two crewmen he had killed were hardly soldiers; they could not be described as casualties of any legitimate war. True, they weren't notable humanitarians themselves; they'd been engaged in ferrying human beings to a dreadful fate at the hands of cannibals. Still, the Immolators *wanted* to be delivered to the abattoirs—and this *was* Sook.

No, his only justification came from one basic consideration. He would kill again with as little hesitation—if it allowed Nisa and Ruiz to live a little longer.

"I regret their deaths," said Ruiz. "Were you in my shoes, would you have done otherwise?"

"Perhaps not," said Gunderd after a moment.

No one spoke again for a long time. *Loracca*'s survivors seemed to be digesting Nisa's revelations with reluctance, but they all watched Ruiz with a greater degree of wariness —even Jeric. That might be for the best; perhaps they would think twice before attempting any treachery. Maybe Nisa's rash claims would turn out to be useful.

Jeric drove the boat northeast, across the diminishing swell.

•   •   •

BY MIDAFTERNOON, THE wind had fallen to a light breeze, barely enough to ruffle the great green backs of the leftover storm swell. The sun had broken through, and only a few wispy clouds marked the verdigris sky.

Ruiz sat in the bow, watching a seabird wheeling high above the mast. He remembered earlier, less complicated times: the dusty roads of Pharaoh, the Expiation at Bidderum, the paddock in the Blacktear Pens where he had nursed Nisa back to health and where they had become lovers, Corean's silk-upholstered apartment where he and Nisa had spent their longest time alone together . . . and best of all, the barge trip through beautiful wild country to SeaStack.

It occurred to him that he had never completely enjoyed those sweet lost days—at the time, he had been so full of schemes, so taut with violent anticipation, so wary of his enemies, that the best times had slid away from him, leaving only a sketchy residue of memory. Of course, he and Nisa were still alive because of these relentless preoccupations, so perhaps he had made a fair bargain. Still, he wondered briefly if it was the best possible bargain. He thought of that starry night on the barge, when he lay in Nisa's arms. He remembered feeling that if he were to die in that moment, he might never find a more suitable moment in which to depart his long strange life—that a measure of safety from future evils could be found in such a death.

Ruiz shook his head angrily. Such thoughts were a slow poison, a weakness that would steal away his future with Nisa. He must cling to his wariness, his treachery, his brutality—until a time came that those qualities no longer served them, until they could finally escape from Sook and return to some less dangerous world.

He looked at her as she slept, her head pillowed on her hands, her features obscured by a tangle of thick black hair. All he could see of her were her slender strong arms and the white vulnerable curve of her neck. He felt an odd constriction of his throat, a mixture of grief and tenderness so powerful that his vision swam with tears. He was astonished; he hadn't cried since his long-ago childhood.

He was distracted by a sudden change in the pitch of the boat's engine, which then rapidly lost speed and began to emit an unpleasant grinding sound.

"What is it?" he asked Gunderd, who had leaped to the nacelle and flipped up the latches.

Gunderd grunted noncommittally and ducked his head into the engine compartment.

The engine fell silent. From the compartment came a series of peevish clatters, and then Gunderd emerged, face blackened with grease. "Dead," he muttered. "Wasn't the fuel cell, after all."

"Now what?" asked Svin the cabin boy, suddenly looking even younger.

"Now we put up the sail and hope this wind holds."

Ruiz helped Gunderd retrieve the gear from the cuddy. They assembled the jointed spars and set the brown lateen sail. Gunderd sheeted it in and the boat moved off, though more sedately than before.

Ruiz looked over Gunderd's shoulder as he fiddled with the boat's minimal navigation module. "Just enough juice left to run this for a few hours," he said, adjusting the scale of a small electroluminescent screen. Gunderd's thin brown finger stabbed at a cluster of wavy lines at the upper right-hand corner of the chart. "Here, the edge of the Dayerak Shelf." His finger moved down. "Here, us." A tiny green dot marked their position, two hundred kilometers off the Namp coast.

Gunderd shut down the display. "We'll save the power until we get into the shoals—that's when our piloting must be accurate." He grinned. "There's not enough juice for the radio—but that's a small loss, since at the moment our only potential rescuers have pointy teeth and big appetites."

Ruiz smiled back. "Have you always been a philosopher?"

"Always. But back to the matter at hand . . . can you steer a course?"

"More or less."

"Good!" Gunderd patted Ruiz tentatively on the shoulder. "Will you stand a watch at the helm? Jeric and I have been alternating since *Loracca* foundered, and we're both tired. Svin is unreliable—we might wake to find ourselves sailing back to the Blades—and Marlena seems to be present in body only. Einduix . . . well, he is as he is. Whatever that is."

"I suppose so," said Ruiz. He was tired, too; he had been unwilling to test Jeric's restraint so early in their association. Still, he couldn't refuse to do his fair share; that would only inflame the resentments against him.

He shifted aft and took the tiller from Jeric, who relinquished it with a grimace of barely restrained violence. The seaman went forward, where he glared truculently at the Pharaohans before settling himself on the floorboards. Dolmaero, who was apparently recovering at last from his bout with seasickness, returned an expression of wary reserve. Molnekh grinned cheerfully and nodded a greeting.

Nisa, who had awakened during Gunderd's examination of the engine, looked bewildered . . . and then disdainful. She rose unsteadily and came aft to sit near Ruiz.

He couldn't help smiling.

But then his attention was caught by the glitter of Jeric's eyes within his hood, and by the ugly comprehension that came over Jeric's face as he looked from Ruiz to Nisa. A chill touched Ruiz, and he wondered how best to deal with the seaman. Sooner or later he must sleep, and what would happen then?

CHAPTER 3

Ruiz steered until dusk shadowed the waves. The wind had held steady from the west all day, and the boat had made surprisingly good progress, cutting a sizzling white furrow through the sea.

When Gunderd relieved him, he took Nisa's hand and led her forward. Dolmaero sat on a thwart, gazing out at the crimson and gold sunset. The Guildmaster seemed much recovered—perhaps the easier motion of the boat under sail had helped. Ruiz was relieved; he wouldn't want to lose Dolmaero's comforting presence.

"So," said Dolmaero, when they had settled themselves, "how are we doing?"

"Well enough," said Ruiz.

"In what way will our situation next deteriorate?" Dolmaero asked. "I don't mean to seem ungrateful, but I'd like to know what new torments await us." Ruiz saw that the Guildmaster had yet to recover his equilibrium. Ordinarily Dolmaero would never have spoken so bitterly.

"Actually, I hope for improvement soon," said Ruiz.

"At least we're alive, which is more than can be said for the rest of *Loracca*'s company."

"Yes," said Molnekh. "Let's be thankful for that."

Ruiz nodded. He was very tired; if he did not rest soon, his judgment would begin to deteriorate dangerously. "Listen," he said. "I need to sleep for a bit. You'll have to take turns watching the crew. Especially Jeric. The others may be harmless. Dolmaero, you take charge of setting the watches. When Gunderd needs me at the helm again, he'll tell you. You wake me; don't let him or one of the other crew near me."

He settled himself in the curve of the bows and shut his eyes. Almost instantly he slept.

WHEN HE WOKE, it was to a feeling of intense danger and a tumble of unidentifiable bodies, rolling over him in the darkness. He rose up, striking at the nearest—but at the last instant he diverted the blow so that his fist clanged uselessly into the lifeboat's alloy. He couldn't tell who his attacker was, or even if he was being attacked. Maybe he was being defended.

Before he could sort out the situation, something cracked against the back of his head and he fell bonelessly into the boat's bilge, his last emotion an unfocused astonishment that he had been so easily bested.

WHEN HE REGAINED consciousness, he was still astonished —though now the source of his amazement was that he was still alive. He still lay in the bilge, but his head rested in Nisa's lap. She looked down at him with a mixture of relief and apprehension.

Dolmaero leaned over him. "You're awake. Good. We wondered if we might lose you."

Ruiz struggled to raise his head, then looked aft. Gunderd steered; he made a jaunty gesture of greeting. The cabin boy Svin huddled beside the mate, his face white and strained. Einduix looked down at his flute; he wore a somewhat pensive expression.

Ruiz looked forward. Molnekh sat in the bows, grinning with his usual aplomb.

Jeric was nowhere to be seen. Nor was the catatonic purser.

"What's happened?" he croaked.

Dolmaero shrugged. "None of us is sure. But Gunderd has your little gun, and he took away our knives."

"The crew attacked us? Who was on watch?"

"I was," said Dolmaero. He looked down, clearly ashamed. "But I was looking up at the stars when it happened. Someone threw a canvas over me and knocked me down. By the time I got untangled and stood up, it was over."

"What was over?" Ruiz struggled to a sitting position and touched the back of his head gingerly. It was crusty with dried blood, but his probing fingers found nothing more alarming than split skin. His head ached horribly, so that he found thought difficult.

"The killing," said Gunderd. "Your crew fared better than mine, Ruiz. Yours are still alive, but two of mine are gone."

"Gone where?" asked Ruiz.

"Fed to the fishes," said Gunderd. "They were thoroughly dead. The purser's guts were lying in her lap. She probably never noticed, but I'd guess Jeric noticed when someone cut his throat. Neat job, too; whoever did it left him on the gunwale so he bled out overboard. Considerate."

Ruiz rubbed his pounding head, trying to massage some clarity back into his thoughts. "Did you see what happened?"

"No." In the cold dawn light, Gunderd seemed much older and more vulnerable, despite the splinter gun tucked into his waistband and his air of nonchalance. "I was asleep. But I can theorize, up to a point. I think Jeric lashed the helm when your man's attention wandered, and went forward to revenge himself on you. Apparently he was surprised by someone. I heard a scuffle—and a classic gurgle—as I was waking. And then you started to get up and I heard the sound of wood on skull. I made a light and went forward cautiously, to find you unconscious and Jeric dead."

"I see," said Ruiz. What had happened? "You found no other indications?"

"No . . . the cutter was very clean. No one had bloody hands, except for Jeric. His own, I suppose."

"Who hit me?"

Gunderd shrugged. "No one will admit to the deed. But whoever did the cutting, the whack was delivered by one of yours. Svin and Einduix were aft when you went down."

Ruiz looked at the others. Nisa wore an expression of frustrated concern. Dolmaero looked embarrassed . . . but Ruiz saw no trace of guilt. Molnekh seemed his usual cheerful self. "Did any of you see anything?" he asked.

No one answered.

"Svin?"

The cabin boy shook his head vigorously. Gunderd laughed. "As well to blame it on sea wights as to suspect Svin. Remember, the deed was performed with élan and skill."

"Einduix?"

The cook looked up from his seat in the waist, smiling without a trace of comprehension.

Gunderd snorted in disbelief. "Einduix. A remote possibility. He's a butcher, I'll grant you that, but an entirely incompetent one. That he could have made two such neat cuts . . . it seems a foolish speculation."

A silence ensued, during which it gradually came to Ruiz that Gunderd probably suspected Ruiz of somehow engineering the deaths of the two crew members. "Me? Don't be ridiculous," he snapped. "How do you suppose I managed to cut up your people . . . and then arranged to get my head broken?"

"I haven't figured that out—though perhaps one of your confederates assisted you into slumber. But no. Despite the dire reputation your woman gives you, I can't figure out why you'd bother with subterfuge. You had the gun."

Ruiz shook his head and winced. "True. A mystery."

Gunderd nodded. "As you say, a mystery. We'll talk later, when you've recovered your wits."

The morning passed in a dull misery. With stinging salt water, Nisa bathed away the blood that caked his head. He sipped cool water from the boat's recycler and nibbled on a nutrient bar. He slowly began to feel a bit better. He couldn't think of anything to say to anyone.

The wind held and the boat made good progress to the northeast and the Dayerak Archipelago. Gunderd steered with the casual intensity of the experienced helmsman, but by afternoon he began to show signs of fatigue. "Come," he said. "Take a turn, Ruiz Aw. I must get my rest before nightfall, I think."

Ruiz made his way aft and took the tiller. Gunderd moved warily away, his hand on the splinter gun. Ruiz could hardly blame him for being cautious, and smiled ruefully.

Gunderd settled himself on the far side of the helmsman's thwart. He watched Ruiz for a while, apparently to judge the quality of Ruiz's helmsmanship. Abruptly he tapped Svin on the shoulder and said, "Go forward with the others, boy. The slayer and I must talk of things which don't concern you."

Svin went slowly, as if reluctant to lose contact with the mate. Gunderd laughed and prodded him with his boot. "Hurry up! Remember, they may kill you, but they probably won't eat you."

Gunderd cast a speculative glance at Einduix. "Hmm . . ." he said. "I would swear the little snake doesn't know a word of pangalac, but why take a chance? . . . Go forward, Einduix." He made shooing gestures at the cook until Einduix got the idea and went.

"Now," said Gunderd in a low voice. "We must speak as frankly as our hearts permit us to. I don't believe you killed my people; but someone did. If it was one of yours . . . that person is a threat to you as well as me. Someone isn't telling all they know."

"So it seems," said Ruiz. He had been avoiding examining the implications of the past night's murders. His head still hurt; he felt weak and unready for any confrontation.

Gunderd looked away, across the sunlit sea. "I must tell you, Ruiz Aw . . . I think we have a monster among us. I can understand the killing of Jeric, who craved your blood. Whoever cut him was protecting you. But whoever killed Marlena—he was ridding himself of a minor annoyance. True, she stank, and she took up a little room, but she wasn't dangerous to anyone. A cold deed."

Ruiz nodded reluctant agreement.

"Let me tell you what I've thought. The cutter was fairly strong—strong enough at least to pick up Jeric and put him across the gunwale. Probably any of your people could have done it, even the woman. She looks strong for her size. And the fat one might easily have struck from beneath the canvas he claimed was thrown over him. So," said Gunderd, "let me ask you. What do you know about your people that might shed light on the matter?"

Ruiz took a deep breath. Almost against his will, a memory rose up in his mind's eye: the monster maker Publius dying. Raving. Telling Ruiz that one of the Pharaohans had been processed by the Gencha.

Should he tell Gunderd? In all likelihood, Publius had simply taken one last opportunity to hurt Ruiz.

His mind refused to work properly; he could not foresee the implications of revealing this suspicion to Gunderd. On the other hand, it was very possible that one of the Pharaohans was no longer his friend, since none of them would admit to striking the blow that had put him down. And none of them had contradicted Gunderd's version of the night's events.

Gunderd seemed as trustworthy as anyone he was likely to meet on Sook; he appeared to have no agenda beyond simple survival.

"All right," Ruiz said finally. "There's a small chance that one of my people—I don't know which one—has recently undergone deconstruction at the hands of the Sea-Stack Gencha."

Gunderd's eyebrows rose to the top of his forehead. "Really? And who is the primary?"

"Probably a slaver named Corean Heiclaro. Have you heard the name?"

Gunderd went slightly pale. "Does she own a big Moc and a famous face? Yes? Then I know her." He drew the splinter gun from his waistband and pointed it forward. "Duck, Svin," he barked.

It almost happened too fast for Ruiz to react. He slammed the tiller across just before Gunderd fired, catching the second mate in the ribs with enough force to catapult him overboard. The gun flew in a bright arc and plopped into the sea.

Ruiz sighed regretfully.

Gunderd's head popped up in the white wake. The mate was floundering ineffectively, apparently losing the struggle against the weight of his gold chains.

After an instant's hesitation, Ruiz came about and heaved to. "Toss him a line," he told Svin, and the cabin boy threw the mate a rescue buoy.

When Gunderd was back aboard, shivering and clutching his ribs, Ruiz let the sails draw, and the boat returned to her course.

Minutes passed in silence, except for the crunch and whisper of the boat, making her way over the waves.

Finally Gunderd raised his eyes and attempted a wry smile. "I begin to believe in your effectiveness, Ruiz Aw. It seems your woman doesn't exaggerate. But I was only acting sensibly. Kill them all and we're sure to get the Genched one. It was a sensible plan."

"Perhaps so," said Ruiz.

"Well, I see that considerations beyond naked pragmatism move you, Ruiz Aw. I should find this reassuring, shouldn't I? At any rate, thank you for fishing me out." He took a handful of clasp knives from his sodden pocket and offered them to Ruiz. "Here. I don't think they give me a significant advantage." His smile grew crooked. "I may as well try to curry favor while I can."

Ruiz took one of the knives and pocketed it. He returned one to Gunderd and pitched the others overboard.

Gunderd qurked up his eyebrows. "Well, then," he said. "Let's be allies. I promise to make no more precipitous decisions, if you'll try to do likewise."

"I'll try," said Ruiz, somewhat ambiguously.

Gunderd shot him a sharp glance, but then he smiled and pocketed the knife. "That's as fair as I could ask," he said. "Given the circumstances. I was attempting the direct solution to the problem."

"I understand that," said Ruiz. "But it may not be true, and I value these people."

"Ah," said Gunderd. He lowered his voice to a confidential whisper. "The value of the woman is obvious, even to me . . . though for a fact she seems not too friendly. A lover's quarrel?"

Ruiz scowled.

Gunderd held up his hands. "None of my business, of course. But after all, even if one of them is Genched, it's not the decay of the universe. I once had a good friend who was Genched."

It was Ruiz's turn to look surprised.

"Oh yes. It was an odd situation, no doubt of that. He was a soldier in the Triatic Wars, outbound for Jacquet's World. He was an assassin, aimed at the High Poet of Bist, and Genched for the part of a talented minstrel, so as to gain the confidence of the Poet. The war ended before he was given his final instructions, and then the lander crashed during his recall to Soufriere. They thought he was dead, so no one attempted to retrieve him and he lived out his life there on Soufriere's Midsea. A fine fellow—a voice like sea foam and moonlight. He was a better man than most men, because he acted as he believed he should act, and not as he wanted to."

Ruiz found this an odd story—he thought of Genching as an end to humanity, and of the Genched as organic machines, unalterable and dead. "Interesting," he said. "So you're from Soufriere?"

Gunderd nodded. "Yes. Can you believe it? I was a fisherboy on the warm Midsea; all I knew was nets and longlines and fishergirls. How I ever came to this terrible world . . . well, we all have our stories, don't we? But to return to Genching, do you know of Aluriant the Ambitious, who had himself Genched into a saint? The Gencha will take anyone's money."

"I suppose so. It occurs to me that even if one of mine is Genched, then it's very likely that they've never been in contact with their primary."

Gunderd's eyes brightened. "Really? Then we may have no great problem. The person will have to act as he supposes Corean would wish him to act. Were any of your people close enough to the slaver to have a good idea of what she would wish?"

"Possibly not," said Ruiz. "They were her slaves, kept in the Blacktear Pens with others of their culture."

"Better and better!" But then Gunderd looked perplexed. "Something doesn't fit here. If one of your people is Corean's creature, why did they protect you from Jeric?"

Ruiz shivered involuntarily. "I suppose it seems clear to him that Corean wants me alive, so that she can redress the wrongs I've committed against her."

"Makes sense," said Gunderd. "What, if I may ask, did you do to earn Corean's enmity?"

Ruiz answered distractedly. "I stole her slaves and her airboat, killed several of her people, ruined her business, stranded her in SeaStack . . . maybe got her killed, though that's probably too much to hope for. This and that."

Gunderd's eyes grew large. "Oh. Well, if she's in Sea-Stack, we won't have to worry about her coming after you any time soon. The city's in a terrible ferment." He still looked puzzled. "All right. Jeric died because he was about to steal Corean's fun. But why Marlena? She was harmless."

Ruiz didn't answer. He was thinking about that long-ago day in the pens, when Corean had come into the paddock and casually destroyed an incapacitated slave.

Suddenly he found himself believing Publius's dying words. One of the Pharaohans was no longer human.

A terrible pressure squeezed his heart. He looked forward at the three of them huddled in the bows. Molnekh seemed his usual bland cheerful self, which meant nothing. Dolmaero stared at his feet, a dour empty expression on his broad face. Nisa watched Ruiz with an unnatural intensity, her lips trembling between a frown and a smile.

Which one?

Ruiz turned back to Gunderd. "Say nothing that might

alert the creature to our suspicions. We may as well try to keep it off its guard."

FOR RUIZ, THE afternoon passed in a haze of sad speculation. He kept his eyes fixed on the tiny grid of the steering compass, shutting out the sounds and smells and sights of the sea through which they passed, though it was a beautiful day, with a soft steady breeze, the sky a lustrous peacock green, the sea a deep silvery azure.

Who was it?

Now Nisa's withdrawal, the absence of that warmth that had always glowed between them, took on a different aspect. True, she had gone through unhappy events in Sea-Stack, but others had suffered as much, or worse. Did it mean anything, beyond the possibility that she was a weaker and less faithful person than he had supposed her to be?

And Dolmaero, who had always before seemed so steady, so unflappable, and who was now so darkly pessimistic—did his illness account for all of the changes in his manner?

Even Molnekh's unchanged persona took on a sinister quality. Was he less affected by their trials than the others, because he was no longer driven by human considerations?

Ruiz's thoughts scurried in circles, like dancing mice, reaching no useful conclusions.

By the time Gunderd took the tiller again, Ruiz had exhausted his capacity for speculation. He found that his hands had clamped the tiller so tightly that they had become stiff and painful.

He massaged blood back into them and looked around, oddly surprised by the change in the light. The sun drifted toward the western horizon behind them. The swells seemed shorter and steeper, as if they had come onto the shelf of the Dayerak Archipelago—and the sea was a different color, a murky green, wormy with floating brown weed. He looked at Gunderd questioningly.

"Yes," said Gunderd. "We'll make the shoals tonight.

Ordinarily, I'd heave to and wait for daylight for our land-fall, but in this case I'll be grateful for darkness."

Ruiz nodded. He found it difficult to concentrate. Perhaps, he thought, he should put the matter away and give thought to what might happen in the coming night. He resolved to do better, to go forward and act as if nothing were wrong, but he was still sitting in the stern when Gunderd shouted happily, stood up, and pointed into the water.

"Look! Neon demons," said Gunderd. "Fine eating!"

Ruiz looked down and saw a trio of large fish, each a meter and a half long, swimming easily beside the boat, just under the surface. Two of the fish had brilliant blue and gold striations on their flanks, but the third had furrows of ugly scar tissue above and below its ventral line, sunk deep, as if the wounds had taken most of the muscle on that side of the fish.

Ruiz wondered how the fish had lived through such trauma. Gunderd saw the direction of his gaze. "Neon demons are the most vital fish that swim Sook's oceans, Ruiz. But their flesh doesn't keep, so when the margar hunters catch one, they just rip a filet off and throw the fish back. They like to swim with the boats, for some reason, and they can keep up until they've lost three of their four filets. Even when they're just a sac of organs hung on a skeleton, they keep trying to follow. . . . It's very strange."

Ruiz felt a sudden rush of horror, an emotion wildly out of proportion to the ugly image Gunderd had summoned. The maimed fish rolled its golden eye up at the boat; it might have been looking at Ruiz. He had a sudden morbid fantasy—that its cold primitive brain held pity for Ruiz.

He shuddered and looked away.

"Take the helm," said Gunderd. "I'll get the fishing gear and we'll eat well at least once before we get to the islands."

"No," said Ruiz, abruptly revolted by the idea of taking the last of the fish's flesh. "We should rest, eat moderately. Be ready."

Gunderd settled back, looking disappointed. "Perhaps

you're right. Yes, you're probably right." He looked wistfully over the side. "Yes."

Ruiz got to his feet and went forward. Svin and the cook
scurried aft. The cabin boy began whispering to Gunderd,
throwing cautious glances over his narrow shoulder at
Ruiz. Gunderd patted him and began speaking earnestly
and reassuringly.

Ruiz settled himself beside Dolmaero—the Guildmaster
was probably the least physically dangerous of the three, at
the moment—though it occurred to Ruiz that if Dolmaero
were Corean's machine, he might be feigning his illness.

He shook his head, feeling a sour dry frustration. He
looked across at Nisa, who returned his glance without
expression. For the first time he wondered, would he still
love her, if she were no longer human? *Of course not,* he
thought, angry at his own foolishness.

But then he looked at her again and wasn't so sure. If
she turned out to be Corean's creature, he might have to
kill her, as much for the sake of the Nisa that had been as
for their safety.

If it came to that, he would be killing his own heart,
tearing away his own flesh.

"Why so grim?" asked Dolmaero. "Surely you don't
fear treachery; not on this civilized world."

Dolmaero spoke with a terrible despairing contempt,
and Ruiz couldn't think of a response.

"No, Ruiz Aw is safe enough for a time," said Nisa
darkly. "We journey into more blood; true? Ruiz is our
only weapon. Would you throw away your biggest gun and
then go a-hunting dustbears? No."

Dolmaero smiled a twisted smile. "A good point, Noble
Person. Well, then, I am encouraged."

"I, too," said Molnekh, without a trace of irony.

Ruiz could think of nothing to say. His head still hurt,
he was exhausted, his will was eroded. He decided to rest.
He made himself as comfortable as he could and shut his
eyes. He would rely on Nisa's logic to keep the knife from
his throat.

As he drifted into sleep, he felt a small trickle of amazement—that he now cared so little for his life.

CHAPTER 4

W HEN Ruiz Aw woke, the sky was black except for a few dim stars and the glittering pinpoints of the Shard orbital platforms. He felt a small cold surprise that he was still on Sook. Had he awakened from some unremembered dream of another, better place?

He sat up and happened to nudge against Nisa, who was huddled motionless by the gunwale, wrapped in a square of canvas against the night wind. She accepted the contact for a moment, then jerked away. Ruiz felt a disproportionate sense of isolation. "I wouldn't hurt you, Nisa. Truly." It seemed an awkward speech—he didn't want to think it was necessary to reassure her of his good intentions.

"I know," she said, in a soft neutral voice.

In the darkness he couldn't see her expression.

"Truly," he said again, but this time she didn't answer.

He waited a moment longer; then, feeling foolish, he made his way aft, climbing carefully over the snoring forms of Dolmaero and Molnekh. Perched on a midships thwart, Einduix the cook nodded affably. It occurred to Ruiz that he had never seen the little orange man sleep.

Svin slept by Gunderd, looking so much like a puppy at its master's feet that Ruiz smiled. The mate still held the boat on its course, though the wind had dropped and the boat moved sedately at best. "Ruiz Aw," he said. "At last. For a while there I thought I'd have to send someone to wake you. I was wondering whose loss would be more bearable, should the messenger step on one of your vipers. A difficult decision: Svin is useless, of course, but at least he's never tried to poison me."

Gunderd seemed to speak with unforced geniality. Ruiz settled himself and took the tiller. He noticed that the course was south of east, an odd direction for their purposes. "What's going on, Gunderd?"

"Look to the north. Do you see the loom of the bane-lights on Roderigo?"

Ruiz looked and saw a glimmer of cold pale green on the horizon, wavering at the edge of visibility. He felt a sudden hollowness in his stomach, and the curious sensation of sweat breaking out on his brow, though the air was cool. "Ah," he said.

"Ah?" said Gunderd. "You're a cool one. When I saw it, I resurrected my father's gods and started to pray—hoping that perhaps they'd established a franchise on Sook. After all, they're water gods, and we sail through a substance that resembles water, at least superficially."

Ruiz was forced to laugh.

Gunderd's discolored teeth gleamed in the darkness.

Ruiz looked again at the banelights. "How did we come so close? Your course appeared to give Roderigo a good offing."

Gunderd's smile disappeared. "The nav console is dead, Ruiz, but before it died, it seemed to show us well off. Two explanations occur: a strong uncharted current after the unit died—not improbable—or . . . the possibility that the Roderigo hetmen detected us and slaved the console to their purposes."

"Oh no," said Ruiz.

"Indeed," said Gunderd. "Indeed."

"What can we do?"

"Not much. Hope it was a current. Flee with as much alacrity as the wind allows. Get religion."

"Ah."

Gunderd snorted. "You're no conversationalist, whatever your other talents. I go now to slumber; it may be my last night as a free man. Steer the course, and wake me at dawn, unless the wind shifts."

He wrapped a blanket around his shoulders and appeared to be asleep in moments.

After a while, Einduix took his delicate little flute from his pocket and played a thready minor key melody, skillfully enough to take Ruiz's mind from his immediate concerns. For an hour the old cook played simple variations on the same theme, and Ruiz never grew tired of listening. Finally he stopped and nodded at Ruiz, who had been his only audience—unless Nisa was still awake.

Ruiz steered southeast, and the banelights faded.

JUST BEFORE DAWN, Ruiz heard an ominous rumble—the sound of powerful engines.

The Roderigo catchboat appeared out of the darkness, showing no lights on its squat steel hull. A harsh voice spoke through its hailer, directing them to heave to and prepare to be boarded.

Ruiz threw the tiller over, feeling a terrible sense of defeat. The Roderigans would be equipped with electret snares and sticky-shock nets; resistance would be futile. He stood up, and for a moment it seemed to him that he was very tired. Perhaps the simplest solution for him was to fall backward into the sea's embrace and let his life finally stream away from him.

"What's happening?" asked Nisa, in a thin frightened voice. The cabin boy choked back a sob.

Ruiz drew a deep breath. *Don't be foolish,* he told himself. Besides, the Roderigans probably carried seeker fish, which would drag him back to life.

"No heroics," Gunderd whispered. "It could be worse. Some of us may live, if we submit and prove trainable."

"Yes," said Ruiz.

Gunderd patted his arm. "I'm sorry, Ruiz. I'd hoped for a better ending."

Ruiz shook himself. "I know." He tried to make himself think, to remember all he could about the Roderigan slave depots. He had never had any personal dealings with the Roderigans on any of his earlier missions to Sook; his employers were no more ethical than any other multisystem corporation, but they had *some* standards.

The Roderigans were notorious for their involvement in a broad spectrum of slaving activities. They maintained a breeding program for several proscribed human types, they supplied Castle Delt with mindwiped shock troops, they ran elimination trials of the most brutal sort. They covered their overhead by fattening human cattle for the cannibals of the Namp coast.

They would supply doppelgängers for any purpose, at a price. Many wealthy cowards came to Sook solely to acquire from the Roderigans a vengeance puppet of their most hated enemy. Star-crossed lovers came, bearing a lock of their beloved's hair.

Perhaps their most notable contribution to the art of exploiting human suffering was the multiple ransom. When they acquired a major prize, the child of a particularly wealthy pangalac citizen, they often cloned a series of duplicates. After the ransom was paid and the original child was returned to its parents, the Roderigans would begin their campaign to extort further money. They would holotape the torture and execution of the first of the duplicates, and then send the recording to the parents. It was a rare parent who could dispassionately observe the destruction of a child that in all meaningful respects was his or her own.

The range and depravity of the Roderigan enterprises had required them to build extremely good defenses and even better security—more than one anguished parent had chosen to spend a fortune on the destruction of Roderigo. But apparently the hetmen still flourished on their steel and concrete island.

On the catchboat's deck, two men in bright mirrorsuits appeared, carrying heavy grasers.

"All right," said the taller one. "Come aboard. One at a time."

A ladder extruded from the boat's high topsides.

Gunderd flashed a smile at Ruiz. "If I don't see you again . . . it's been an interesting time, Ruiz Aw."

Ruiz didn't answer; he was concentrating on his affect. He slumped his shoulders, curved his back, allowed his hands to tremble. He let his face slacken, as if in helpless terror.

Nisa and the other Pharaohans looked at him first in amazement, and then in contempt. Even Nisa turned away from him, her mouth twisting.

Thereafter, Ruiz didn't have to work very hard to make his eyes fill with tears.

Gunderd climbed slowly to the catchboat's deck, where the men grabbed his arms and hustled him over to a line of vertical restraint floaters waiting along the cabinside.

They strapped him in with the efficiency of long practice and returned to the rail. "Next!" barked the talker. "Don't drag your heels, or we'll touch you up with the nerve lash."

Ruiz was the last to depart the lifeboat, clinging to the ladder and fumbling as if his legs and arms would barely obey him. He almost fell over the rail, and the man who clamped his arm muttered in disgust, "Come on, what's the matter with you? A grown man acting like a baby."

"I'm sorry, I'm sorry," Ruiz babbled. He darted a look about, and his heart sank. Along the bridge deck, automated weapons pods tracked him. Underfoot the deck showed the distinctive pattern of a stun grid. His acting abilities, such as they were, would do him no good, at least for the time being.

The restraints snapped shut around his limbs, locking him to the pallet. One of the mirrorsuited men passed a detector over the prisoners and relieved Gunderd and Ruiz of their knives.

When he came to Einduix's flute, he shrugged and pitched it overboard. Einduix made a strangled sound of rage, and Ruiz, looking around, saw in the tiny man's face such a deadly intent that he was genuinely shocked. But almost before Ruiz had seen that look, the cook's face smoothed over and he smiled blandly at his captor.

An uneasy feeling touched Ruiz; apparently they all carried secrets, and perhaps none of them were what they appeared to be.

He found that he was very tired of ambiguity. Still, he had no choice but to think in those tangled terms, so when the taller Roderigan stood before him with a dataslate and asked him his name and profession, Ruiz replied in a bright, frightened voice, "Ruiz. Comfort boy, please sir."

It seemed to Ruiz that he could feel the astonishment of the others, but no one spoke to give him away.

The Roderigan nodded, apparently unsurprised, and made an entry on his slate. "And you?" he said to Svin.

"Svin, apprentice seaman," answered the cabin boy.

Ruiz had the impression that beneath the mirrormask, the man grinned with pointed teeth. "You'll find the stockyards to your liking, boy. All you can eat. A short and merry life."

He seemed pleased also to find a Pharaohan conjurer and Guildmaster in his catch. "Valuable properties," he said.

When he asked Nisa her occupation, she tossed her beautiful head and answered, "Nisa. Princess."

Amusement seemed to seep through the featureless glitter of the mask. "We get a lot of those, Your Majesty. Let us hope that you show talent in other areas, or you'll be joining Svin in the stockyards."

Gunderd spoke next. "Gunderd. Exty scholar."

Ruiz again reminded himself not to be surprised by anything.

Finally the Roderigan stood before Einduix the cook and asked his question.

The little orange man smiled and shook his head, his incomprehension so obvious that Ruiz was automatically suspicious.

The Roderigan produced a multichannel translator and spoke into it. It regurgitated the sentence in dozens of languages, some of which were unfamiliar to Ruiz. Einduix remained cheerfully uncommunicative. After a while, the man drew a nerve lash from his mirrorsuit and shook it in the cook's face, which prompted Einduix to shout incomprehensibly in a thin cracked voice.

"Well, what shall we do with him?" said the taller Roderigan.

"Don't know," said the other. "It's certain they'd not want him in the stockyards. Perhaps he's collectable; we'll just mark him 'unknown' and leave it at that."

"As you say."

The man with the dataslate touched his wrist and the restraint floaters rose up and moved toward an armored hatch that peeled open in the side deck.

Ruiz Aw was the first to go down into the below-decks darkness. A familiar stench filled his nostrils: the smell of the slavehold, compounded of organic substances and the unmistakable bouquet of hopeless misery.

THE HOLD WAS dank and lit only by red glowplates. After the Roderigans had secured them to bulkhead racks and gone away, no one said anything for a while. The catchboat's engines revved and the boat began to pitch up and down in the seaway.

Finally Nisa started to speak. "Why did—"

She was interrupted by Gunderd, who spoke in a loud jovial voice. "Well, well; now we are embarked on a new and exciting life. Our careers will be whatever we can make of them, and we must never forget that our new supervisors will weigh every aspect of our behavior, so as to find the best possible use for our talents. Why, even now they probably listen and evaluate. And why not?"

Ruiz realized with a small start of surprise that Gunderd had not yet given up, that he hoped that Ruiz Aw, slayer extraordinary, might arrange a miracle and get them away from Roderigo alive.

Svin spoke in a small voice. "And what of me? My career is to be the stockyard. What does that mean, do you think?"

The cabin boy meant nothing to Ruiz Aw, but he pitied Svin. He didn't know what to say.

Gunderd answered in the same cheerfully brassy voice he always used with Svin. "Who can say? Perhaps that is their term for their holding area, where they keep folk whose talents have yet to be gauged. Be content; if anyone can find a use for you, the Roderigans surely will."

The cabin boy seemed somewhat heartened by Gunderd's attempt to comfort him, though Svin would have to be improbably stupid to swallow Gunderd's words completely, Ruiz thought. The hold had such an air of malevolent purpose; Ruiz could almost feel the ghosts of former passengers, crowding around him, touching him with cold bloodless fingers.

He shivered and tried to form a plan. Nothing came to him; he could only hope that somewhere along the line, the Roderigans would think him harmless and relax their security sufficiently to give him an opening. Unfortunately, everything he had ever heard about the Roderigans led to pessimistic thoughts. Many assassins had been sent against the Roderigan hetmen, for millions had reason to hate them. But as far as Ruiz knew, the hetmen lived as long as they chose, until the weight of their deeds bore them down into extinction.

In less than an hour, the drone of the engines dropped in pitch and the motion eased, as if they had come onto the smooth water of a harbor. The engines rumbled to an idle and then stopped. They heard the clatter of people on deck, shouted commands, the whine of windlass motors.

Finally the sounds fell away, replaced by an ominous silence.

The hatch slid open, admitting a harsh ray of sunlight.

"Good-bye, everyone," said Gunderd. "I'll miss your company. Even the vipers. Even Svin. Even, gods help me, Einduix the poisoner."

"Good-bye," said Ruiz, in a suitably tremulous voice.

No one else seemed inclined to farewells.

In the hatch appeared a pair of magnificently embroidered margar-web boots, followed by their owner, a woman in the black shipsuit of a Roderigan hetman.

She descended the access ladder with sinuous grace and

turned to inspect the prisoners. For a moment she stood in the light, as if to permit their admiration.

Despite his certain knowledge that she was a great monster, Ruiz felt compelled to an abstract admiration. She had a dark harsh face, framed by an artfully wild tangle of hair falling below her shoulders. At the crown her hair was an arterial red, muting to rusty brown at midlength. At the ends it was as black as Nisa's. Ruiz suddenly realized that the hetman's coloring recapitulated the progressive hues of drying blood.

She wore a cluster of rubies and tiny white feathers from her right ear, and on one high cheekbone a triple chevron of thin white scars. Her body was strong and spare, without any apparent softness.

The impression was of barbaric splendor. Someone spoke in a soft detached voice. "Light."

Overhead lamps came on, so that brilliance filled the hold and Ruiz was blinded for a moment.

When he could see again, the hetman stood before Ruiz's floater, staring at him with stony black eyes. Another Roderigan had joined her, a man of great apparent age, white-haired and wrinkled, his body knotty with wiry muscle. He had a clever vulpine air, and eyes that darted everywhere. Ruiz identified him as the hetman's personal tongue and security chief.

"I am Gejas," said the man, in that incongruously gentle voice. "I speak for your new keeper, The Yellowleaf." He made a courtly half-bow to the hetman.

She nodded and turned, to give each prisoner a deliberate expressionless look. Then she returned her cold gaze to Ruiz, who had no difficulty in adopting a look of barely restrained terror. He told himself there was no special malevolence in her attention, but he wondered why she was so single-mindedly focused on him.

A minute passed with excruciating slowness. Ruiz found her face baffling—if there was any expression at all, it appeared to be a sort of rapacious curiosity. She finally turned away and went back up the ladder, moving with a powerful agile grace. Ruiz felt an involuntary shudder run through him. He thought, *She's probably as dangerous as any creature on Sook.*

Gejas waited until the hetman's boots had disappeared before he spoke again. "Roderigo's pens overflow with stock at the moment. You will all therefore be held in our intake area until training slots open up. It is my job to teach you to survive this initial procedure. Your survival is probable, providing you follow this simple rule."

He gave them a small chill smile. "Never attempt to harm or disobey or annoy any Roderigan. Or you will die. Does anyone not understand? Are there any questions?"

Svin said in a small tremulous voice, "Sir? I—"

Gejas moved so quickly that even Ruiz was surprised, and before Svin could speak another word, Gejas had dexterously opened his throat, using a small sonic knife. A single spurt of blood escaped the wound before Gejas attached a self-sealing drain, which pumped away the cabin boy's blood as quickly as it flowed, down a thin clear tube, into a receptacle at the foot of the rack.

Unable to look away, Ruiz watched the boy's white, horrified face. Svin wheezed and choked, unable even to scream; apparently Gejas's skillful knife had destroyed his larynx. His arms jerked in their restraints, a little blood trickled from his mouth, and then his eyes went dull, his body relaxed.

"So," said Gejas. "A useful lesson here. The wise trainee asks no questions; he simply does what is required. A few of you may think yourselves more valuable than this person, who was destined to be meat in any case—but you should remember that there is always an empty hook waiting for you in the holds of our freezer ships. Roderigo is rich, and will survive even if we must sell your carcass to the Blades for a pittance."

Gejas smiled again, projecting an air of repellent charm. "Now, you go to Intake. You will go sleeping; security requires that no one see more of us than is absolutely necessary." He touched a control pad at his wrist, and an injector at Ruiz's shoulder sighed.

Ruiz made no effort to fight the darkness.

*   *   *

COREAN FELT A huge bubble of joy well up in her chest, squeezing her heart, almost painfully. "They have him?" she asked again, breathlessly.

Marmo shifted uneasily, his ancient servomotors whining. "But consider carefully. The hetmen have set an absurd price on Ruiz Aw; furthermore, they are demanding you come to Roderigo to claim him. How can we know their purpose in this? Why will they not simply ship your properties back to you?"

Corean regarded Marmo with impatience. "We must take precautions, of course; I'm not so foolish as to show up at Roderigo, hat in hand, trusting in the hetmen's good faith. As to the price, they must know that the Lords want him. And they're a cautious folk, by all accounts—which may be why they want to sell him away from SeaStack, where the Lords can't try to steal him. But none of that matters. I'd climb down the throat of Hell to get Ruiz Aw."

"Reassuring, to hear that," Marmo said dryly. The old cyborg turned away, his chassis catching a dull gleam from the overhead light. "And what is your plan? I must tell you, Corean, I'm not so brave as your esteemed self. The Roderigans frighten me; you will have to have a very good scheme before I will agree to go with you."

Corean felt an astonishment as vast as the joy she had felt on hearing of Ruiz Aw's capture. In all the years he had served her, Marmo had never spoken so to her.

CHAPTER 5

RUIZ Aw came to himself more slowly than was usual.

He opened his eyes to a dim bloody light. The warm air smelled of disinfectant. The only sound he heard was a low murmur of voices, so soft and so numerous that the sound seemed a natural phenomenon, bereft of content, like surf or the rush of wind through a forest.

He raised his head and looked about. The others lay beside him in a neat row, on a riser of some soft gray plastic. They all still slept and, like him, were naked. Behind them a wall of monocrete rose up to a low ceiling.

The room was vast, its farthest reaches invisible through the mist that rose from the thousands who filled it. Everywhere were clumps of naked humans of all races, genders, ages. Only a few moved about; the others either sat in watchful silence or huddled together, whispering.

Ruiz sat up slowly, muscles protesting. He wondered how long the Roderigans had kept them under; he felt worse than he might have expected after an hour or two of unconsciousness. Perhaps Gejas had ordered him injected with debilitating drugs, just in case he proved more dangerous than he pretended to be. He massaged his limbs, trying to work the stiffness out and restore some circulation, and gradually he began to feel a little better.

By the time Gunderd began to stir, Ruiz felt well enough to stand up and stretch.

"Oh," groaned Gunderd. "Was this necessary?"

"So our keeper said," replied Ruiz in a timorously hopeful voice, keeping within his chosen role as a helpless comfort boy.

"Give it a rest." Gunderd grunted. "They don't monitor these cattle pens, except under extremely unusual circumstances. Unless the universe has gone crazy, we're of no great significance to the Roderigans. Control your grandiosity and help me to sit up."

Ruiz reached down a hand. "How can you be so sure?"

"The Roderigans were among those races I studied at the university—before I came to my true calling as a paid hand on the worst rust-bucket to sail Sook's seas. Anyway, my professors generally agreed that the hetmen are no longer human—in any important sense—so we were required to take a section on Roderigo. 'Transitional Alienation-A Study in Self-Willed Evolution'—I think that was the course title."

Ruiz felt a small twinge of hope. Once again a trace of luck had clung to him, in the midst of a terrible situation. Surely Gunderd's knowledge would prove helpful. "What else do you know?"

As if reading Ruiz's mind, Gunderd looked at him in bleary disapproval. "If anything useful occurs to me, I'll certainly tell you—if you promise to control your overly decisive nature. We won't live long if you can't."

"I'll do my best," said Ruiz.

Nisa was the next to waken. She sat up abruptly and stifled a gasp, face pinched with pain. Then she apparently noticed that Ruiz and Gunderd were naked, and she shrank away.

"Don't worry," said Gunderd. "Even if I weren't a man who prefers the love of men, you'd be safe from any unwanted attentions. Or wanted attentions, for that matter," he said, shooting a wry glance at Ruiz. "Our keepers take a dim view of unauthorized entertainment, so they infuse the atmosphere with drugs which inhibit desire."

"I see," she said, but her face was still stiff with wariness.

Ruiz looked at her, and though she was as beautiful as before, he took only an abstract pleasure in her beauty. He felt no desire for her, but he found he could feel a bitter anger for those who had stolen from him that precious heat.

Something of his reaction must have shown in his face, because Gunderd tapped him on the arm and said, "Control, Ruiz Aw. Above all, control. The Roderigans leave us very little to control; we must do the best we can with what's left."

Ruiz took a deep breath and nodded.

The others slowly woke, groaning and coughing, except for Einduix, who remained as still as a small orange statue. After a while, Ruiz began to wonder if perhaps the cook had succumbed to the disabling chemicals they'd been dosed with. He went over and knelt beside the little man.

If Einduix breathed, it was very slowly indeed. Ruiz reached out and touched the cook's neck. After a moment he detected a slow faint pulse.

As he drew back, he thought he saw the cook's right eye open, just a slit, barely noticeable—but behind that slit was the watchful darkness of a pupil, not the blank white of unconsciousness. Before he could be sure it had happened, the eye shut again . . . but Ruiz felt an odd certainty that the cook had winked at him.

"Does the poisoner live?" asked Gunderd.

"I think so," said Ruiz. "Well, what now?"

Gunderd laughed sourly. "We wait; what else?"

Molnekh stood up and stretched his cadaverous frame. "When do they feed us?" he asked, in his usual cheerful manner.

Ruiz shrugged. "Gunderd is the expert; ask him."

Molnekh looked to Gunderd, eyebrows raised.

Gunderd frowned. "I'm no expert. I've spent thirty years forgetting what I once learned—and I've done a fair job of it. However, to answer your question, I seem to remember the Roderigans use an on-demand feed system. Somewhere nearby you'll find a hopper full of pellets. Search it out."

Molnekh seemed undisturbed by Gunderd's unfriendly tone. "Thank you. I will," he said, and wandered away, his eyes darting from side to side hungrily.

Gunderd followed him with hooded eyes. "Of all your vipers, that one I like the least, Ruiz Aw. He looks too much like Death's homely brother."

Dolmaero sat up finally, face white and beaded with sweat. "Appearances deceive, sometimes," he said in a weak voice. "Of the conjurors I've known, Molnekh has the best heart—at least he doesn't treat common folk like bugs."

"Perhaps. You know him better than I," said Gunderd. "But he makes me uneasy, and it's not just his handsome face."

"You're not so handsome yourself," said Nisa tartly.

Gunderd laughed, this time with genuine amusement. "True. However, it may be that I'm more handsome than I was." He opened his mouth, displayed gleaming white teeth. "They took my tooth skins; now I look a less authentic buccaneer, eh? And if any of you were carrying implanted weaponry, or subdural cerebral enhancers, or anything else you didn't grow yourself—you haven't got the gear anymore. Apparently none of us depends on mech organs, since here we are."

"What's he talking about?" asked Dolmaero, rubbing his head as if it ached.

"Some pangalacs carry devices within their bodies—weapons, or communicators. And those who can't afford autocloned replacement organs for, say, a damaged heart, must make do with mechanisms."

Nisa looked at Ruiz with serious eyes. "So your heart is flesh, and not steel?"

"Flesh," Ruiz said.

She tipped her head to the side and gave him a long speculative look. Ruiz wondered what thoughts that lovely head held, and how she had become such a stranger. The speculation frightened him. Were the Gencha to blame?

Dolmaero looked up. "What's the matter, Ruiz Aw?" the Guildmaster asked.

"Nothing," Ruiz muttered.

"Ah. Well," said Dolmaero, turning to Gunderd, "you seem to know a lot about our captors. May I ask a few questions?"

"Let me ask Ruiz if he thinks it wise," said Gunderd. "Ruiz?"

"Dolmaero is a thoughtful man," said Ruiz soberly. "He has a unique perspective and a supple mind. Who knows, he may provide useful insights. Why not inform him?"

Gunderd nodded affably. "Why not? Ask away!"

Dolmaero rubbed his chin thoughtfully. "We are among slavers?"

"They are that, at least," agreed Gunderd.

"And they intend for us . . . what?"

Now Gunderd looked a bit uneasy. "Ordinarily I could answer with a high degree of certainty: They will market us to the highest bidders, or ship our meat to the Blades if no one offers them a sufficiently profitable price. But . . . now I'm not entirely sure; there are oddities here."

Ruiz felt something stir deep in his mind, that paranoid part of himself which resonated to the possibility that the universe might conspire to snuff out the small particle of itself called Ruiz Aw. Ordinarily he sternly repressed such ideas; that way led to madness and, worse, ineffectiveness. *But,* he thought, *times might have changed.* "What do you mean?" he asked, as casually as possible.

"Well, there's The Yellowleaf. Why would a hetman of that rank take any interest in a randomly collected scraggly little group such as ours? Begging your forgiveness, but none of us seems a truly valuable specimen."

Dolmaero frowned. "Ruiz Aw informs us that we, as key members of a Pharaohan Expiation troupe, have considerable value."

"I don't doubt it," said Gunderd. "I don't mean to demean your value; still . . . the hetmen deal in very large affairs indeed. The ordinary business of the island is left in the hands of tongues like Gejas."

" 'Tongues'? What does that mean?"

"Ah. This is one of the more interesting elements of Roderigan society," said Gunderd, adopting a professorial tone and shaking his finger for emphasis. Ruiz suddenly had no trouble seeing him as the scholar he claimed to have once been—though to the casual eye he might still appear to be a thin naked scoundrel with the crude tattoos of a sailor.

"You see," Gunderd continued, "Roderigo is a place of intrigue, brutality, betrayal, all to a degree of intensity found in few other places in the human galaxy. The hetmen are obsessed with security, with secrecy. When a new hetman is initiated, he must accept the surgical removal of his tongue and larynx, so that never will the new hetman be tempted to speak a secret. Thus the 'tongues': persons trained to anticipate the hetman's wishes and speak them."

Dolmaero's eyes widened. "The hetmen never speak again?"

"Never. Of course, in a way it's a largely symbolic mutilation, since at need the hetman can communicate directly through dataslate or manual vocoder. Still, it's one of the reasons why we think the Roderigans have evolved away from humanity."

"I don't understand," said Dolmaero. "I've known men unfortunate enough to be born dumb; they seemed as human as anyone."

"Of course," said Gunderd. "And they are, they are. But, I understand you come from a client world where life extension is unknown, where all die after a natural span, no matter how rich they might be."

"True," said Dolmaero shortly.

"So an affliction with which a man can cope over an ordinary life—though such men may in their loneliness be more different than you imagine—becomes, in a thousand years, something else entirely." Gunderd's voice dropped to a hoarse whisper. "How important is language—the exchange of ideas that raised us above the beasts? In its absence, can we retain those other qualities that distinguish us from the beasts: compassion, remorse . . . love? Perhaps their never-ending silence somehow makes the Roderigans strong enough, cruel enough, *bestial* enough to perform their terrible deeds. Who knows?"

Dolmaero looked shaken. "What deeds are these, worse than slavery and cannibalism?"

"They're not cannibals; in fact I understand that they subsist on vegetable matter, finding the flesh of animals too disgustingly mortal to take into their bodies. Strange, that. As to their deeds, I find that I cannot recount any of them, at the moment. I'm already too frightened, and I don't think I can bear to be more so." But he smiled at Dolmaero. "Later, perhaps, when I've grown used to the fear. We're so constructed, we humans, that even in the most fearful situations, we eventually grow calmer."

"I have enough to think about, for a while," said Dolmaero.

Molnekh returned soon after. He looked happier; his stomach bulged slightly. "Yonder is the nearest feeder," he said, pointing to the left along the wall. "The pellets are much better than I expected—sweet and savory at the same time."

Gunderd grinned, not pleasantly. "I see that you intend to cooperate with our keepers."

"How so?" asked Molnekh.

"You're fattening yourself for the hook. Notice how plump our fellow prisoners are, for the most part." Gunderd made a gesture indicating the other humans that filled the hall.

Ruiz looked, and saw that it was true: They were surrounded by hundreds of terrified fat people.

Molnekh looked only briefly uncomfortable. "Always have I eaten gluttonously; never have I fattened."

"You're lucky in your metabolism, then," said Gunderd.

GEJAS SAT ACROSS the wide armorglass table, watching the vastly subtle expressions of The Yellowleaf. His mind had gone to that place where he was no longer Gejas, but an organ of his hetman, more facile to her use than the tongue gone from her mouth had once been.

He spoke into the screen, to a beautiful madwoman in SeaStack. "Corean Heiclaro, The Yellowleaf hears your petition with favor. She is unoffended by your whining; after all, Roderigo is strength personified, and you would be foolish indeed not to perceive your own weakness in any dealings with us."

It was his life's work, to read faces, and the little slaver's face was transparent, a thin lovely veneer over a writhing snake's nest of bitter passion. He judged that she possessed enough cold amorality to take a small place in Roderigan society, but not enough discipline. Why else would she allow her vengeful lust for the Dilvermoon slayer to so override her sense of self-preservation?

Her mouth twisted into a sour shape, but otherwise she ignored his insults. "Then we have an agreement?"

"Yes. But . . . our sources tell us the battle is still raging, that more of SeaStack turns to ashes every day. The surviving Lords grow more desperate, do they not? More terrified that someone will escape with their great prize, whatever it is. Are you not afraid to leave your own interests there unprotected?"

"No," she answered, in a convincingly careless tone.

TIME PASSED IN dim red tedium. Ruiz sat on the plastic riser and tried to force his brain to work, without much success.

The others seemed as lethargic as he felt. Dolmaero lay back, apparently asleep. Molnekh leaned against the wall, face blank. A few meters away, Gunderd and Nisa spoke together in low voices, and Ruiz wondered what they could possibly find to talk about. Einduix the cook remained quiescent in his odd coma.

It occurred to Ruiz that he was probably as close to death as he had ever been—but the notion carried no urgency. He considered that, his thoughts painfully sluggish. Drugs? Cerebral suppressor field? Terminal weariness? It hardly mattered, if he could not somehow push himself past the cobwebs that wrapped his mind.

The clatter of steel-shod boots echoed through the hall, much louder than the soft shuffle of bare feet. He looked up to see a pair of mirrorsuited guards moving toward them.

They halted in front of him. "Come," one said.

He got to his feet, feeling dizzy. The guards turned and moved away; Ruiz staggered after. As he passed Nisa, he glanced down. She looked up at him, eyes huge, beautiful mouth trembling. She reached toward his hand, but he was already past and her fingers missed his by a meter.

He didn't dare turn back.

THE GUARDS CONDUCTED him to a transport coffin, an alloy box with padded restraint cuffs. He considered escape just before they thrust him into the coffin, but the thought of a naked man whose muscles could barely respond to his will attacking two well-trained armed men in mirrorsuits—it was so ludicrous that a smile twitched at his mouth, even as they closed the lid.

He waited in the darkness of the box, a stink of ancient terror filling his nostrils.

After a while the box jerked, and they began to move. Ruiz tried to feel the changes of direction, to get some notion of where they were going, but several times they paused and the box whirled, so that Ruiz was completely confused long before they reached their destination.

He waited in stillness for another measureless time.

Finally he heard the clatter of latches as the box was opened. Light flooded in, stabbing his eyes.

He squinted, and after a moment he saw the affable face of Gejas peering into the box. "Ruiz Aw?" asked Gejas. "Comfort boy?"

Something in the tongue's manner told Ruiz that his small deception had collapsed, but he had no choice but to play it to the end. "Yes, sir."

"Come out, then," said Gejas.

Ruiz stumbled forth, almost falling in his weakness.

Gejas caught his arm in a crushing grip. "Steady, Ruiz," he said.

Ruiz raised his eyes. He was in a small sumptuous room, lit softly by golden lamps, which threw their light up against sparkly white quartzite walls. A desk of polished copperwood filled one end of the room. He stood ankle deep in a carpet of some soft blond fiber, fine as baby hair. He looked down and shuddered. Perhaps it *was* baby hair.

Gejas shook his head. "This will never do. Presently The Yellowleaf will arrive, and you must be coherent." He took a small skinjector from his pocket and pressed it to Ruiz's thigh.

Almost instantly Ruiz began to feel better. Gejas released him and stepped back. The Roderigan's eyes glittered and to Ruiz he suddenly seemed an avatar of alertness, wariness personified—as though he could never be taken by surprise.

"Stand easy, now, Ruiz Aw," said Gejas. "The Yellowleaf comes."

At the far end, behind the desk, a door slid open silently, and The Yellowleaf stepped through. She wore the same shipsuit, but now her ear ornament was a string of tiny jade beads, from which hung a black opal carved in the shape of a rose.

Ruiz glanced aside at Gejas and was caught by the strangeness of the tongue's affect. That preternatural wariness had shifted and narrowed its focus; Gejas appeared to be oblivious of everything but the hetman, eyes shining, vulpine features alight with concentration. Ruiz had the impression that he might do almost anything, and Gejas would not notice, could not notice. It occurred to Ruiz that for each new defensive adaptation, a new vulnerability appeared.

On the other hand, if he were now to attempt to wring Gejas's neck, The Yellowleaf would surely notice, and *then* Gejas would know.

He shook himself. Were these pointless fancies the result of the drug Gejas had used to revive him? Even if he managed to best Gejas, The Yellowleaf was probably at least as formidable physically, and surely her safety was guarded by automated weapons systems.

"The Yellowleaf greets you, Ruiz Aw," said Gejas in a voice subtly different from his own—slightly breathless, a little higher pitched.

Ruiz was unsure of the proper etiquette, so he smiled as obsequiously as he could and bobbed his head.

Without seeming to take any of his concentration from the hetman, Gejas swung his fist up and into the back of Ruiz's head. Ruiz found himself on all fours, shaking bright spots from his vision. Apparently the drug hadn't entirely restored his strength.

"Kneel to greet The Yellowleaf," said Gejas.

Ruiz nodded groggily. Gejas's boot lifted him off the carpet and he landed on his back, clutching his ribs.

"Say 'Yes, Master.'"

"Yes, Master," said Ruiz. He wondered how they managed to get the bloodstains out of the thick carpet; it looked so clean.

"On your feet," said Gejas.

"Yes, Master." Ruiz struggled to his feet and found that he could stand up, despite the pain in his ribs.

He looked up to find The Yellowleaf examining him with an intensity almost as great as Gejas had directed at her. Her regard was a vastly colder thing, however, and in that passionless gaze Ruiz felt small and insignificant.

Ruiz looked back at her as humbly as he could, but he was conscious of a great fascination. What did Gejas the tongue see in those frozen eyes, that still face? What dreadful deeds had she ordered with that nonexpression? Had Gejas ever misinterpreted her will, and what had the consequences been for the tongue? His manner suggested a man trapped in an obsessive passion; how much was love and how much was terror?

"The Yellowleaf asks: You claim to be a comfort boy named Ruiz Aw; is this true?"

"Yes, Master."

She smiled a tiny cruel smile. Gejas said, "The Yellowleaf asks: Where have you plied your trade?"

"Master, I've worked on Dilvermoon, in Bo'eme . . .

at the Palace of Passionate Pulchritude, at the Club De-
mesne, at the Red Donkey. I've also served on SeedCorp
liners, though in an unofficial capacity."

"The Yellowleaf observes: An engine-room whore."

"Yes, Master."

Her smile widened fractionally. Gejas spoke on. "The
Yellowleaf observes: A rough trade. The Yellowleaf asks:
How did your beauty survive intact?"

"Master, I was lucky enough to obtain a patron."

"The Yellowleaf asks: How did you come to Sook?"

"Master, my patron sold me."

"The Yellowleaf observes: An old story."

"Yes, Master."

A silence fell. In that small room with two other people,
Ruiz had never felt so alone. The air seemed charged with
communication to which he was deaf; but he could feel it,
like a bone-deep shiver.

Finally Gejas spoke again. "The Yellowleaf mentions:
She has a squad of Daccan shock troops who have recently
worn out their playpretty. Perhaps she will give you to
them. The Yellowleaf asks: Would you like that?"

Ruiz knew he must respond or be hurt, but it wasn't
easy. Several times he had come into unwilling contact
with Daccan troops; they were little better than flesh and
bone killmechs, living only for cruelty and the most basic of
pleasures, bred down to loyal bestiality. They were a poor
choice for a tactically demanding mission, but excellent for
punishing helpless conquered populations.

"Yes, Master," he finally said. What choice did he have,
but to play out his role?

The Yellowleaf smiled a little more broadly, showing
red-enameled teeth.

"The Yellowleaf observes: You are either incredibly
brave or abysmally stupid. The Yellowleaf asks: Which is
it?"

"Master, I'm not brave."

The Yellowleaf laughed soundlessly, an eerie thing to
watch. But almost instantly her face smoothed back into an
expressionless mask.

"The Yellowleaf states: You have been briefly amusing,

but now it's time to get down to business. You are not Ruiz Aw, comfort boy with a high pain threshold. You are Ruiz Aw, once an unsuccessful emancipator, of late a slayer under contract to the Art League. Abandon all pretense; henceforward it will earn you nothing but pain that even you will be unable to endure."

"Yes, Master," said Ruiz numbly.

"The Yellowleaf informs you: We attempted to peel your mind, without significant success. We find certain aspects of your mind intriguing. It may be that you will find yourself serving Roderigo in an important capacity."

Here Gejas paused, while The Yellowleaf continued to watch him with her dead eyes.

"Yes, Master," Ruiz said.

"The Yellowleaf elaborates: A situation exists in Sea-Stack. Roderigo is interested. The Yellowleaf has recently been entrusted with the responsibility of clarifying this situation. The Yellowleaf asks: What do you know of the matter which has caused the Lords of SeaStack to destroy each other with such reckless ferocity?"

"Master, almost nothing."

"The Yellowleaf states: This may be the truth. We could find no evidence of such knowledge in your peel. The Yellowleaf asks: Would you accept a contract from Roderigo to obtain this knowledge?"

Ruiz felt an absurd twinge of hope. "Yes, Master." He would agree to anything, if it meant a chance to get away from Roderigo.

"The Yellowleaf laughs. The Yellowleaf states: The only way you will ever leave Roderigo's control is as a mindwiped body, or on a hook in the freezerhold. But if you agree to attempt a job for us, your life, as long as you may live, will be easier and more comfortable. This is the best you can hope for. The Yellowleaf asks: Is this so negligible?"

"No, Master," said Ruiz, sadly.

"The Yellowleaf elaborates: On the island of Dorn, there once existed a great library. Now nothing remains but ruins and a repository virtual, unfortunately damaged in whatever catastrophe destroyed the library. Roderigo has reason to believe that data pertaining to the SeaStack matter resides in this virtual. A number of submen such as Gejas have been sent to consult the virtual; all have been killed or mentally damaged. No useful data has been obtained. Recently a hetman was sent, The Redrock, a person of obdurate power. He returned in a nonfunctional condition, and we were forced to rusticate him to his dacha in the north mountains. He can almost feed himself."

Gejas paused. Again Ruiz sensed the communication between tongue and hetman, a current that sparkled unseen beneath the surface.

Finally Gejas spoke again. "The Yellowleaf states: Your mind combines several uncommon features. It is so well protected by self-circuited traps and synaptic lockdowns as to be virtually impenetrable, barring destructive deconstruction. Yet you retain a remarkable flexibility; you have one of the highest adaptability indices our technicians have ever recorded. You are a valuable prize indeed. If you were not crippled by your unevolved ethical constructs, you could expect a bright future on Roderigo. Still, we must make the best possible use of your talents. We will get our use of you, one way or another."

"Yes, Master," Ruiz said uncertainly.

"The Yellowleaf emphasizes: Do not think to deceive us with a facade of cooperation. We understand that you would agree to anything that offered a chance of escape. No such chance will ever come to you."

"No, Master."

Gejas tore his attention away from the hetman with a grimace, as though the act caused him physical pain. He touched a control pad at his wrist, and the wall to Ruiz's right opened. Inside a dark niche sat a restraint chair fitted with a crude holomnemonic probe.

Gejas seized Ruiz's arm and thrust him down into the chair. In contrast to the hygienic purity of the room, the niche and chair were spattered with dried blood and other unpleasant substances. A thick crust covered the seat of the chair and scraped at Ruiz's naked skin.

Cuffs snapped shut on his ankles and wrists, and the

probe's hood descended over his face. The stink of death was so strong in the hood that he gagged.

"The Yellowleaf asks: Will you accept this assignment: to be transported to Dorn and taken to the virtual, there to merge with it and seek the data we require, with no hope of later reward other than the treatment we accord any valuable property?"

The hood was like a grave, slimy with the juices of corruption. "Yes! Yes, Master. Yes!"

Ruiz felt himself to be smothering in the ghosts of all those the hetman had given to death in this place; he could barely breathe. It seemed a very long time before Gejas spoke again. "The Yellowleaf speaks with anger: You are insincere."

"No! Master!" And in fact, Ruiz felt that he would do anything to get out of the terrible embrace of the probe.

"The Yellowleaf states: You have yet to realize the parameters of your situation. Were you an ordinary property, you would now become a carcass for the freezerhold. The Yellowleaf demonstrates flexibility: You are remanded to another job which exploits your unique skills, until such time as you gain an appreciation for your altered circumstances."

Ruiz heard the hiss of a skinjector against his neck, and he fell down a long dark tunnel.

CHAPTER 6

RUIZ woke. At first he was blind, but gradually a low red glow illuminated his surroundings.

He sat in a cold metal chair, still naked. An armored cable connected the chair to a steel band welded around his waist. The band was so tight it cut into his ribs if he slumped even slightly. He straightened up and looked about.

The chair sat on a platform, perhaps three meters square, with a double railing on three sides. At the open end of the platform, a conveyor rail passed at waist height.

He could see nothing else. The conveyor came from darkness and disappeared into a deeper darkness.

A horrible smell hung in the silent air—fresh blood and old decay and excrement—a hideous abattoir stink.

He stood and went to the conveyor rail, pulling his cable behind him. It gave him just enough slack that he could stand beside the rail. A metal pier supported the rail at the platform; to this pier was riveted a box, from which the handle of a knife protruded. Ruiz jerked it out, examined it. The blade was thin and displayed the fine glitter of a monomol edge—a well-equipped butcher might own such a knife. The lid of the box had a catch; he turned it.

Inside was a curved piece of plastic, to which was attached a length of clear tubing. He drew it forth. Where had he seen a similar thing recently? He began to have a very bad feeling.

"Can you guess what it is, Ruiz Aw?" Gejas spoke from someplace close, startling Ruiz so that he almost dropped the knife.

Gejas clicked on his floater's lights, revealing his presence only a few meters away. He wore a mirrorsuit, causing Ruiz to suppress his first wild impulse, which was to fling the knife.

Gejas seemed to sense his impulse; a throaty chuckle came from the faceless mask of the mirrorsuit. "Can you guess?" he asked again.

Ruiz looked at the plastic thing and a memory suddenly returned to him—Gejas cutting the throat of the cabin boy Svin and saving the blood. "Yes . . . Master," he said, feeling a cold stomach-turning dread.

"You needn't be so formal with me," said Gejas cheerfully. "We're just submen together, eh? Still, I have all the power, so perhaps it's wise for you to show me as much respect as you can stomach."

Ruiz was too busy examining the implications of his situation to answer. What "job" had The Yellowleaf assigned him?

As if reading his mind, Gejas said, "You're our new knacker, Ruiz Aw. I'll explain the procedure. The cattle come down the conveyor and pause by your station. You cut their throats—I'll show you precisely how it's done—and then you apply the leech. That's all there is to it. The blood, by the way, is jellied and sold to the Blades as a condiment. Strange folk, the Blades. We could do the knackery much more efficiently; we have one of the finest automation systems in the pangalac worlds. But the cannibals want bled-out meat, done the old-fashioned way—and the customer's always right. Right? Besides, they sometimes send inspectors."

Ruiz couldn't speak. He stood there clutching the knife

in suddenly nerveless hands, mouth hanging open in horror. How could they make him do it?

The answer came swiftly. Pain flowed into him, beginning at his waist, under the metal band. It exploded up and
down his body, a pain compounded of every variety of agony, in every level of himself. His joints felt as if they were
being torn apart; his internal organs felt distended by a
terrible pressure, as though each were on the point of
bursting. His skin seemed to be on fire.

Ruiz fell to his hands and knees, dropping the knife to
the platform. The breath went out of him, but he hurt too
much to scream; there wasn't enough of him left for anything but feeling the pain.

"We also have good neurostimulators—pain is the basis
of our business," Gejas said, though Ruiz heard him only
dimly.

The pain stopped, and Ruiz drew a great breath. For an
instant he felt lighter than the heavy air, as if he could float
up and away from everything. But then he felt the cold
metal under his hands, sensed Gejas hovering closer. The
tongue stepped onto the platform.

"Stand up, Ruiz Aw," said Gejas.

And he did.

"Pick up the knife."

He did.

"Here comes your first customer."

A low rattle came out of the darkness, and a conveyor
gurney slid into the dim light, bearing a fat middle-aged
woman.

The gurney slid to a stop in front of Ruiz, its brakes
squealing a little. The woman seemed only half-conscious.
Her eyes were unfocused and appeared not to see Ruiz.

"They're drugged, as you see," said Gejas. "Otherwise
the flesh would bear an unsavory bitterness—too much
fear. The Yellowleaf wants you to learn a lesson—but not
at the expense of our product quality, in which we take a
certain pride."

Ruiz looked down at the woman, wondered who she
was, and what her dreams had once been. Certainly she
had never expected to end her life in such a dreadful way,

her significance reduced to her value as meat. To her dressed-out weight. "I'll do the job you wanted me to do—I'll consult the virtual. This isn't necessary. It isn't necessary."

"You and I, we can't be the judge of that, Ruiz Aw. Such decisions are for the hetmen," said Gejas. "Give me the knife." He extended his mirrorgloved hand.

Ruiz reluctantly laid the knife's haft there.

"Watch, now," said Gejas.

Moving at a deliberate pace, Gejas set the knife against the sagging skin under the woman's ear. He cut carefully, made another cut on the other side. The woman stirred, and a little more awareness came into her eyes. No great amount of blood flowed yet, but then Gejas took the leech, applied it to her throat. He gave a strong downward push, and the arteries burst, filling the leech with bright blood.

The woman kicked briefly and expired.

"That is my technique, which I recommend to you, Ruiz Aw. If you cut all the way into the arteries with your first stroke, you'll get a lot of blood on you, and waste a good bit, too."

Gejas wiped the blade off on the woman's short gray hair and handed it back to Ruiz.

"I cannot do this," Ruiz said.

"You can't? Well, I assure you, you must. You will. The pain will stay with you until you do your job. It will come if you perform with unsatisfactory efficiency. Yes, you will come to love your work. Oh, yes!" Gejas spoke with just a hint of anger, the first real emotion Ruiz had ever noticed in that smooth voice. Gejas boarded his floater. "You're a brazen sort, I must tell you. You would have to work here for *years* before you would equal the number of murders you've already committed. We know your reputation and record, Ruiz Aw. You've spread death across the human galaxy for centuries, haven't you?"

"That was different."

"Was it?" Gejas turned out his lights and disappeared. Ruiz heard the whine of the floater's drive fade away into the silence of the slaughterhouse.

.   .   .

THE CONVEYOR RAIL carried the corpse away, and nothing happened for a while.

Then Ruiz became aware of an ache in his middle, under the metal band that connected him to his chair. Minutes passed, and the ache grew worse until he had to sit down, huddled around the pain, sweating and grinding his teeth.

He began to look up the conveyor rail, and to listen for the rattle of the gurney.

When he realized what he was doing, a sob escaped his clenched teeth.

THE PAIN INVADED his body, a slow relentless conquest that eventually reduced him to a gasping mindless creature, empty of everything but pain. When the gurney finally brought him his first victim, he at first felt no emotion but a confused relief. He staggered to his feet as the gurney stopped at the platform's edge.

The pain stopped. A dreadful buoyant joy possessed him. He strode across the platform, lifting the knife.

The child seemed not as heavily drugged as the woman had been, and smiled sleepily up at Ruiz. He had dark curly hair and blue eyes; he might have been eight or nine standard years old. The straps that held him to the gurney seemed much too large.

The joy evaporated, leaving only a weary horror. "No," he said.

Pain returned, a tidal wave of agony. His legs turned to jelly and he fell to the steel, unable to do anything but twitch. He couldn't breathe; if anything, the pain was worse than before. He tried to say something, but he had no breath. His vision darkened and he fell into blackness.

When he woke, he heard the little boy crying, a soft muffled sound that seemed to fill the slaughterhouse. The pain was gone, at least for the moment. He sat up carefully.

The box that held the leech whirred and extruded a

small directional speaker. Gejas's voice issued from it, a tinny whisper. "See what you have done? The child's trank has worn off; now he must die in fear, and it's your fault."

"Please," said Ruiz Aw.

Gejas laughed, a low soft sound, full of delighted amazement. " 'Please'? You astound me, Ruiz Aw. Begging the hetmen for mercy . . . even that boy would not be so foolish. No, you must do the deed. And continue, until The Yellowleaf deems you properly educated."

"No, no . . ." Ruiz said. But he got to his feet and picked up the knife, hiding it behind him.

"No? The hetmen don't understand that word, Ruiz Aw. And consider. If I give you pain again, the boy must lie here a while longer until you recover. You make frightening noises when you're full of pain. Do you wish his suffering to continue?"

"No." Ruiz stood over the boy, looking down at the small tear-stained face. The little boy had stopped crying, though his mouth trembled and his blue eyes were very wide.

"Go on," said Gejas. "He is meat, whether by your hand or another's. The pain will kill you eventually, and The Yellowleaf has instructed me to give you pain until you do her bidding."

Ruiz didn't answer. He laid the knife aside. He smoothed back the little boy's hair as gently as his trembling hands would allow. The child spoke, asking him a question in a language he couldn't understand. Somehow that seemed an insupportable brutality—that he couldn't even offer the boy a word of intelligible comfort.

"Do it," said Gejas impatiently. "Your next job will be here soon."

"A moment," said Ruiz. "Don't be afraid," he told the child in as soothing a tone as he could manage. He brushed away the tears, then held the small face between his hands.

The boy gave him a tentative smile, and Ruiz smiled back. He slipped his long assassin's fingers up under the ears, pressed down on the arteries.

The blue eyes went dreamy; the lids flickered shut.

Ruiz held the pressure a moment longer—not long

enough to stop the child's heart—then picked up the knife and did the rest of the work.

"Don't you feel better now, Ruiz Aw?" said Gejas, and laughed.

The gurney jolted into motion and took the meat away. Ruiz went to his chair and sat. Time seemed to have stopped. He succeeded in thinking about nothing at all.

A few minutes later his next job arrived and he did it.

After a few hours the faces blurred together, became the same hopeless nonhuman shape, nothing but a landmark for his knife.

THE SUBMARINE SCRAPED along the side of the stack, eight hundred meters under the surface. Corean nudged the controls, sweat glistening on her expensive face. Marmo played his endless games against his own processors, in a shadowed corner of the small chamber.

The sub came away from the stone, and Corean fed a tiny bit more power to the silent impellers. "Better," she said.

Marmo looked up from his screen. "Will we survive, then?"

"Of course," she answered. "Haven't we always?"

Marmo glanced up at the steel deckhead, as if observing the carnage that raged at the surface, throughout the ancient marine city of SeaStack. "Thousands are even now saying the same thing. They'll be dead soon."

She gave him a glance compounded of vexation and impatience. "We're smarter, stronger, luckier."

"No one is as lucky as Ruiz Aw," Marmo said heavily. "If by some miracle we get out of SeaStack, let's run for the north launch rings, go back to the Blacktear Pens, collect our belongings, and leave Sook. Doesn't that plan have a certain beautiful momentum? Don't you want to live?"

"Not without Ruiz Aw to entertain me," she said shortly.

She looked at the old cyborged pirate and saw in his half-mech face a look that she had detected with increasing frequency over the last weeks. *You're mad,* it said.

But Marmo apparently knew better than to say such a thing out loud; he went back to his games.

NISA'S WORST EXPECTATIONS had proven prophetic. Again Ruiz Aw had taken her to a terrible place and left her alone.

The stockyard seemed the most dreadful place yet—suffused by such an atmosphere of hopeless brutality that she found it almost impossible to retain any shred of hope that Ruiz Aw would once again find a way for them to survive. His small miracles seemed insignificant beside the horror of the stockyard—the function of which she had gradually come to understand. At first she had refused to believe that people could be as depraved as the Roderigans appeared to be; after all, they *seemed* human.

Gunderd instructed her. "They're not human, Nisa-the-princess. Oh, at any time in the history of the human race, creatures have walked among us that were nonhuman by any reasonable standard: joykillers, for example, who have been with us since we came down from the trees. But Roderigo is one of those places where inhumanity has been institutionalized. Venerated. It's passed beyond aberration here."

She could only shake her head, perplexed.

The day after they had taken Ruiz away, three hugely fat men had visited her little group.

They stood above her, staring down with small cruel eyes. "Yes," said the largest. "You are still beautiful. You will come with us and entertain us in our last days. We are ripe."

She felt somehow more naked under their cold stare. "No," she said, drawing up her knees. She turned to Gunderd. "I thought you said there were no rapists here, that the hetmen medicated the air."

Gunderd shrugged.

The fat men looked scornful. The largest one spoke again. "We would not so waste our precious remaining time. We will play more interesting games." He reached down for her, and she scuttled away.

Abruptly Molnekh jumped up and moved in front of the fat man. "Go away. You can't have her."

The fat man chortled in mild amusement. "Don't be foolish, stick man. Those who watch might punish us . . . but only if we break your bones badly enough to keep you from crawling to the hoppers, or injure your innards so that you can't eat. Otherwise we can hurt you all we like, which we'll do if you obstruct us in any way. We are ripe—ripeness has its privileges."

Molnekh seemed serious to the point of grimness, quite unlike his usual genial self. "You can't have her. She's a famous slayer's woman. If you annoy her, he'll break your bones, and worse—without regard for the feelings of those who watch." He turned to the others. "Think! What will Ruiz Aw do to *us,* if we allow her to be molested."

Gunderd rubbed his chin thoughtfully. "A good point." He stood and faced the fat men. "Go away," he told them.

Dolmaero also rose, glowering and clenching his fists.

They slowly backed away, bewildered hurt on their great shiny faces. "This is incorrect," said one, before he turned and shuffled off. "We are ripe. . . ."

Somehow she found it impossible to feel any real gratitude toward the others, though she knew she owed it.

GEJAS AND THE Yellowleaf watched the screen in her apartments, deep under Roderigo. The screen enhanced the dimness of the slaughterhouse, transmuting its grays and blacks into brilliant fluorescing colors.

Ruiz Aw filled the screen, moving in a slow jerky dance, as if to some unheard music. His body was an electric sapphire, and the blood that covered his arms and chest was a smoky crimson, the color of dying lava. In one hand he held his knife, a violet flame; this he used to draw complicated symbols in the air.

Gejas felt The Yellowleaf's dissatisfaction, a cold wind on his mind. "Don't worry, Master," he said, with as much sincerity as he owned. "The indices remain stable—he's not as mad as he seems."

She turned and gave him a dark-eyed look, full of meaning. He heard her words as clearly as if she had whispered them in his ear: *You must hope that you are correct. If he is broken, we lose a great opportunity.*

"He has always been a murderer, Master. We force him to embrace his true identity. One day he will thank us for his liberation, and he will be a fine tool indeed."

She nodded, a tiny inclination of her noble head, and he felt bathed in the watchful warmth of her confidence.

RUIZ AW HAD hidden himself a long way away from the grotesque actions of his body, the carrion stench of the slaughterhouse, the blood. His hiding spot was warm and bright, full of sweet rich music, and had the clean vital scent of flowers, but otherwise his sanctuary had no physical attributes. He felt safe there, but he wasn't entirely happy . . . he was alone. Occasionally he wondered why he couldn't have company, and then his thoughts strayed into a darker place, where the face of a beautiful woman could be seen through a haze of uneasiness.

He always pulled himself away from that image, with as much shame as fear.

Now and again, he was forced to watch his body perform an awful act, and for a bit he couldn't quite believe in his sanctuary—not while his victims groaned, not while their blood spattered over him.

But the jobs were soon finished and the evidence carried away into darkness, so that he could forget again.

TIME PASSED SLOWLY in the dim red light of the stockyard. Nisa slept, woke for a few endless hours, slept again. The others visited the feed hoppers, but she had no appetite. Dolmaero brought her a handful of pellets, but the food lay beside her on the plastic riser, untouched.

"At least have a drink of water," Molnekh urged her. "When Ruiz Aw returns for us, we must be ready to act, not weak from moping."

She looked at him with dull amazement. How could he

be so foolish as to expect Ruiz Aw to return? "He's dead or far away," she said.

Molnekh frowned. "We don't know that. How many times has Ruiz Aw surprised us?"

"I think the surprises are over," she said. "We'll never see Ruiz again." But she got up and went to the nearest tap. The water was cold and sweet, with a slight resinous tang.

She felt a little better after she had drunk her fill, a little more alert.

She was the first to notice the return of the mirrorsuited Roderigans. The sound of their boots sent waves of silence spreading through the cattle.

They seemed to be coming straight toward her. She scuttled back to the others, but the guards changed course accordingly, closing the distance with quick strides.

She wanted to run, but what good would that do?

RUIZ AW BEGAN to feel that familiar terrible impatience. The metal band around his waist sent a pang; it felt as though invisible fingers probed at an ancient unhealed wound. He began to listen for the rattle of the gurney.

When he heard it, he leaped to the edge of the platform, knife raised, anticipating the stroke that would free him from the ache of the band. He felt his face twist into an unnatural shape, halfway between a grin and a silent scream.

The next job slid into the dim illumination, and he bent over, touching a soft throat with trembling fingers.

The face was only a white blur through the tears which still came each time he did a job, for some reason he no longer understood.

"Ruiz?" The voice was softer than the throat, uncertain, slurred.

Other jobs had spoken to him, begged for mercy, cursed, raved. He had paid them no attention; what could he do but end their suffering? But this voice was different. Memory tugged at him, stayed the stroke of the knife for a moment.

He rubbed at his eyes until the tears cleared.

The woman was beautiful, with tangled black hair and dark eyes. Her face bore such an incongruous expression of dreamy horror that he had to look away from her.

The band sent him pain, and it forced the breath out of him, so that he bent over, pressing his arms to his stomach.

"Ruiz . . . it *is* you. What have they done to you?"

Her voice seemed almost as sweet as the pain was bitter. He looked up again, and some tiny degree of recognition filtered into his mind. Nisa? Was that her name? What was she to him?

NISA REGARDED RUIZ AW with unwilling recognition. He was naked but for a metal band around his waist, and was covered with dried blood, black in the dim red light, his hair a spiny snarl, as though he had rubbed the blood into it and then twisted it into spikes. He was surely mad; his eyes were very wide, white showing all around the pupils, and his lips were pulled back from his teeth in a straining rictus. He clenched a knife in one large hand, and both hand and knife were clotted with coagulated blood, so much blood that the shape of his hand was obscured.

No demon from Hell could have seemed more dreadful, and even in her sedated daze she was terrified.

"Ruiz," she said again, less certainly. Could this monster really be Ruiz Aw? Surely not, she thought. Surely this was just a torment devised by her captors for their own mysterious reasons, some automaton made in the shape of Ruiz.

His face twisted even more, and he fell to his knees, making an odd grunting sound, his breath whistling as though he could barely catch it.

She heard a small tinny voice near at hand. "Do it!" it demanded.

THE PAIN WAS eating him, devouring his substance. Soon there would be nothing left of Ruiz Aw but an empty skin. He wondered vaguely if that bag of skin would still stand

and slash . . . but then he realized it didn't matter, that he would be gone, safe from both pain and the knowledge of the deeds he had done. He felt a dull amazement that he hadn't seen this escape before. How easy it was going to be . . . to let the pain drain him away into nothingness.

Another hand would take Nisa's precious life, but not his. Not his.

He couldn't understand why this was so important, but he knew that it was, and so he sank toward death, almost content.

CHAPTER 7

GEJAS shivered in the chill of The Yellowleaf's displeasure.

"At once, at once," he said, the words forced from his mouth by the pressure of his fear. He switched off the neurostim and watched the man on the platform slowly subside into a boneless heap.

"You're right, of course," he said. "But the specimen is essentially undamaged, despite appearances, Master."

The Yellowleaf touched her dataslate, called up the specimen's indices. Each string of numbers glowed red at the last entry. A flashing warning bar read: PERSONALITY TERMINATION IMMINENT.

"I'm sorry, Master," Gejas said faintly. "I underestimated his attachment to the primitive woman. Who could have known? He's such a secretive creature; he hides from himself almost as well as he hides from us."

He watched her face; it remained cold and distant. He felt a bubble of desperation form in his chest. "But I can repair the situation, I'm sure," he said. "I'll place him back in the group he arrived in, intact. A sort of family, to heal his hurts and allow him to regain hope. Perhaps his bonds to the others of his group are stronger than we had assumed; perhaps we can use his loyalties to control him.

"I know; this is less satisfactory. If only we had more time. . . . We'd have no trouble breaking him to the leash, I'm certain. But time grows short. SeaStack burns. The pirates decimate each other, each day more passionately. We must learn what we can, Master."

She finally turned her head and looked at him with a terrifying degree of appraisal.

"Oh, it will surely work, Master," he babbled, believing it with all his might.

NISA STOOD AGAINST the wall, arms wrapped around her chest as if she were cold, though the air still held the moist animal heat of the stockyard. In fact, she had grown used to the warmth, and now in the rough coveralls provided by the guards, she was too warm.

The others, except for Einduix the cook, stood looking about the three rooms they had been brought to. Their faces revealed varying degrees of relief and apprehension. The guards had deposited Einduix on one of the cots in the second room, where he still lay in his deathlike sleep.

Gunderd touched her shoulder, and she jumped.

He held up his hands in a disarming gesture. "Sorry. I didn't mean to startle you. What can you tell me about the change in our accommodations?"

She shrugged. "How would I know anything?"

"Well, the guards come for you, take you away, and a few hours later we're escorted from the stockyard and installed in what for Roderigo must be termed palatial quarters. What happened to you? Perhaps it has a bearing on our new circumstances."

"I don't want to talk about it."

He frowned. "Listen, Nisa-the-princess. We have very little chance of survival, and even if we do survive . . . on Roderigo our lives will torment us until we die." He looked about the rooms, as if searching for something. "Our hosts listen, but I speak an obvious truth, so they will probably not punish me for stating it. At any rate . . . you must overcome your petulance and risk your dignity, if you have any hopes involving the future. Our only tools are what knowledge we can share. Tell me what you can, please."

She wanted to reply that she had discarded hope, but in his thin rough face she saw a great terror, held barely in check. She felt a pang of unwilling admiration for him, that in his more certain knowledge of their plight, he could still keep his wits.

"All right," she said. "The guards took me to a small room and strapped me to a wheeled table. They sent me along a track, through a hole and into a dark place. After a while I saw a dim red light and a naked man dancing on a platform in the middle of the darkness . . . though I could hear no music. I was drugged, I'm sure—nothing seemed to matter very much and I felt little fear. Then my table stopped by the platform and I saw the man more clearly. I thought it was Ruiz Aw, though I couldn't be sure. He was covered with black blood. He held a knife high. He took me by the throat, and I thought he would kill me then. I called to him and he stopped. . . ." She shook herself. "But I don't believe it was Ruiz, now. The man's face was very strange. Then he fell down; perhaps he was dying. My table took me away after a while, and the guards brought me here."

Gunderd looked no less puzzled when she had finished. "I wonder what it means?" he said, his eyes unfocused. "I wonder—"

The doors opened with a clang, and two guards carried Ruiz in, unconscious. Old blood crusted on his body. He stank of the abattoir. She looked into his face and saw a frightening absence there, worse than just a common senselessness.

It disturbed Nisa more than the mania she had seen in the slaughterhouse.

They dumped him on a cot next to Einduix and went away.

The others looked at Nisa, as if asking her what they should do. She went in the other sleeping room and lay down. Let them deal with whatever Ruiz had become.

*   *   *

UP THROUGH A terrible dark dream, Ruiz Aw swam toward the light.

He dreamed he was a great monster, knee deep in the sea, his head above the last icy wisps of atmosphere, thrusting out into the cold brilliance of space. He looked down at the misty surface of the world, so far below, and laughed a wild laugh.

The texture of the dream was a mad hopelessness, compounded by a ferocious amusement—though he couldn't say what he found so amusing.

He laughed again, a belly-bursting laugh that seemed to go on too long, until he felt the world wavering, until it seemed he had lost a lifetime's breath. He looked down at himself and noticed the shuddering of his flesh, like the slow-motion chaos of an earthquake—and then he saw his skin begin to tear open under the wrenching of his laughter.

He expected to see the ordinary things to be found inside a body: flesh, bone, blood. But there was nothing inside him but a darkness more absolute than starless space. He stopped laughing, but it was too late. The ruptures spread, and he felt his body begin to collapse, to fall back toward the world, dissolving into shrieking tatters.

HE WOKE FLAILING and gasping for air.

Dolmaero and Molnekh held him down for a moment, before releasing him and jumping back. "Be calm," said Dolmaero. "We weren't attacking you, Ruiz Aw."

Ruiz realized that he had been striking at them; a welt bloomed on Molnekh's cheek and Dolmaero had suffered a split lip.

For once, he could recall a few fragments of his dream, though already he felt the details slipping away. What did it mean, that he dreamed and remembered? Were the doors of his mind finally crumbling?

"Sorry," he muttered.

He was sitting in a hygiene cubicle, where apparently

the two Pharaohans had been trying to wash him clean.
Rusty water had splashed high on the cubicle's plastic
walls, but he was still stained with the product of his labor.

He held up a trembling hand and examined the matter
that caked under his fingernails.

Memory clubbed him, and he bent over, retching.

"Can we help you, Ruiz Aw?" asked Dolmaero uncertainly.

"No," he gasped, "no. Leave me. Please!"

The two of them went out, closing the cubicle's door
behind them.

How many had he murdered? He hadn't even kept a
count. A hundred? A thousand? How many lives had he
ended this time, just to save his worthless self some pain?

And Nisa? An involuntary sob forced its way past his
clenched teeth. Had he killed her in a mindless involuntary
spasm, or had he left her to Gejas? Surely she must be
dead.

Why wasn't Ruiz dead, too? He surely deserved to be,
and the Roderigans weren't known for capricious mercy.

He took a deep breath and leaned back against the
plastic wall. He was still alive, which meant that he had a
chance, however small, to make the Roderigans pay for
what they had done. Comforting visions rose up in his
mind's eye: Gejas crucified on a neurostim cross, body
spasming frenetically. The Yellowleaf throttled with her
own slimy guts. Roderigo itself blooming into fiery beautiful destruction, its bunkers and tunnels cleansed of the
horror that now inhabited it.

He tried to smile, to take some comfort from those
lovely images, but he felt a curious distance from them, as
if they were too far removed from any possible reality to
satisfy him.

Finally he stood up and turned on the cubicle's shower.
The hot water pounded him, and he stood there, scrubbing
until his skin was almost raw, until he was as clean as he
would ever be.

Warm air swirled around him, and he closed his eyes,
waiting without thought until he was dry.

When he emerged from the cubicle, Gunderd handed

him a pair of gray coveralls. As he put them on, he looked about the room. Everyone was there but Nisa. He struggled to control his urge to cry out, to smash something. What had he expected?

"She's in the other room," said Gunderd.

He took two long strides and reached the door. She lay on a cot, her back to him, and he could see that she breathed.

That was enough, for the moment. He backed slowly away. If she could find refuge in sleep, he wouldn't disturb her.

"You're pleased," said Gunderd. "Are you sure you should be?"

Ruiz turned to the former second mate. "What does that mean?"

Gunderd glanced uncertainly at the other Pharaohans. "Remember your suspicions?"

Ruiz couldn't bring himself to care. His former worries seemed remote and unimportant compared to what had just happened to him on Roderigo. So what if one of them had been to the Gencha? If one of his companions had become Corean's creature? He couldn't imagine how such a small thing could affect him now.

"What is he talking about?" asked Dolmaero.

Ruiz sat down on the nearest cot. He didn't want to answer, but he found the thought of continuing to deceive Dolmaero repellent, even if Dolmaero were the one who belonged to Corean. Deception was part of his old life—along with the violence, the death.

That life was gone, for better or worse. It came to him that his dreams of vengeance were just that: dreams. In his present state of mind, he would be incapable of bringing destruction to Roderigo, should an opportunity miraculously present itself. He sighed. He didn't even care that the Roderigans were surely listening.

"Publius told me something," Ruiz said.

Gunderd raised his eyebrows in a quizzical expression, as if he questioned the wisdom of revealing this, but he said nothing.

"What?" demanded Dolmaero.

"He told me that Corean sent one of you to the Gencha minddivers. Which one . . . he didn't know, or wouldn't say."

A silence followed. Dolmaero seemed to sink into thought, and his broad face closed in on itself.

Finally he spoke again. "Do you believe this?"

"I didn't," said Ruiz. "Until someone killed the folk in the lifeboat."

Dolmaero rubbed his face, an uncharacteristic gesture, and Ruiz saw sweat glisten on his jowls. "You spoke of this once. Long ago, it seems now."

"Yes."

"The Gencha take a man's self, you said. They steal his soul and leave nothing but the urge to please his master."

"Yes."

Dolmaero shuddered. "Tell me. Would a man know if he had lost his soul?"

Ruiz shrugged and did not answer.

"Not necessarily," said Gunderd in a pedantic tone. "Only if his master commanded him to recognize the fact. If his master told him to conceal it, no one could tell, not even the Roderigans . . . perhaps not even another Gencha practitioner."

Dolmaero went to his cot and sat heavily. He stared at the floor, apparently empty of questions, for once.

Even Molnekh seemed sobered. He said nothing. After a while he went to the food hopper and got a handful of pellets, which he ate without his customary relish.

"I wonder what our hosts think of your revelations," said Gunderd, glancing about the room.

GEJAS WATCHED THE specimens. He touched his slate and linked to The Yellowleaf's data retrieval locus. "Master," he said. "We've confirmed the connection."

He watched her beautiful, terrible face. "Yes, as you suspected, Corean is involved. Your plan is vindicated, Master. It only remains to set it in motion."

She looked at him with eyes full of dreadful promises, and he was very afraid. "Oh yes, Master," he said. "Ruiz

Aw will play his part, however it goes at the virtual. If he returns with the data we need, well and good. If not, we'll use him to hook the slaver."

GEJAS WALKED IN, his gait as springy as ever, his face full of alien cheer. "Everyone up!" he called. "Time to go on a journey."

Ruiz got carefully to his feet, still sore from the neurostim, from the straining of his muscles in their attempt to escape the pain. Hatred flooded into him, but it was an odd hatred. He couldn't imagine any way to ease the emotion, to satisfy his need for retribution. His earlier fantasies now seemed pale and colorless in the light of the tongue's actual presence.

Crucifixion seemed far too gentle a punishment, for Gejas.

He could barely see the tongue's grinning face. Other faces—pleading, hopeless, numb—seemed to float in his vision.

"Come, come," said Gejas. "No time to waste. Let's go, all!"

Ruiz felt a shudder of rage pass through him. He tried to speak, but his throat seemed full of some burning substance, and he made a foolish croak. Gejas turned to him, crooking his eyebrow up in an inquisitive gesture. "What?"

Ruiz cleared his throat, tried again. "Where do we go?"

Gejas frowned. "Why haven't you learned the unwisdom of questions? And where is the respect you should show me?"

"Fuck you, Master," said Ruiz carefully. "If you didn't need me very badly, I'd be dead. So you must be content with what respect you deserve. Answer my questions, or do without my cooperation."

Gejas's face twisted into a predatory mask, but only for an instant. "Ah. Well, yes, we need you. So! We go to Dorn to consult the virtual."

"All of us?"

"If you wish. The Yellowleaf is merciful, and permits you to enjoy the comfort and company of your friends

while you prepare for your mission." Gejas looked at
Einduix, comatose on his cot. "Though why burden yourself with the little turnip? We'll send him to the composter.
No profit in slaughtering such an odd specimen . . . the
cannibals are surprisingly conservative in their tastes."

"No," said Ruiz. The cook was nothing to him, though
he had enjoyed the little man's music. But he wanted to
frustrate Gejas in every possible way. "We'll take him. And
what payment will you offer me for this job?"

"We've already discussed this," said Gejas in a soft
deadly voice. "Your life. That's all you may expect to gain."

Ruiz laughed, a sour hollow sound. "Insignificant—
you've made me worthless to myself. You must offer something I value more."

Gejas snapped his fingers at the guards. "Bring out the
woman."

They brought her forth, twisting and struggling, her face
full of fear.

The rage and hatred in Ruiz Aw congealed into something much colder and stronger, an emotion he could put
no name to. A great distance opened between himself and
his feelings; the situation took on an unreal, abstract quality. Without effort, he adopted an expression of sneering
condescension.

Gejas gave him a curious glance, as if the tongue's expertise in reading faces had suddenly deserted him. He
frowned and looked at Nisa. "This is the woman you would
have died for. I believe I can buy your cooperation with her
pain, if necessary."

Ruiz laughed, a metallic sound.

Nisa looked up at him, and he was strangely pleased to
see that she regarded him almost without recognition.
"Then you are wrong. What are these creatures to me?
Phantasms, no more. Their lives are nothing notable, a
blink of tedium between unbeing and the grave. At best
they're symbols of my power over you. I insist on their
preservation . . . but only because I take my only remaining delight in annoying you and your hag."

Gejas's face darkened, and Ruiz smiled a smile that hurt
his face. He turned to Nisa and struck her across the

mouth, so that she sagged and a trickle of blood ran down her chin. Her eyes grew enormous and bewildered.

He felt a sickness that never reached his face. It wasn't just Nisa's confusion and hurt—it was the blood. But he thrust the sickness away. "See?" he shouted, his voice trembling on the edge of a happy mania. "Mine to hurt. Not yours."

He whirled and seized Gejas by the silky material of his shirt. "Do you see?" he screamed into the astonished tongue's face. "Fuck with me and I'll sit down and die right here. Do you doubt I can do it?"

Gejas picked ineffectually at Ruiz's hands. "Be calm, Ruiz. No, I don't doubt you. We peeled you well enough to see that you have all the skills a famous slayer requires."

Ruiz pushed his face into Gejas's until their eyes were no more than a few centimeters apart. In the Roderigan's gaze Ruiz saw ferocity and uncertainty, contempt and fright. *Good enough, for now,* he thought, bending down. He jerked Gejas close and lunged.

Cartilage crunched, as his head flattened the tongue's nose.

He stepped back with a high-spirited giggle and folded his arms. Gejas stumbled back; his eyes went wide and then ignited. He snapped his arm straight and a sonic knife dropped into his fist. With flickering speed, he drove it toward Ruiz's throat.

Ruiz waited for the blade, still as stone.

A low bone-trembling tone sounded, and Gejas dropped as if dead, the blade grazing down the front of Ruiz's chest. Ruiz felt a cold stinging pain and looked down to see if his innards were still in his belly. The knife had barely broken the skin.

"Ooh," said Ruiz. "Synaptic decoupler. The Yellowleaf seems to be keeping an eye on you, shithead—and a finger on your button. Nice for me."

The two guards finally reacted. They started into movement that seemed painfully slow, pulling out neural whips and starting toward Ruiz.

"No," croaked Gejas from his sprawl on the floor. "The

Yellowleaf permits this activity." He started to rise, as carefully as if he were made of glass.

Ruiz skipped forward and kicked Gejas in the ribs, so that he rolled across the room and thumped into the far wall.

"What fun," Ruiz said brightly. He took a small detached pleasure in the tongue's humiliation, but again the blood sickened him, even though it was his enemy's blood. What was wrong with him?

"Stuns only," said Gejas, wheezing and clutching his ribs.

The guards pointed their stun rods at Ruiz.

He faded away to a single point of triumphant futility. And then to nothing.

THEY WAITED ON the streaming deck of a Roderigan submarine, looking through a misty darkness at the deeper smudge of land. Gunderd stood by Ruiz; the others gathered in an anxious clump a few steps away. The only illumination came from the glow of green ready-lights on the weapons of the Roderigan guards.

"Dorn," said Gunderd. On the whole, the former sailor seemed more cheerful than he had since the sinking of the *Loracca*. Perhaps, Ruiz thought, Gunderd was just happy to be away from Roderigo's dungeons.

"The devil you know is only preferable when you can tolerate it," Ruiz muttered.

"Eh?" asked Gunderd.

"Nothing," said Ruiz. "So, you're a scholar. What do you know of Dorn?"

"Very little," said Gunderd. "Ghost stories, mostly. I'll tell a few when we're sitting round the campfire. Do you suppose they'll allow us a campfire?" He pulled his coveralls tight and shivered. "It's cold."

"We'll have a campfire, then," Ruiz promised.

Gunderd gave him a speculative glance. "I confess to astonishment. How did you come to have such influence with the hetmen? I mean, we're alive, most of us. More or less." He glanced at Einduix, strapped to a floater on the deck.

Ruiz shrugged. "They need me, for some reason. They want information from the virtual, and none of their own can get it. For some reason they think I can."

"Ah," said Gunderd, but he looked no less confused.

Gejas climbed over the rail. The tongue wore a black shipsuit and a helmet haloed with sensors. "Come," he said. "The lander is ready." He pointed at Ruiz. "You first."

Ruiz laughed. "Me last."

Gejas tensed and moved toward Ruiz, baring his teeth. A neural whip appeared in his hand.

Ruiz stepped back, seeking better footing on the water-slick deck, but he bumped into one of the dozen mirror-suited guards that waited with them. The guard shoved him with the butt of his graser. Ruiz kept his balance and turned to the guard, planning some satisfyingly destructive act.

A hatch in the conning tower hissed open, and The Yellowleaf stepped forth, clad in light armor of some dead-black composite. An impressive collection of weapons hung from harness points on her torso. She carried her helmet under one arm.

Gejas stopped and looked at his master. Ruiz could see nothing at all in her stony eyes, but apparently Gejas read some dire message there. He dropped his head and said in a voice shaking with fear, "The Yellowleaf states: You may go last, if you wish. The Yellowleaf states: We must board the lander quickly. Persons unfriendly to Roderigo patrol Dorn's waters. They will attempt to prevent us from landing if they find us."

Ruiz faced the hetman. "We have not yet negotiated my fee for this job."

"The Yellowleaf states: We will do so before you enter the virtual."

Ruiz hesitated. "All right," he said finally. "Why not?"

He couldn't avoid an uncomfortable thought: that in agreeing with the hetman in the slightest degree, he was taking another step along the path to oblivion. He still hoped to survive long enough to give Nisa a chance at life —however unreasonable that hope might be.

He glanced at her as the guards took them to the boarding ladder. She looked back at him with a smooth passionless expression, as though his were a passing face in a crowd of strangers. He was suddenly reminded of the look she had given him in Bidderum, on her way to her Expiation . . . and to her first death.

THEY LANDED ON a beach of gray cobblestones just as a dim pearly light began to lighten the mist. The half-dozen guards went ashore first, their mirrorsuits detuned a little, so that they looked like wisps of fog. When they were deployed into a perimeter a hundred meters from the lander, The Yellowleaf stepped onto the beach.

She stood without movement for a long minute, then motioned.

"Out," Gejas whispered urgently.

Ruiz sensed a genuine apprehension in the tongue, and so he decided to save his next defiant gesture for later. He nodded and went down the ramp behind the others. He took a remote pleasure in discovering that the Roderigans had enemies dangerous enough to make such precautions necessary.

With the thought came a lift of irrational optimism . . . but he put it away. "Not yet," he muttered.

"What?" The tongue stood at his shoulder, peering into the mist, a small ruptor strapped to his left forearm.

"What are you so afraid of?" asked Ruiz.

"Probably nothing," said Gejas, his eyes darting from side to side. "Anyway, nothing for you to worry about."

Ruiz shrugged and stepped aside as the first of the landwalkers bumped down the ramp, carrying racks of gear on its low steel back. The next one carried Einduix's litter, strapped to its underside.

Gunderd stood beside him. "He fears Castle Delt. Delt and Roderigo were the principals in Dorn's destruction.

Both claim the island, and both fear the other will discover how to exploit the virtual."

"I see," said Ruiz.

THEY FOLLOWED THE four landwalkers in a single file, flanked by the unseen guards. Ahead of the landwalkers, Gejas picked a path through tumbled stones and thorny scrub. The mist still lay heavily on the island, but the sun was soon bright enough to make the going fairly easy, though the waist-high scrub eventually soaked Ruiz and the others.

They climbed into an area where the stones were larger and showed the marks of tools—though the stones had long ago weathered into anonymity. Here and there, holes yawned; apparently the ruins had deep roots. Ruiz couldn't tell a pillar from a paving stone, but the place had a melancholy sense of antiquity, as if sad ghosts watched from beneath every dark heap.

The land rose slowly and the mist grew thinner, until it floated in tattered streamers across the ruins, and Ruiz could see the sea, shining below them. The island's central massif became visible: once-jagged peaks of black basalt, now worn into gentler contours. Everywhere were the remains of ancient structures, reduced to dimly seen patterns amid the stony wastes.

Ruiz walked almost blindly, trying to think nothing, feel nothing. To a large extent he succeeded. The others said nothing to distract him, although Dolmaero seemed to be having some difficulty maintaining the pace; he breathed in a loud rasp that gradually took on a desperate tone.

Once Ruiz looked up to see Nisa watching him. She looked away instantly, as if her gaze had fallen upon him by accident.

After three hours of steady hiking, they descended into a hollow and Gejas signaled a stop. The landwalkers formed a defensive square. Several of the guards reappeared.

"We wait here for a while," said Gejas.

Dolmaero sat heavily on a flat rock, gasping for air, his

face pale and blotchy. Ruiz seemed to wake suddenly; he saw that Dolmaero was in real difficulty. He knelt beside the Guildmaster and loosened the collar of Dolmaero's overalls.

Gejas watched incuriously.

Ruiz remembered that several hours had passed since he had last baited the tongue. "Give me a medical limpet," he said.

Gejas shook his head. "Medical supplies are reserved for essential personnel."

Ruiz smiled, somehow delighted. "Oh? Give me the limpet. Or do your own dirty work."

Gejas looked at his master. She nodded, a barely perceptible movement, and Gejas hung his head. Ruiz saw that Gejas had changed profoundly over the last few hours; he no longer seemed the perfectly-at-ease monster. In some way Ruiz had disrupted Gejas's world. It seemed an insignificant revenge, compared to what Gejas had done to him, but the thought gave Ruiz a brief chilly pleasure.

The tongue consulted the miniature dataslate he wore at his wrist. "The limpet is in the second starboard pannier on the red-legged landwalker." He turned away and started supervising the guards, who were erecting a canopy of chameleon gauze over the campsite.

Ruiz considered forcing the tongue to fetch the limpet. But then he realized that a tiny traitorous sliver of hope had embedded itself in his heart. He didn't want to risk driving the man to a violence The Yellowleaf might not be quick enough to stop. He looked at Dolmaero; the Guildmaster seemed no worse, but perhaps he should get the limpet without delay.

So he went to the landwalker and dug out the limpet. It was of Dilvermoon manufacture, a model with which he was familiar. He quickly activated it and slapped it on Dolmaero's chest.

The indicators trembled to life, showing an orange-red on several of the scales. Dolmaero looked down, pop-eyed, as the limpet sent several hair-thin sensor wires into his skin.

"What . . . ?" he gasped. Then the limpet took control

of his laboring heart and dulled the pain. He looked more frightened than relieved.

Ruiz watched the indicators fade toward amber, then chartreuse. "You'll be all right," he told Dolmaero. "Your heart is strong. Rest for a bit. Don't touch the limpet." Dolmaero nodded, eyes still too large.

Ruiz rose and went over to Gejas. "Why are we stopping here?" he asked.

Gejas didn't look at him. "The virtual won't open until local midnight," the tongue said, in a thin colorless voice.

CHAPTER 8

Ruiz found a smooth stone and sat. He watched the guards as they set up the camp, and out of the corner of his eye he watched Nisa. She leaned against a low gray-barked tree and gazed out over the way they had come. Molnekh and Gunderd joined Dolmaero on his rock; Molnekh looked at the limpet with bright curious eyes. "Don't touch it," warned Ruiz.

Molnekh nodded easily, but he still seemed fascinated by the pangalac device.

Gejas activated the chameleon gauze, and the hollow fell into an artificial twilight.

Ruiz shivered. In the sunlight, the day had seemed warm.

Gejas set out various sensors around the campsite's perimeter and assembled an elaborate security console in the center of the camp. Over the console a self-erecting weapons arch rose; on top was a heavy ruptor and a brace of antipersonnel grasers. Ruiz was a little surprised by the thoroughness of these precautions. He shrugged. Perhaps this simply reflected a habitual paranoia.

The guards triggered self-inflating shelters, low bubbles of shiny green plastic. From one of the landwalkers, they brought a field autochef; its battered olive chassis reminded Ruiz of a hundred other such machines, machines that had fed him on a hundred long-ago battlegrounds.

He felt a sudden sad nostalgia for the single-minded boy he had once been, the boy who had been able to destroy his enemies with such a clear conscience. He'd felt clean then, so clean, so sure of the rightness of his various lost causes.

He looked down at his hands, which would never be clean again.

Ruiz got up and went to the perimeter, a few feet from Nisa, who still stood looking out over the ruins below.

He was surprised when she spoke. "What's happened to you, Ruiz?" she asked.

"You couldn't understand," he said, attempting to match her detachment.

He made the mistake of glancing at her, and saw that her eyes were swimming with barely restrained tears. "I didn't really believe you'd ever hurt me," she said, looking down.

His gaze fell on a strand of audiovisual sensors almost at his feet. He took a deep breath. "Things have changed. I've changed." He made his voice as cold as he could.

He turned away and saw Gejas watching him with smiling assessment.

THE YELLOWLEAF DISAPPEARED into her shelter when the guards served lunch—a bland hash of reconstituted vegetables with a slab of gray seedbread.

Ruiz sat apart from the others while he ate. He couldn't display any human feeling for them; Gejas was too alert. Already he might have made a fatal mistake in speaking politely to Nisa. He must wear a face of mad unpredictability, of black nihilist joy—and he must, to the best of his ability, *feel* that way. Any other face would give Gejas irresistible leverage.

When he had finished the tasteless food, he sailed the

plate away, as if without thought. It struck the weapons arch just above Gejas's head, and Ruiz turned to give the Roderigan a wide grin.

Gejas glared. A bit of hash decorated his shoulder; he flicked it away with a look of distaste. "Rather than playing silly games, you should be resting, slayer. Midnight will arrive before you know it, and you'll need all your strength."

Ruiz got up and swaggered toward the tongue. "Oh? Perhaps I'll join The Yellowleaf in her shelter. She might find me entertaining."

Gejas laughed uneasily. "Perhaps. But not in the way you mean. You wouldn't find her attentions pleasant, I think. No, restrain your ambitions; go to your own shelter. I'll put the primitive woman in with you." He showed his teeth in an approximation of a smile. "The stockyard drugs have doubtless worn off by now, and you may breed to your heart's content."

Ruiz twisted his face into a contemptuous mask. "Your master's mouth is tongueless; with such a disadvantage she couldn't be very good in bed, eh? I'll leave it to you to go sniffing after the bitch." He glanced at Nisa without focusing his eyes on her. "My slave is untrained and shows little natural aptitude, so I'll rest alone."

He was reassured to see that Gejas once again regarded him with baffled rage. He nodded affably and went into one of the shelters.

Ruiz lay on the pallet, teeth clenched, refusing to feel anything. The afternoon passed slowly.

RUIZ AW EMERGED into the cold twilight, exhausted. He saw that his people sat around a glowpoint the guards had set up in the center of the camp, warming their hands at its feeble heat. A few tiny blue lights hung from the chameleon gauze, shedding a wan light. Someone had moved Einduix's stretcher close to the glowpoint, but the cook was apparently still comatose.

Gejas stood at his security console, studying its readouts intently.

The Yellowleaf stood at the perimeter, looking out at the black mountains. Obeying some dim impulse, Ruiz approached her.

As he came up behind her, The Yellowleaf turned abruptly, her weapons jingling against her armor. She regarded him with her usual opacity.

He fought a sudden urge to attack her. She was, he was sure, as strong, as quick as he was—and she was thoroughly armed. Even if by some stealthy miracle he succeeded in wringing her neck, Gejas would destroy him an instant later.

So he adopted an insolent smile and said, "Time to bargain."

If she reacted at all, he couldn't see it. Her face was disconcerting in its unreadability.

Gejas relinquished his console to one of the guards and came trotting over. "What is this?" he asked in a breathless voice. "You must not speak to The Yellowleaf directly —that is disrespectful and will bring severe punishment."

Ruiz laughed. "I've already been severely punished. Therefore I must perform sufficient disrespectful acts to balance our accounts. Not so?" He turned to Gejas. "We're a long way from even, tongue."

Gejas frowned. "You should stop this foolishness. We have serious matters to discuss."

"Indeed we do," Ruiz said. "What will you offer me for my help? And please, not my life, nor the lives of my worthless companions. Something better."

Gejas watched The Yellowleaf's face. "The Yellowleaf asks: Why do you hold them in such low esteem?"

The question surprised Ruiz a little, but he let all the bitterness in him boil up and answer for him. "Why? Let me tell you about them." His voice swelled into a shout. He turned and saw that the others were watching, wide-eyed. "Look at them! Let me number their virtues. There's Gunderd, a failed scholar hiding from his inadequacies, playing make-believe sailor. His only noticeable skill is cheating at cards. There's his cook, the small orange vegetable there, whom we dragged along just to annoy you. There's Molnekh the all-consuming, a gangly dirtworld norp, a walking appetite who to my knowledge has never spoken a sentence more intelligent than 'Feed me.' And Dolmaero, his loyal dirtworld dog, a snake oil addict, a dour lump of a man who hasn't smiled more than twice since I've known him."

Ruiz turned his attention to Nisa; he hardened his heart to the necessary degree and went on. "And look at that: the dirtworld princess. Grew up in a fly-specked hovel of a palace in a shit-soaked stone town, and is therefore certain that she is the galaxy's highest form of life. Managed to push her ignorant arrogance far enough to get herself put to death for excessive whoring, and then some idiot revived her, on the slaveship that was hauling her corpse to Sook."

Ruiz turned back to The Yellowleaf, so he wouldn't have to look at the faces of his friends.

Gejas spoke. "The Yellowleaf muses: And yet, in the slaughterhouse you refused to cut her throat."

Ruiz shrugged. "A handy symbol, nothing more. A logical stopping point. I'd cut far too many throats. Had you not sent her, another throat I could not cut would soon have arrived." He looked at The Yellowleaf, feeling a bright crazy burning in his eyes. "I'm not even sure I could cut your stringy throat, if you offered it to me. I've changed." He said it for effect, but as soon as the words were out of his mouth, he was afraid it might be true.

An expression appeared on The Yellowleaf's face at last. Ruiz hoped for fear or hatred, but then he saw it was a sort of disgusted pity, the expression of a person who has seen a broken-backed dog lying in the gutter.

Anger flared through him. It felt oddly pleasant.

"The Yellowleaf admonishes: Put aside your grievances and attend to your negotiations. The Yellowleaf offers: Free passage back to SeaStack for you and your people."

Ruiz laughed incredulously. "Really? Aboard a Roderigo vessel? Do you take me for a complete fool?"

"The Yellowleaf responds in the negative. She has hired an independent transporter, unaffiliated with Roderigo."

"Oh, of course. Would it surprise you to learn that I don't wish to return to SeaStack?"

"The Yellowleaf asks: Where would you wish to go?"

"Off Sook."

"The Yellowleaf states: This is acceptable. She will arrange passage to the nearest launch ring. There you will be given funds sufficient to take you and as many of your people as you wish off Sook—but you must personally arrange for any further travel."

"That's easy enough. . . ." Ruiz said slowly. "But how will she convince me to trust her?"

"The Yellowleaf states: She would not expect you to. She will make herself hostage. She alone will accompany your people to the transport she has contracted, there to wait for you. When you have completed your mission and have the requisite information, she will release your people to you, and provide you weapons with which you may defend yourself against any treachery."

It seemed a surprising offer. What, Ruiz wondered, was the catch? "Who will provide this transport?"

"The Yellowleaf reiterates: An independent contractor, whose identity is immaterial. They lie offshore in a submersible, awaiting our signal. When you have gone up to the virtual, The Yellowleaf will go down to the sea with your people. You will be provided with a comm device, with which you may make arrangements for the exchange when you emerge from the virtual. Do you wish to speak with the contractor now?"

Ruiz was amazed at the thoroughness of the hetman's arrangements. It was almost as if she intended to play fair. "Why not?" he said.

Gejas produced a small transceiver and made as if to strap it to Ruiz's upper arm. Ruiz snatched it, smiling brightly, and then examined the mechanism carefully. He could find nothing obviously wrong with it—no explosives, no drug injectors, no neural dampers. It seemed to be exactly what the Roderigans had claimed: a simple short-range transceiver.

"No video," he said. Instead of strapping it to his arm, he knelt and put the adhesive band around his boot. Perhaps the thick plastic of the boot would thwart any dangerous mechanisms.

Gejas snorted. "The Yellowleaf states: You are properly

cautious, but no treachery is intended. No, there's no video, but the scrambling is sophisticated. To activate the device, enter the following sequence on the keypad." And Gejas spoke a string of numbers.

Ruiz tapped them in; the unit's ready-light glowed green.

"Yes?" The voice, tiny and distorted by some cloaking device, issued from the speaker.

Ruiz took a deep breath and then, in a creditable imitation of Gejas's soft light voice, said, "Repeat your instructions."

Gejas seemed startled but unalarmed. The Yellowleaf's face, as ever, was unreadable.

A moment passed, then the speaker rattled and the distorted voice answered, "We are to take on passengers, for a destination to be given us by a final passenger, who will notify us on this frequency when we are to pick him up."

"And?" Ruiz couldn't believe that was all there was.

A pause ensued. Then the anonymous voice answered uncertainly, "Do you have further instructions for us? If so, we may need to negotiate additional fees."

"Never mind," Ruiz said. "Stand by."

He clicked off the communicator. The Yellowleaf watched him without expression, but Gejas wore a twisted smile.

"The Yellowleaf asks: Are you satisfied with these arrangements?"

"Not particularly." Ruiz considered the situation. "Tell me. Why did you bring us up here?"

"The Yellowleaf states: Dangerous folk frequent the seashore. Here we are safest."

"Plausible," Ruiz said. What would prevent The Yellowleaf from issuing new instructions when she and the others reached the sub? "Let's do this a little differently," he said.

How could he maintain a reasonable degree of control over the situation? "How about this?" he said. "The hetman disarms herself and comes with me. One of my people comes along to keep an eye on her until I return from the virtual—that person must remain sufficiently intact to give me a report of the hetman's activities during my absence.

Clear so far? We'll exchange hostages when I've got the information you require." He spoke without the slightest hope that the hetman would agree.

Gejas looked at his master, and his mouth dropped open. "The Yellowleaf will consider your proposal." The two walked to the other side of the camp, and Gejas spoke in an animated whisper, gesturing wildly.

Apparently, Ruiz thought, the tongue was unhappy with the revised plan.

Eventually Gejas fell silent and the Roderigans returned. "The Yellowleaf states: Your proposal is acceptable, on one condition. The Yellowleaf must retain her armor."

Ruiz was unable to conceal his astonishment. "All right," he said.

"The Yellowleaf asks: May we now see to the details? Time is passing, and the virtual opens at midnight."

COREAN SLAPPED MARMO jovially, her rings clattering on his metal torso. "It was him! He disguised his voice but it was Ruiz Aw. I know it!" She turned away from the communicator and looked at the screen, which showed a wide-angle view of Dorn.

The island seemed to float above the star-silvered sea, a featureless mass. She wondered: Where on those dark slopes did Ruiz Aw wait for her?

Marmo cleared his throat and spoke with his usual deliberation. "Then you're pleased?"

"Of course. Why shouldn't I be?"

The old pirate sighed. "Don't forget, the Roderigans will surely try to cheat you. And your previous jousts with Ruiz Aw have never gone as you expected."

"How kind of you to point this out. However, we're well armed." She patted the sub's wide weapons console. "The Roderigans believe we're in a lightly armored little seabus —they won't be expecting *this*. We have the Moc, if it comes to hand-to-hand. We have the Genched Pharaohan in place, if treachery is required. And Ruiz has no reason to suspect that we're the ones who've been hired to 'transport' him." She shrugged. "What can go wrong?"

"I've heard that question before," Marmo muttered. "Usually on the eve of some great disaster."

"THE YELLOWLEAF ASKS: Will you come into the shelter, so we can discuss the information you must obtain from the virtual?"

Ruiz nodded and followed the hetman into her shelter, Gejas at his heels.

As he lifted the flap to go inside, he saw that the guards had begun to serve dinner.

The Pharaohans had turned away, but Gunderd grinned and gave him a wink.

Inside, The Yellowleaf indicated a low chair, and Ruiz sat.

The hetman took a chair across a small glowpoint, but Gejas stood. "The Yellowleaf states: The data we require has to do with the Gencha enclave which exists under the fortress of Alonzo Yubere, in SeaStack."

Ruiz heard this with no great surprise; he no longer expected anything else. It was as if his existence had become some sort of inept drama, which kept returning doggedly to the same unsolvable problem. "I see," he said.

"The Yellowleaf elaborates: We wish to know four things. One, how many Gencha live in the enclave? Two, what defenses protect the enclave? Three, why have these defenses never been penetrated and the enclave raided? Four—and most important—what is the great secret connected with the enclave? Can you remember these things?"

"Yes," said Ruiz. "What makes you think this knowledge lies in the virtual? What if it doesn't?"

"The Yellowleaf promises: If you fail, you will be given to Gejas for his amusement."

Ruiz laughed. "An effective threat indeed. Well, then, tell me what I need to know about the virtual."

"The Yellowleaf states: Very little. In a little while, you'll set out for a certain cave on the mountainside. There at midnight the virtual field will envelope you. Your mind will dream with the virtual—it will be as if you have returned to the days of Dorn's glory, when the island was encrusted with libraries and the villas of the keepers. Or so our information leads us to believe."

The Yellowleaf stood abruptly and began to remove her weapons, laying them on an armory rack. The process took several minutes. When she was finished, she turned and raised her arms.

"The Yellowleaf permits you to examine her for compliance."

Ruiz got up and approached the hetman reluctantly. He felt the same reluctance to touch The Yellowleaf that he might have felt toward a venomous insect. But he forced himself to loosen the latches of her armor and slip his hands inside.

It struck him as terribly unnatural that she should possess so human a body—tautly muscular, but with small soft breasts. The bizarre intimacy of the moment made his stomach heave uneasily. This was the creature who had ordered him to the slaughterhouse—what odd perversity of fate now caused him to caress her as a lover might? He felt slightly dizzy, but finished, finding nothing.

He noticed that the armor seemed slightly vulnerable over the lower ribs, where it was segmented for mobility. He filed the datum away for later consideration.

"Give me your hands," Ruiz said.

With barely perceptible reluctance, she held them out. He examined them carefully and, in place of the left index finger's last joint, found the too-regular shape of a one-shot graser.

"Kill it," he told Gejas.

The tongue opened his mouth to protest, but apparently read agreement in the hetman's face. He took a pinbeam from the rack and did the job.

A tiny plume of steam jetted from The Yellowleaf's finger; a faint smell of cooking meat hung in the air for a moment.

The hetman took her helmet from the rack and settled

it over her head. Gejas scurried to her and helped her refasten her latches.

The helmet, of silvery alloy, covered her head completely, replacing her enigmatic face with the image of a grinning snaggle-toothed ghoul, artfully carved in an exaggerated surreal style. She drew on beautifully made alloy gauntlets. When she was done, only the tangled black ends of her mane remained unprotected by her armor.

"So, how do you read her face now?" Ruiz asked Gejas. "Is she as jolly as she seems?"

"Shut up," snarled Gejas, apparently on his own. "Outside."

"CHOOSE YOUR MAN," Gejas said, gesturing at the other prisoners.

In the wan blue light, the camp seemed a tableau of accusing faces and cold eyes. Only Gunderd appeared at all amiable. Perhaps, Ruiz thought, events had already diverged so greatly from the scholar's gloomy expectations that he now looked forward to the next amazing incongruity.

If so, Gunderd wouldn't be disappointed. Ruiz gazed at the others, and considered: Who would best guard his interests while he dreamed in the virtual? Gunderd might be the most capable, but what could he do against the armored hetman?

If they'd seen through his invective, the Pharaohans might still be loyal—except for the one who wasn't.

Then an odd thought came to him . . . and then matured almost instantly into a plan. He turned it over in his mind; except for the possibility that one of the Pharaohans was a Gencha puppet, what was wrong with the scheme? Nothing obvious, he thought, suppressing an impulse to grin. "I'll take the dirtworld princess," Ruiz said.

Gejas responded with gratifying astonishment. "What good will she do you?"

Ruiz shrugged. "She's somewhat observant, easily frightened, and naturally suspicious. All I want from her is an accurate account of your hetman's doings while I'm in the virtual."

Nisa stood up, her face set in angry lines.

The tongue's mouth pursed, as though he had detected a smell, faint but very bad. "You plan some trick; so much is certain. It won't work."

"Probably not," said Ruiz, adopting his most lunatic smile.

"And don't think to run away. The Yellowleaf would catch you; she is very fast. Besides, we have very good tracking tech; this is my personal specialty." Gejas patted his security console affectionately.

The Yellowleaf made an impatient gesture. Gejas ducked his head. "Time for you to go," he said, pointing up the dark mountainside. He picked up a metal canister by its sling and proffered it to Ruiz. "Here," Gejas said. "An energy cell; you'll need to connect it to the virtual's receptacle. Payment in advance—the only sort the virtual recognizes."

"I wonder why," Ruiz muttered, but accepted the cell and slung it over his shoulder. He turned to Nisa. "Come with me."

She glared at him for a long moment, and he was afraid she would refuse to go, and that he would have to force her.

But then her face crumpled. She looked down at her feet, shuffled forward.

His heart felt as if it were being crushed between two cold stones, but he kept his voice light and easy. "So. Shall we go?"

At that moment Gunderd laughed and pointed to the landwalker that held Einduix's litter. "Look! The cook awakens. Guard your victuals, everyone."

It was true. The small orange man had somehow unfastened the straps securing him to the litter and was crawling out from under the landwalker, eyes still cloudy. He looked up at Ruiz and smiled, an odd rueful expression.

Then his arms seemed to lose what little strength they had, and he sagged, still smiling.

It seemed to Ruiz that Einduix laid his cheek against the stony ground in a strangely tender manner.

"Take charge of him," Ruiz said to Gunderd. "Get him to the transport."

"As you say," Gunderd answered. He helped the cook to sit up. "Despite your unflattering opinion of me, I wish you good luck, Ruiz Aw."

"Yes," said Dolmaero grudgingly, but the Guildmaster didn't look up.

Molnekh waved, waggling his fingers, then returned to the remnants of his supper.

Ruiz turned to The Yellowleaf. "We're ready," he said cheerfully.

CHAPTER 9

A T first the three of them climbed through a pathless jumble of stone and scrub. Nisa followed at the hetman's heels, stumbling frequently, but falling only occasionally. When she did, Ruiz picked her up without ceremony and gave her a light push.

The hetman's helmet lamps shed a dim red light at their feet, just bright enough to keep them from stepping in any deep holes.

A few minutes later, they came upon a faint track. Other footpaths joined the track, which gradually grew broader and smoother, so that they were able to walk less cautiously. Walls rose up on either side, almost intact. Soon they were walking in an ancient lane, worn deep by countless footsteps.

"I don't understand where we're going," whispered Nisa after a while.

"Doesn't matter," said Ruiz lightly. "But I'll tell you. I'm going to consult a man-eating library. Our hosts are afraid to do it themselves."

"Why are you doing *anything* for these monsters?" She

seemed more puzzled than angry now. "After what they've done to you."

Ruiz forced a laugh. "The hetman has no tongue, but you should remember that there's nothing wrong with her ears. You're not so casually attached to your life as I am to mine. But to answer your question: Why not? Is there anything you wouldn't do to get off Sook? And after all, what did they do to me?"

She didn't answer for a bit. When she finally spoke, her voice was very low. "They made you a butcher, Ruiz."

"No," he said, in a foolishly gentle tone. "I was already a butcher. They showed me what I was. That's all they did."

EVENTUALLY THE LANE led to a portal in a basalt cliff. The gate had once been impressive. A tall bronze slab, half-open and slumped from some ancient fire, hung drunkenly from corroded hinges. Carving in shallow relief had outlined the dark rectangular opening . . . but it had long ago worn to an unidentifiable suggestion of pattern.

The Yellowleaf paused for a moment, as if listening for some faint sound, and then went inside.

Ruiz and Nisa followed, and he held her arm firmly. He told himself that it looked right, as though he merely took precautions against her bolting . . . though actually he just wanted to touch her. Well, why not? In a short time they would likely both be dead or crazy and it seemed an innocent indulgence. She gave no sign that she detested his touch, though he would have found such detestation understandable. Perhaps she simply hid her feelings well.

The floor of the tunnel was damp and spotted with patches of phosphorescent slime, so he picked his way carefully, staying close to the pool of light shed by the hetman's lamps.

Once Nisa slipped and only his grip kept her from falling. He took the opportunity to pull her a little closer— and felt a guilty twinge of pleasure.

A hundred meters inside the mountain, the roof lifted and they came into a great circular hall. A shoulder-high band of small lume panels gave a sickly green light, and the floor was dry and level.

The hall seemed full of an impalpable presence, and after a moment Ruiz recognized the sad unmistakable aura of vanished magnificence. Time pressed down from the blackness above and muffled the sound of their steps. Here Ruiz fancied that the ghosts watched more openly, disdaining concealment, as if they were specters of aristocratic rank.

Ruiz wondered how long the island had been dead. Carpets had turned to dust, the paneling on the walls had decayed to a few splinters of dark punky wood. Amazing, he thought, that the island's machinery had survived so long untended.

"What now?" he said. His voice echoed and died.

The Yellowleaf pointed, then led the way toward the far side of the hall and a curtain wall, where three low openings glowed with a stronger light, which shone up the high walls behind.

As they neared the wall, a strong smell of death met them. It was enough like the stink of the slaughterhouse to stop Ruiz in his tracks. "No," he said, his will deserting him.

The Yellowleaf stood by the arch of the center niche and made a peremptory gesture. Ruiz shook his head, unable to speak. He felt his face writhing with some betraying expression.

Nisa moved to stand in front of Ruiz, and she looked up into his face. "What's wrong?" she asked in a soft voice.

"I've changed," he muttered, as much to himself as to her. "Too late or too soon, but it's happened."

She touched his shoulder, then turned and went into the niche. Ruiz felt compelled to follow, then.

The niche seemed at first glance to be the den of some fearsome mythical beast, an ogre perhaps, or a dragon. Bones littered the floor, broken and scattered. In the center of the niche a softstone couch rose waist high.

The couch was currently occupied by a corpse in an ugly stage of decay. It wore Roderigan armor of some silvery alloy. It lay in a relaxed posture, head tipped back, arms flung wide. Maggots crawled over its exposed face, and the eyes were gone.

The Yellowleaf unceremoniously rolled the corpse aside and it fell with a clatter. The softstone was stained and crusted with the products of decomposition, and the thought that he must soon lie there made Ruiz's skin crawl.

"Where does this go?" he asked, lifting the energy cell.

The Yellowleaf indicated a bank of circular sockets in the left-hand wall, all filled with discharged cells.

Ruiz jerked one out; it released with a cloud of dust and a waft of acidic corrosion. At The Yellowleaf's nod, he slid the fresh cell in and gave it a turn to lock it into its contacts.

For a moment the lights wavered, and then a faint hum filled the niche.

The Yellowleaf pointed urgently to the couch.

Ruiz turned to Nisa, who stood along the wall, arms wrapped around herself. He felt an impulse to go to her, to press himself against her, to ask her to put her arms around him. He couldn't. Even were the hetman not watching, alert to any exploitable weakness . . . he was too dirty, he would never be clean enough to hold Nisa, never. But he smiled and spoke cheerfully. "Keep a close eye on the hetman. Remember everything she does, so you can tell me when I come back."

She nodded. "So you plan to come back?"

"Why not?" he said, and lay down, ignoring the stink that enfolded him, ignoring the slimy surface of the couch. He thought, *This is what I deserve, to receive Death's decaying kiss. I've served so faithfully.*

The niche grew brighter, the hum rose up the scale.

The lights flared a brilliant white, and he was elsewhere.

RUIZ OPENED HIS EYES, which he had shut against the painful glare of the virtual's activation. He seemed to lie on the same couch . . . but the carrion smell was gone, and the bones. A soft radiance streamed down, colored in a thousand subtle shades, as if by stained-glass windows high above. He squinted his eyes, but the lofty ceiling was obscured by a misty brightness.

He levered himself upright and saw that he was alone.

The niche was hung with heavy tapestries, worked with red and gold designs, angular abstractions. The floor tiles were an interlocking pattern of umber and cerulean, inlaid with sunburst medallions of polished bronze. A pure white coverlet draped the couch.

No sound penetrated the curtains, and he wondered if something stealthy waited for him out in the great hall.

He swung his feet down, but felt no great urge to get on with his business. From the grim attitude of the Roderigans, Ruiz had expected the virtual to be a dreadful place.

So far it seemed the most peaceful place he had visited since coming to Sook.

The change was so profound that he found it a little difficult to believe that his body still lay on that festering slab . . . and that his mind now inhabited a synthetic reality. He looked down at himself and observed that he wore a pair of white cotton trousers and a loose-sleeved open-necked shirt. On his feet were canvas sandals. His fingernails were neatly trimmed, his face smooth-shaven. The bruises and aches he had collected during his sojourn on Sook were all gone.

"Tidy folk," he muttered. He drew a deep breath and stood up.

WHEN HE STEPPED out through the curtains, he saw that the beauty of the niche was only a small reflection of the glory outside.

High above, a great rose window filled the ceiling, a design of vast interlocking complexity, rivers of glowing color. It was through this window's magnificence that the light poured down on a hall filled with concentric circles of thronelike chairs, all facing inward toward a tall central pulpit carved from the twisted white trunk of a dead tree.

He walked forward to admire the nearest of the chairs, a sinuous construction of forged black iron, set with translucent panels of russet agate, accented with pink moonstone cabochons. The small round cushion was of inky purple velvet. He felt that he could almost see its owner's ghost, a complicated person with a strong supple mind and a stony will, sitting erect and composed.

Ruiz thought it the most interesting chair he had ever seen, until he looked at the next one. The high back was a thin curved shell of laminated wood, a lustrous lavender gray, inlaid with intricate spiraling designs in silver wire. The slender elegant legs seemed to be cast from opalescent glass, and the heavy feet were carved into the semblance of human fists, knuckles down. Ruiz touched the chair, let his fingertips slip across the warm silky texture of the wood and the cool polish of the silver. He closed his eyes, and a fanciful picture filled his mind's eye: a beautiful woman in silks and jewels, imperious and languid.

Ruiz wandered toward the central pulpit, marveling. Each of the hundreds of chairs was a remarkable object, each showed a dazzling brilliance of craft, each seemed to cloak itself in a distinctive humanity, to announce its owner's character in an unmistakable voice.

By the time he reached the open space at the hall's center, his thoughts were cloudy with ghosts. He stood looking up at the pulpit, admiring the way it seemed to soar up into the light of the great rose window.

"We called it the Tree of Knowledge." The voice was high-pitched but pleasant. "Though actually I think it was a Sook-adapted hawthorn of some sort."

Ruiz turned to see a person standing in the dark opening at the far side of the hall. At first glance, he seemed a young boy with yellow skin and dark sloe eyes. He wore a white unisuit, and his woolly black hair was cut in fanciful puffs and spires, a sort of cranial topiary. In his left hand he held the right paw of a small doglike creature, which stood, incongruously, on its hind legs.

The boy seemed somehow as unthreatening as any being he had ever met, so Ruiz attempted to make a polite response. "The Tree of Knowledge?"

"Yes," said the boy as he came toward Ruiz, leading the animal like a child. "We took the name from an Old Earth myth about the origin of curiosity. In that case, some barbarian god got angry with his people for tasting the fruit of the tree. Did nasty stuff to them: kicked their ungrateful curious butts out of paradise and gave them suffering and death." He laughed softly. "We saw it as an interesting irony. We never thought it would happen to us."

The boy held out a slender hand in greeting, which Ruiz took without thinking. "By the way," the boy said, giving Ruiz's hand a decisive shake and then dropping it, "I'm Somnire, your host. Welcome to all that's left of the Great Compendium."

"I'm Ruiz Aw," Ruiz said, bemused by Somnire's nonchalance. At closer sight, Somnire seemed older, though his skin was unlined and he moved with the easy grace of youth.

"Yes, I know." Somnire stepped forward, patted the tree affectionately. "Oh, we had a lot of fine times here, no doubt about that. The dons would relax in their chairs and the stackfolk would pass among us with trays full of goodies and wine. We'd all get drunk and then we'd take turns climbing the Tree of Knowledge—each of us would tell a joke or sing a song. Pretty soon the dons would be rolling around on the floor under their chairs, fornicating joyfully, and the stackfolk would bring coverlets for afterward. There'd be music and dancing and games. Fine times. . . ." His black eyes went dreamy for a moment, as though he were too full of remembrance to see.

Ruiz felt somewhat confused by these confidences. "I thought this was a library."

Somnire grinned and gave Ruiz an amused look. "Are the librarians small gray people, juiceless and timid, where you come from? Not so here! We accepted none but the best: comets in the universe of knowledge, great roaring fires of curiosity and ambition."

"I see," said Ruiz. He hardly knew how to respond.

Somnire chuckled, a pure melodious sound. He released the animal's paw and it dropped to all fours, slowly and carefully, as though the movement hurt it. Ruiz saw that the twisted stumps of membranous wings sprouted from its withers. It looked up at him with its doglike eyes, and he saw no more intelligence than he would expect from a dog.

"Run along, Idirin," said Somnire, making shooing motions at his pet. "We have business to transact."

It laid its blunt head against Somnire's leg for a moment, then stumped away stiffly.

Somnire watched the animal go, and a trace of sadness flitted across his childish features. "She's too attached to me. It's because she can't fly with the other sarim. Perhaps I ought to put her ghost to rest, but I'm afraid I'd be too lonely without her."

Idirin paused and looked back at her master, and then shimmered and disappeared.

Somnire straightened his shoulders abruptly and turned to Ruiz. "So! You're here to gather data for Roderigo?"

"No," said Ruiz. "I'm just trying to live a little longer." He felt he had to defend that ambition, so he went on. "I have people depending on me."

"Yes, I know," said the boy. "I know. Actually, I'm just teasing you a little. If you were really working for Roderigo, you wouldn't be *here.*" Somnire waved his hand, a gesture that took in the hall, the chairs, the rose window.

"Oh? Where would I be?"

"In Hell. Or anyway, the closest thing to Hell that a bunch of imaginative, slightly crazy folk could design. Close enough." A grim thoughtful look settled over Somnire's face, and suddenly he looked ancient. "Anyway. What do you think Roderigo wants to know?"

"They want to know what's so important about the Gencha enclave in SeaStack."

"Ah. And you? What did you come to the Compendium to learn?"

Ruiz shook his head. "How to survive. A little longer."

"Maybe we can help you," said Somnire.

NISA WATCHED AS the hetman tore the armor off the decaying corpse, digging through the corruption with her gauntleted hands.

Squatting there, The Yellowleaf looked like some bright

mechanical carrion bird, happily selecting the best gobbets. Nisa shuddered, and wondered what the woman searched for.

Her curiosity was satisfied a moment later, as the hetman found a long thin-bladed dagger, which she wiped clean on the corpse's hair. Then she slipped the knife into a slot in her calf armor. The hetman looked at Nisa, her ghoulish faceplate gleaming in the dim blue light, and Nisa imagined that behind the metal she was smiling.

"I don't think you have to worry," Nisa said. "I think you've broken him. I never thought that would happen."

The Yellowleaf shrugged and sat down, her back against the darkest wall. Nisa remembered that the hetman couldn't speak.

Nisa looked down at Ruiz's sleeping face. He seemed a great deal younger, as though the dream he now lived in was a pleasant one. Perhaps, she thought, that was the danger here: The dreamer might not want to wake.

She felt as if she had just awakened from a dream she would have wished to continue: the dream in which Ruiz Aw loved her.

"WOULD YOU LIKE to see the city?" Somnire asked. "Come outside. I'll be your tour guide and we can talk." He put a light hand on Ruiz's arm and tugged him gently toward the exit.

When they came to the great bronze door, Somnire touched it and it swung open. A small two-passenger flier sat between the deep walls, and Somnire led Ruiz to it.

"Let's go," the ancient boy said. "Don't be afraid. I'm an excellent pilot, and besides, none of this is real." He winked cheerfully and slid into the left-hand seat.

"So, why don't we just sprout wings and float away?" Ruiz asked.

"Would you like that better? No? I didn't think so. Let's try to preserve our illusions."

They lifted above the walls, into the sunlight, and Ruiz thought, *How beautiful, how strange.*

The island was a living confection. From the surf that

rolled in from the blue-green sea to the crown of shining black cliffs that rose above, palaces of brilliant white stone frosted the steep slopes. Everywhere flowering plants spilled from terraces and windows and walls, and their spiciness thickened the air, so that it almost made Ruiz dizzy.

The oddest sights of the city were the great white flying buttresses that rose from the sea and swept upward in a fine vigorous curve until they met the basalt of the cliffs. These massive structures, spaced a half-kilometer apart at the base, apparently served as apartments for thousands of dwellers; windows glittered in the sun, and innumerable small balconies broke the sheer faces.

They rose higher and began to drift sideways above the palaces.

Ruiz looked down, to see more of the small animals the boy had called sarim. They sat on ledges, sunning themselves, huge iridescent wings spread—or flitted from balcony to balcony, chasing each other playfully. High above, a dozen others circled lazily in the rising air currents. The city seemed otherwise empty, and Ruiz wondered who tended the plants, until he remembered that none of this was real.

"Ah, but once it was," Somnire said.

Ruiz jerked his head to look at the boy, full of a sudden unsettling suspicion.

"Oh, of course I know what you're thinking," said Somnire with a careless smile. "Your consciousness now exists in the mind of the Compendium; what would you expect? I lie to myself and pretend that I'm a man named Somnire, who once called himself the Head Librarian—but in fact I'm only a subroutine in the virtual. There are no rules for me!" He laughed. "For example . . ." His face shimmered, became a chitinous insectile nightmare, all fangs and spines, the eyes huge compound jewels. An instant later it returned to its pleasant youthful humanity. "See? I couldn't have done that so easily when I was real. So, I have access to every ripple that slips across your mind. Please remember this, should you be tempted to think unkind thoughts of me."

Ruiz sighed. He had grown terribly weary of things that weren't what they seemed; he could barely bring himself to notice them.

"I'm sorry," Somnire said. "I shouldn't have done that. And I think we can help you, I really do. After all, the Compendium contains all the knowledge a thousand years of searching could collect—and what's more powerful than knowledge? Other than guns and bombs, I mean." Somnire's voice had darkened. Just for an instant the beautiful city seemed to waver and Ruiz caught a glimpse of the emptiness beneath.

"Roderigo did it, you know," Somnire went on. "That's why we won't help them. Roderigo and Delt. Well, they had many allies—all the folk of Sook who couldn't stand to see knowledge freely shared—but they were the organizers, and they were the ones who broke the stones and butchered all the stackfolk."

Ruiz felt a small curiosity. "Why would you build your library on Sook, of all places?"

"Ah! Where else? You must understand, we had only one rule: We would give any knowledge we possessed to anyone who asked for it. No pangalac world would have suffered our presence."

Ruiz must have shown his perplexity, for Somnire laughed, a trifle bitterly, and went on. "For example: You want to build a hellbomb? We'd tell you how. You want to know where the fissionables can be bought? The price? How to arrange secure transport? Do you see why we would be unpopular? But the Shards don't care who lives on Sook, as long as they obey the rules."

"Oh," said Ruiz. "Then why won't you tell the Roderigans what they want to know?"

The ancient boy gave him a long unfriendly look. For a minute he didn't answer; then he said, "That was then, when the Compendium was alive. We've since learned a certain self-protective pragmatism. The truth didn't save us.

"Now we're ghosts. Vengeful ghosts. You should remember that, if you want our help."

"I will," Ruiz said.

•   •   •

THEY FLEW ON in silence, and Ruiz wondered if he had fatally offended the ancient boy. He didn't care very much.

They gradually circled the island, and it appeared to Ruiz that the island must once have housed hundreds of thousands, though now all the palaces and courtyards and gardens were empty of human life. The only movement came from the sarim, who played everywhere in the deserted city.

Once a flight of the creatures winged by just below the flier, and Somnire sighed. "Beautiful, aren't they?" Sunlight glowed in the wings, throwing back a subtle prismatic dazzle.

"I suppose," said Ruiz. "Are you alone here, except for them?"

"No, I have a few companions—though they dwindle. At one time there were many of us, most of the dons and many stackfolk." The boy shook his head, and his face was dark and cold. "But the laws of time and energy are stronger than anything else, stronger even than all the varieties of truth we harvested here."

"Ah," Ruiz said, though he didn't understand what the boy was talking about. "These stackfolk . . . your slaves?"

Somnire jerked around to glare at him in irritation and amusement, an odd mixture. "Slaves? There were no slaves on Dorn. The stackfolk were a race designed to care for the Compendium—they did that job better and more joyfully than any other race could have . . . but no one but a fool would describe them as slaves. You have an unhealthy obsession with slavery; you see slaves everywhere." He grinned. "Look at me; do I really seem a slave?"

"It's hard to tell sometimes," Ruiz said. "But, no."

"And yet my parents were stackfolk. I was a stackperson until I became a don."

"Oh," said Ruiz.

On the far side of the island were vast sea caves, like fanged mouths biting the ocean. Long breakwaters radiated outward from the openings. "There ships from every land on Sook docked," Somnire said. "That was a gentler time on Sook. Before the pirate Lords had grown so great. The Blades of Namp were nothing but a mob of ragged crazies, too weak to eat any but their own. Castle Delt was only an evil dream of the SeedCorp factors, a few troops marching up and down the beach and playing soldier." Somnire drew a deep breath, and his elaborate coiffure wobbled. "Roderigo was already strong, however."

Abruptly the boy released the controls. "This is a foolish waste of time and energy," he said. "Why should you care about our lost glories?"

The world shimmered and grew dim, and Ruiz felt an instant's vertigo.

HE AND SOMNIRE stood in one of the city's courtyards. A flaming bougainvillea vine spilled down the sunniest wall, and a still pool full of cerise water lilies reflected the ancient stones on the shady side.

A tall angular woman came from a high doorway.

"This is Leel," Somnire said. "She'll try to make you well."

Ruiz looked at Leel and thought of the wood and silver chair he had touched in the hall of dons. She was handsome in a spare understated way, her hair a translucent cloud, her eyes a soft earthy green, her mouth pale coral. She wore a thin artless shift that fell halfway down her slender thighs and left her arms bare.

"I'm not sick," Ruiz said.

"Don't be silly," said Somnire. "Your heart is leprous with regret; your mind is hibernating. Your soul is so dark you can't find it. You may have hard jobs to do soon. In your present state, I don't think you could act with your former admirable ruthlessness."

"I have no time," said Ruiz, a little desperately.

"Time is elastic in the virtual. How long do you think you've been here? An hour? Two? Thirty seconds! In the niche, your enemy is searching her countryman's carrion for his knife. The woman you love is watching your sleeping face; she has yet to form her first sad thought. So, take some time. Rest. Gather your thoughts. Your resolve." Somnire patted his shoulder.

"Come," said Leel in a low sweet voice, and took his hand in her cool fragile one. "It's not as if you had any choice." She gave him a smile so warm and unforced that he was charmed against his will.

When she drew him toward the doorway, he went without further protest.

CHAPTER 10

As he passed through the doorway of Leel's house, Ruiz heard music, a soft sweet murmur of strings and chimes. It seemed to swirl forth from a fountain that played in the center of the room. The white-plastered walls had no windows, but a pure bright light fell from high clerestories.

The fountain rose in languid jets from a shallow basin set in the red tiled floor, and after a moment Ruiz realized that the water of the fountain was moving far more slowly than was natural on a world of Sook's mass.

He must have frowned or made some other gesture of distaste, because Leel gave his arm a little shake and looked at him with mock severity. "No, Ruiz, it's not another of Somnire's little liberties with reality. I allow none of his nonsense in my house; I live as I did in life, as much as possible. The fountain has a gravity filter under it. I thought it pretty. Isn't it?"

She pulled him forward to stand in the cool air that billowed around the basin. "Yes, it's pretty," he said. The fountain, seen up close, seemed a confection of flowing glass, and he had the illusion that if he touched it, the glossy ribbons and upwellings would have a dense impenetrable surface. He reached out and learned that it was just water, though his hand felt very light when it passed through the shimmering curtain.

As his hand disturbed the fountain, the music fell into a dissonance, but it recovered its sweetness as soon as he pulled back.

"I read all sorts of omens into the music," Leel said. "It always seemed remarkable to me that the universe is tied together with webs of gravity, and that whenever the farthest star trembles, my fountain shivers in response. I put the gravity filter under it not just to make it pretty, but to insulate my omens from the evil old mass of Sook, and make the stars' messages stronger. Silly, right?"

"Doesn't seem at all silly to me," said Ruiz. He looked aside. Leel's attention was fixed on the fountain and her face was full of a fresh vivid delight. *This is a ghost*, he reminded himself.

But she seemed as alive as anyone he had met lately. He wished, with a sudden stark intensity, that he felt half as vital as she seemed to be. He felt an odd shift in his perceptions. She became irresistibly desirable.

She looked so clean. He couldn't imagine her with sour sweat greasing her face, with dirty feet, with lice in her translucent curls. With blood on her long fine hands.

I'm a ghost too, he thought, but it was an idea without significance.

He was horrified, ashamed of the lust that surged out of some deep place in his heart. His vision seemed misty with it; he heard the pulse pounding in his ears.

"Tell me," he said thickly. "Are you a mind reader too?"

She gave him a quick bright look. "No. That's Somnire's sole privilege—and burden. Who would want that?"

He felt a certain relief, though the lust seemed as strong and hot as before. "Good," he muttered, returning his attention to the fountain.

"Well," she said. "Are you hungry?"

He shot her a sharp glance. Had she lied about the mind

reading? But then he realized that she was asking if he wanted food. "A little, maybe."

"Come to the kitchen, then," she said, and led him from the fountain room.

HER KITCHEN WAS small and intimate, and it seemed to Ruiz that there was nowhere he could look that didn't show him some desirable part of Leel. She seated him at an old table, its wood worn white with scrubbing. She arranged three sprays of tiny gold-red blossoms in a round blue vase and set it before him. She brought pale gray plates of an antique mannered design, and mugs of celadon porcelain. Her long legs carried her around him in a kind of graceful domestic dance. His desire seemed, impossibly, to intensify.

When she bent over him to set the silver, her shift fell open and he caught a glimpse of tiny breasts, puffy pink nipples. Her scent was of the sea and sunshine and something darkly sweet, like night-blooming flowers.

She laughed and laid her arm delicately across his shoulders. Her face was only a few centimeters from his, and he felt pleasantly engulfed in her smile. "Tell me," she said. "Would you rather eat or go to the bedroom?"

An image filled his mind and pushed Leel from the center of his thoughts: Nisa in the bone-filled niche, watching him with strange eyes. A cold hand squeezed his heart and he looked down at his fists, clenched on the table.

"All right," said Leel. "Perhaps I was wrong." She seemed unoffended. She went to her stove, an archaic mechanism with nickel-silver fittings and blue enamel oven doors. She broke a pink egg into sputtering oil, she buttered toast, she poured a glass of amber fruit juice.

It was all so heartbreakingly ordinary.

"IS THAT ENOUGH? It's easy to make more, if you're still hungry." She sat across from him, nibbling at a pastry filled with scryfruit and sweetened with a glistening smear of lime-blossom honey.

For a moment he didn't answer—he was too fascinated by the pink tip of her tongue, licking up the crumbs that stuck to her lower lip. "No, that was fine," he said.

"Good." She put the last bite of pastry down and then took the dishes to the sink.

When she began to wash them, his bemusement spilled over into speech. "Why do you do this? Why eat? Why cook? Especially, why wash dishes?"

She turned gracefully, still swabbing at one of her antique plates. "When all you have is the illusion of life, you guard that illusion fiercely." Her eyes were dark and deep and he regretted that he had asked her the question.

"I see," he mumbled.

"No, you probably don't," she said. "Somnire doesn't try to fool himself . . . but Somnire is the closest thing we have to a saint. The rest of us can't be the way he is. We'd go mad. Of course, he's more than a little mad, isn't he?"

"I'm no judge," he answered.

"And I hope you never become one," she said cryptically. "The flesh is so great a gift. . . . But those who wear it rarely appreciate it." Her mouth trembled, and she went back to her dishwashing with a somewhat forced air of concentration.

"I'm sorry," he said, though he was unsure of his offense.

"Never mind," she said, and smiled. "Listen, why don't you sleep for a while? Somnire gave me a précis of your recent memories, and I'd like to look over them, to see what weighs so on your soul."

"I'd rather you didn't," Ruiz said. He felt a shudder of hot shame, that this clean lovely person might learn of the terrible things he had done.

"I must," she said. "It's my job."

She took him to a cool dark room in the center of her house, where a narrow bed waited. "Sleep as long as you like," she said. "Somnire has explained the elasticity of time here, so don't fret about wasting it. We'll have you back in your body before your muscles have a chance to cool off. We want you spry when you return to the niche."

He sat on the bed and tugged off his sandals. The white sheets drew him almost as passionately as Leel's body had.

She went to the doorway and reached up to untie a curtain. The light shone through her shift, so that for an instant she seemed luminously naked.

Just before she went, he spoke. "Why? Why are you doing these things?" he asked. It seemed the only important question.

She shrugged. "Can't you guess? We want to hurt Roderigo, and you can do it for us. Or so Somnire believes, which is good enough for me." She smiled and waved her hand. "Sweet dreams," she said, and then she was gone, the curtain fluttering.

RUIZ WOKE IN a sweat, though the room was still cool. He sat up and wiped his face with trembling hands. Oddly, he felt a little better after his imaginary slumber, though still far less than well.

After a while, he rose and went out.

The house was silent, but for a thread of the fountain's music, almost inaudible.

He wandered down the hall, which was lined with waist-high pedestals, each of which supported a crystal belljar. Under each jar was some enigmatic object, extraordinary only for the value evidently placed on it by its owner. Here was a tiny bedraggled baby shoe, with laces of rainbow shimmerglass. Next, a black hat with a narrow soft brim, sweat-stained and dusty. An empty wine bottle. An old leather dog collar with a rhinestone bauble. A rusty trowel. A tangled nest of fishing line, from which a gaudy treble-hooked lure peered with bulging black eyes. Crumpled blue panties, entangled in a worn-out work glove. A silver-framed flatgraph of Leel, wearing ragged shorts and nothing else, leaning from a sunny balcony, a look of contentment shining from her face.

A fascination grew in Ruiz as he went from pedestal to pedestal, trying to imagine the significance of the objects. It was oddly entertaining, a sort of archaeological voyeurism, and it diverted him from his weariness.

So absorbed did he become in his speculations that he jumped when Leel spoke. "More silliness," she said. "I anchor my memories as best I can. But it helps. Some of us here have grown very strange. Forgotten our names, and even our humanity." She stood in the far doorway, arms folded.

He wanted to ask her about the objects, or about the strange virtual-dwellers, but then he decided his curiosity might seem rude.

"Well," she said. "Let's talk. Come in my bedroom. I won't make indecent advances, unless you're very charming."

He had to smile at the absurdity of it all.

Her bedroom was spacious and full of light. Ornate glass doors led out to a flagstone terrace, and thick rugs of brown and maroon wool covered the floor. Leel waited on her bed, gracefully cross-legged in the center of a faded patchwork quilt. Spread in a semicircle about her were a dozen squares of smoky plastic. "I made Somnire give me your memories in these," she said, laying her hands on two of the squares. "He wanted me to experience them directly, but I wouldn't. I know I'm just a pattern of electrons in the circuits of the machine, but I refuse to have it demonstrated to me more forcefully than is absolutely necessary." She patted the bed and said, "Sit."

He sat uncomfortably at the bed's edge.

She picked up one of the squares. "I believe Somnire when he says these magic mirrors hold a fair sampling of your memories—though no sampling could be completely fair, I suppose. Still, in Somnire we trust. Right?" She flexed the plastic square and it threw moving light on her features—though Ruiz could see nothing of the images that shifted through the square.

Ruiz wondered what she watched; her expression was unreadable.

She looked up at him and smiled, without mockery. "By any humane standard, you've been a great monster, Ruiz Aw. The things you've done. . . ."

"Yes," said Ruiz. "A monster." He felt only a sort of detached discomfort.

"It doesn't matter," she went on, "that in most things you meant well—at least until you went to work for the Art League. Monsters are as monsters do. Many monsters are loving to their families, take good care of their pets. So strange."

Ruiz looked down at his hands, confused as to the purpose of the conversation.

"I should, really, detest you," she said. "But for some reason I can't."

"Why not?" Ruiz asked, intrigued. Who, knowing what he had done, would not detest him? "Are you also a monster?"

She laughed. "I don't think so—though for a fact, monsters generally don't think themselves monstrous. You're unusually forthright in that respect. Maybe that's why I like you. And also, despite what you've done and been, there's still a sweetness to you. A decency. Very strange, but there it is."

A silence grew, while she picked up one square and then another.

He grew uncomfortable. "I don't understand any of this. Why should you care? If I'm a monster, give me what I need to hurt Roderigo and set me on them. Why all this, this . . . discussion? Dissection?"

"Well, for one thing, I'm curious about you," she answered. "Strangers come infrequently to the virtual—or anyway, strangers we can entertain. Will you humor me? And besides, have you not felt a lessening of effectiveness, a blunting of purpose lately? Perhaps discussion will help a little."

"Perhaps," he said, grudgingly.

She held up a square, and in it he saw the farmhouse where he'd been born a slave. It was early morning, just after dawn, and the light lay silver on the old stones.

"Tell me about this," she said in a terribly gentle voice. He felt tears of remembrance cloud his eyes.

LEEL WAS FAR more thorough than any minddiver, even Nacker the Teach. She turned the stones of his memory

over, and seemed unrepulsed by all the ugly things that
scurried from the light. She reviewed his childhood as a
slave, his youth as a bondservant to a senile aristocrat, his
career as a free-lance emancipator—his scarce and empty
triumphs, his betrayals and disappointments. When he
took his first contract with the Art League, she seemed
only puzzled. She asked an occasional question, but mostly
she listened without response to his terse summations.

When Leel saw his memories of the empty world where
he had lived alone for so many years, she seemed to take
an unforced pleasure in touring the gardens he had culti-
vated there.

"If you live, and escape Sook . . . will you go back
there?" she asked, a little wistfully.

"Perhaps," he said. The idea seemed as fantastic as any
fairy tale.

"I would, too, were I you," she said. "I love to grow
flowers, and here I'm always aware that it's just a game,
that the flowers don't depend on air and water and soil, but
on my remembrance of real flowers. It subtracts much of
the joy from them, though they're still beautiful, I suppose."

Curiosity scratched at him. "Tell me. Did you always
look as you look now?"

"Exactly so, since I came to the Compendium," she
said.

"You're never tempted to improve anything?" he asked,
looking away.

"Such as?" Her voice had a slightly tart edge.

"I don't know," he muttered. "The color of your hair?
Your nose, perhaps . . . a little smaller, a little larger?
Something."

"My nose?" She giggled and looked down. She pulled
the thin fabric of her shift tight over her breasts, so that the
soft swellings and the puckered nipples became obvious.
"Too small? Don't you think they're pretty?"

"Yes," he said, his hands knotted in his lap.

"I'm sorry," she said, sobering. "May we go on? Even if
it does you no good at all, I'm fascinated. Do you know,

when the Compendium was still alive, I was a specialist in human adaptation?"

"Really?" The information made him uneasy, as though she saw him as some sort of fungus, evolved to thrive in blood and bitterness.

"Really." She picked up another memory square and saw the Gench who had installed the League death net in Ruiz's mind. "Hideous creature," she said.

She put it aside, gazed at another. "And here, poor Auliss Moncipor, who probably still dreams of you, in her sterile little cube of air and light and warmth, up in the blackness over Pharaoh."

She patted his hand. "I find it easy to put myself in her place—and when I do I know she still thinks of you as a handsome prince from a far country, who might someday return and save her from her tedious destiny. Even though you so rudely departed the platform, without so much as a good-bye."

"She was a slaveholder. She bought children for her pleasure and never gave a thought to what she did." Ruiz recalled the anger and disgust he had felt—long ago it seemed—that night on the platform.

"So she was shallow—and a woman of her time and culture. Your self-righteousness is incongruous, to say the least." But Leel's tone was more amused than malicious. "Let me ask you this: Why do you not condemn your Nisa for holding slaves?"

He shook his head; he'd never really considered it.

"I think *I* know. Nisa is from another time and culture, so you make excuses. Auliss was a pangalac like you, so you could not forgive her for failing to share your sensibilities."

"Perhaps," Ruiz said.

"Well, then, I can make excuses for *you.* You're not of my time and culture, after all," Leel said. Her eyes twinkled, and Ruiz was forced to return her smile.

She went on to show him the stony face of Pharaoh, the tragedy of the play in Bidderum, the Blacktear Pens, his foolish escape attempt, his time with Nisa in Corean's apartments.

"She's quite beautiful, Ruiz," Leel said, studying an image of Nisa dressed in one of the glittering gowns she'd invented to pass the time. "She's unmodified, true? Born that beautiful . . . a rare thing."

"Yes," said Ruiz, gazing at the Pharaohan princess, who gazed out of the memory square with soft fond eyes. He felt a rush of hopeless longing. Could she ever look at him like that again? He shook his head, as if to drive such foolish thoughts from it.

Leel flexed the square, and she faded, to be replaced by his memory of Corean as they had boarded the airboat for SeaStack.

"Also beautiful," said Leel. "But not as good to look at."

Ruiz drew a deep breath. "She's probably dead, for which I'm grateful. A dangerous woman."

Leel regarded him sidelong. "I understand The Yellowleaf is quite handsome, in her harsh Roderigan way. How is it that you have so many perilous entanglements with beautiful women?"

"You say that as though it were a bad thing," said Ruiz with a wry smile. At that moment, Leel seemed very beautiful herself.

"Well . . . when I look through your memories, I see that various disasters seemed to follow these entanglements. Perhaps there's no connection."

"An evil destiny," Ruiz said. "But there are compensations."

"So I see," said Leel, looking at the final square. After a long moment she turned it so Ruiz could see what she watched.

It was that night on the Deepheart barge, when he and Nisa had made love on the upper deck. Her dark head tossed, thrown back, her hair an obscuring cloud against the star fields. Her white breasts swayed as she moved her beautiful strong shoulders. . . .

Ruiz made an odd choking noise; it forced itself from his throat against his volition, and he couldn't seem to find his breath, or get it past the swelling in his throat. His eyes clouded with tears, and he rubbed fiercely at them.

"Lovely," Leel said in a sad small voice.

She turned the square facedown on her quilt, slowly and reluctantly.

"Ruiz," she said. "Somnire gave me other memories, and colorful memories they were . . . but this is the last important one. I know . . . you suffered and did terrible things: the murders in SeaStack, and on the barge. And of course the time you spent in the Roderigan slaughterhouse —though surely you understand that you were no less a victim there than those whose throats you cut."

He laughed, a sour bitter sound. "It hurt me more than it did them, is that it?"

She shook her head, the translucent curls bobbing. "What else could you have done? Could you have saved any of them? The Roderigans are a pestilence on the universe. A plague that strikes down innocents at random, and what can be done? All anyone can do is try to survive."

"Maybe you're right," he said. "But I'll never feel clean again."

Her green eyes flashed, and he felt her anger, like hot breath. "Did you feel clean before? Then you were a monster indeed. How many innocents have you killed, over the years—or caused to die?" She bared her white teeth at him.

"I never claimed to be a saint," he said.

"Did you claim to be human?"

Now he felt an answering anger. "Yes. I did."

She flailed at the memory squares, scattering them off the bed. "These tell a different story, Ruiz Aw!"

"I didn't force you to look at them," he said stiffly.

The room seemed chilly. Ruiz wondered how he could have begun to feel comfortable in this foolish dream. He looked around; he seemed to be able to see through the imaginary walls of Leel's house, to the tumbled stones that remained.

But Leel finally reached out and patted his arm—and her hand was as warm as a real woman's hand. "I'm sorry, Ruiz. It's not for me to judge you and what you've done with your life. My life was so different. I grew up on Becalt —a long-settled world, stable and prosperous. My family was wealthy and loving. I went to the university. I did my graduate work on Dilvermoon. I never knew a day of hunger or physical fear. All my crises were manufactured by myself: puppy loves, striving for status, social slights. During a long life in the pangalac worlds, I never saw a dead person."

She took his hand and squeezed it. "Here, the same. My life ran down smooth channels and the only sorrows I knew . . . small things, compared to yours. A setback in my research. Envy of my more talented colleagues. A less than perfect party . . . similar small embarrassments. An unhappy love affair or two."

"Well," he said, wondering why she was telling him these things. "Not your fault if you had an easier life."

"Oh, it didn't *seem* easier, at the time. No, I was sure my little sorrows were as deep as anyone's. . . . Anyway, this personality matrix, all that's left of me now, was taken several months before the Roderigans and their allies destroyed the Compendium and slaughtered the people. So I have no direct memory of the end . . . of our lives. But Somnire made us watch recordings."

"Ah," he said.

Her face was a mask of tragedy. She twisted her hands together and didn't look at him.

"That must have been difficult," he said.

"I didn't see my own death; Somnire was kind and edited the recordings. But I saw the ruin of all that I loved."

"I'm sorry," he said.

"I'm telling you this because I want you to know that I can feel, just a little, the things that drove you to be a murderer. I know a little of how it must feel to know that no matter what you do, it can never be enough, can never balance the scales, can never make your life right again." She again gripped his hands in hers and pulled them into her lap. Her eyes searched his. "I know a little, just a little. If you showed me every Roderigan hetman, bound and helpless, every Roderigan neck stretched on a block, I couldn't cut their evil throats, as much as they deserve it. Though I'd cheer if *you* could; I'd weep for joy."

It seemed a charming picture to him, and he must have smiled in a way that disturbed her, because she looked aside and shivered. She didn't push his hands away, however, and he began to feel a bit overwhelmed by pleasant sensations. He could feel the hardness of her hipbone against his wrist, the softness of her belly, the resilience of the thick curls that covered her mound.

This is foolish, he told himself, and would have drawn back. But she wouldn't let him go. She gazed fiercely into his eyes. "Listen, Ruiz," she said. "None of that really matters, not anymore. You've been the knife in so many hands, for so long—but you don't have to be, not anymore."

"What are you talking about?" he asked roughly. "You don't want me to hurt the Roderigans? Somnire wouldn't like to hear you talking like that. Would he?"

"No, he wouldn't. But I think you'll hurt the Roderigans sufficiently to satisfy me, just by denying them your use. Never mind that; I promised I wouldn't go into it . . . my point is, you can stop. You have your salvation, if you're smart enough to seize it."

"Salvation?" It seemed a ridiculous word to apply to his situation, and he had no idea what she meant. "Will you let me stay here and listen to your fountain, forever?"

She shook her head and smiled a bittersweet smile. "No. You can't stay here. But you have a better refuge. You have Nisa."

Now he did jerk his hands away from her. He was filled with a formless frustrated rage. "Really?" he asked, almost shouting. His eyes watered and his voice shook. "Do you think so? 'The love of a good woman,' is that what's going to save me? What a lovely romantic . . . maudlin, pitiable, pig-stupid idea. You know nothing about it—she doesn't trust me and I don't trust her. For all I know, she's a Gencha puppet. And we're both going to die on Sook."

Leel seemed undisturbed by his outburst. She picked up the memory square that held the night on the barge. "I know whatever *you* know about it, Ruiz Aw. And it doesn't really matter what she thinks of you—though I can't believe she's as cold as you fear. It doesn't matter whether or not you trust her. What matters is, do you love her?"

He shook his head, unable to speak.

"Well, I didn't really need to ask," said Leel, smiling, as

she laid the square aside. "Love is far rarer than most people suppose, but also more easily identified."

He stood and went to the glass doors, looked out over the white slopes, down to the sunny sea. *All imaginary,* he thought. *I'm listening to an imaginary minddiver, who's telling me that love conquers all.* The sad futility of it made him want to cry, and all his anger seeped away.

A few silent minutes passed, during which Ruiz noticed a curious regularity to the surf that broke around the roots of the great buttresses. *Of course,* he thought. *The simulation is limited, after all.* He wondered if every semblance of sanity in the universe was as unreal as the Compendium. Somewhere, he was sure, people lived lives of peaceful fulfillment, going through their days in safety and contentment. Surely there were such people; but in his present state of mind they seemed as bizarrely unnatural as the monstrous Shards, who rode their weapons platforms above Sook, who enforced their alien laws on the pirates, the slavers, the cannibals—and the innocents—who struggled over the surface.

He pushed open the doors and went out into the sunlight and sea breeze. He stood gripping the balustrade, between two terra-cotta urns full of pink cinnamon-scented flowers. The next palace was far below; three sarim with iridescent wings wheeled in the lucent gulf.

He felt Leel's presence at his back, then her arms went around his waist and she pressed her thin body to his.

After a while he spoke musingly. "What would happen if I jumped off?"

"You'd fall for a while—until you'd passed from my domain. Remember, I cultivate realism here. But then I suppose Somnire would catch you. Knowing him, he'd probably appear as a mighty angel, and bear you aloft in a cloud of glory." She hugged him a little tighter. "He has an odd sense of humor."

Ruiz took a deep breath and closed his eyes. He rubbed at them with the heels of his hands. The pressure felt as real as it ever had; he felt as firmly held in this imaginary body as he ever had in his real one. Leel continued to hold him tight, and he became uncomfortably aware of her warmth, of the long thigh touching the back of his leg, of her slender hands crossed over his belly.

"Come back into my bedroom, Ruiz," she said, in a different voice. She slipped her hands under his shirt and slid them upward.

He wanted to, very much. To lose himself in her handsome body, her cleanliness and sweetness . . . to drive all thought from his aching head, submerge his anguish in lovely imaginary sensation. But some bitter hardness in his heart made him laugh and say, "Part of the therapy?"

"No," she answered, without any apparent resentment. "No. You're a beautiful man, and I want you. Please."

She pulled him around to face her, and he looked into her face. Her cheeks were flushed and a dew of perspiration glittered above her mouth, though it wasn't warm on the terrace. Her eyes seemed unfocused with desire. She pushed off the straps of her shift so that it fell to her waist. She guided his hands to the soft buds of her breasts. "What does it matter to you?" she asked breathlessly. "It's all pretend, anyway. I'm a ghost, a dream. No different from a joygirl in a pornsim."

"You're different. Very different," he said. Her breasts seemed to burn his hands.

"Then let's give each other this gift," she said, and kissed him, hard enough to bruise his lips.

He was about to say, *Why not?* But then he just shut his foolish mouth and let her draw him inside.

CHAPTER 11

LEEL was sweet and fierce and tender. She made love with such a desperate intensity that Ruiz forgot his suspicions, finally convinced that there was nothing merciful in her passion. She was everything a lover ought to be, and Ruiz burned away his sadness in her fire.

When they eventually drew apart, resting in a tangle of sheets and pillows, he felt a small healing begin in his heart.

She rolled her long sweat-slick body over his and took his face between her hands. She looked into his eyes and smiled. "So, did we please each other?" she asked, in a voice like winter sunshine.

"It seemed so to me," he answered.

She put her head down on his chest. "To me as well," she whispered.

Before long her breathing softened and became regular. A little while later he drifted into sleep, his arm across her back, his fingers brushing the elegant rise of her buttocks— and his last stumbling, slightly wistful thought was, *This is far too pleasant to be anything but imaginary.*

•   •   •

RUIZ LIFTED HIS head to find himself sitting on a bench in Leel's courtyard. Beside him sat Somnire, wearing an ornate silver and garnet crown, his hair dressed in lank braids. Around the Librarian's shoulders was an ermine cloak. At his feet lay the maimed sarim, watching Ruiz with its wise dog eyes.

The water in the little pond was black and the bougainvillea dead.

"So," said Somnire, smiling. "How are you?"

A shudder of distaste ran through Ruiz. "Don't you know?"

"No. Leel made me promise not to peek, during or after. A funny girl, she was."

"Was? What's happened to Leel?" Ruiz felt a sort of sick dread.

The smile disappeared, and Somnire looked very old and very tired, despite his boyish face. "Leel is dead, Ruiz."

"I thought you were all dead," said Ruiz in a low voice.

"Well, of course we are, of course, but there are several levels of death here, and I'm sorry to say that Leel has descended to a lower one."

"I don't understand." Ruiz rose and would have run back into Leel's house, but the frail-seeming boy put a restraining hand on his arm, and it was as if he had been gripped by a killmech's steel claw.

"Leel is gone," Somnire said gently. "Her house is full of empty rooms and dust. Sit down and I'll explain."

Ruiz sat numbly.

"It's time and energy, Ruiz. Time and energy," Somnire said. "When the virtual was built, its designers thought of it as an emergency data backup system, not as a refuge for dead librarians.

"The virtual is powered by magma taps, with the bulk of the energy earmarked to maintain static data storage. The personality support functions are less well endowed, since they were merely a convenience for users, none of whom were expected to reside for long within the virtual.

"The tap that powers the remaining personalities is failing, very slowly . . . but steadily. Occasionally we have a lottery, to see who goes into cold storage. The winner's pattern is retired, to be resurrected if ever we get a new source of energy. Leel won the last lottery—or lost it, you would say. She was nearly ready when you arrived."

Ruiz absorbed the information gradually. At last he glanced down at the Librarian's pet and said, "Why didn't you put the sarim into storage and let Leel stay a little longer?"

Somnire looked down at Idirin and his eyes glittered with what Ruiz saw to be tears. "It's an idea I've several times proposed. And in fact, most of the island's sarim *are* in cold storage. They were our dearest symbol, beautiful fliers who gifted us with their grace and loyalty . . . the other dons couldn't bear to see the virtual completely emptied of them. Anyway, they're simple creatures, they're dim candles to the fiery furnace of a human being's personality, so it doesn't cost us much to keep a few of them flying."

"I see," said Ruiz. He felt a terrible weight of disoriented denial. Only a few minutes ago, he had lain in Leel's bed; he could still feel the comforting weight of her body. "And I thought I'd left the monsters outside."

"Monsters? You call us monsters, you who have been on Roderigo? All we did was take you in and give you a respite, some breathing room."

"Why?" asked Ruiz. "Why did you go to the trouble, you and Leel?"

Somnire seemed almost haggard. "Leel's reasons were different from mine. I told you I was a vengeful ghost." He made a swirling gesture with his hand, and a concrete-lined pit opened up at Ruiz's feet.

Ruiz looked down and saw two long-legged reptilian creatures tearing at each other in a bloody blur.

"Lervals," said Somnire. "People bet on the outcome. At first they simply dumped the lervals into the pit and let them fight to the death. But then the handlers discovered that if they separated the creatures after ninety seconds and returned them to the company of their packmates between rounds, the lervals would fight much harder and much longer, until they were nothing but clots of raw meat. It's a little like what the Roderigans were doing when they spared your folk. All I had for you . . . was Leel."

The pit closed, became the flagstones of the courtyard again.

"I see," said Ruiz. He began to feel a slow hot anger.

"Do you? I want you to be my weapon against the Roderigans. I've waited centuries for you, and I would have put your edge to the grindstone any way I could. You were dying, looking for a place to lie down and rot. Not much use to me or anyone else. Now you're mending. Look in your heart and tell me I'm wrong."

Ruiz could not. "What were Leel's reasons?"

Somnire shrugged and spoke slowly. "Leel was exactly who she seemed to be: a sweet loving person, who helped me only because she couldn't see how it could harm you. And because she thought you a beautiful animal, too fine to be allowed to die of a broken heart."

A little twisty wind swirled through the courtyard, scattering the dead leaves.

"Couldn't you have let her say good-bye?" Ruiz asked finally. "Did you have to take her while I slept?"

"She chose the time, Ruiz."

RUIZ FELT A moment of vertigo; then he and Somnire stood on a slender high-arched bridge above a foggy chasm. Both ends of the bridge were lost in misty darkness; the light was vague and sourceless.

The bridge seemed too fantastic to be real, built of lacey black wrought-iron, as delicate as a spider web. Ruiz grabbed at the slim guardrails, and the whole bridge quivered.

"It's safe," said Somnire over his shoulder. "Let's go. We need to get down to business, Ruiz Aw."

Ruiz moved carefully, still clinging to the rails. He looked down at the roiling mist and fancied that he could see ominous shapes, almost recognizable. The mist swirled, threatened to coalesce.

"Don't look down," said Somnire. "It's one of my safeguards, in case the Roderigans somehow managed to inject an independent entity into the virtual. I don't know how they could do that, but why take chances?"

Ruiz fixed his eyes on Somnire's ermine-clad back until they reached the far pier.

They stepped down onto a path paved with opalescent glass, lit from beneath. The glass rang under their feet, as though each slab of glass were a great gong.

"I like a little drama," said Somnire.

A hundred paces took them to a   brazen door, carved with a many-times-life-size portrait of Somnire.

The carving's eyes appeared to be of flesh, and they fixed a bloodshot disapproving gaze on Ruiz as they approached the door. Ruiz almost expected the carving to speak, but it remained mute, even when Somnire reached up and tweaked its large nose.

The door swung open on a well-lit room filled with flatscreens and holotanks. Somnire led the way inside and sat down before a big dataslate. He took off his crown and set it aside.

"So, welcome to my inner sanctum," Somnire said.

Ruiz wondered why he had ever thought the Librarian a boy. The smooth youthful face was alight with an ancient craftiness. A thousand years of cunning seemed to glow in Somnire's dark eyes, and the Librarian had an almost hysterically cheerful look.

"And why not?" Somnire asked. "How often do I get to stick Roderigo in the eye with a sharp stick? Why shouldn't I take delight where I may? You must strive to do the same!"

"I'll try," said Ruiz, a bit resentfully. He still couldn't get used to the way Somnire responded to his thoughts instead of to his words.

"You try, yes," said Somnire. He seemed to shake himself, and then he spoke in a less gleeful tone. "I suppose the armor is the first problem. Can't make an omelet if you can't break an egg."

"What?" Ruiz didn't understand the reference, but Somnire was bent over the screen, tracing the columns with a finger.

"Why do you use the screen? It seems a pointless rigmarole. Why not just pull the data from its matrix directly?" Ruiz still felt a degree of annoyance with the Librarian.

Somnire grinned his strange ambivalent grin. "I do it for your comfort. Would you rather fly the electron storm with me, blowing through the decaying synapses of the machine, formless and elemental? Ah . . . forgive my occasional lapses into purple speech—a hazard of my occupation." He laughed darkly, and turned his attention back to the screen. "It's all right with me, if you're brave enough, but I should tell you that we sometimes drive our enemies mad in exactly that way. They become holy fools, of course . . . fortunately none of our enemies have any respect for holy fools, so they never learn to use their fools against us."

"Never mind," said Ruiz meekly.

"Ah," said Somnire. "Here it is. She's wearing Axolotl Light Intertribal armor, Mark IV version. Roderigo is frugal. Old, old equipment, but very good. She's probably had the armor since she was a girl. Axolotl went out of business before we did." He sighed. "Anyway. Designed for use in urban guerrilla conflicts. Twisted carbon monomol fiber. Most effective against light energy weapons and high-speed low-mass projectiles like splinter guns. Tough stuff."

"She let me search her for concealed weapons," Ruiz said. "The articulation under her ribs looked weak."

The screen flickered, showed an image of the armor. It expanded into individual components, each tagged with stress engineering data. Somnire tapped the rib plating with a delicate finger. "No. You might break them open with a crowbar, but there's nothing strong enough in the niche. Besides, I don't think she'll sit still while you pry."

"Probably not," Ruiz agreed sadly.

"Hmmm," said Somnire. "Let's take a different approach." He pressed at the screen's touchpoints, and the armor was replaced by the still image of an old man with a harsh dark face and the slashing cheek cicatrices of a Madeline Wreaker. "General Savin," said Somnire. "He's one of millions of personalities recorded in the Library's Anthroreplicant files. A military genius. He fought a notable campaign on Juneau almost three thousand years ago. The rebels were equipped with Axolotls. Let's see what advice he can give us."

The screen flickered, and then the old man moved, raised his sunken eyes to Ruiz. "What? What do you want?"

"The Axolotl Mark IV. How do I disable a woman wearing it? Bare-handed?" asked Ruiz.

"Almost impossible." The old man stared intently into Ruiz's eyes, as if seeking something.

"Wait," said Somnire to Ruiz. "Did I tell you that she found a wireblade on the corpse? She has it in her right calf sheath. Could you get it, if you surprised her?"

"Possibly," said Ruiz. "But she's alert, quick, and probably very strong."

General Savin grunted. "With a wireblade, there might be a chance. The helmet latches on the Mark IV are less than optimal—their cams were slightly weakened by the fanciful carving on the helmet's faceplate."

The old man disappeared, was replaced by an image of a soldier wearing the armor—though the legs and arms were banded with bright primary colors and the torso had a blue and yellow flag painted across the chest. A pointer appeared, touched the helmet at its lateral attachment points.

The general's voice continued: "A sharp blow here, at a fairly precise angle of one hundred and ten degrees to the column of the neck and with a slight anterior component, has been known to loosen the latch sufficiently to allow a knife between helmet and seat." A red arrow appeared, pointed at the latch to show the proper vector; the image rotated to show the arrow from three angles. The vector fired and the helmet cocked up a centimeter on that side.

"So?" asked Somnire.

Ruiz nodded.

Somnire turned back to the screen and the old man reappeared. "Anything else, General?"

"The Mark IV was not designed for hand-to-hand. Get the helmet loose; then you might be able to break her neck, if you can hit her with a sufficiently massive club, or use her own weight against some immovable object."

"We'll keep it in mind, General," said Somnire, and without ceremony he switched off the screen.

Ruiz fancied that the general had worn a faintly desperate expression, as though he didn't want to return to the dreamless limbo of the files.

"They don't know where they are," said Somnire, still reading his mind. "We don't let them wake long enough to think about it."

Ruiz had an uncomfortable thought. "Is that where Leel has gone?"

"Yes," said Somnire. "But I won't call her back from her rest, just so you can say good-bye. That wasn't her wish."

"I see," said Ruiz unhappily. "Well, now what?"

"Now we send you back to your body, so you can have a go at the hetman." Somnire lifted his arm and a large brass chronometer appeared on his wrist. "Been about four minutes since you entered the virtual, real time. She won't be expecting you back so soon. Most of their people we keep for days, just to inflict as much madness as possible on them." The chronometer wiggled and disappeared in a puff of pink smoke.

"I'm curious; why do the Roderigans keep coming to the virtual, if all they ever take away is madness?"

Somnire laughed rather maliciously. "Oh, we don't always destroy them completely—and sometimes we give them some relatively harmless scrap of information. Just enough to keep them from destroying the inducer and sealing us off forever. And we do what we can to keep Roderigo and Delt at each other's throats."

"Oh," said Ruiz. "Well, do you know the answers to their questions? What's going on under Yubere's fortress? Are you going to give me anything to bargain with, if I can't deal with the hetman? She promised me transport off Sook if I could get the information. Or can you give me a plausible lie—something to work with?"

"Are you still mad? Roderigo would never keep its bargain." Somnire gave him a hard, somewhat unfriendly look. "I have great hopes for you, but you may fail. The information they seek is too important to give you, unless

you can kill or incapacitate The Yellowleaf. As for fooling
Roderigo . . . a callow hope indeed."

Ruiz reluctantly saw the sense of it. Still, more than The
Yellowleaf stood between him and escape. "But if I *can*
best her . . . what then?"

Somnire grew agitated and, throwing off his ermine
robe, paced back and forth among the holocubes and flatscreens, muttering to himself. Finally he threw up his arms
and said, "All right. I've been living at a much higher rate
than you since the moment I left you at Leel's, so that I've
had a week to wrestle with my conscience—which isn't
what it once was, not at all. It's a terribly dangerous secret,
more dangerous than you can possibly understand now.
But it's out, it's surely out. The things your friend Publius
told you, the conflict in SeaStack, the slavers conspiracy—
all these things convince me that the secret is out.

"A disaster if the Roderigans find out for sure . . . but
also a disaster if anyone else finds out." Somnire fixed Ruiz
with a baleful gaze. "I don't admire you, Ruiz. You're what
I abhorred above all else, a man of violence. For all the
changes that have touched you lately, you're still a murderer. Your heart is open to me. You'd kill me in an instant
if it would save you and your friends. Oh, you'd rationalize
it until it didn't seem like murder, if you could: 'He's just a
pattern in the machine, not really alive,' and so forth, but
you'd do it, rationale or not."

But then the fire went out of Somnire's eyes and his
shoulders sagged. "Still, there's some decency in you. Even
I must admit that. So. If you're successful against The Yellowleaf, I'll give you the secret, and you must do with it
what your violent heart tells you to do. You may find unexpected help among the ruins, so be alert." He took Ruiz by
the arm and tugged him toward the nearest holotank.
"Look," he said, and brought the tank to glowing life.

Ruiz saw the niche, in half-life-size scale. His body lay
on the softstone slab, apparently resting in easy slumber—
though at first his body seemed as motionless as death.
Then Ruiz detected a slight slow rise of the chest, and
Nisa, who had been standing beside his body, facing away,

commenced a painfully slow turn toward his viewpoint. "Time differential," he said in realization.

"Yes, yes," said Somnire. "Didn't I say so?"

"So you did." Ruiz stepped quickly to the far side of the holotank, so that he could see Nisa's face. She was looking down at his body as she turned, and there was an unmistakably tender expression on her patrician features.

Ruiz felt a pleasant pain in his heart.

He glanced past Nisa and saw The Yellowleaf sitting against the far wall, ghoulmask glinting in the uncertain light.

A serious doubt struck him. "What about surveillance devices? It'll do me no good to kill the hetman if her guards come running in a moment later. Gejas surely has a man outside the cave."

"Probably," said Somnire. "But no spy devices are permitted in the cave—if we detect any, the virtual won't activate. If any appear after activation, we shut the field down abruptly, which almost always kills the visitor. They've learned to respect our notions of privacy, over the centuries."

"Oh," said Ruiz. He turned his gaze once more to Nisa and felt himself smiling foolishly.

"All right, Ruiz—pay attention," said Somnire impatiently. "First neck-breaking, then happy reunions. The order of your universe, I suppose. Now do pay attention." The Librarian produced a light wand and used it to point to a particular heap of bones and rubbish in the darkest corner of the niche. "If you survive, look here. There's an inductor helmet, voice only, hidden here. Put it on; we'll talk. I won't bring you back into the virtual—that costs too much energy and the cell you brought is long since exhausted."

"All right," said Ruiz, still looking at Nisa, who had begun a gesture that would eventually become a pat on his arm. Her expression was shifting by subtle degrees toward worry.

Somnire snorted, his youthful features wearing an incongruously cynical cast. "Ruiz. You must concentrate on the task at hand. I'll leave you for five minutes. Gather your will, make your plans, compose yourself. Lie down so that you won't jerk about when I return you to your body."

Ruiz pulled his attention away from Nisa. "Yes. Well, I'll do my best."

Somnire regarded him seriously for a long moment. "Good luck, then," he said finally, and before the sound of his voice had entirely died away, he was gone.

IT *HURT*. RUIZ couldn't entirely suppress a hiss of pain when he returned to his body. It was as if all his bones had been broken and reset, all his joints dislocated and restored.

Agony turned his muscles to nerveless jelly for long heartbeats. When the first twitch of returning control shuddered through him, he turned his head and saw The Yellowleaf rising, her hand dropping toward the hidden wireblade.

He thought of his time in the slaughterhouse, and the madness that had swept him away. He could still feel it, a great infected bruise under the lucid surface of his mind.

He closed his eyes and let the madness well up, a black volcano erupting from his holomnemonic ocean, belching red horror. He released his face, felt it turn monstrously gleeful.

Terrible sounds forced their way from his throat, and he opened his eyes again. The Yellowleaf was sliding her wireblade back into its calf sheath, her body relaxing into disappointment.

He couldn't look at Nisa, but he heard a broken-off sob, and a soft "Oh, no. Oh, no."

The Yellowleaf came closer, and he let the madness dance. But underneath it, he pitted his muscles against themselves, flexor against extensor, a motionless clenching that drove blood and life into them. Sweat broke on his face and his lips writhed back from his teeth.

The Yellowleaf raised her gauntleted hands toward his neck, as though reaching for his carotids.

He waited until her body passed the balance point and her hands had almost touched his neck.

He exploded from the table, all the madness compressed into that one movement, expelled from him in one tearing burst.

He struck her breastplate with his shoulder, driving upward so that she lifted from her feet for a precious instant, could not gather her strength against him. The heel of his right hand smashed upward against the side of her helmet, and he felt the latch break, a tiny triumphant *snick*. But the helmet stayed on, held by the remaining latches, and now The Yellowleaf got her feet under her and rotated, snapping her armored forearm around, catching him under his still-raised arm.

The pain took his breath for a moment and she thrust him back. He wondered if his ribs were broken, but the thought fled as the hetman bent, quick as a snake, for her wireblade. It came from its sheath with a sizzling metallic sound, and she flicked it up, reversing it with easy dexterity, so that the needle tip plunged toward his heart.

At the last instant, he parried the stroke, but the impact of his unprotected wrist against her armor made his hand go limp and numb.

He was losing, he was losing. After all that they had gone through, he was going to die. He grabbed desperately at The Yellowleaf's knife hand, managed to get it locked between his damaged left wrist and his right. He clung to it with all his strength, but she was stronger. She bent him backward over the softstone slab, she put her other hand behind her knifehand, and pressed him down until the tip of the knife trembled over his breastbone, and he knew it was all over. The ghoul carved into her helmet leered at Ruiz like a demon welcoming him to Hell. The armorglass eyeslots winked blue light. His strength ebbed.

A glittering blur caught the corner of his eye, just before it crashed into The Yellowleaf's helmet. Her helmet cocked over farther, and the pressure of the knife lessened. Then the hetman tried to pull loose, but Ruiz clung to the wristlock he'd achieved—and again something smashed into her helmet, making an even louder sound.

Ruiz felt a great astonished delight. The force of the mysterious blow had twisted the hetman's helmet to the side, too far to the side, and he felt the first tremors as the hetman lost control of her muscles. The wireblade fell loose; the hetman's knees buckled.

He shoved, and the body crashed down, legs jerking, making a terrible clatter amid the bones.

Ruiz turned and saw Nisa, still holding aloft one of the corpse's long greaves, as if she meant to make sure of the hetman.

"She's dead," Ruiz said.

Nisa lowered the piece of alloy slowly, then let it fall from her hands. "Good," she said in a muffled voice.

Ruiz massaged his wrist as the hetman's corpse grew still. "That was well done," he finally said.

Nisa didn't answer at first. Finally she turned toward him and spoke in an almost inaudible voice. "Are you badly hurt?"

Ruiz flexed his left hand; the numbness was fading. He lifted his right arm and winced. He might well have a broken rib or two. He probed with his fingers, but discovered no evidence of splintering. He could still function, as long as he took no more heavy blows on that side. "I'll live," he said.

"That's good," said Nisa neutrally.

Ruiz bent, ignoring the pain in his ribs, and picked up the wireblade. Nisa took a step backward.

"What?" he asked, bewildered by her fearful expression.

She took a deep breath. "You should have seen your face when you woke. Anyone might have been frightened."

"Yes," he said sadly. "I suppose so. But I would never hurt you intentionally."

"Is that true?" she asked, unsmiling.

"It's true."

She wrapped her arms about herself, as if she were cold, and he noticed that the air had grown chill and damp.

"Well," he said. "We won't be here much longer."

Ruiz went to the corner and threw aside the rubbish. Underneath, he found the tarnished wire mesh of the inductor helmet.

He lifted it up and wondered if Somnire planned some

trick. Certainly the Librarian was devious enough. Perhaps Somnire was content with The Yellowleaf's destruction; perhaps he meant now to get rid of the evidence. If Ruiz were retaken by the Roderigans and brainpeeled, he would reveal the Compendium's adamant hostility to the hetmen. From Somnire's viewpoint, it might be safer to eliminate that possibility.

Even worse, Somnire might now impart some knowledge to Ruiz that would burden him with yet another responsibility. His strong impulse was to drop the helmet and run away.

But where would he run to? Were there any hiding places on the island where he and Nisa would be safe? He imagined Gejas's ferocity when The Yellowleaf's corpse was discovered. A shudder ran through him.

And beyond all pragmatic concerns, did he owe Somnire something? Or Leel? He had entered the virtual as a cunning madman; he had returned as a human being —or as much of a human being as he had ever been.

"What's that?" asked Nisa, pointing to the helmet.

"Trouble." Ruiz sighed. But finally he lifted the helmet and set it on his head.

CHAPTER 12

As the weight of the helmet settled on his skull, Ruiz heard Somnire's voice fade in. "Ruiz?" The sound was thin, as though the helmet had partially failed, but the clarity was adequate.

"Well," said Ruiz out loud. "The job's done."

"Yes, I watched. She's a fire-spitter, that Nisa. Of course, she comes from a primitive world, so I suppose it's an admirable trait, in her."

Ruiz felt a rueful amusement, remembering Leel's observations on cross-cultural tolerance.

"Yes, Leel was wise," Somnire said, and Ruiz detected a note of sadness in his voice. "Perhaps wiser than I. Anyway, how do you propose to elude the rest of the Roderigans?"

Out of secretive habit, Ruiz attempted to keep his mind empty, but enough of his plan must have seeped through for Somnire to grasp the essence. "Ah!" said Somnire happily. "Very clever. It might even work."

Ruiz sighed. Nisa was watching him intently, as if she expected him to momentarily collapse into a frothing fit.

He gave her a weak smile, to which she did not respond. "So, what's the terrible secret?"

Somnire's voice went dark. "It *is* a terrible secret, Ruiz Aw. I hope we haven't misjudged you. Leel said I could trust you to do what is required. I don't know that I trust *you,* but her instincts were always excellent." Nothing came through the helmet but the hiss of transient currents, for a minute; then Somnire continued. "I'm only a ghost in a dying machine, but I still feel a loyalty to the universe of living beings we left so long ago."

"Get on with it," Ruiz said impatiently. "The sooner I get moving, the more surprised the hetman's people will be."

"Yes, of course. So: In the Gencha enclave, under the stack you know as the late Alonzo Yubere's stronghold, there exists a device. They call it the Orpheus Machine. My data don't cover the origin of the Machine; nor, of course, do they reveal any clue as to why the Machine is again being used, after all these centuries. Anyway. Anyway. This Machine—and I have no description of the appearance of the device—allows a Gench to perform its minddiving functions with no expenditure of vitality."

Somnire fell silent, and Ruiz tried to understand. For some reason he had difficulty focusing on the Librarian's words. Perhaps the wreckage of the death net still cluttered the depths of his mind, because a shrill tide of alarm was rising in him, threatening to drown out rational thought.

"Yes, you understand," said Somnire. "The Machine allows any Gench to perform an unlimited number of deconstructions. The process is swift and automatic. In fact, there's convincing evidence that mass deconstructions are possible."

"Oh no," said Ruiz.

RUIZ FELT A sort of odd paralysis. He wanted to throw the helmet down and walk away and never think about the Gencha again.

But his mind betrayed him with its irresistible compulsion to extrapolation, and so he could not avoid seeing the consequences of Somnire's information, spreading out through the human universe. Suppose Roderigo obtained control of the machine and its Gencha—or what if Castle Delt did, or even one of the pirate Lords?

Someone would be able to rebuild all the dangerous folk of Sook into deadly machines. Would forge Sook into an irresistible hammer. World after world would be crushed under that hammer, and the hammer would grow mightier.

Someone would eventually dominate all the worlds.

Ruiz looked more deeply into that strange future. It seemed to him that someday the human universe might become one vast organism, a far-flung body serving one mind, changeless forever.

He wondered who that absolute ruler would be. In retrospect, it was clear that his old ally and enemy, Publius the monster maker, had intended to seize that evolutionary pinnacle.

"Emperor of Everything," Ruiz whispered to himself, finally understanding what Publius had meant.

It occurred to him that it wouldn't matter who got control of the Gencha machine—the end would be the same. If a saint took the machine, all would be saintly. If a demon, all would be hellish. But in either case, in all the universe only one human being would remain to be exalted or tormented. Everyone else would be a flesh-and-blood machine.

Slavery would no longer exist, he realized. Only sapient beings can be enslaved. Wasn't that a good thing, in a way?

Ruiz shook his head violently. He felt shadows cloud his mind, and he tried to stop thinking. He couldn't seem to get his breath.

One final hideous idea occurred to him. What if it had all happened before, so long ago that memory of that time was gone? What if an ancient godmind had grown tired of its absolute rule and one day spoken to its body and said, "Go now and do as you will"? If so, was it any wonder that no one now understood the irrational intricacies of human behavior?

"Ruiz, Ruiz," said Somnire, breaking into his spiraling

dismay. "Calm yourself, please. Attend to the business at hand: survival, escape . . . and then the destruction of the Machine." The Librarian's voice seemed suddenly weaker, as if the ancient mechanisms of the helmet were finally failing.

"All right," said Ruiz slowly. "Can you tell me anything else? Anything I might find useful?"

Somnire cleared his throat, and Ruiz wondered why an electronic ghost would make such a sound. "The habits of the body persist, Ruiz," said Somnire. "Anyway. Do you understand the phenomenon of mindfire?"

"To some extent," said Ruiz.

"Then a brief overview: The pheromonic exhalations of a large number of Gencha, confined within a limited airspace, cause in unprotected humans intense perceptual distortions, similar but not identical to certain recreational hallucinogens. The primary difference is this: The visions and delusions stimulated by the mindfire do not originate entirely within the affected human's brain. The pheromonic net carries information within its structure. The visions may be purposefully imposed by a concerted Gencha effort, or may derive from past events, re-echoed over years or even centuries."

In his present state of mind, Ruiz felt no particular dismay at Somnire's description. How distressing could these visions be, compared to the realities he had recently witnessed? "Anything else?"

"Do not be complacent, Ruiz Aw," said Somnire, whose voice now carried undertones of impatient anger. "If you reach the enclave, carry clean air. If you run out, be prepared to see things as terrible as any you saw on Roderigo. Remember that Roderigo, for all its evil, can do nothing quite so dreadful as the thing the Orpheus Machine can do. And that Roderigo is one small island, on one sparsely populated backwater world. Regarding the mindfire: The Gencha are olfactory creatures; their worldview is supplemented primarily by visual sensory input. Therefore the mindfire distorts most vividly, for humans, in the visual range. Auditory distortions are mild compared to the visual ones, so that if you *hear* something clearly and strongly, you may assume its reality."

"I understand," said Ruiz.

"Finally, finding the Machine will not be easy. Pay close attention, while I tell you what is known of the enclave's geometries." And Somnire spoke at length, constructing a mental map for Ruiz, pausing frequently to assess Ruiz's memory. His voice grew fainter, and the static more distracting.

"The helmet's failing," Somnire said. "What I've told you must suffice." A long pause ensued, during which Ruiz began to think the helmet had already died. "Remember us," Somnire finally said.

"Always," said Ruiz, from his heart.

"Good luck!" Somnire's voice was almost gone. A thin heterodyning screech came through the helmet—then nothing more.

Ruiz removed the dead mechanism.

Nisa stood close, her eyes wide with concern. "What is it, Ruiz?"

He sat down. "A very bad thing, Nisa."

"RUIZ," NISA SAID more urgently. "What is it?"

Ruiz raised his gaze to her. What was going on behind those lovely dark eyes? Was it human concern, or was it inhuman calculation?

He couldn't risk the possibility that it was the latter, so he temporized. "The situation has become difficult."

"What was it before?" she asked.

"You have a point," he said. "Well, we must get started, anyway." He got up, and his bruised ribs flared with pain. He knelt by The Yellowleaf and unfastened the remaining helmet latches. When he pulled the helmet loose, her head rolled like a broken-necked bird's. Her face was as uninformative in death as it had been in life, the eyes staring coldly, the mouth slightly open.

His stomach churned at the thought of what he must do next. Close at hand was a chunk of masonry; he lifted it and smashed it down on the hetman's skull. Bone cracked and the once-handsome head deformed. He heard Nisa make a gagging sound, and he felt almost as sick himself.

But he took the wireblade and opened the broken skull, slicing the scalp along the fractures. Then he chopped through the brain until he found the synaptic decoupler, a small black ovoid trailing a pseudoneural filament.

"No good," he said, sighing regretfully. "I'd hoped it used some sort of electromechanical trigger, so we could use it against Gejas." He started to crush the thing, but then it occurred to him that perhaps it incorporated some sort of tracking device. He wiped it clean on a wad of the hetman's coarse hair and handed it to Nisa. "Put this in your pocket. Who knows? It might help."

He rolled the body over and rotated the catches that held the dorsal plating to the plastron, then began to pull the pieces off.

"What are you doing now, Ruiz?" Nisa asked in a troubled voice.

He looked up and saw that she was pale. "I'm retrieving your new wardrobe."

He was pleased that she offered no hysterical objections. She stood still for a moment and then nodded jerkily. "I see."

"It's the only chance we have to approach Gejas, I think," he said. The armor was accumulating in a little pile beside The Yellowleaf, who had begun to look smaller and less important, as corpses always did.

When the body was stripped, Ruiz stood up and handed the first piece of armor to Nisa. She took it. Apparently she had been watching, because she donned the pelvic girdle without fumbling.

"Good," said Ruiz. Nisa was a bit smaller than the hetman, but her bulky unisuit would pad the armor well enough for their purposes. Her breasts were larger, but her chest was not as deep, so the plastron seemed not too uncomfortable.

She dressed rapidly, without wasteful movement, and Ruiz found himself envying her apparent calm—no matter the source.

When she was done, except for the helmet, she stopped and looked at Ruiz. "Do you think this will work?"

"I hope so," said Ruiz. "It's all I can think of."

She frowned. "I have a question for you, Ruiz."

"Can't it wait for another time?"

She shook her beautiful head. "There may not be another time, Ruiz. Your luck can't last forever. I need to know: Did you mean those terrible things you said, at the camp? You were very convincing."

Ruiz shook his head violently. "Oh no, no . . . how could you think so? It was necessary, to keep the Roderigans from knowing how I valued you. They would have used you to destroy us both." He looked at her and remembered all the sweetness they had shared. He felt weak dangerous tears cloud his vision.

She looked away, as though embarrassed for him. "But it was true, what you said about me dying in Bidderum? Yes? Well, I think I always knew that I was dead when you found me. And that you had given me a second life. I always knew. Sometimes I wonder if I got a second soul as well; I don't seem to be able to touch it."

He didn't know what to say.

Finally she said, "I realize you can't advise me. I think you're none too sure about your own soul."

"That's true," he said in a somber voice. "Nisa . . . I want to apologize for striking you on Roderigo."

"I'm sure you thought it necessary."

"Yes, of course. . . ."

"Then why apologize?"

He tried to smile. "I feel the weight of it on my heart."

She shrugged. "What do you expect me to do about it?"

"I don't know," he answered humbly. "I suppose there's nothing to be done."

She looked at him with an ambiguous expression, part pity, part anger.

He couldn't bear to see that look, whatever it meant, and he closed his eyes.

In the next instant his head rocked back, as she struck him across the mouth with her gauntleted hand.

He touched his lip where it had torn and looked at her, too surprised to speak.

She smiled—a cool smile, but unforced. "Now we're even," she said.

To his further astonishment, she bent and kissed him . . . just the lightest touch of her mouth on his.

Then she lifted the helmet and drew it down over her head.

RUIZ FOUND A length of half-rotted rope and knotted one end around his neck. He used the wireblade to slice through the fibers, so that the loop hung by a few fibers. He handed the other end of the rope to Nisa. "I'm your prisoner," he said, with a hopeful smile.

He regarded her critically. The ends of her hair fell lower on her torso than had The Yellowleaf's; he took the wireblade and hacked them off. He slid the wireblade up his sleeve and tightened the cuff.

She was as perfectly disguised as he could have hoped. In fact, had the hetman's mutilated corpse not lain between them, he might have thought The Yellowleaf still regarded him through the eyeslots of the ghoul mask. Nisa's regal carriage seemed an eerily close approximation of the hetman's style, so close that it gave him a shiver.

"Listen," he said. "You must walk as if you owned the world, as if everyone else was shit on your shoes. Can you do it?"

"Of course," she said. "I remind you: For most of my life this was my attitude exactly—until quite recently, in fact."

"I forgot," he said, smiling more broadly. "Well, good, then. The other thing you must remember is this: Never speak. When we come out into the open, the Roderigans may have a spy bead or long-range monitors on us, so we must play our roles to perfection. No matter what happens, no matter what I do, remember to act as the hetman would."

"I'll remember." There was a short silence; then she spoke again. "I'm pleased to see you more yourself, Ruiz

Aw. You've seemed so cold, so distant, since we left Sea-Stack—I hardly knew what to say to you. Something good must have happened in your dream world—something that healed you a little." Her voice had a somewhat ambiguous quality, as if she were pleased but also apprehensive.

"Yes . . . a pleasant dream," Ruiz said, thinking of Leel and her serene imaginary life. He hoped Nisa wouldn't question him further. Though he was tired of telling lies, even kind ones, he could see no point in telling her of Leel.

But she didn't ask anything else, and after a moment he said, "Time to go. You lead, I'll follow." Then he had her knot another decayed length of rope around his wrists so that he would seem to have his hands bound behind his back. With care, the rope wouldn't break before the time was right.

"One last thing," he said. "If things go badly, if I'm killed or captured, try to get away. The armor should protect you from most long-range weapons, short of a direct ruptor hit. You'll have a chance." He didn't suggest any good place she might run *to;* probably there was no place of refuge on the island. Still, he wanted her to live as long as she could.

She nodded, the ghoul mask gleaming.

GEJAS WALKED NERVOUSLY back and forth beneath the weapons arch, pausing occasionally to glance at his surveillance screens.

His tracking screen signaled him with a low chime when The Yellowleaf's implant began to move. It seemed very soon; he had expected to camp in the hills for several days at least. He waited impatiently before another screen, which displayed the transmission from a spy bead hovering on the slope above the tunnel.

When The Yellowleaf emerged from the tunnel leading the madman on a choke rope, he felt a wave of relief wash through him. He wondered briefly what had become of the primitive woman, but then his attention was attracted by a subtle wrongness in The Yellowleaf's movement. She seemed to walk with a slightly easier, more sexual motion, as though her hips had been oiled. The relief he had felt was replaced by a furious envy. She had obviously indulged herself, had required the madman to please her, there in the cave of the virtual.

He told himself that he was angry because she had so casually risked Roderigo's interests. What if the madman had hurt her, or escaped? He was quick and strong—and dangerous as only the utterly reckless could be. But now Ruiz Aw hung his head and stumbled, as if exhausted.

When Gejas began to wonder exactly what The Yellowleaf and the madman had done together, he turned abruptly from the surveillance screen and shouted to the nearest guard. "Get the landwalkers ready. We meet the hetman on the beach."

He went to the center of the encampment, where the prisoners huddled around a glowpoint, attempting to stay warm. The little orange subhuman still lay on the ground, eyes half-open, obviously too weak to walk.

"Up," Gejas said. "We go."

The fat old Pharaohan gestured toward the orange one. "What of him, Master?"

He would have harvested any ordinary prisoner who asked such a question, but he restrained the impulse, remembering that the Pharaohan was part of the bait they were dangling before the slaver Corean. "Leave him," he said, and turned away.

OUTSIDE, THE NIGHT was clear, and the starlight bright enough to illuminate the path.

By the time Ruiz and Nisa reached the site of the encampment, the Roderigans and the other prisoners had been gone for a long time. Besides the beaten-down scrub, the only evidence of their presence was a bit of rubbish—food wrappers, discarded ammo packaging, scraps of paper—and the prostrate body of Einduix the cook. At first Ruiz thought the little orange man must be dead, but as they passed, Einduix rolled over and showed Ruiz a feeble smile. On Einduix's chest, Ruiz caught the glitter of the limpet—Dolmaero must have given it to the cook.

Ruiz resisted an impulse to stop. He didn't know what he might have done for the former sea cook—perhaps nothing—but in any case he couldn't risk an act that Gejas might perceive as uncharacteristic. Surely stopping to aid a discarded prisoner was not the sort of thing that would ever occur to The Yellowleaf.

Nisa played her role well, not even glancing aside as they passed Einduix.

Ruiz was certain that they were watched. The more he thought about it, the more foolishly optimistic his plan seemed. Could a man like Gejas, who for a lifetime had studied the hetman with an obsessive intensity, be deceived? Ruiz found it increasingly easy to play the demoralized prisoner; unfortunately, his performance was not the crucial one.

They continued down the path toward the water, and now Ruiz heard a rustle to one side. He presumed this indicated the presence of one of the mirrorsuited Roderigan guards.

With all his heart, he hoped that the guard would be incautious enough to approach them before they reached the beach.

COREAN WATCHED THE beach through her light-multiplier. The ghostly figures of the Roderigan party had appeared ten minutes before, and now they had settled on a terrace just above the high-water mark. Four landwalkers were arrayed in a defensive formation, and she saw a fairly sophisticated weapons arch visible above the alloy backs of the machines.

"Not too bad," she said, chewing distractedly on her lip. "We seem to have the firepower edge. But where is he?"

Marmo shook his head stiffly, engrossed in his perpetual processor games. Lately the old cyborged pirate seemed less and less interested in the real world. Corean wondered if he had finally become a liability. She contemplated him for a moment, and he glanced up sharply.

Still alert, then, she thought, and returned her attention to the multiplier. "Where is he?" she whispered.

DAWN GLIMMERED JUST below the eastern horizon when Ruiz and Nisa stood atop the last foothill ridge and looked down at the beach, where Gejas had reestablished the camp. Under the weapons arch, the tiny figure of Gejas hovered over the dim blue glow of his screens. The three remaining prisoners waited fifty meters down the beach, in a little dismal huddle.

"Let me catch my breath, please, Master," Ruiz said in pleading tones—just in case anyone was listening. He collapsed dramatically to his knees and hung his head. The path here went through deep beach grass, which now rose chest-high on Ruiz.

Nisa nodded, a disinterested gesture. Ruiz was a little surprised that she made such a convincing hetman. But then he recalled the first time he had ever seen her, when she had played the goddess Hashupit so well. That day in dusty Bidderum seemed a very long time ago now . . . it might almost have happened to someone else.

The rustles in the underbrush had grown closer as they approached the beach, but now Ruiz heard nothing. He tried to gather his thoughts. How could he get past Gejas and aboard the waiting transport? How could he ensure that the transport took them where they needed to go? How could he prevent Gejas from pursuing them when the Roderigans arrived?

He breathed deeply, trying to suck inspiration from the air. It proved as dry of ideas as his own brain.

He leaned his hip against a square of broken paving stone that jutted from the sand. He noticed that it was loose and not too large to be lifted.

Abruptly, a plan suggested itself to Ruiz. He went over the idea, and quickly detected a dozen ways it could end in disaster. However, surely the same would be true of any plan he could devise. He should probably consider himself lucky to have hatched any scheme, however farfetched.

He glanced up at Nisa. Could he rely on her to keep

silent if he startled her? He couldn't explain his plan in advance. Gejas surely watched and listened—in fact Ruiz's plan depended on it.

He probably should have gagged her before they had left the cave. He sighed. Hindsight was always so clear, and so useless.

Nisa faced away from him, still watching the beach. He snapped the rotten rope that bound him. He took the stone in both hands and rose up, lifting the stone high. He brought it down in a vicious arc that just brushed the back of her helmet, managing in the same motion to snap his left shin across the backs of her knees so that she collapsed as if from the force of the descending stone.

As she fell into the deep grass, he waited for her to cry out. But she didn't, she didn't—and his heart gave a hopeful leap. He raised the stone high again and smashed it down into the sand beside her head. He crouched over her, hidden by the grass.

She turned over and looked at him, and he was glad he couldn't see her face. He held an admonitory finger before his mouth before he remembered that the equivalent Pharaohan gesture put the finger under the chin.

She nodded slowly, and he smiled in what he hoped was a reassuring manner. Then he slithered as silently as possible into a slight depression a few meters away.

He waited.

GEJAS TRIED NOT to look at the screen that showed The Yellowleaf and the slayer, but occasionally he felt the compulsion to glance that way.

Eventually The Yellowleaf and her prisoner stood on the last ridge above the beach. When he looked again, they had both disappeared.

He swore and cued the playback mechanism.

For a long breathless moment he found himself frozen in horror. He watched the crazy slayer jump up, he watched the huge chunk of stone descend, he watched The Yellowleaf fall bonelessly into the long grass.

The terrible stone rose above the grass, fell again.

And then, nothing.

Gejas clawed at his communicator, keyed the channel of the guard he'd detailed to flank The Yellowleaf's return. "Herin, The Yellowleaf's been attacked by her prisoner. She's down. Go to her aid, kill the offworld slayer if you can get a clear shot—but above all, take no risks with The Yellowleaf's safety. Be very careful—the slayer is dangerous."

The remaining guards ran up. "Irsunt," Gejas barked. "Man the weapons arch—but hold your fire, unless I'm killed. Then burn them all. Call the sub right now, and let them know what's happened."

The guard set down his ruptor and started warming up the heavy weapons.

Gejas was delayed for precious seconds, looking for a medical limpet. Finally he found one and stuffed it in his jacket. He took the guard's ruptor, slung it across his back, and started running toward the ridge. If The Yellowleaf was seriously hurt . . . his vengeance would be monumental. He couldn't yet consider the possibility that she was dead.

SOMEONE CRASHED THROUGH the bushes toward them. Ruiz rose to a half-crouch and waited, wireblade in hand.

The guard was no more than a glimmer in the starlight, his mirrorsuit making him almost invisible—but his progress was so noisy that Ruiz had no trouble finding him.

Just before the guard reached him, Ruiz felt a disorienting intensity of perception. The night air was chill on his suddenly sweaty skin; he heard the movement of the guard and the sound of Gejas's approaching feet, thudding on the sand. The dry clean scent of the beach grass filled his nostrils. The tautness of his muscles, the readiness, the focus—all these seemed for that instant to return him to a comfortable reality he had almost forgotten.

All kill-thrilled, he thought in disgust. A sudden bleakness washed over him. *Never mind. Never mind.*

He forced himself to leave thought behind. He leaped

as the guard passed, knocking the man off his feet and into the concealing grass.

The man writhed under him and attempted to bring his weapon to bear, but Ruiz once again moved in the illusion of invincibility that had served him so well over so many years. He smothered the man's struggles and punched the wireblade through the tough fabric of the mirrorsuit, up into the man's vulnerable throat.

Ruiz twisted the blade and the man died. Blood ran smoking over his hand and he felt an unexpected weakness.

His energy sagged away, but only for a moment. Gejas was much closer, though the rhythm of his footsteps had moderated to a more cautious tempo. Ruiz pried the guard's weapon loose from the clenched hands and crawled back to Nisa's side.

There he examined the weapon, and discovered to his disappointment that it was a splinter gun, deadly at short range, relatively useless at over fifty meters.

And he could no longer hear Gejas. Either the tongue was moving more carefully, or he had deduced his mistake in sending the guard against Ruiz and was waiting just out of range.

Ruiz ground his teeth together. What now?

As GEJAS RAN, it occurred to him that he had been very stupid. The slayer had bested *The Yellowleaf*, after all. What chance would an ordinary guard, unarmored and unaugmented, have? He had probably just armed the slayer with the guard's weapon.

He crouched on the sand and used his communicator again. "Herin," he barked. There was no answer. Gejas groaned and ran on.

He took cover behind one of the huge boulders that edged the top of the beach, gripping the ruptor in sweat-slick hands. What should he do? If he went blundering up to the ridge, the slayer would surely chop him down. But

The Yellowleaf might be badly hurt; he *must* get the limpet to her before it was too late.

Fifteen seconds passed before his fear for The Yellowleaf grew too great to contain. "Ruiz Aw!" he shouted in a voice hoarse with hate and apprehension. "Speak to me, Ruiz Aw."

CHAPTER 13

Ruiz heard Gejas with a certain relief; at least the tongue wasn't sneaking up behind him.

Nisa turned her masked face toward him. He shook his head and made another shushing gesture. He examined his alternatives, found them discouragingly few. He sighed and made ready. He rolled closer to Nisa and disengaged the latches on her helmet, creating a gap between helmet and seal just wide enough to admit the muzzle of the splinter gun.

"You're dying, but you're not dead yet; maybe your tongue still values your stringy carcass," Ruiz said roughly. He hoped that Nisa would understand without any more explicit hint, and that Gejas, if he was still listening, would be further alarmed.

He shifted the transceiver from his boot to the back of Nisa's helmet, where he could use it without being seen by the tongue.

"Let's get up," he said, lifting her, his arm around her waist. As they rose above the grass, he jammed the splinter gun into the opening in her armor and swiveled her so that she shielded Ruiz from the tongue.

She played her part beautifully, hanging from his arm as if barely conscious, unable to hold herself up—though actually she was supporting a good bit of her own weight.

"What would you like to talk about, Gejas?" Ruiz shouted in a cheerful brassy voice.

"LOOK!" SAID COREAN, gazing into the screen, full of amazed delight. "He's somehow captured the hetman. What a dire creature he is! See, his luck assists *us* now. Surely whatever treachery they planned for us has been disrupted."

Marmo seemed skeptical, though he watched with almost as much interest as she did. "Perhaps," he said. "Though things aren't always what they seem."

GEJAS FELT AN ambiguous exultation—The Yellowleaf lived. But how could he free her from the mad slayer? It was clear Ruiz Aw was capable of anything.

To gain time, he shouted, "You don't know what you're doing. If you release The Yellowleaf and throw down your weapons, I can promise you an easy death. If not, you'll live in Hell forever. Once a year, on the High Day, we'll take you out and let you scream, as a lesson to those who would obstruct Roderigo."

The madman laughed, a trembling breathless sound. "You paint a vivid picture, tongue. But I've got my own ticket to oblivion, right here in my hand. After I turn the hetman's head to slush, I'll do the same for myself."

"We'll torment your clones, then!"

"You do that, tongue! I'd expect no less from Roderigo. But I'm a man without imagination, so the thought holds no terror for *me.*"

Gejas felt the truth of it. He bit his lip. "What will you accept in exchange for The Yellowleaf's life?"

"I don't know that you possess anything I want more than her death," said the slayer cheerfully.

"There must be *something*!" Gejas shrieked, panic clouding his vision.

A silence ensued. Gejas couldn't really see the madman's expression in the darkness of the ridge, but he sensed that the man was considering, and hope flared.

"Well," said Ruiz Aw. "I'd still like to bid Sook farewell —though the idea seems no more than a dim fantasy. . . . Let's see. I seem to hold the whip hand. So, cast away your ruptor."

"How can I do that? You'd just kill me," Gejas responded.

"No! Tell your man at the weapons arch to blow us all to bits, if I do that."

Gejas considered. Somewhere there was a flaw in the plan—perhaps the madman just wanted to be sure he could kill both hetman and tongue. But what other choice did he have? He could almost feel the madman's anger, a black pressure pulsing in the night. At any instant, he might decide to finish murdering The Yellowleaf, or she might succumb to the injuries he had already inflicted on her.

"All right," Gejas said. "Give me a moment." He bent over his communicator. "Irsunt. The Yellowleaf has been taken hostage, and I must disarm myself to get close to her. Before I can attempt her rescue. Direct all your weapons at the crazy slayer. If he attacks me, destroy him instantly. If he removes his weapon from The Yellowleaf's neck, pinbeam him instantly."

Then he stood up and moved away from his cover behind the boulder.

"Throw the ruptor away," said his opponent. Now Ruiz Aw sounded just a little less mad, a little colder. More in control.

Gejas took the ruptor by the barrel and smashed the mechanism across the boulder before he cast it out upon the sand.

"Now what?" he asked, folding his hands on top of his head. He half-expected to be cut in half. "What do we do next?"

•   •   •

RUIZ WAS PLEASANTLY surprised when the tongue stepped into the clear and destroyed his ruptor. Probably the tongue had other weapons hidden about him, but the Roderigan seemed remarkably biddable. Perhaps Ruiz had underestimated the tongue's loyalty to his hetman.

He sighed. He counted the guards at the weapons arch; all of the remaining Roderigans were there, apparently trusting to the armament of the arch and the cover of the landwalkers.

Now he came to the part of his plan where he must rely on a little luck—though surely it was reasonable to assume that anyone who dealt with Roderigo would be untrusting, would come to the meeting armed to the teeth. He must hope so, and hope that the transport was indeed not Roderigan. He keyed in his transceiver code and waited for the transport to answer.

The transceiver burped, and the thin sexless voice emerged. "Yes? Shall we send an autoboat to the beach now?"

"No," whispered Ruiz Aw. "No, the Roderigans plan a betrayal. They boast of how their fleet will be augmented by your craft, and their stockyards by your crew. If you wish to thwart them, I've arranged that their weapons currently bear inland. Destroy the arch, now!"

As he spoke, he shoved Nisa ahead of him, down the path toward the waiting tongue.

COREAN LEANED OVER her screens, concentration furrowing her brow. "What do you think, Marmo?"

The cyborg watched Ruiz Aw march the captured hetman toward the beach. "I don't know. The arch *is* focused inland; that much is true. But I still fear his luck—and his guile."

"Yes," said Corean slowly. "But do you not also fear Roderigo's treachery?"

The old pirate sighed and turned away. "Of course, of course. Treachery is only another name for Roderigo, and from the beginning of this mad adventure I warned they would never deal fairly with you."

"Then I suppose we must do as he bids us." Corean felt a sense of dislocation at that unpalatable thought. It seemed so strange, so uncanny, that Ruiz Aw had again found a way to compel her.

But she unlocked her fire control board and armed her weapons.

"Let's go up," she said.

OUT ON THE sea, the light had strengthened enough that Ruiz saw the boil of white foam when the submarine broke the surface.

It was still too dark to see the vessel clearly, but there was some disturbing familiarity to its ominous shape—though it was not the Roderigan sub that had put them ashore on Dorn.

He had time only for a flash of uneasiness before the submarine's big grasers fired.

Gejas whipped his head around, mouth dropping open. He stood frozen as the weapons arch and the remaining guards were consumed in orange glare. Ruiz wrenched the splinter gun out of the crack between Nisa's helmet and collar.

For a crucial instant the front sight caught on the collar and the gun refused to come free.

Gejas recovered and dove for the cover of the big boulder, just as Ruiz finally cleared his weapon and snapped off a burst. The spinning wires struck sparks from the boulder and flung the Roderigan's legs backward, but Ruiz couldn't be sure he had wounded the tongue seriously, and now Gejas was hidden behind the boulder.

Ruiz pushed Nisa flat and hid behind her armored body; Gejas might have another weapon ready.

He felt a deep sense of regret. He had probably failed to kill the tongue. How could he have been so inept?

He listened. He could hear nothing but the crackle of flames and the groan of tortured metal.

Indecision plagued him. Should he go after the tongue?

Or should he wait for the man's wounds to weaken him? Apparently the transport was not Roderigan, but could he now trust them to do their part? Might they not think it safer to burn all the witnesses? They had breached their contract with Roderigo, a very dangerous thing. He risked a peek above the beach grass. The three surviving prisoners still huddled by the water's edge, apparently unharmed —perhaps a good sign.

He reached up and refastened Nisa's helmet as best he could, so that she would have whatever protection it still offered. "Listen," he whispered. "We have to act soon, before the Roderigans send reinforcements. But I'm not sure I got Gejas."

"You seem to miss quite often," she said dryly.

"It does seem that way, doesn't it? I blame it on the superhuman agility of my enemies." Ruiz smiled at her and imagined that she was smiling back.

He keyed the communicator again and said, "Send the autoboat. I'm coming down to the beach with a valuable Roderigan prisoner. One of the Roderigan landing party may have survived—destroy him if he shows himself."

"As you say," the neutral voice agreed.

GEJAS STARED AT the burning ruins of the camp, shocked. He couldn't imagine what had gone so terribly wrong. He turned his gaze to the black submarine that now lay just outside the surf line. How could such a potent vessel belong to the slaver Corean? *Inexplicable,* he thought.

A wave of dizziness broke over him and drew his attention back to his wounds. He peeled back the tattered fabric over his right thigh and saw the pulsing of arterial blood.

He clutched at the medical limpet in indecision. He had intended the limpet for The Yellowleaf—but if he didn't use it in the next few seconds, he'd pass out and then die. And who would help The Yellowleaf if he were dead? He peeled the limpet's wrapper off and set it over the wound. He set its parameters to preclude anesthesia or sedation, and activated it. Instantly its probes slid into the ragged flesh and pinched off the artery.

He inventoried his weapons: a knife, a couple of stun grenades, a short-range one-shot pinbeam, a carbon-fiber cestus, a chemical interrogation kit. He cursed his improvidence. How, injured and with such pitiful armament, could he hope to best a man as deadly as Ruiz Aw?

He was barely clinging to consciousness. It occurred to him that he'd better hide or Ruiz Aw would find him helpless as a rabbit. He gritted his teeth and squirmed off through the boulders, careful not to expose himself to the sub's eyes.

He eventually found a place beneath a tumble of eroded concrete, from which he could watch the beach. He lay there, trembling on the edge of a blackout, wondering what new disaster would assail him.

A sponson on the sub's armored flank lifted up to reveal a small automated longboat. The longboat sped toward the beach, bursting through the surf in a high plume of spray and then grounding on a bar a few meters off the sand.

Gejas saw Ruiz Aw and The Yellowleaf running across the beach toward the other prisoners.

Then he saw how he had been deceived. The black-haired primitive woman wore the hetman's armor; she ran at an awkward shuffling pace, completely unlike the easy predatory lope of The Yellowleaf. Apparently the armor fit her poorly.

The Yellowleaf was dead—how else could the locator beacon have been extracted from her brain? That was his last desolate thought before darkness came down to cover him.

RUIZ FELT NAKED. As they ran, he tried to keep Nisa between his unprotected body and the boulders Gejas had taken refuge in. Her armor might turn away the tongue's fire; if not, Nisa wouldn't long survive Ruiz's death.

But nothing happened. They reached the others, and Ruiz shouted, "Into the boat, everyone!"

Molnekh and Dolmaero gaped at him, bewildered by the apparition of The Yellowleaf trotting obediently at

Ruiz's side, but Gunderd jumped up and began wading out toward the autoboat.

"Come on," Ruiz urged, and, taking Nisa's arm, splashed through the knee-deep water.

The others finally began moving, just as Gunderd pulled himself over the gunwale. The scholar turned and held out a hand to help Nisa aboard, and Ruiz boosted her in unceremoniously.

Dolmaero was a little harder to hoist, but between them, Ruiz and Gunderd managed. The instant Molnekh and Ruiz clambered aboard and settled on the metal benches, the longboat shuddered and backed off the bar with a grating sound.

"Where are we going?" Dolmaero asked.

"I don't know," said Ruiz. "But it's almost certain to be better than Roderigo."

Gunderd rubbed his chin in a now-familiar gesture. He looked over his shoulder at the grim shape of the sub. "On any other world but Sook, I would have to agree with you, Ruiz Aw."

Ruiz shrugged. "What else can we do? Even if we're giving ourselves to some ordinary slaver, it's still an improvement over Roderigo." He saw that Nisa was struggling with the latches of her helmet and he laid his splinter gun aside to help her.

She pulled the helmet off with a gusty sigh of relief. "It stank in there," she said.

The neutral voice came from a grill built into the forward bulkhead. "Welcome." It sounded slightly less anonymous, as though the unseen speaker had cut back the filtering. Perhaps, Ruiz thought, a person who knew the speaker well might guess his identity. "We'll have to get you aboard as quickly as possible; the Roderigans got off a distress call before I destroyed their comm unit. Their vessel is just over the horizon, coming fast."

The speaker seemed businesslike and unthreatening, but Ruiz felt the anxiety in his stomach twist a few turns tighter. He detected a tantalizing familiarity in the disguised voice.

They were halfway to the sub, moving rapidly. Ruiz put his hand down for his gun and it wasn't there.

He looked up slowly. Molnekh, two benches forward, held the splinter gun in a steady hand. The cruciform eye of the muzzle watched Ruiz, unwavering. Molnekh wore an odd smile on his cadaverous face, an expression compounded of happy achievement, faint embarrassment, and caution.

Dolmaero shook his head in bewilderment. "Molnekh? What are you doing?"

"My work, as is proper," said the voice from the grill.

Molnekh nodded contentedly, but his attention never left Ruiz.

Ruiz finally recognized the voice. "It's Corean," he said. "It's Corean on the sub." Shock made him breathless. How had he been so easily translated from the uncertain reality of the desolate island, into this familiar nightmare? His thoughts slowed, seemed to linger over irrelevancies.

"Molnekh?" asked Dolmaero.

"Molnekh belongs to Corean now," Ruiz said to Dolmaero in a faint voice. "The Gencha remade him."

Dolmaero put his hand to his mouth and regarded Molnekh with an expression of fascinated loathing.

Ruiz glanced at Nisa and saw that she was very pale. Her mouth was a taut line, her eyes huge. He felt a sort of abstract relief that she was still herself, still human—and at the same time a great regret. That they should have struggled so, across the hostile face of Sook, only to return to Corean . . . it seemed a sad dreadful futility. For a few heartbeats, he lost all will to resist.

Gunderd, who sat just forward of Ruiz, looked at Molnekh, and his face showed nothing but a sort of bland curiosity. *Always the scholar,* Ruiz thought, with a touch of bitterness.

The boat was no more than fifty meters from the sub, and slowing to come alongside, when a pneumatic hiss sounded across the water. The sponson armor lifted to reveal the old cyborged pirate, Marmo. Marmo waved his ruptor in an oddly comradely manner.

Ruiz almost waved back.

Gunderd turned to Ruiz, so that Molnekh couldn't see his face. The scholar smiled and winked, to Ruiz's puzzlement.

Gunderd looked forward and pointed. He spoke in a voice brimming with pleasurable discovery. "So that's the beautiful Corean!"

Molnekh turned to look, as if compelled.

Ruiz went over the side.

As he plunged down in a thrash of bubbles, he heard the thrumming sound of the splinter gun.

NISA CLOSED HER eyes as parts of Gunderd's left arm spattered her and a few splinters ricocheted from her armored torso.

Gunderd screamed, a dreadful throat-tearing sound— but a moment later he was drowned out by the giant amplified voice of Corean. "You idiot!" she roared. "Oh, you worthless dirtworld moron."

Nisa slowly opened her eyes, afraid of what she might see. It was bad enough. Gunderd, white with shock, clutched at the stump of his arm, trying to stop the blood that spouted from it.

But Ruiz was gone. When she started to lean toward the gunwale that he had rolled over, to see if there was any blood in the water, Molnekh jerked his gun toward her. His eyes weren't human, not at all. Apparently he had taken his owner's criticism to heart. "Sit still," he hissed.

RUIZ SWAM DOWNWARD through the black water, trying to get as deep as he could. He didn't know why. Shortly he would be forced to surface and Corean would take him; he was only postponing the inevitable.

He took some small comfort from the fact that he had at least been decisive. His old self wasn't entirely gone, apparently, even if in this case he hadn't made a very good decision.

When he crashed into a crumbling slab of ancient meltstone, he cracked his wrist painfully enough to force a cloud of bubbles from his straining lungs. He flailed helplessly for a moment, disoriented; then his hand caught the edge of the slab and he held on. Barnacles cut his hand. He floated to an angle that suddenly allowed cold salt water to fill his nose. He almost choked, but some long-ago training supplied a reflex that allowed him to clear his nose without losing all his air, and he managed to keep his grip on the slab.

He began to feel the chill of the water. His ears hurt and he swallowed to equalize the pressure. His chest was already aching with the need to breathe, and he felt a dismal certainty that he had only prolonged his freedom by a few insignificant moments. He attempted to investigate the underside of the slab, to see if he might somehow wedge himself under it and stave off capture until he was thoroughly drowned, but his hand encountered something unpleasant, a stringy mass of pulp—and he drew back hastily. Then he wondered how salt the sea was on Sook. Were it no saltier than Old Earth's, his densely muscled body would sink, once he had filled his lungs with water. No, he would probably float to the surface. Sook was a very old world, her seas thick with antiquity. . . . Ruiz realized his mind was wandering, and tried to focus his attention outward.

He listened. At first all he could hear was the pounding of his own blood, and then an odd squeaky sound. It was, he realized, his own throat, trying to open and let the sea in.

COREAN WATCHED HER exterior screens in familiar disbelief. How many times would Ruiz Aw escape her before he gave up, before he realized who he belonged to?

"He won't get far," she told herself. She consulted her infrared detectors and quickly located the slayer fifteen meters below, his body a hot crimson shape against the cold blue-green of the rubble-strewn bottom. He floated head down, clinging to a stone like a man-shaped oyster.

She smiled at the image. "I can wait longer than you can hold your breath," she said.

She glanced back at the exterior screens and saw that Marmo was hustling the survivors aboard. The wounded man tried to climb up onto the sponson shelf with the others, but the old pirate shoved him casually back into the sea and secured the longboat.

She touched the switch that carried her amplified voice on deck. "Wait," she said. "We'll pick up the slayer when he comes up for air. Take a catchwire and a stunner."

Marmo looked up at the camera, and his head gave a slight weary shake. Still, he started to follow her directions, though without any visible enthusiasm.

Alarms wailed, and most of Corean's screens shifted viewpoint to show the Roderigan submarine rushing up over the horizon. Almost immediately, she saw the twinkle of ranging lasers from the Roderigans' deck guns.

They hailed her. A harsh voice demanded her surrender.

She slapped at the main touchboard, closing the sponson armor, charging her heaviest weapons, cranking up her defensive screens.

One last longing look she gave to Ruiz Aw, still clinging to his rock. None of her weapons were small enough, delicate enough, to use against him. The water was too shallow; her vessel could be damaged by reflected energies. Besides, that wasn't the sort of death she wanted for Ruiz Aw. She wanted the slayer to die from the touch of her hands, with the sound of her laughter in his ears. She would have to let him go, this time. *What a sorry thing,* she thought.

"Don't die yet," she said to him, almost tenderly, before she engaged her engines and fled.

RUIZ'S AWARENESS HAD contracted to the burning in his chest. His fading volition struggled to keep his throat closed. He had almost decided to breathe the sea, to attempt to die purposefully, rather than in an unconscious spasm . . . when he heard the rumble of engines. He was only dimly conscious, but it seemed to him that the sound meant something, that he might as well try to live.

He let go and rose with agonizing slowness toward the surface, now silvered by the strengthening daylight. He tried to relieve the pain in his lungs by allowing the air to trickle from them, and it was almost a fatal mistake. By the time his lungs were empty, he was still several meters below the surface and with the loss of buoyancy his ascent had slowed. His vision darkened, but he thrashed upward with the last of his strength.

He burst through the surface and the sweet air shrieked into his lungs.

Of all the breaths he had taken in his long strange life, this, he was sure, was the finest. He marveled that he had never before truly noticed what a wonderful thing it was to breathe. Just to breathe.

At that moment he didn't really care about anything else.

But after a few blissful moments, he regained his sanity and swirled around, trying to find Corean's sub.

A glare lit the sky to the west, drawing his attention, and there he saw the larger Roderigan vessel pursuing Corean's sub, both boats speeding over the sea on hydrofoils, throwing plumes of spray high. Occasionally a beam would flash between the two combatants, to no obvious effect.

Corean's sub had apparently reached the edge of the offshore trench, because it came off its foils and sank below the waves. A moment later the Roderigan followed.

Ruiz floated alone, two hundred meters off the beach.

Was he alone? He heard an odd gasping sound, and his mind filled immediately with thoughts of margars and other large pelagic predators. But then he saw a head bobbing amid the waves. After a moment, he realized that it was the scholar Gunderd.

It took Ruiz three minutes to approach the scholar, who, without his gold sailor chains, was apparently floating without great effort.

When he reached Gunderd, Ruiz noticed with dismay that a red cloud stained the water, spreading from the ragged stump of the scholar's left arm. "Gunderd?" Ruiz said.

Gunderd lifted his eyes, and Ruiz saw that the man was

almost dead—he wore that look of calm regretful acceptance that the best soldiers took into oblivion.

Ruiz wondered how many times he had seen that look. *Far too many,* he thought.

He swam close to Gunderd, ignoring the possibility that predators might be attracted to the blood. He put a supporting arm across Gunderd's chest.

"Ruiz," said Gunderd, in a voice almost inaudibly faint. "Glad you survived."

"For the moment, anyway," Ruiz said, and started to sidestroke toward the shore.

Gunderd struggled feebly. "No," he whispered. "Don't drag me . . . foolish waste of strength."

"I'm just trying to get you away from the worst of the blood," said Ruiz. "I don't want the margars to eat us." *And maybe,* he thought, *you'll live to reach the beach, and can die a less frightening death.* He remembered that conversation he'd had with Gunderd on the *Loracca,* when the scholar had explained why he wanted to die swiftly if he were ever lost overboard. *The long slow falling away from the light . . .* Gunderd had said.

"Ah," said Gunderd. "For a slayer you have a good heart."

Then he died.

Ruiz felt the transition from life to death, a sudden weight, an unmistakable laxity. He stopped swimming, turned Gunderd to face him, saw the emptiness in the scholar's face.

"Well," he said aimlessly, and released the body. It floated facedown, leaking blood at a much slower pace.

Ruiz swam toward shore, as fast as he could.

When he reached the waist-deep shallows and stood up to wade ashore, he heard a thrashing flurry. He looked around to see something scaly take the body down. The sight stimulated him to a mild panic, and he splashed the last few meters, knees pumping high.

Once on dry land, he kept running until he had reached the cover of the boulders at the high water line.

CHAPTER 14

NISA watched Corean as she would a poisonous reptile. A few minutes before, the sounds of weapons and engines had ceased. Now the slaver walked up and down the narrow corridor between the cages that held Nisa and Dolmaero. The cyborg Marmo floated beside the forward bulkhead, attending his mistress.

Several hours had crept by since she and the Guildmaster had been herded into separate cages by the old man-machine. Nisa had passed the time by imagining that Ruiz Aw was still alive, that he would come after her, would rescue her from the woman who now held her.

As if she could read Nisa's mind, Corean stopped and glared in at her. "He's surely dead, bitch. He surely is." The slaver's face had undergone some destructive metamorphosis, so that she was no longer beautiful, in any human sense. The planes of her face hadn't changed, but whatever veneer of sanity she had possessed seemed now to have evaporated, and the madness writhing beneath the skin had become too insistently visible.

Nisa shook her head slowly. The slaver was probably right—but she wouldn't believe it, not yet.

Corean seemed to swell with rage, her face almost puffy with emotion. "You doubt it? Really? If he didn't drown, then the Roderigans have him. Better for him to be dead, if so."

Nisa looked away, as if terribly interested in the rusty steel in the corner of her cage.

The slaver sighed, and it was so incongruous a sound that it regained Nisa's attention. Corean had grown abruptly pensive, and Nisa had great difficulty in reading the expression on that perfect face. Corean looked at her so strangely that Nisa felt a greater degree of uneasiness than she had when the slaver had seemed full of violent anger.

Corean finally spoke in a voice softer than she had ever before used in Nisa's presence. "No, dirtworlder, I think you're right. He's still alive. His luck is uncanny—why shouldn't he survive the margars and the hetmen? Minor perils for him, eh? Foolish of me to think that the story is ended."

Suddenly it occurred to Nisa that Corean, in some dreadful way, loved Ruiz as much as she hated him. *How very odd,* she thought. *I never realized monsters could love.* But then she thought, *Why not? Isn't Ruiz a monster, in many ways? And doesn't he love me?* That train of ideas made her very uneasy, and she shut it off, though not before she thought, *As monsters go, Ruiz Aw is a kindly one.*

The cyborg made an uneasy throat-clearing noise. "Corean? What are your orders?" For once Marmo used a very ordinary voice. He sounded to Nisa like a tired old man, an old man who wanted nothing but his bed and an end to turmoil. "Shall I set the course to Port Ember? We can get a good price for the sub there, and safe passage offworld."

Corean whirled. "What? No, no. What are you talking about?"

The cyborg made a shrugging gesture. "Corean. We were lucky to get away with our lives. You wouldn't be thinking of returning to SeaStack, surely. We might not get

away a second time. Neither can we go back to the
Blacktear Pens; Roderigo will be waiting for us there.
We've lost all that, now."

Corean sidled a few steps toward Marmo. "Yes, of
course—but you can't believe I would give up now. After
everything Ruiz Aw has cost me? Are you crazy?"

Marmo drew back slightly and didn't answer. Corean
stepped closer, her hands clenched. For some reason, Nisa
remembered something she had once seen on Pharaoh,
just before her eighth birthday. A caravan of charlatans
had come to her father's palace, and though their sleights
had been unimpressive, they owned two great arroyo lizards, which they displayed in gilt cages. To her eventual
regret, she had gone to watch them being fed their monthly
meal of stonemole puppies. The deliberate movements of
the arroyo lizards as they approached their prey, the frozen
fascination of the puppies—there was something in the
present situation that resonated with that long-ago memory.

"Corean," Marmo said. "Please. What do you intend?"

"Isn't it obvious? We return to SeaStack. Ruiz will come
for his woman, or to take the Gencha . . . and we'll get
him. This time." Corean spoke a bit breathlessly.

"Oh, no. Corean," said the cyborg, "you must be mad.
SeaStack is a charnel house. Ruiz Aw has to be dead, or
otherwise beyond your revenge. But at least we're still
alive. Don't let his ghost drag us to our deaths. My life isn't
much, I admit. But it's all I have and I want to keep it."

Nisa watched in horrified fascination. The slaver stood
very close to her henchman, looking into his metal eyes.
"Marmo. You've been with me so long. I never thought
you would desert me." She spoke in a voice of cool
bemusement.

Marmo shook his head. "I haven't deserted you,
Corean."

Corean put her hand to his cheek, where the metal met
the flesh.

It ended so quickly that Nisa wasn't completely sure
what she had seen. The slaver's hand dropped to the

cyborg's throat. Nisa heard a buzzing whine. Marmo jerked and then became still.

A small amount of blood trickled down the front of his battered chassis.

When Corean turned around, Nisa saw tears shine briefly in her blue eyes.

RUIZ CROUCHED AMONG the boulders, listening, trying to filter any alien sound from the slap of waves, the cries of seabirds, the whisper of the offshore breeze in the beach grass. Nothing.

He still had the wireblade; doubtless Gejas, were he alive, was more formidably armed. Maybe the tongue was dead or too badly hurt to oppose him. Ruiz felt a slight degree of cheer at the thought.

As if that small encouragement had unlocked his heart's armor, he thought of Nisa, whom he would never see again. Corean would surely flee to the farthest corner of Sook, or at least as far as her sub's energy reserves could carry her. She might sell Nisa—or perhaps Corean would ease her frustration in torment.

The latter seemed most likely, when he remembered the lunatic sound of the slaver's voice. He supposed he should hope that Molnekh's burst had caught Nisa as well as Gunderd . . . but he couldn't do it.

You're wasting time, he told himself, and began to slither as silently as he could through the boulders.

When he reached the path he became even more cautious, alert for sensors and trip wires. Gejas was probably equipped with such devices; what good Roderigan soldier wouldn't be?

But he found nothing and after a while he decided that Gejas must still be hiding in the rocks. He started to run up the path toward the campsite.

By the time he reached the clearing, his damaged ribs were hurting him badly. Einduix was gone, and as Ruiz sat on a rock to catch his breath, he felt a certain relief. If he'd had to nursemaid the little man, his minute chance of survival would shrink to nothing.

He heard a stealthy movement and dropped to the ground behind the rock, gripping the wireblade.

Einduix raised his fuzzy head above the brush ten meters uphill, a quizzical expression on his wizened features.

Ruiz remained cautious. Was the little man alone? Was he perhaps a decoy for Gejas? *No,* he thought in mild embarrassment. *Gejas would have potted me by now.*

"Einduix," he said. "Come out; it's all right."

Einduix shuffled toward him, scratching his head and smiling a wry smile. Ruiz sat back down.

Einduix sat beside him, small thin hands on his knees. He turned his face up to Ruiz and his mouth worked, as though he were chewing a mouthful of pebbles. Eventually his mouth opened, and he spoke. "Gunderd?" he asked in a voice squeaking with disuse.

Ruiz was a little surprised, but the cook's concern was transparently genuine. "Dead," he said. "He died to give me a chance. I'm sorry."

Einduix's face fell, but he didn't seem surprised.

"I wish you could tell me what's been happening," Ruiz said.

Einduix cleared his throat at some length, then spat decisively. "I can tell little," he said. His accent was archaic, but he spoke the pangalac trade language understandably.

Ruiz was quite startled. "You speak?"

Einduix frowned at Ruiz, as at a willfully slow child. "So it would seem."

"Then why did you pretend . . . ?"

Einduix made a curious flapping gesture with his hands, as if waving away a bad scent emanating from Ruiz. "Do you see no advantage in such a subterfuge?"

Never had Ruiz expected such a conversation, there on the dead hillside. "I guess I do, but was it worth the . . . lack of companionship?"

Again Einduix made his disrespectful gesture. "What lack? Need you jabber with your friends to know their love? Gunderd did not." Einduix smiled painfully. "His jibes? Only affection, which he gave me in his own manner. True, as a chef I possessed little talent, but never was I seasick, so my food—such as it was—appeared with regularity. No more important quality is there, at sea."

This long speech had apparently exhausted the little man, because now he hunched down into his shipsuit like a skinny orange turtle.

"I see," said Ruiz. "Why are you speaking now?"

Einduix curled his wrinkled lip. "I am past all ruses."

Ruiz felt a touch of disorientation. He shook his head violently and attempted to return to the business at hand. "Have you seen the tongue Gejas? Or anyone else?"

"No one. And will the hetman soon be here, to bite out our hearts?" Einduix seemed more annoyed than terrified by the possibility; he gave Ruiz an odd wry smile.

"I don't think so," said Ruiz. "I killed her some hours ago."

A wide yellow-toothed grin lit the tiny face. "Ah? I am delighted to hear this. My deadliest enemy always has been Roderigo—a pestilence on them and may their years be numbered. Because our captors were Roderigo, I slept the sleep like death, so as to deprive them of my torment." He cocked his head to the side, looking like a clever curious monkey. "But then . . . who did I see in the hetman's armor? Your love?"

"My love," Ruiz said sadly.

"A fine ruse," said the cook, who now seemed a great deal friendlier. "It worked well?"

"To a point."

"Ah," said Einduix in a tone of deep commiseration. "And your love?"

"Gone now, where I cannot follow," said Ruiz, who suddenly wanted to cry.

"I am sorry, truly." Einduix patted his shoulder, his hand as weightless as a little bird.

The two of them sat together in a mournful silence that Ruiz somehow took comfort in.

It was Einduix who finally turned and said, "So what will you do, now?"

Ruiz shrugged. "I'd like to live a while longer. I expect that to keep me pretty busy. How about you?"

Einduix pursed his mouth judiciously. "I have no particular plans." Then the little man looked out over the ruined slopes, lit kindly by the golden morning light. "It is enough that I have come home. To the island's scent my body woke."

Ruiz looked at Einduix, puzzled. Then the image of Somnire came into his mind, with his odd yellow skin, his black eyes, his puffs of fuzzy hair. What might a long hard lifetime on the sea do to a person of Somnire's race? Might it not burn his skin orange, bleach the color from his hair, give him a thousand wrinkles?

"You're a stackperson," Ruiz said, astonished that he had taken so long to make the connection.

Einduix's eyes narrowed to slits and he jumped up. "Where did you hear that term, barbarian?"

"From Somnire, in the virtual."

The cook's eyes grew wide and his mouth dropped open. "Somnire? You spoke to him?"

"Yes," said Ruiz. "He gave me a job to do, but I don't know how I can do it now."

"Somnire," said Einduix, and now tears trickled down his small worn face. "Somnire, so glorious once. How fares he in his dream?"

"Well, I think," said Ruiz. Then he thought of Leel. "Though he must sometimes make ugly decisions."

Einduix flapped his hands. "What being does not? Somnire . . . to think you bespoke Somnire last night. And the city? Beautiful still?"

"It was," said Ruiz. He felt a sudden urge to give the little man a gift of some sort. "Somnire took me flying above the city, on a fine day. He showed me the white palaces, the shady courtyards. The sarim flew the air. Music rose up from the fountains and perfume from the flowers."

Einduix sat heavily and lowered his face into his hands. Ruiz began to wonder if perhaps he had been cruel.

But finally Einduix looked up, and his face showed some warm transformation. "You have been gracious to me, Ruiz Aw. And this task?"

"I don't know how I can do it now. It requires me to go to SeaStack." Ruiz was surprised by his own words. When had he decided he must see to the purging of the enclave alone?

Einduix stood and threw back his narrow shoulders. "Come with me. Friends will guide you by secret ways to a place of leaving."

Ruiz smiled. "Lead on, then." He stood abruptly and winced.

"You are injured? Here." Einduix took the limpet from his pocket. "See? I am useful already."

GEJAS LIMPED UP the trail in the noon sunlight. The limpet had restored his vitality sufficiently that he could go in search of The Yellowleaf. He took no precautions against ambush. If Castle Delt had landed a sweep team, he would soon be dead no matter how carefully he hid, and as for Ruiz Aw, he was sure the slayer had left the island in the submarine. *May you suffer a long time in Corean Heiclaro's hands, Ruiz Aw,* he wished. The thought gave him little pleasure; he would not witness the slayer's expiation, and no matter how passionate Corean's cruelty might be, her expertise would fall far short of Roderigo's.

He reached the campsite in the hills, and paused to rest for a bit. He settled on a rock and extended his throbbing leg carefully. The limpet still covered the torn flesh; he could feel the peculiar itchy pain of accelerated healing.

His eye fell on the octagon of crushed grass where The Yellowleaf's tent had been. Was it only the night before that the mad slayer had swaggered into The Yellowleaf's tent and made his outrageous demands? Gejas shook his head wearily. Sook had turned for a few hours, and his life had torn. Had gone with The Yellowleaf, away.

She was dead, she was dead. He accepted the fact, though he didn't understand how such a magnificently vital being could have disappeared so suddenly from the universe. The stars had not trembled in their courses, the sky had not split open.

He looked out at the sea far below, and saw that it was feathered with whitecaps. He wondered how much Ruiz

Aw had hurt her. The slayer had sufficient reason to hate The Yellowleaf.

Gejas stared at his feet, almost ready to select a fatal soporific from his interrogation kit, to abandon the tatters of his life.

Then he saw a curious thing, a boot print in the loose soil, its edges crisp, uncrumbled by the night's dew. Gejas bent, the better to examine this anomaly.

When he straightened up, he knew that Ruiz Aw was still on the island. A fire kindled in his belly, and he smiled.

"First to the cave," he whispered to himself. "To see what you've done, slayer. Then I'll start to find you."

He felt better. As he climbed quickly up the path to the virtual, he hardly noticed the pain in his leg.

RUIZ FOLLOWED EINDUIX through the rubble, down into a valley where the stones lay thick and tumbled. The little man took him into a pathless thicket, pushing the thorny branches carefully aside. "Not to break," said Einduix. He pointed at Ruiz's feet. "Don't scuff. Delt and Roderigo would hunt us, could they find the way."

Ruiz nodded and took care to leave no marks.

At the bottom of the valley, where a gully undercut an almost intact wall, Einduix stopped and rapped at a slab of black meltstone. His knuckles sounded out an odd syncopated rhythm. Was it a signal? Ruiz couldn't imagine who or what the cook hoped to notify.

Einduix squatted beneath a little tree, offering no explanation. Twenty minutes passed and the only sound was the buzzing of flies.

When the slab grated back into a slot, exposing a dark opening, it so startled Ruiz that he jumped up and grabbed at his wireblade.

"No, no," said Einduix. "These will be friends."

Two faces looked out, eyes blinking against the glare of day. One emerged into the light: an old man who looked a great deal like Einduix, except for the color of his skin, which was a pale citron.

"You I recognize, Einduix-who-fled. Who might the barbarian be?" The man's voice was deep and measured, larger than his stature. He held a splinter gun of antique design; the muzzle was fixed on Ruiz. He seemed poised to kill, though it seemed an oddly dutiful readiness, completely dispassionate. "Never may barbarians enter the Remnant. Have you forgotten?"

"No," said Einduix. "But he carries the commission of Somnire the Glorious."

The man's eyes opened very wide, and the muzzle dropped—but only for an instant. "Truth? How verified?"

"The Roderigans sent him into the virtual. He has returned whole. He spoke of the city in its glory . . . spoke as only a loving visitor could. He has slain Roderigans; he has caused great frustration to Roderigo."

"Ah!" Now the old man glowed, lips curling back from the black stumps of his teeth. But he still held the splinter gun ready. "Name yourself, barbarian."

"Ruiz Aw. And yours?" Ruiz made his voice polite and easy. What an irony it would be for Ruiz Aw to be killed by an elderly unemployed troglodyte librarian.

"Not important, to one who may soon die. Answer this, for your life: What did you see beneath Somnire's bridge?" The old man leaned forward in his intensity, so that the light fell brighter across his face. Ruiz saw that ancient scars seamed his face.

So eager was the old man to hear his answer that Ruiz thought he might easily disarm him, unless the man had abnormally fast reflexes. Ruiz controlled the impulse. What good would that do him? If he didn't get some help, he was finished. At worst, the librarian would execute him with more kindness than Roderigo.

"Somnire told me not to look," Ruiz said slowly. "But before he warned me, I think I saw terrible things. Things that I had made."

The muzzle sagged. The old man's eyes grew wet as he returned his weapon to its sling. "Glorious Somnire . . . how does he fare?"

"Well enough," Ruiz answered—though in truth he did not understand how Somnire managed to live with a heart so badly broken.

"What else can you say?" said the old man—and then in an uncanny parallel to Ruiz's thoughts: "I would ask you more, but I would only break my heart. Hard wisdom. Come below, and we will help with Somnire's commission." He moved back.

Ruiz stepped inside the tunnel, stooping to clear the low ceiling. Einduix followed. There were a half-dozen little people in the tunnel, all silent, all armed. He lifted his arms and they searched him, relieving him of the wireblade and prodding at the limpet. Einduix spoke. "A medical device only." The old man nodded and they left it in place over the injured ribs.

The slab slid shut with an ominous sound. "Thank you," Ruiz said.

The old man made Einduix's fart-flapping gesture. "Don't thank us. Be grateful to Somnire the Glorious."

Ruiz nodded, though he had an impulse to describe the nature of Somnire's commission in other than grateful terms. "How should I address you?"

The old man frowned. "Call me Joe," he said, finally. He turned to Einduix. "So, have you returned full of energy wealth, as once you swore you would do?"

Einduix shrugged. "I own a tidy sum, in the Northring Mercantile Bank. But I came home only by accident, naked of energy."

Joe made a sound of derision. Then he jerked his head and they set off down the tunnel by the light of pale green lanterns.

Some of the tunnels were so low that Ruiz was forced to waddle through them like a duck, and twice he had to get on his belly and crawl a hundred meters through an ancient conduit barely wide enough to pass his shoulders. At intervals he felt a movement of air and the pressure of unseen eyes. It came to him that the conduits were actually very ingenious defensive structures. How could any attacking force survive a passage through such a tunnel?

Finally he followed the old man into a corridor lit by tubes of some blue bioluminescent algae.

Joe stopped at a steel door and several of his followers put their shoulders to it. It slid aside with a screech of protest.

"Wait here," he said to Ruiz. "I will speak to you later, after Einduix-who-fled gives explanation."

"All right," said Ruiz a bit apprehensively. He stepped inside.

A dusty plastic bench stood in the center of the otherwise unfurnished room. Ruiz sat down.

The old man nodded, and the door slid shut, wrapping Ruiz in a dense velvety darkness. Locks clattered.

RUIZ FOUND HIMSELF finally alone with his thoughts, bereft of distractions. He remembered the days of the recent past, trying to slip lightly past the dreadful deeds he had done, the madness he had retreated into during his time in the slaughterhouse. But it seemed impossible; the more he tried not to think about his bloody hands, the red glee he had felt . . . the more those memories seized him.

He felt himself beginning to rock back and forth in the darkness. He bit his lip until the blood flowed, trying to feel the pain and nothing else.

When the limpet's tendril touched his mouth he jerked. A shuddery frisson of horror ran through him before he realized what it was.

It explored the jagged flesh, then applied a coagulant and anesthetic. He felt the sting of sutures, little ghostly pains that made his lip itch.

A sedative jetted into his bloodstream, bringing a sense of warm detachment. He sighed and wiped the blood from his chin as best he could. There was no point in cultivating the appearance of a self-destructive madman, even if that was what he was. Especially if that was what he was.

His thoughts drifted now along more comfortable paths. He remembered Nisa, but perhaps because of the drug, his memories were sweet, untainted by the pain of her loss.

Time passed indefinitely, and Ruiz dwelled in loving recall. After a while he began to wonder why he had chosen to give Nisa so much of his allegiance. She was beautiful.

But the universe was full of beautiful women. She was brave, but though bravery was a rarer quality, he'd met many brave persons. She was intelligent, warm, witty. None of those qualities were so unusual.

Was it all just a tangle of erotic coincidence? He shook his head. Difficult to believe. But other explanations trespassed into the realm of mysticism, in which he could put no belief.

"Well, what does it matter?" he said. He took a deep breath and let his mind empty, until he was just a man waiting in a dark room.

BY THE TIME Einduix came back, Ruiz had lost all sense of time.

"Ruiz Aw, hello!" said the little orange man. He seemed to be alone; he held a lantern full of glowing worms, a squirming tangle of greenish light. He carried in his other hand a covered tray.

"Hello," Ruiz said sluggishly. He found it difficult to think; perhaps he should instruct the limpet to discontinue treatment, now that he had enough light to reset the limpet's parameters. He fumbled under his shirt and clicked it off. He felt slightly painful tugs, as the tendrils withdrew from his body—but his ribs seemed much better. He poked at them, found only a little lingering soreness.

Ruiz dropped the limpet in a pocket. It might later come in handy; for now he would conserve its limited capacity.

Einduix thrust the tray at Ruiz. "Breakfast," said the little man. "Eat quickly."

Ruiz peeked under the cover. There was a bowl of yellowish porridge and several strips of what appeared to be dried fish. A deep cup held water.

"Eat!" said Einduix, so Ruiz did. The food seemed tasteless—or perhaps he was paying no attention. When he was done, he felt marginally more alert.

"So . . . are you ready?" said Einduix.

"Ready?"

"Yes! You must go to SeaStack; so you claimed when we met on the hillside."

"Ah," said Ruiz. "And how will I go?"

"Those-who-stayed took counsel. Aid will be given, as I promised. They can spare you no weapons; they have too few already. But they will help as they can. Follow!"

Ruiz got up and followed. Perhaps, he thought, Einduix was incapable of explanation. In any case, he lacked the energy to interrogate the little man.

The two of them trudged through kilometers of dark tunnels, a maze of mouldering machinery and sealed doors. They met no one.

Ruiz thought about his benefactors, since he had nothing better to do. Obviously a remnant of the stackfolk survived here, down in the deepest rubble of the Compendium. But to what purpose? He could not imagine such blind loyalty, at least not to a thing that had died so many centuries before. After a while he stopped thinking about it; the universe was full of inexplicable things.

After what seemed hours, Ruiz became aware of a faint shuddering sound, rhythmic and diffuse, almost too deep to be heard with the ears.

"What is it?" he asked.

Einduix glanced back. "The sea. Do you not voyage to SeaStack?"

"Such is my hope," said Ruiz glumly.

"Then follow," Einduix said, lifting his pale lantern and moving off.

The sound of the sea grew louder. Presently the walls of the tunnel began to tremble with it.

Ruiz was ready to ask Einduix another question, when they rounded a curve and came to a gate, a tall slab of monomol secured by heavy cross timbers.

Here a party of stackfolk waited, armed and nervous. The old man named Joe wasn't with them, and Ruiz felt an unexpected flicker of disappointment. *What an odd thing,* he thought. *What is he to me?*

"This is . . . what?" asked Einduix of the woman who stepped forward. She had a worn defeated face, but she stood straight-backed and held her old punchgun with an air of familiarity.

"Escort," she said. She handed Ruiz his wireblade. "No activity along the beaches. Roderigo delays; Delt ignores."

Ruiz shook off his dangerous passivity. "Wait," he said. "I must know what you plan. This is my area of expertise."

Einduix frowned at him. "Out into the Sea Caves we go. Where once flourished trade. Where once vessels in great numbers called. There, sealed safe against the ages, low-tech escape boats are hidden."

"Ah," said Ruiz. "Well, then, how many are required to obtain one of these?"

"You could do it alone, had you the knowledge."

"Do you have the knowledge?" Ruiz asked Einduix.

"For a certainty."

"Then let us go alone. We'll have a better chance of escaping notice."

"Agreed," said Einduix. The woman argued with him, but without enthusiasm.

In the end, the two of them slipped unescorted through the gate into the Sea Caves.

CHAPTER 15

THE Sea Caves formed a vast natural cavern system. Einduix led them down a tall narrow corridor. Stalactites hung down like hungry teeth. Black iron railings were in places buried under a half-meter of white flowstone, and Ruiz wondered how long it had been since humans had walked this route.

They passed numerous junctions; the path changed levels several times. "Are you sure you remember the way?" Ruiz asked.

"Yes," said Einduix. "Never can a stackperson forget; otherwise we would lose our way in the stacks."

Eventually they came to a crawlway, where the ceiling pressed close to the floor, creating an opening like a wide frowning mouth.

Einduix stopped, looked at Ruiz critically. "It is possible that you are too large. We must try, however. On your belly! You first; then I will follow, the better to pull you out if you become stuck."

Ruiz took a deep breath. He had never liked confined

spaces. But he got down and wriggled under the overhang and began a long painful crawl over sharp gravel.

Only once did he find himself jammed between the overhead and the gravel. For a moment he couldn't seem to get his breath, and he almost sobbed, trying to fill his lungs. The stone seemed to press down on his back, and he had the terrifying illusion that it had settled a little closer to the gravel and was about to crush him. Was the island subject to earthquakes? He struggled to no avail, writhing like a bug under a giant thumb.

"Ruiz Aw! Attend!" Einduix spoke sharply. "Let out your breath. To the left is more clearance."

Ruiz controlled himself, realized that he had been holding his breath, as if that small pneumatic pressure could hold the stone up. He concentrated on emptying his lungs, and the stone released him.

When they emerged into another high-ceilinged room, Ruiz felt a joyful sense of release. They rested on a flat-topped formation for a few minutes, though Einduix seemed untaxed by the crawl, despite his age and apparent frailty.

The thunder of the sea shook the stone here, an insistent vibration, as if the stone under Ruiz's hand were the skin of some living creature. "How close are we?" asked Ruiz.

"Close," said Einduix. He frowned and gave Ruiz a searching look. "On the lifeboat, after *Loracca* died, you seemed to own some small knowledge of the sea. True?"

"I've sailed several seas," said Ruiz. "I claim no great expertise, but I can navigate well enough to find the coast."

"The escape boats are uncomplicated—but old and somewhat fragile." Einduix got up and pointed. "We must go, and hope that Roderigo waits elsewhere."

They walked the last hundred meters on condensation-slick rock and came out under the great dome of the Sea Caves, filled now with the gray cold light of dawn.

They stood among the ruins of warehouses, now reduced to a few low walls. Among these remnants huge pillars rose to the roof high above. These appeared to be natural formations, once carved with decorative reliefs.

Ruiz stepped closer to one of these, but the carving was obscured by delicate calcite veils, evidently formed since the destruction of the Compendium.

Long piers had once extended from the warehouses into the sea; these lay in broken tumbles, submerged for the most part.

A mild surge ran into the Sea Caves. It seemed the worst of the booming surf broke on the windward side of the island, just east of the caves. The sound was very loud, as if the arch of the cave somehow focused and amplified it.

Ruiz could see a small arc of horizon beyond the entrance; the sea was frothed with whitecaps and the sky had a brassy dangerous look.

"The weather does not entirely bless us," said Einduix. "But at least Roderigo does, by its absence."

"I should go as soon as possible, bad weather or no," said Ruiz. "Roderigo will be searching for me."

"True. So, follow!"

Einduix set off through the ruins, zigzagging from one pillar to another in an apparently random pattern. Ruiz followed, feeling somewhat foolish. How could anything useful survive in the midst of this destruction and decay?

By the time Einduix stopped before a pillar, Ruiz had begun to wonder just how sane the stackfolk could be, after all this time spent hiding and brooding.

Einduix picked up a jagged stone and chipped carefully at the calcite. In a minute he had uncovered a dim carving of a mermaid. "Ah," he said, and pressed it. Nothing happened. He frowned and tapped fussily with his stone. He pressed again, and the carving sank into the stone.

Einduix stepped back nimbly, as the pillar hissed. Calcite fell from its side in glittering fragments; a seam opened. A tall narrow door swung out, to reveal a long bundle wrapped in mirror-finish monomol.

"Escape boat," said Einduix, with evident satisfaction. "Help me to assemble it."

      •   •   •

WHEN THEY WERE done, a graceful catamaran lay on the wet stone. Seven meters long, laminated wood hulls like two bright curving knives, a spidery platform of carbon-fiber slats linking them—the boat seemed extravagantly beautiful, to Ruiz's anxious eyes. A tall wingmast of some clear composite material rose from the platform, controlled by a crank wheel at the helmsman's station. A tiny jib hung from the forestay.

"She is fast," said Einduix. "Once she was strong. Use care, Ruiz Aw. The fibers of her hull were encapsulated with inert resins, but time is time."

Then the little man demonstrated the controls, showed Ruiz the survival capsule, with its ancient water canisters and nutrient blocks, its charts and compass, its sextant. He smiled at the navigation almanacs, so long out of date. On a chart he pointed out the course Ruiz must take.

"Do you proceed direct to SeaStack?"

"Yes," said Ruiz. "If I'm right, the pirates will still be letting traffic in; they'll need soldiers and slaves. My biggest worry is getting too close to the Namp shore. Other than that, I should be all right, if no margar hunters stumble across me."

"She is radar-transparent, but not invisible," said Einduix, patting a gunwale. "You'll need some luck, Ruiz Aw."

JUST BEFORE THEY picked up the catamaran and slid its hulls into the green sea, Ruiz took Einduix's small hand between his. "You're staying?"

"Yes," said Einduix. "Here is my place, if only to die. But we stackfolk live a long long time; what use ephemeral librarians?" He laughed. "So I can hope to see Roderigo's death before my own."

"I hope for the same," said Ruiz. "Well, thank you. And thank Joe for me."

A strange look crossed Einduix's ancient face. " 'Joe' never was his name, Ruiz Aw. You should understand: In a time long lost, in a place long dead . . . far away from the sadness here and now, Somnire the Glorious was his name."

Einduix gave his hand a little shake. "Good luck to you, Ruiz Aw, and good-bye."

GEJAS HAD BURIED the sad ugly remains of The Yellowleaf under a cairn of heavy stones, to keep the scavengers away from her until she could be returned to Roderigo.

And then, not knowing what else to do, he had climbed up to the heights, so that he could look down on the island. So that he could see Ruiz Aw when the slayer finally crept from his hiding spot.

The sun set, the sun rose, and still the slayer had not shown himself.

By midmorning Gejas began to grow restless. What would he do if the slayer had met some accident among the ruins? A pack of joykillers from Delt, perhaps? Or maybe he had fallen into some pit; the island was riddled with caves. Had The Yellowleaf inflicted some wound on the slayer, some slow-to-kill injury, and did Ruiz Aw now lie in some unfindable place, bright with fever or dull with lost blood?

These thoughts moved Gejas to a great anger. "No!" he shouted, raising his face to the sky. "You *will* live, until I find you."

When he looked back down at the north headland of the island, he saw a tiny boat make out from the cliffs.

Who else could it be? His fury increased; what could he do to prevent the slayer's escape? Nothing, nothing.

His head buzzed; he clamped his jaw so tight his teeth creaked. All he could do was watch the slayer sail away, unpunished.

As he watched, the boat tacked to the east, clearing the headland by several hundred meters. It fell off onto a course that would bring it down the island's windward shore.

After a bit, he could see the slayer's small figure, crouched over the tiller, feathering the wingmast into the strongest puffs. The boat was very fast, slashing over the sea, throwing roostertails of spray several meters into the air.

In minutes Ruiz Aw would be gone. But then Gejas realized something that gave him hope. The boat was sailing to the southeast, in the direction of SeaStack.

SeaStack. Gejas's anger was gone, replaced by a sort of violent contentment. Soon Roderigo would send a boat for him. They would make him suffer for The Yellowleaf's loss, they would hurt him and try to break his mind; that was Roderigo's way, and a good one.

But he would survive. Because The Yellowleaf—and by extension, her tongue Gejas—had been Roderigo's greatest student of that strange city, eventually they would allow him to take a force into SeaStack.

Where Ruiz Aw was bound, for reasons Gejas could not comprehend. Because of his dirtworld woman? Because of the slaver Corean? It didn't matter.

Gejas turned away from the sea and made himself comfortable, to wait.

RUIZ AW HAD his hands full with the catamaran. The lee hull sliced deep into the waves, pressed down by the weight of the wind. Einduix had warned him about allowing the lee bow to dig in; apparently the boat was capable of tripping over its nose. The weather hull hissed along the surface, trembling. Ruiz could feel its willingness to rise, to capsize the boat laterally.

He cranked the wingmast out a few more degrees to spill a little wind, and the weather hull settled a bit more firmly into the sea.

He began to get a feel for the boat's helm, and some of the tension drained from his muscles. If the wind grew no stronger, he should be able to manage.

In the early afternoon the wind dropped, and Ruiz was able to lash the tiller for a while. He swallowed a mouthful of antique water, but was unable to bring himself to try the nutrient block. It had a gray, mummified quality and a musty smell. For all he knew, it had always been that way, but at his present speed he'd reach SeaStack long before hunger became a serious problem.

He took a sight with the small bubble-sextant, crossed the position line with his dead-reckoning track. He marked the fix on his chart with a certain satisfaction; for the past three hours he had averaged fourteen knots. He began to feel an ambiguous hope. It seemed he might survive to reach SeaStack, and that was good. But then he would find himself in SeaStack, facing an impossible task.

He unlashed the tiller and concentrated on the task at hand, and in that concentration he found some comfort. He passed the afternoon in a state of almost pleasant thoughtlessness.

As night began to fall over the sea, low clouds raced across the horizon to the west, and the wind grew heavier. The waves grew taller and began to break with a tumbling hiss.

Ruiz shivered, and feathered the sail into the wind, adjusting its camber to its maximum flatness. Still the boat rushed along in a welter of foam, quivering with the urgency of its passage. Ruiz grew more anxious.

With complete darkness, the speed became more frightening, and the growing seas more ominous.

Ruiz struggled with the helm, trying to take the seas consistently on the quarter, so that their force shoved the boat harmlessly ahead. But the sound of the wind sang a higher note, and the boat was beginning to move so fast that Ruiz worried it would fly down the face of a wave and bury itself in the back of the next wave.

He tried to remember what to do, tried to pick the bones of memories from a long-ago time, when he had fought a campaign on a water-world.

Finally it came to him. He waited for a lull. When it arrived he cranked the jib slightly to weather, put the tiller down to leeward.

The boat paused in her headlong rush, spun up into the wind, and sat there, riding the waves like a duck.

Ruiz lashed the tiller down, wiped the spray from his eyes, and crawled into the coffin-sized berth in the weather hull. He latched the hatch carefully and lay down on the thin cushion.

For some reason, a thin thread of happiness ran through him. He didn't know why. The boat jounced violently, the wind shrieked, breaking crests thumped the topsides.

But after a while, remarkably, he slept.

HE SLEPT, IN fact, until well after daybreak, and it was the silence that finally woke him.

When he went on deck, he found that the breeze had dropped to a zephyr, and the boat sat on a glassy sea. A leftover swell lifted the boat up and down, and Ruiz was once again glad he didn't suffer from motion sickness.

He unlashed the tiller and set his course toward Sea-Stack.

His progress was less impressive than it had been the day before. He could coax only three or four knots from the unsteady wind. He experimented with the wing. He trailed a fishing line, with no results. He took a sun sight and pored over his charts. He couldn't be certain how much the storm had set him to the east until he could get a crossing line in the afternoon. He kept glancing to port, as if he expected the low coast of Namp to appear there.

In the early afternoon he saw a margar, a lone bull who came to the surface to clear its spiracles, two kilometers off the starboard bow. The great reptile rolled on the surface in a thrash of foam, its spiracles moaning, one upraised vane catching the sun with a white glitter.

Ruiz held his breath until it had submerged. Had it seen him? Would it be interested in his insubstantial craft?

Time passed and he remained uneaten.

He was beginning to relax when he saw a slim black hull on the eastern horizon.

When it suddenly veered toward him in a cloud of spray, he wondered if perhaps it might have been better to be a margar's dinner.

No, he thought fiercely. *None of that.* He checked his wireblade.

In a few seconds he could see clearly the glaring raptor

eyes painted on the approaching boat's bow. *Castle Delt,* he thought, shocked. The vessel was a small, fast, open-cockpit squirtboat, used for reconnaissance and infiltration. Two armored figures crouched behind the boat's windscreen.

He touched the haft of his wireblade—an absurdly inadequate weapon. He cast about desperately for a plan, but nothing came to him.

Eventually he decided that his best course would be to present the appearance of helplessness and hope that the Deltans grew careless.

He pinched his cheeks until a prickling warmth told him they were pink, and combed his fingers through his tangled hair, smoothing it as best he could.

The boat came alongside, sending a wave splashing over the catamaran's port hull. Its engine roared and then fell to a low throb. Grappling pitons fired into the catamaran; their lanyards retracted, jerking the boats together.

Ruiz smiled brightly at the boat's crew—two black-masked Deltans, their light armor painted in black and fluorescent green stripes. Red chevrons on their masks identified them as members of the officer class known as Sub-Dominators: young, untried, platoon-level commanders. They weren't wearing their helmets; apparently they considered him easy prey.

One held a splinter gun in his hands and played carelessly with the safety lever.

"Hello," said Ruiz, standing up, hands clasped at his breast. He pitched his voice as sweetly and hopefully as he could. "I'm so glad you've found me!"

One of them laughed, with a somewhat forced harshness. Ruiz could imagine him in a classroom, with some scarred veteran saying, "Laugh to curdle the blood! All together now: laugh!"

His hopes rose.

"Yes," said Ruiz. "I don't know what I would have done." He simpered, and thrust out his hip and made his body seem as soft and vulnerable as he could.

"What are you doing out here, boy?" demanded the one with the splinter gun.

Ruiz assumed a theatrically tragic expression. "Roderigo harvested our village, kind sir. I escaped, through great good fortune—or so I thought. . . . And then I found myself out on the sea, alone. With no protector." Ruiz licked his lips, widened his eyes.

The laugher practiced his bloodcurdler again, this time with more confidence. "We'll protect you," he said. "Come aboard."

Ruiz clambered over the gunwale, moving with an eager dainty awkwardness, as if the hard steel of the rail hurt his hands. "Oh, thank, you, kind sirs, thank you," he babbled.

The one with the splinter gun latched back his safety and fired an economical burst, cutting the catamaran in half. Ruiz concealed a wince; he had grown fond of the fragile thing.

"Perhaps you have something I could eat; I've drifted for days and the emergency rations were unbearable." He rolled his eyes and smiled, as he settled between the two Deltans.

The laugher stood and began to unbuckle his armor's pelvic girdle. "I've got something you can eat," he said jovially.

"Oh no," said the one with the gun. "I don't take your leavings this time. Me first." He didn't exactly point his weapon at the other Deltan, but the muzzle wandered close.

"Sirs, sirs," said Ruiz nervously. "No need to quarrel. I can surely satisfy you both at the same time. For what other reason did the deities give us more than one erotic orifice? Women are more blessed in this regard than we are—but there are only two of you."

They both laughed, less harshly—Ruiz detected a note of relief. The one with the gun locked it to a retaining clip, and they both unlatched their armor.

The laugher stretched out in the bows; the other stood behind Ruiz, fingering himself.

It was too easy. But he accepted his good luck, as he was required to do. The wireblade slipped from its hiding place and he stabbed backward into the groin of the one there, ripping the blade transversely free. He reversed the point and drove it up into the laugher's belly.

Almost before the man could react, Ruiz sawed the knife back and forth, withdrew it, and turned to finish the man who had carried the gun.

He hardly noticed the screams, even though they were more bloodcurdling by far than the laughs had been.

WHEN IT WAS over, and the corpses gone over the side, Ruiz examined his prize. The squirtboat seemed in fine condition, apart from the blood that spattered it. Its fuel cell registered a full charge, the engine purred. He rummaged through the lockers and found a good selection of weaponry in the portside one: splinter guns and ruptors, monomol garrotes and elbow axes, stun grenades and nerve lashes.

In the starboard locker he found pouches of irradiated rations and cases of potables. He opened a pouch of stew and a chillcan of beer, but he suffered from an odd lack of appetite.

His eyes wandered about the cockpit, lingering on the splashes of blood, the heap of armor he had taken from the taller Deltan. He felt almost sick to his stomach; finally he drained the beer and threw the stew overboard.

After a while he stirred himself and began to perform the necessary tasks. He rinsed the armor clean and buckled it on. In one of the armor's storage slots he found a wad of SeaStack currency; apparently the Sub-Dominators were on their way to a SeaStack vacation. He tried a harsh laugh, and to his ears it sounded infinitely more menacing than the laugh the dead Deltan had been practicing.

"Well, I'm an experienced monster," he said, as if to an invisible companion, and smiled. His face felt odd, so he stopped smiling.

He took a bucket and washed the rest of the blood down into the bilge, where an automatic pump whirred and discharged it into the sea.

Despite the sleep he had gotten the night before, he felt a feverish exhaustion. But he sat down in the helmsman's seat and saw that the navigation computer was already set up with the coordinates of SeaStack. Before he pressed the execute bar, he had a thought; he looked under the dashboard and saw a black box with Delt's logo: a remote controller. He pried up the connector and jerked the datacable loose.

The boat was now his—or so he hoped.

He buckled on the restraint harness and sent the boat arrowing over the sea at its maximum speed. The sensation was like riding a skipping stone at seventy knots.

He and the bruises he would collect would arrive at SeaStack in the morning, provided he avoided enemies with speedier boats.

RUIZ DROVE THE boat through the night in a state of comatose vigilance. He submerged his thoughts in the sensations of speed, narrowing the focus of his mind to throttle and wheel and the heaving surface of the sea.

He was quite surprised when the dawn showed him the tips of SeaStack's tallest structures, rising above the horizon.

He jerked back on the throttle bar and the boat came off the plane, settling into the sea with a flare of spray. The engine's scream dropped to a mutter.

What was his plan? At that moment his head was filled with a terrifying indecision, and nothing else. He had promised Somnire something . . . hadn't he? No, actually he hadn't said he would do anything; Somnire had told him he must do as his heart directed.

At the moment his heart told him to flee as far from SeaStack as he could get, to run away from Sook, to hope that he died a peaceful death long before humanity was consumed by what lay under Yubere's stronghold.

He sighed. No, it wasn't his heart speaking—it was common sense.

For some reason he thought of his foolish youth, when he had called himself an emancipator, when he had still believed that the institution of slavery could be destroyed. He thought of the pain, the disappointment, the blood spilled, the friendships betrayed, all in the name of that hopeless chimera.

As he mused, he discovered to his surprise that he no longer regarded that younger self with his customary bitter contempt. Something had changed. Something had thawed the ice that had filled his heart for so long, and now his heart demanded that he go into Sook and do his best to destroy the Orpheus Machine. "How strange," he said aloud, and his voice shook a little.

He laughed, then, and had a pleasant thought. Perhaps Corean had sold Nisa somewhere; perhaps in SeaStack he could consult the market listings, if the market still survived the disturbances in the city. Maybe he could still find her.

When he began to wonder where he could access the market datastreams, the beginning of a plan formed in his mind, just a faint glimmer of possibility—but it was better than no plan at all.

Ruiz Aw took the Deltan's helmet from its locker and settled it over his head. He took a deep breath and shoved the throttle bar forward.

CHAPTER 16

SEASTACK grew until its towers eclipsed half the sky. Ruiz Aw approached the security perimeter, where he expected some sort of challenge from the floating forts which formed the city's seaward defenses.

Dead ahead was a fort of burnished rose-colored alloy; it presented a low rounded profile, like a turtle of mythic proportions. He slowed the squirtboat and waited for the fort's garrison to hail him.

But as he drifted forward, he began to notice ominous details.

No one moved along its armored battlements. Scorch marks licked up from several observation ports. As he floated a little closer, he saw that twisted wreckage had replaced the fort's weapons emplacements.

He brought the boat to a halt, reversing its impeller momentarily. Had the fighting gotten so out of hand that the pirate Lords no longer controlled the perimeter?

A breeze eddied around the twisted shapes of Sea-Stack's towers and brought him the smell of decay. He gagged, then forced himself to be calm. *I'm not the man I was,* he thought, but he felt no great regret.

He swung the squirtboat in a wide circle and passed the fort without incident.

WHEN HE NEARED the first of the great stacks that gave the city its name, he looked up with his usual amazement; it seemed impossible that a structure so spindly could reach such an enormous height.

Then he looked down into the murky water that surged against the stack's base, and thought how deep the stack reached into the sea. He remembered the job he had done for Publius the monster maker, breaking into Yubere's stack at its roots—and how it had felt, to be surrounded by the impersonal relentless pressure of the deep.

In retrospect, his assassination of Yubere appeared a rather lighthearted adventure, compared to the things he had lived through since then.

Perhaps those memories retained a certain warmth because of his conviction—at the time—that Nisa waited for him if he returned. He had no such reward before him now . . . nothing beyond mere survival, a prospect in which he found insufficient motivation.

He searched himself for will. Why should he again go down into SeaStack's depths? What reasons compelled him to try?

For a while nothing significant came to him. He had made a half-promise to a ghost. What of that? He also hoped to spite Roderigo—but revenge had, very strangely, ceased to move him with any great intensity.

Then he remembered that the universe was surely full of men and women who loved as passionately as Ruiz and Nisa, who hoped to live out their lives together without brutality and coercion. Could he act on their behalf? "Better than nothing," he whispered. Did he feel a little stronger? Perhaps.

He shook himself. Now wasn't a time for pointless speculation. Now was a time for caution, scheming, sharp observation.

He looked up at the stack again. What was different from the way it had been when last he had passed this way, a passenger on the barge *Loracca*?

Then the terraces had been green with crops and flowers, spilling perfume and color into the air. Now the steep sides of the stack were brown and dead, and no farmers moved along the terraces in their eternal stoop.

Then music had floated down from the habitations higher in the stack, faint and sprightly. Now the silence was so deep as to raise Ruiz's hackles.

He passed the entrance to an interior anchorage; the metal gates were half-melted from their hinges, and the tunnel seemed blocked by a wrecked airboat, barely awash.

He saw his first corpse, a legless woman with a face so bloated she no longer looked at all human. In the old Sea-Stack, corpses never floated long enough to decay significantly—the margars took them down. Were the margars so gorged they could no longer keep up with their task?

Ruiz Aw hunched down in the cockpit and kept to the shadows, as he made his way deeper into SeaStack.

HE TRAVELED AMONG the spires for an hour, and in that time he saw no one, heard nothing but a single distant explosion. A few minutes after that deep dangerous sound, his boat shuddered as a confused wave pattern passed beneath it.

Where were the sampans, the armored barges, the freighters that once swarmed through the city's channels? The city wasn't dead, he was sure of that. Ruiz felt nakedly vulnerable; he was certain that hidden multitudes watched him and weighed his intentions. Why didn't they attack him? His paranoia ran wild, so that by the time he reached his destination his face had developed a painful tautness, and his shoulder muscles twitched.

The gate into Deepheart's lagoon was still open, he saw with a surge of relief—though one phallic gate post was broken off, and the other drooped at an exhausted angle.

He passed within slowly, trying to look in all directions

at once. As he recalled, the lagoon was a perfect spot for an ambush.

When last Ruiz had seen the lagoon, it had been lit by low red lights—but now it was dark as a cave, and he could see nothing at all.

He switched on the squirtboat's spotlight. He played the beam slowly around the lagoon's perimeter.

A great face looked back at him from the far side—the bow of a Deepheart effigy barge. It lay along the quay, half-submerged, the black water lapping over its chin. Its heavy-lidded erotic languor seemed tragically inappropriate, and a wild laugh forced its way out of Ruiz's throat.

The sound echoed across the otherwise empty lagoon. Was Deepheart deserted? If so, his plans would need reformulating.

He heard the hum of a switched-on loudhailer an instant before the voice boomed across the lagoon. "Deltan! Show empty hands and make no sudden moves! Irresistible weapons are locked on you. What are you doing in Deepheart?"

Ruiz laughed again, this time with relief. He stood up and tugged off the Deltan helmet. He raised his hands high and shouted: "It's Ruiz Aw. Let me in."

RUIZ LEFT THE squirtboat moored to the quay, hidden behind the sunken barge, where it would not be immediately visible should enemies visit the lagoon.

He was met at the blast doors by a fragile-looking young woman in scarred servo-armor. He didn't recognize her, but she opened her faceplate and spoke in a whispery voice.

"Ruiz Aw. I'm oddly happy to see you again."

"Again?"

"It's me, Hemerthe. Your friend from before."

The first time Ruiz had seen Hemerthe, he had been a tall green-eyed man. "Ah," said Ruiz. "Hemerthe. How are you?"

"Personally, well enough," she said, her narrow face

dimpling. "SeaStack has become dangerous—as you surely saw. Did you have any trouble reaching us?"

"The city was very quiet," he said.

"Sometimes it is. At first the fighting was constant and bloody. Now it comes in great spasms that fill the channels with corpses and shattered war machines. Between times they lay low and plot the next frenzy of killing. They grow exhausted, but their ferocity doesn't fade, at all. No one can understand it."

"Yes," he said. "I need to talk to the Joined. About what's going on in SeaStack."

"All right," she said. "We wondered if you would return to us. Come."

Just inside the blast doors, they passed a squad of armored men and women, crouched behind the shield of a heavy ruptor. They looked up at Ruiz through cloudy faceplates, and in their eyes he recognized suffering puzzlement.

RUIZ FOLLOWED HEMERTHE down the spiraling corridor into Deepheart, remembering his first visit. He and Nisa, with Dolmaero and Molnekh and the treacherous conjuror Flomel, had walked this same path, afraid and expectant.

His frame of mind then seemed, in retrospect, inexpressibly innocent, as remote and forever lost as childhood's innocence. They had escaped from the slaver Corean and survived a trip across Sook's violent lands. Ruiz and Nisa had found a deep closeness—never in his long life had he been as happy as he had been on that night aboard the Deepheart barge.

As he walked behind Hemerthe, he felt his mouth pull down into a strange sad shape.

Hemerthe spoke over her shoulder. "We've gathered the Joined to hear what you have to say. Don't be too surprised by what you may see."

They reached a cross-corridor, turned left, and eventually reached a set of ornate brass doors, carved in low relief. A number of naked smiling people, artfully intertwined, copulated in a variety of imaginative ways. Such cheerfully ribald icons were common in Deepheart.

Hemerthe pushed the doors open, flinging them back and raising her thin arms high. Ruiz smiled a little. They loved drama in Deepheart.

"The slayer Ruiz Aw," Hemerthe announced, and swept one hand down to point at him with a quivering finger.

Ruiz looked up at the platform where the Joined sat in a half-dozen chairs. He felt a disorienting shock of recognition.

Nisa sat in the leftmost chair, regarding him with sleepy eyes. She looked as though she had just been roused from a nap; her hair was still pleasantly tousled.

He started forward, to sweep her up, to touch her, to feel her life—but then he remembered where he was and stopped. She was watching him with impersonal hostility—nothing more.

"Yes," whispered Hemerthe at his side. "Jufenal wears the body of Nisa. The body has just become available and Jufenal, because of her position as leader of the Joined, had first claim. We would not have purposely arranged it so, but you arrived suddenly."

"I see," said Ruiz painfully. Somehow he had avoided thinking about the clones he and Nisa had given to Deepheart in return for their freedom and Deepheart's help—even though his half-formed plans had included one of those clones.

Jufenal-Nisa stood abruptly. "What do you want here, Ruiz Aw? It was an ill day when you came to us the first time."

The other members of Deepheart's ruling council were nodding. Jufenal went on. "Your arrival signaled the beginning of the convulsion that is destroying SeaStack—and now rumors reach us that the pirate Lords search for a Dilvermoon slayer named Ruiz Aw. That he has something to do with this great treasure they are killing each other to find." She gave him a look both severe and despairing. "It's only a matter of time before they trace you to us. And what will we do then?"

Ruiz looked up at that collection of grim faces and wondered what he dared tell them. Would their unique perspective, their commitment to an extreme form of personal freedom, make them immune to the temptation of the Orpheus Machine? He sighed. It was not his nature to trust, and now what choice did he have?

"I must tell you a terrible story," he said finally.

WHEN HE WAS done, when he had answered all their disbelieving questions, when he had seen skepticism replaced by horrified acceptance . . . a silence filled the almost empty hall.

"Why have you come to tell us this monstrous thing, Ruiz Aw? Why *us*?" asked Jufenal, after a long time.

Ruiz was beginning to wonder the same thing. As he had retold the story, all the unlikely coincidences that had brought him his knowledge of the Orpheus Machine, he had begun to feel a treacherous doubt. Was any of what he believed really true, or had the events on Roderigo broken some essential part of his sanity? Had he made it all up, seeking some justification for the suffering he had endured, the death he had inflicted on so many innocents?

He shook his head. What did it matter? He must act, if there was any chance that Somnire existed and that his information was correct.

"I've come for your help," said Ruiz.

Jufenal shook her lovely head, and Ruiz's heart ached to see a gesture so much like one Nisa might make. "What help can we give? It's all we can do to defend our lives, and we don't know how long we'll be able to do that."

"I don't want anything you can't give." He looked down at his hands. "I need an armored submarine. Weapons. A light flatscreen camera with a transceiver powerful enough to be received here—even if the cam is a thousand meters down in the roots of a stack."

Jufenal looked puzzled. "Why a camera? I had not thought you so eager for fame."

Ruiz laughed bitterly. "No. Of the things left to me, anonymity is what I value most. But the camera will serve two purposes. I'll be going down into the Gencha enclave.

To survive there, I may have to abandon what shreds of sanity remain to me, and I'll need someone at the other end of the link to tell me which things really exist—and which are hallucinations." He looked at Jufenal. "The second purpose is yours. The camera can document the destruction of the Orpheus Machine, so that the pirates will cease their struggles and SeaStack will survive."

"If you succeed," said Jufenal. "And is that the entirety of your list?"

"No," said Ruiz. "I don't think I can do it alone. I want to borrow the use of my clone. Body and personality. I need someone I can trust at my back."

Jufenal blinked. "You regard yourself as trustworthy?"

Ruiz shrugged. "I've tried not to betray myself . . . not always succeeding, I'll admit. Is what I propose so different?"

"I'm not sure; it's a confusing idea," said Jufenal. "Well, you must give us time to discuss these requests. Go with Hemerthe; she'll get you a room and see to your other needs." The familiar wonderful face grew stern. "If you plan some treachery, control the urge. You cannot evade our surveillance."

"I plan no treacheries against Deepheart," said Ruiz in a small tired voice.

HEMERTHE CONDUCTED HIM to a small suite. "Here, the hygienic facilities," she said, indicating an oval door. "Here, an autochef; ask for anything you like."

She gave him a warm smile. "Here, the bedroom," she said, standing in the doorway. "Come, we'll see if the bed's comfortable."

There was nothing but kindness and uncomplicated desire in her voice, Ruiz was sure—but he felt no interest at all.

"I'm sure it's comfortable enough for someone as tired as I am, Hemerthe," he said, trying to smile at her as pleasantly as she had smiled at him.

Apparently he succeeded in his attempt at tact—or else

she wasn't unduly sensitive. "Sleep well, then," she said, and went out.

When she was gone, he sat down in the lounger and looked about in a sort of bemused amazement. He saw all around him the conveniences of civilized pangalac life; it was as if the monstrous realities of Roderigo and Dorn had been nothing but bad dreams.

He had a very unsettling thought, sitting there safe and at least temporarily at rest. *Why,* he wondered, *have I so many times left my comfortable retreat on the empty world, my flowers and my vistas?* What had he ever accomplished, beyond the ending of a few evil lives—and far too many innocent ones? What had driven him here to Sook, where he must attempt to do a job that all the pirates in SeaStack had failed to do?

He shook his head slowly. Bizarre beyond words, his life had been . . . and had he ever really noticed that before?

Ruiz felt smaller and less significant at that moment, than he could ever remember feeling. A long time passed before he could get up and go wash the stink of the Deltan armor from his body.

As TIRED AS he was, he slept only a few hours before restlessness drove him from his bed.

He wandered aimlessly about the suite, idly shuffling through his memories. He ordered a meal: noodles with fish and mushrooms, a meal from his childhood. It tasted not at all as he remembered, but it was good and he felt a little better.

He discovered a datalink screen concealed behind a framed print, and to his amazement it responded to his touch.

His surprise diminished somewhat when he saw that it was locked to input only—he could observe the datastream, but post no responses. The security people of Deepheart were subtle, he thought. He could send no treacherous messages, but they could monitor what he viewed, and thereby glean clues to his purposes.

"Well, why not?" he said. He focused the screen's retrieval algorithm on the latest offerings in the SeaStack slave market. He began to page through the offerings, surprised at how few items appeared in each category. The disturbances had severely curtailed business, evidently.

A new image formed, and Ruiz's heart thumped.

It was Nisa, staring moodily from the screen. In her lovely eyes was a look he recognized: controlled anger.

Was this some cruel Deepheart trick? He shook his head violently and looked at the datatag at the bottom of the page.

Member of Pharaohan royalty, it said. *Perfect health, well-developed sexual skills, intelligent, biddable.* Biddable? Ruiz smiled and read more. *Available for viewing. Make appointment.*

A datastream address followed, a code which meant nothing to Ruiz. He attempted to search for a real-world address, but the limited capacity of the screen defeated him. Finally he made a note of the code and sat back, looking at her face.

If this wasn't just some manipulation by Deepheart, then Nisa was alive and in SeaStack. Did it change anything?

Finally he sighed and said, "No." The task he had set himself must still come first. If by some miracle he survived the trip down into the enclave, then he could go find her.

"I'm sorry, beloved," he said to her, and shut off the screen.

IN THE LATE Alonzo Yubere's dungeon, the sound of fighting was only a distant thunder. To Nisa's ears, it was no louder than the storms that sometimes rumbled through the steams of Hell, far below the edge of the world where she had been born.

She had not seen the slaver Corean since their return to the Yubere stronghold.

Corean had thrust her into this small room. "I'll get around to you, slut," Corean had said, smiling in an odd lopsided manner. "Now I've other things to do." She had slammed the steel grate and locked it and gone away.

Nisa was glad to see Corean go, despite the unpleasant promise implied in her parting words. The slaver had acquired a brittle volatility of manner, since killing the old cyborg; no longer was she the calm confident murderer she had once seemed. Whatever sanity Corean had once possessed seemed lost forever.

Nisa speculated that the old pirate had meant a great deal more to Corean than the slaver had understood.

She had little else to do but speculate. Her cell was reasonably comfortable, if bare. The light never changed. The food was some bland anonymous paste, the water tasted faintly of some astringent chemical.

So she spent her time thinking about the strange circumstances that had brought her here, and inevitably her thoughts centered on Ruiz Aw, that strange, strange man.

It occurred to her after a while that he had meant a great deal more to her than she had realized. In retrospect, it seemed to her that she had been very foolish to treat him so coldly during the last days of their time together.

She imagined how it could have been. Aboard the *Loracca,* they might have spent several nights together, several precious nights. Would those nights have been as wonderful as the night aboard the Deepheart barge?

She shook her head. Perhaps not—how could anything surpass that? But what did it matter, these subtle degrees of perfection? Now, in this barren dusty room, when she would never see Ruiz Aw again . . . just to touch him, to hear his voice, to see his quirky smile—these impossibilities now seemed terribly dear. Her memories of him glowed more vividly than all the things she recalled from her former life on Pharaoh.

"That was the dream," she said, sadly. "And this is the truth." She looked around the cell. How childish she had been to blame Ruiz Aw because he could not protect her from all the dangers of Sook. On this terrible world, there was no safety, no refuge—not for more than brief sweet moments.

She had learned that truth too late. Too late. She put her face in her hands and cried.

CHAPTER 17

"W E'VE decided," said Hemerthe as she came through his door.

Ruiz Aw sat in a chair, where he had been waiting for hours. "And?"

"We'll help." Hemerthe perched on the arm of Ruiz's chair. "What other choice do we have? If we do nothing, would we survive? Probably not. At least you've given us the opportunity to do *something*. Even if it's the wrong thing, at least we'll have a comforting illusion. Right? Besides, if you *should* actually reach the enclave and broadcast the location of the Machine, no one will come looking for it in Deepheart."

"I guess not," said Ruiz. "What now?"

"We're trying to contract for a sub, first. Meanwhile, would you like to meet your clone?"

Ruiz frowned. Perhaps at another moment, in another place, he'd be curious. All he felt now was a vague weary dread. "All right," he said finally.

She got up. "Then let's go. To his suite, if you don't mind. We've told your clone nothing except that you're here and you want his help. You'll have to convince him to help you; we can't compel him. So go easy on yourself." She grinned, as though she had uttered a great witticism.

HEMERTHE STOOD ASIDE and Ruiz went through the door. His clone was sitting before a datascreen; he rose and turned to face Ruiz. Ruiz looked at that dark uninformative face and felt no sensation of recognition. The face seemed to belong to a person to whom self-doubt was unknown, for whom failure was unthinkable. *Did I ever look so blindly confident?* Ruiz shook his head in wonderment.

Hemerthe glanced from Ruiz to his clone. "Well," said Hemerthe. "I suppose introductions aren't in order, are they?" She laughed mischievously. "I'll leave you to get acquainted."

When she was gone, the clone nodded carefully. "Hello," he said.

"Hello," answered Ruiz.

"Sit down," said the clone.

They sat and observed each other in silence. After a while, the discomfort of seeing a stranger with his face began to fade a little.

"This is very odd, isn't it?" Ruiz said.

His clone nodded somberly. His face was unreadable, which struck Ruiz as terribly wrong. This was a mind identical to his own; how could it be so inaccessible? Had he really changed that much in the weeks just past?

Finally Ruiz spoke again. "What shall we call each other?"

The clone shrugged. "You choose; you're the senior entity, according to the Fuckheads."

Ruiz smiled. "What if I call you Junior, then?"

The clone smiled back. "Shall I call you Dad?"

Ruiz laughed. For some reason he had begun to feel a bit better. "If you like."

"So, Dad," said Junior, "what's this job you want us to do?"

"It won't be an easy job," Ruiz said. "I've promised to destroy a machine." He looked at his clone. How much of the deathnet remained in that duplicated mind? What could he do but ask? "Does the League deathnet still function?"

The clone shook his head a bit doubtfully. "The Deepheart Gench claims not enough remains to kill me. We're not completely identical—something is always lost or skewed in translation, and my edges are not as sharp as yours were. My lights not so bright, my darks not so deep." He gave Ruiz a critical glance. "Though I have to say that you seem quite different from the self you gave me. You look a little worn. Somewhat broken. Your body is damaged, but that's the least of it, isn't it? It worries me. I can't help wondering what could do that to *me*."

"We've been wounded before, body and soul," said Ruiz a bit defensively.

"Of course, of course . . . perhaps it's just the perspective," said Junior.

"Perhaps," said Ruiz. "Anyway, this is the story."

He told the clone a greatly condensed version of the events of the past weeks, since their memories had diverged. He saw no point in mentioning his involvement with Publius—and the things Publius and Ruiz Aw had done to each other. He said little about his time on Roderigo. He said less about his traveling companions. He devoted considerable description to his visit to the Compendium, though he had not meant to—but he mentioned Leel only in passing.

When he finally told the clone what Somnire had told him, the clone shuddered and his eyes rolled back into his head for a moment. His color faded to a dirty gray and he almost fell out of the chair.

Ruiz caught him and eased him back into a more comfortable position. He felt a strange reluctance to touch his own cloned flesh, so he propped his other self upright in the chair and stepped back.

After a bit, the clone drew a ragged breath and seemed to regain his composure.

"A little of the net remained?" Ruiz said.

"Apparently." The clone rubbed his neck.

"You're all right?"

"I suppose. The weight of it is gone." Junior's mouth twitched into a small smile. "I'd almost forgotten how heavy it was."

"Good," said Ruiz. "It almost killed me, several times."

Junior gave him a somewhat cool stare. "You risked my life without a lot of soul-searching, didn't you?"

"Perhaps," Ruiz said impatiently. "But this is important. If we don't destroy the Orpheus Machine, humankind will become a slave race."

"Yes, yes," said his younger self wearily. "I grant you it's important. Why must we be the ones to do something about it? Why not return to the pangalac worlds and organize a well-equipped force?"

"There's no time," said Ruiz. "By the time we could get home and find help, Roderigo might have the Machine. Or Delt, or one of the pirate Lords. Besides, who could we trust with such a secret? Who could resist the temptation to seize the machine and use it to make the universe a sweeter place?"

The clone looked at him with a look of resignation. "Ah. I see. We two, who know nothing of constructive solutions, are perfect for the job. All we know about is destruction—the only safe alternative."

"Do you think I'm wrong?" asked Ruiz.

"No, no."

"Will you help me?"

"If your plan seems feasible," said the clone. "You have to trust your own judgment, I guess—especially if you're twice the man you once were." He chuckled.

Ruiz felt no great sense of achievement. Rather he felt a more intimate premonition of disaster—the time when he must go down into the Gencha enclave was now a little closer.

For a while it seemed there was nothing left to say, but Ruiz felt an unexpected curiosity. "Tell me," he said. "How did it feel to become a person so suddenly?"

"You haven't thought this through," said Junior. "It didn't feel any particular way at all. The Joined chopped my memories at the point of our arrival in Deepheart. We took a nap and then I woke up and Hemerthe was there.

She—well, she was a man at the time—explained that I was Ruiz Aw the Second. And that you had sold me to Deepheart in return for their help."

The dark face tightened and the black eyes grew even more unreadable. "So I was henceforth a Fuckhead, like it or not. It was something of a shock, I'll admit."

"I guess so," said Ruiz faintly. When he had departed Deepheart, he had never imagined he would one day have to face the result of his bargain. He wondered if he would have made the same decision, had he known how things would eventuate.

Junior showed him a quick humorless smile. "Well. Don't waste any energy sympathizing with me. From what you say . . . and what you don't say, your escape has been more of a trial to you than my time in Deepheart has been to me. After all, I've only been out of the replicant tank for a few days, which is why I'm still in this body. The nights have been . . . interesting. During the day I train defense teams, so I'm still working at our old trade, in a way." He laughed a bit sourly and looked away. "And if Deepheart survives SeaStack's destruction, Hemerthe has promised to teach me how to make porcelains."

Ruiz could find no appropriate response. The clone's face was desolate.

Finally he said in a hesitant voice, "And Nisa? What of her? Have you seen her clone?"

Junior's manner became hard and distant. "No. I try not to think of her. Tell me your plan for penetrating the enclave."

RUIZ EXPLAINED HIS less than exhaustive plan.

When he was finished, the clone nodded his elegant predatory head in understanding. "Holes exist into which we will likely disappear. But as you say, we have little time. How long, I wonder, will it take for Deepheart to charter a sub? If it takes a few days, we can work on your plan, grind a few of the burrs off of it."

"All right," said Ruiz.

The clone pondered. "We need intelligence. Deepheart

has a fairly passive security apparatus—though it's good for what it is. Get them to comb the datastream for us. I don't think they'll find out much—the Lords are suffering from extreme paranoia at the moment, and all their sensitive communications are going by courier."

"Good idea, anyway. How do we learn more?"

"There's no one here who could go out into SeaStack and survive long enough to bring back any useful news." The clone smiled a bit sadly.

"One of us will have to go, then," said Ruiz, full of sudden apprehension.

Junior shrugged. "I suppose. How else are we to make our plans? For all we know, Yubere's fortress has fallen to one of the Lords, and who knows how far down the stack they've penetrated? If the Machine has already been captured and adequately fortified . . . then there's no hope."

"You're right."

They looked at each other in sober assessment.

"Do you want to go?" asked Ruiz.

"Yes, actually I *would* like to go. However, my personality isn't yet perfectly integrated with my new body—or anyway that's what Deepheart's technicians tell me. There's a lag in perception and reaction. It's a terrible feeling, and sometimes embarrassing. A few of the men and women I'm training can best me at hand-to-hand; any competent slayer would chop me up.

This was an unpleasant revelation. Ruiz frowned. "How long before you recover your skills?"

"Not long. A day or two, I'm told. I'm much better than I was, and it's an accelerating process. When I first came from the tank, I could barely walk."

"Ah," said Ruiz. He felt a dull dread. He had hoped to rest in Deepheart for a few days. Clearly he hadn't been thinking.

Already the clone had been useful.

Ruiz was about to get up when the clone spoke again. "I can't help this, I must ask you. What has become of Nisa? Your Nisa, the original?"

For the first time, Ruiz could read the clone's eyes; he felt the same bittersweet pain.

"I lost her," he said. "She was with me, she helped me escape the Roderigans. I'd have died on Dorn, without her help. But—and this will strain your credulity—she was taken by Corean. Corean."

"How?"

"I don't know. Corean must be mad, to have followed us to Roderigo. But she has Nisa, and Dolmaero. We didn't know it until we were almost in Corean's hands."

The clone stared at the floor. "This is difficult to grasp. So much must have happened to you since our lives divided."

"I suppose so."

"Where do you think she is now?"

Ruiz saw again her picture in the datastream. "She's here. In SeaStack. She's for sale. She was listed in today's market offerings."

The clone leaned toward him, eyes glowing. "Who owns her?"

"There was a datastream code . . . but my screen is locked to input only, so I couldn't look for her."

The clone settled back. "Mine too. They say they'll trust me one day." A small sad smile twitched up the corners of his mouth. "Well, you probably think the same thing I do: that she's bait. Corean must be fishing for you."

"No doubt," said Ruiz.

"So you'll ignore the whole thing?"

Ruiz looked at his younger self, frowning. "Of course."

When the clone started to laugh, Ruiz held his frown for a heartbeat. Then the laughter began to bubble out of him, escaping from some secret place, where it had hidden for most of the time since he had arrived on Sook.

If he laughed a little bitterly, that was not so surprising.

"ANOTHER NIGHT TO rest," Ruiz told Hemerthe, as she walked him back to his room.

"That seems reasonable," she said. "And then?"

"Weren't you listening?" he asked.

She had the grace to look uncomfortable. "Well, yes. But I'm a polite person. I like to observe the civilities."

"Oh?"

"Yes!" She saw that he was smiling. "Well, I do. We all do."

"I know," he said. "You were the only people in Sea-Stack that I thought I could trust with my story. Maybe there are other decent folk in the city, but I wouldn't know where to look for them."

"Nor do we, which is why we're so untrusting," she said, wryly. "So. What did you think of Ruiz Aw, the famous slayer?"

"He isn't me," Ruiz answered instantly. "I find it hard to believe that we were ever alike. He's so young. I was never so young."

"You think so? He's *you*—as you were when you came to us. Or as close as makes no difference."

Ruiz shrugged. "Maybe . . . but I don't recognize him."

They reached his door. It slid aside, and Ruiz turned to Hemerthe. "Tell me something," he said.

"Almost anything," she answered.

"My clone . . . is he happy? Is he adapting to life among the Fuckheads? Will he want to stay, if we survive?"

She dropped her eyes. "That's hard to say. We have anxieties about him. He still lives in his birth flesh, of course, so we don't know what will happen when he cuts those bonds and flies free. Perhaps he'll learn to appreciate our life, then. Of course, if he doesn't survive . . . or runs away, one of his clones will eventually adapt. We keep trying."

Ruiz frowned. Somehow he hadn't pictured his clone's future in quite those terms. Apparently Deepheart would contain a Ruiz Aw for as long as it existed.

"And Nisa? Is she happy here?" He had asked almost casually, but now he found that he wanted to know the answer, very badly.

Hemerthe seemed indecisive; she had the look of one who contemplates a kindly lie. When she answered, he wasn't sure if she had succumbed to that impulse. "Again, hard to say," she said. "You may ask her, if you wish."

"No," he said quickly. "There's no point to that."

In truth, he had no desire to see Nisa looking out at him from a stranger's eyes. No desire at all.

He stepped inside his room. She laid a hand on his sleeve. "I'll stay with you, if you wish."

He shook his head. "Thank you, but—"

She smiled brightly. "Would you prefer another? I can advise you."

"No, no. I know you mean well. But the one I want doesn't live in Deepheart."

"You're making a tragedy for yourself, Ruiz Aw." She seemed not at all angry, only a little sad. "Love exists only where you find it. Nowhere else."

"I'm sure you're right," he said heavily, and started to close his door.

"Wait," she said. "We've decided to give you some information; we judge its effect will be motivational. The address where your darling may be found—it originates from the Yubere stronghold."

Ruiz's head jerked up. After a pulse of disbelief had passed through him and then evaporated, he felt a strong sudden conviction: that the story of Ruiz Aw and Nisa remained unfinished.

"Thank you," he said, and went inside.

When he lay down, he fell into the soundest sleep he had known for weeks. If he dreamed, his dreams were the sort that ease troubled hearts.

IN THE MORNING he called Hemerthe.

When Hemerthe appeared in the datascreen, Ruiz discovered that she had changed bodies. Hemerthe was now a short broad man with large square teeth, a swarthy face, and ruby earclips. He wore his gray hair in alternating spikes and sausage curls. It was a remarkably unflattering style; it made Hemerthe's head resemble some sort of odd sea creature.

"What do you think of my new body?" asked Hemerthe in a deep gravelly voice.

No diplomatic remark came to mind, so Ruiz confined his response to a careful nod.

Apparently his amusement was visible, because Hemerthe scowled. "Life goes on, slayer. We have a saying in Deepheart: 'The body is a play; the mind an actor.' A great actor can bring beauty to the most ordinary drama."

"I'm sure that's true," Ruiz said in placating tones. It occurred to him that as much as the denizens of Deepheart took pride in the mastery with which they moved from body to body, the bodies still exerted some influence on the minds that rode them. This Hemerthe seemed noticeably more aggressive than the Hemerthe who had inhabited the slender woman.

Hemerthe shrugged his heavy shoulders. "It is. And now, what do you need?"

"A selection of paints—suitable for redecorating my Deltan armor."

"We can find you better armor."

"I'm sure—but I plan to pose as a deserter from Castle Delt."

"Oh," said Hemerthe.

HEMERTHE BROUGHT HIM the paints a few minutes later. He seemed to have gotten over his pique. "These should bond to the monomol without difficulty. I have brushes, aerosols, a color wand. Which will you use?"

Ruiz picked up a brush. "This will do."

"May I watch?" asked Hemerthe.

"Why not?" Ruiz said.

Ruiz claimed no great skill as an artist, but in this case a crude design would suffice. He'd already laid out the dull black-and-green-striped armor on the floor, latched together into a hollow man.

He cast his thoughts back over the years and remembered a world he'd fought on, long ago. The slaveholders there had invested all their wealth in the latest killmechs, rather than in living soldiers. Ruiz's emancipators had defeated them easily, by retreating into muddy swamps where humans could survive and machines could not. Still, the first time Ruiz had seen one charging toward him across a green swale, he had been frightened into witlessness. At least part of that terror had arisen from the hideous armored Death painted on the huge chassis.

He picked up the helmet and turned it in his hands. He dipped his brush into a container of white paint and began.

An hour later he was done, and the armor carried, superimposed on its smoothly functional monomol panels, a crude depiction of ancient plate armor, the sort of cumbersome armor worn only on worlds so primitive that they had yet to reinvent gunpowder—armor encrusted with useless spikes and fins and knobs. Jagged holes gaped here and there, through which imaginary bone showed: a shattered femur, a few ribs, the articulation of a shoulder. On the helmet Ruiz had painted tattered plumes above a grinning skull.

"Not bad," said Hemerthe judiciously, turning his head this way and that as he examined Ruiz's efforts. "Vigorous and direct. I'll abandon my plans to teach you to make porcelains. You show promise as a painter."

Ruiz laughed. "Your way of life breeds tolerance in abundance."

"True. Well, what else do you need?"

"Perhaps a skinmask. If the Lords are after me, I'd better not look like myself."

"Who would you like to resemble?"

"I don't know. What about you?"

Hemerthe laughed. "You're a diplomat. By the way, we've chosen a person to sit at the other end of your camera link. We asked for volunteers. Only one seemed suitable. You know her."

"Oh, no."

"You object?"

Ruiz shook his head, finally. "No," he said. As he spoke, he felt both the foolishness and the inevitability of the decision.

Before he left, Hemerthe seemed to struggle with himself before deciding to speak. "I must ask you, Ruiz. Why did you not arrange for your clone to have the advantage of a camera and an observer?"

Ruiz felt an irresistible impulse toward honesty, which for some reason he was unable to resist. "I'm not sure . . .

unless it's that I cannot entirely trust him, and so I must have an edge. 'An edge'—the phrase sums up my philosophy, doesn't it? You may so equip him, if you think my judgment is flawed."

But Hemerthe only shook his head, a gesture Ruiz was unable to identify. Was it disapproval or pity? Or both?

"You are in charge," said Hemerthe. "However, I must report a disappointment: the armor you requested for your descent into the Gencha enclave is unavailable. Armor equipped with the sort of atmosphere regeneration tech you described is apparently not used on Sook. The best we could do was to install carbon scrubbers and an external oxygen tank into a conventional urban warfare suit. You'll have about three hours of clean air. Will that do?"

"I suppose it must," said Ruiz.

BEFORE HE LEFT Deepheart, Ruiz Aw conferred again with his clone.

"What information will you seek, and how will you go about it?" asked Junior in pedantic tones.

"What do you advise?" asked Ruiz, strangely amused.

Junior smiled ruefully. "Have you noticed? This is like an interior monologue in a bad holodrama. Remember when we fought the campaign on Gwalior? The clone squads they sent against us in the high desert that winter? All the jokes we made about them?" He laughed. "Is this justice?"

"Probably," said Ruiz. "I'm beginning to believe that— if you live long enough—the universe will get even with you for every deed you do. That's a frightening thought, isn't it? For us, especially. Anyway . . . I'm going back to the Spindinny."

Junior frowned. "I wonder if it still exists. Do you suppose there are any uncontracted fighters left in SeaStack?"

"I don't know. . . . Do you have a better approach?"

"Hmm . . ." Junior rubbed his chin thoughtfully. "It's difficult even to attempt the exercise. I can't help thinking that if I could come up with anything, you would have done so already. It takes the edge off my speculations. . . .

Well, if you find anyone alive in the Spindinny, I guess you plan to ask about work, and where the loot lies thickest."

"Yes. Maybe I can find out if Yubere's stronghold still holds out, and if the fighting has descended to the level of our ingress. Without being too conspicuous in my curiosity."

"And if there's no one there?"

"I have a few other avenues I can explore." Ruiz thought of all the recent associates his clone didn't know about: Publius the monster maker and would-be Emperor of Everything, the slavekeeper Diamond Bob, his friend Albany.

On an impulse, Ruiz said to his clone, "Remember Albany Euphrates?"

Junior smiled. "Oh, sure. A pretty good man, for a slayer."

"He's dead."

"How do you know?"

"He was working for me, and one of my enemies took his head."

"Oh. That's too bad." Junior seemed genuinely distressed, as he should have been, but Ruiz detected a trace of superficiality in his clone's reaction. What did that mean? "Did you get even, or are we waiting for the universe to do the job?" Junior asked.

"Well. I didn't kill Albany's murderer . . . but I got to watch him die. Publius it was—"

"Good!" His clone's face showed a degree of satisfaction that Ruiz now found a bit repellent, though he agreed with Junior's basic sentiment. "Publius, eh? I won't ask you about *him*. A greater monster than any of his children."

For some reason Ruiz felt a compulsion to tell his clone about Publius. He debated the wisdom of this only for a moment, and then he told the story: how he had assassinated Alonzo Yubere, how he had lost all his people, how Publius had betrayed him, how he had allowed Publius to die. He told all this in growing shame, but when he was done, there was nothing in his clone's face but bland acceptance. Looking at that face, Ruiz grew a little angry, though he could find no reason for his anger.

A silence followed. Finally Ruiz spoke again. "So, have you any further wisdom for me?"

Junior smiled crookedly. "No, I guess not. I have this urge to tell you not to do anything I wouldn't do. But I can't decide if that would be funny, or not." He made a wry face.

Ruiz got up. He wondered if it would be appropriate to shake hands with himself. "It *is* a confusing situation." He looked down at his clone and thought, *What an oddly vulnerable-looking person, for all that he has the hands of a strangler.* His anger faded into a strange pity. He spoke impulsively: "The Fuckheads told me that Nisa's datastream address is Yubere's stronghold. What do you think?"

Junior's head snapped up. "Really? How interesting." He seemed lost in thought for a moment. "That would seem to mean that Corean holds the stronghold. Or perhaps she *did* hold it, and whoever took it from her is selling off her assets."

"Those probably aren't all the possibilities," said Ruiz.

"No, no. Probably not." Junior gave him a very odd look, and Ruiz had no idea what his clone was thinking. "But if we run across Nisa while we're breaking the Orpheus Machine . . . and we all survive, she'll have a decision to make, won't she?"

"I suppose," said Ruiz. His mouth felt dry.

The look on his clone's face shifted and Ruiz finally made some sense of it. It was compounded of envy and desire, embarrassment and determination. "I really don't like it here, much," said Junior.

"Well, I didn't want to stay here, either."

"Yes. If we all survive, I wonder what will happen. It occurs to me that I'm the man who rescued her from Corean. You're the man who took her to Roderigo and then gave her back to Corean." Junior wore a taut challenging grin.

"That's true," said Ruiz. He felt an abrupt rage, which he struggled to keep from reaching his face. Had he been insanely naive, to think that he could trust his other self?

Junior slumped and dropped his face into his hands.

"I'm sorry. I'm sorry. It's just that I've lost her in a stranger way than you have. That must be why I'm acting this way."

Ruiz's rage disappeared as suddenly as it had arrived. "I understand," he said. "I understand."

When he went out the door, Junior was still hiding his face in his long strangler's hands.

CHAPTER 18

G EJAS stood on the bridge of the destroyer, facing into the wind of their passage, a wide grin frozen on his mouth. He fingered the bandage on his neck, where the hetmen had attached their interrogation devices. He thought of Ruiz Aw and his grin grew wider.

Down below, protected by the destroyer's heavy armor, were ten maniples of brain-chopped cyborg slayers, cocooned in stasis pods. Steel seeds . . . soon they would sprout into blood and pain.

As he had known they would, the hetmen had commanded him to go to SeaStack. Through a tongue who had stared at Gejas with a fascinated revulsion, the hetmen had said: "Gejas Tongue, you have allowed your god to be murdered. In only one way can you make amends. Bring us the treasure hidden in SeaStack."

"I will," he had said. But in his heart he kept a thought hidden, and it had to do with Ruiz Aw. What a pleasant, warming thought it was.

•   •   •

RUIZ DONNED HIS newly redecorated armor, cinching the straps tight with a kind of automatic intensity. But his thoughts were far away from Deepheart and the dangerous job he was about to undertake.

For some reason he kept thinking about Nisa in the canalside fountain on the day after they had escaped from Corean. Her pale perfect body, her smile, the way the water glistened on her skin—pretty memories, almost too pretty to be real.

He shrugged, to settle the gel pads that protected his shoulder. He smoothed the skinmask over his features and looked in the mirror to check its fit. He realigned the mask slightly and nodded at his unfamiliar reflection.

He picked up his helmet. *Time to go,* he thought.

THE WATERWAYS WERE as deserted as before. Ruiz drove the squirtboat through the city and met no one at all until he was within a kilometer of the Spindinny's stack.

Then he saw something that shocked him and made him dodge into the shadowed side of the channel.

A huge old starboat swooped down from the heights, spiraling around the stacks at high speed. Ruiz recognized its jaggedly baroque style, all spines and barbs. It resembled its owners, the Shards, the ancient race who owned Sook and enforced its eccentric rules.

He caught a glimpse of a hideous alien face as the boat sped by. A loudhailer squealed, and then a synthesized voice roared, "Attention, inferior species! Shard law must be observed in every detail, no matter how your enemies press you. All weapons must be line-of-sight and non-nuclear. No surface vehicles may exceed a speed of two hundred kilometers per hour. No air travel from local twilight to local sunrise. No more than three vessels of more than ten tons standard mass shall maneuver as a group. Violators will suffer instant and terminal correction!"

The starboat disappeared behind the nearest stacks and began to repeat its message. Ruiz was amazed. Never before, to his knowledge, had the Shards descended from their orbital platforms to instruct their tenants. How volatile had the situation become? It appeared the Shards had grown anxious about their property.

He went on, exercising even more caution, and finally arrived safely at the Spindinny's lagoon.

The lagoon was under one of the largest stacks in the city and, remarkably, was full of boats. Under the purple glare of the lagoon's lights, the vessels revealed the marks of hard use and battle.

There were no empty berths along the quay. Ruiz passed slowly along the line of boats, which were tied two and three deep to the dock. Why this unusual gathering?

As he passed a large whaleback torpedo boat, a man came from a hatch and stood swaying on its armored deck. The man wore a threadbare shipsuit, patched with the sigils of a dozen obscure campaigns. Ruiz identified him instantly as a mercenary—his face had the hollow intensity of a man who lived by violence. He wore an elbow punchgun, which he didn't aim directly at Ruiz.

"Hoy!" the man said. "Are you here for the meeting? Of course you are . . . throw me your lines; I'll tie you off." His voice was slurred and too loud. *Drunk*, thought Ruiz.

Still, a berth was a berth, so he tossed his mooring cable to the man, who wobbled over to a midships bollard and dropped it over.

Ruiz reached up to the whaleback's rail and heaved himself aboard. "Thanks," he said. What meeting? He wondered how he could find out without revealing his ignorance: suppose this were an invitation-only affair? "So, why aren't you at the meeting?"

The man spat overboard and produced a flask of some pungent liquor from his pocket. "Someone got to watch the boat. Besides, it's all shit; I wouldn't have gone anyway. What are they going to do about the war? Tell the Lords they don't want to fight anymore? That too many of us are dying? Shit, that's all it is. If we won't fight for the Lords, they'll kill us and carry on with their house troops. Shit."

"I can't say I disagree with you," said Ruiz.

The man looked a bit confused, as if he found Ruiz's

position difficult to analyze, but after a moment of brow-furrowing concentration he apparently abandoned the effort and shrugged. "Well. We cast off an hour before midnight—better be back before then to move your boat."

"I will," said Ruiz. "Thanks again."

The man nodded and went below, closing the hatch with a clang.

Ruiz entered the Spindinny with an increasing level of apprehension. The war must be particularly bloody if the mercenaries were considering a strike.

Inside the Spindinny, killmechs manned an armored security cage, and their red-glowing optics locked on him as he passed. Otherwise the warren was silent, an eerie thing in that place of eternal debauchery.

Ruiz went down to the hiring hall, where the Spindinny maintained its computer facilities.

The hall was empty, except for one proctor, who gave Ruiz a suspicious glance. "What are you doing here? The meeting's in the sub-basement auditorium."

The proctor was a thin gray man with a grafted-on third arm protruding from his chest. At the moment, the central arm held a bowl of soup; his other two arms were crumbling crackers into it.

Ruiz took off his helmet and assumed an expression of innocent confusion. "I don't know anything about a meeting. I just got to town this morning; what's going on?"

The proctor snorted and started spooning up his soup. " 'Just got to town'? You can look forward to some surprises, then."

"Really?"

"Really. SeaStack is a grave. Do you claim you didn't notice?"

"No. . . . I saw the scars—and the stacks are silent. Is there no work, then?"

The proctor laughed, spraying a bit of soup from his mouth. "Oh, there's plenty of work, but you might want to wait for a bit before you sign up for it."

"Really?"

"Really. Really. Is that all you can say? Never mind. Go

down to the sub-basement and listen to the fools at the meeting." He went back to his soup, ignoring Ruiz pointedly.

"All right," said Ruiz, striving for just the right note of uncertainty.

He put his helmet back on and scuttled out.

A RUSTY STEEL lift cage lowered Ruiz into the sub-basement, where plumbing and other conduits striated the damp meltstone walls and a smell of ancient garbage filled the stagnant air. Ruiz heard a deep murmur and followed it to the doors of the auditorium.

Inside, the lights were bright. Hundreds of mercenaries milled about, shouting and shoving. Ruiz sidled along the back wall, trying to be as unobtrusive as possible, and found a spot from which he could watch. The crowd was a sea of garish color, twinkling with the glitter of well-kept weapons. An odd stink—composed of unwashed bodies, gun oil, raw alcohol, and ozone—hung thick in the room.

On a platform at the far end of the hall a tiny woman in chromed servo-armor stood at a podium, waving her arms and screeching in a thin piping voice.

"Order!" she shrilled. "Order!" No one paid any attention to her.

A half-dozen other persons sat in a row of chairs behind her. When a scuffle broke out in front of the platform, a large man with a naked tattooed torso and several metal heatsinks protruding from his shaven skull, rose slowly and massively from his chair. He stood looking down at the two scufflers for a moment. When they fell and began to roll around on the floor, he drew a graser from a calf holster and cut them into four parts, which clutched at each other for a moment longer and then subsided into aimless twitching.

The hall fell silent, except for the rattle of drawn weapons and the snick of safety levers.

"Thank you, Sergeant-at-Arms Mondawber," said the little woman in a tone of irritable satisfaction. "I hope no more such disciplinary acts will be necessary. The Lords wouldn't really mind much if we chopped each other up."

A mutter of agreement ran through the hall, accompanied by the sounds of weapons being returned to holsters.

"Now," she continued. "We have speakers pro and con. Give them your attention, so you can convey their arguments to your constituents."

A tall Dilvermoon herman in a flowing crimson robe approached the podium. It carried a thick sheaf of paper, and a groan rose from the crowd of mercenaries.

It smiled disarmingly. "No, no," it said. "You mistake me. These aren't notes, they're handouts—so you won't strain anything trying to remember what I've said." It handed the papers down to the crowd, as low laughter ran around the room.

The herman waited until the handouts had circulated to the far corners of the hall. Ruiz took his in a gauntleted hand and read: "Why We Must Withdraw Our Forces From SeaStack."

The herman cleared its throat. "This is the situation: Our units have all suffered losses far in excess of acceptable rates. Under these conditions, our contracts—most of them, anyway—specify that our pay must increase to a mutually acceptable level, in compensation for the increasingly hazardous working conditions. If our employers are unwilling or unable to raise our pay, we're entitled to withdraw from our contractual commitments."

"They've upped the pay," shouted someone from the floor.

"No . . . they've *promised* higher pay—an important distinction," said the herman. "They cannot deliver on these promises until the situation in the city stabilizes."

It shook its handsome head. "They'll never deliver; this is my opinion. Furthermore, I think the Lords have gone quite thoroughly mad and intend to fight over their obscure treasure until no one in SeaStack is left alive—except the victor. Dead persons cannot benefit from high pay.

"If we wish to survive, we must withdraw our forces from the pirates' strongholds. If necessary, we must fight our way out of SeaStack—or we'll all be dead in a week or two.

"This is my argument—and I think it irrefutable."

The herman sat down, to a renewed babble of contention. The large tattooed man started to get up again, but the babble ceased and he settled back with a glower.

A woman with a tangled mane of white hair and a face like a nicked ax stepped to the podium. "My argument is even shorter. We must continue to fight for our employers, even if it means we must die. That is our function in the universe, and we must not deny it. If we die, we die—but if we slink off, our way of life will begin to die. Who will hire mercenaries if mercenaries cannot be depended upon to honor their contracts?" She sat down amid a chorus of hooting laughter and hisses of derision.

"Dupe!" someone shouted.

"Pirate's dog," shouted another anonymous voice. The white-haired woman stared stonily ahead.

Another woman stepped forward. She wore light armor of an opalescent lavender color, and when she raised her visor, Ruiz was startled to see the pale lined face of Diamond Bob, once the proprietor of a well-respected slave kennel.

"Well," said Diamond Bob. "I can't agree with *that* sentiment. Mercenaries are mercenaries. They fight for pay, but when no hope exists that they will live to spend that pay, intelligent mercenaries 'slink off.' Every time. Our employers are aware of that tradition, you can be sure.

"But another possibility exists. Why can't we put our heads together and figure out what it is that the Lords want so bad? And then take it for ourselves?"

A rumble of confusion ran through the crowd, and then a tentative enthusiasm. But no one spoke.

"How else will we ever survive?" asked Diamond Bob. "How else will we ever get paid?"

"What if we can't figure it out? And who would lead us?" someone asked from the floor.

"Whoever has the most experience," answered Diamond Bob. "We'll see who volunteers, and each candidate can make a pitch. And if we can't figure it out, who can? The Lords aren't cooperating with each other, and they've completely abandoned any attempt to keep SeaStack's commerce functioning, so we can assume the prize is worth more than any of SeaStack's other treasures."

Shouting matches broke out here and there across the hall, and the sergeant-at-arms started to get up again. But the tiny woman laid a hand on his arm and shook her head. She stepped to the podium beside Diamond Bob and spoke quickly: "We'll recess for an hour, to think over what our speakers have said. When we come back in, we'll get down to making a decision."

The mercenaries turned and started jostling their way from the hall. Ruiz stood against the wall, watching Diamond Bob.

After most of the fighters had left, she came down the hall toward him.

RUIZ LET HER pass and then fell into step just behind her.

At the row of lift cages, the remaining mercenaries were jostling for a place. Just as Ruiz and Diamond Bob reached the cage, the last man jammed himself in.

"Come on, old woman," the mercenary said, and made a kissing sound. "Plenty of room."

She stopped. "I'll wait for the next lift," she said, in a tone of fastidious reserve.

He shrugged and slammed the gate shut. The cage lifted away and they were alone.

Ruiz looked about. No one watched, as far as he could tell. He took Diamond Bob's elbow and pulled her toward an open maintenance alcove at the end of the corridor. "I need a few moments of your time," he said brightly. "We can help each other."

She writhed in his grasp and struck up at his neckpiece with a sonic knife. He blocked her thrust with his armored forearm, barely—she was much quicker than he had expected. His forearm smoked and glowed, and the knife made a sound like a hundred grindstones.

He bulled her toward the wall, parrying two more

slashes. He slammed her between the wall and his armored body, letting his momentum and mass do the work. Her armor flexed under the blow and she gasped. The knife fell from her hand and he twisted her arm behind her, levering it back and up, his gauntlet hooked into her armor's neck ridge.

"Be calm," he said as he hustled her through the door into the maintenance alcove. "I mean you no harm; I just have to talk to you."

He kicked the door shut and jammed her into a tangle of monomol pipe while he looked around the alcove. A coil of thin cable caught his eye, and he used it to lash her securely to the pipework.

When he was done, he gingerly raised her visor. She glared at him with the eyes of a trapped beast, her teeth bared in a snarl.

He sighed and took off his helmet. Then he peeled up the skinmask.

Her eyes grew wide. "Ruiz Aw? What are you doing here?"

"Looking for information. Why are *you* here?"

She shrugged as expressively as her bonds permitted. "I'm out of the kennel business. My pens were burned and all my slaves killed or stolen. It ruined my rep and I couldn't get insurance. Pretty soon I owed a lot of money. So here I am, trying to make a living." She laughed, only a little bitterly. "This is a trade I've practiced before. It's not so bad."

"I see," he said. "Well, I'm sorry you've had reverses."

"Oh?" She looked down at the cable that bound her to the pipes.

"I must take precautions, Diamond Bob."

"I'm sure," she said. "Do you know what you're worth, these days? I kept hoping you'd bring me Remint's head and give me a chance to catch you. Then I'd have gone far away. Far away." Her face showed a childlike wistfulness, for just an instant.

"Remint's dead, I think," Ruiz said.

She smiled poisonously. "You didn't kill him, I take it?"

"Only indirectly," he said. "If he's really dead. But never mind that; will you talk to me? I won't try to force you to help me . . . but if you'll tell me what you know, it might help me to put an end to the fighting."

"Why should you care how long the fighting lasts?"

"I don't," answered Ruiz honestly. "If the pirates kill each other completely off, I won't mind at all. But you will, I guess, and if I achieve my goal, the fighting will end."

Her brows drew together. "What do you want to know? From the Lords' urgent desire to meet you, I'd have judged that you know more about what's going on than anyone else."

"You'd be wrong," he lied. He could see no point in telling her anything, since he intended to spare her life, if at all possible. She had, after all, dealt as fairly with him as anyone else on Sook had. "I need to know about the fighting: where it's heaviest, where it's quiet. The patterns of the fighting. The forces involved. Anything you can tell me about this mysterious treasure . . . everything you've heard, everything you've seen."

She chuckled dryly. "When I made my pitch to the mercs, I didn't think anyone would take me up on it so soon. Why don't you volunteer to command us? Most of them have heard of Ruiz Aw by now—they'll believe you know what the treasure is, even if you don't. I won't tell."

He sat down and put his back against a comfortable patch of wall. "Tempting. But I know them. They'd throw a sack over me and haul me in for the reward; they'd go for the sure thing."

"You're probably right, Ruiz Aw. Well, how shall I begin?"

IN THE HALF hour that followed, she gave Ruiz a summary of SeaStack's recent disintegration.

In the week following Ruiz's departure, several prominent Lords had suddenly turned into vegetables.

Their heirs had discovered them to be impostors—gene-carved to resemble the real Lords, then Genched into near-perfect counterfeits.

The survivors had lost their composure completely, lashing out at rival Lords under the assumption that old hatreds had been revived. But gradually this first outbreak of hostilities had waned, to be replaced by a period of watchful paranoia and frenzied espionage. The violence grew sporadic: assassinations, ambushes, killmech skirmishes.

"That's when we started hearing the rumors," Diamond Bob said. "About a treasure, hidden somewhere under SeaStack. But no one knew what it was."

"And now?" Ruiz asked. "Does anyone know?"

"Not that I've heard . . . unless *you* know. Though maybe the Lords know. Or some of them, anyway—but I really don't think so."

"What *have* you heard?"

She dropped her eyes for a moment. "Everyone has a different theory. The least imaginative fantasize about great heaps of rare isotopes, or cisterns full of valuable drugs, or chests of soulstones. That sort of thing. The superstitious believe a god is hiding under the stacks. The romantic think it's a woman or a man of such inhuman beauty as to drive the beholder mad—and the Lords certainly seem maddened."

"So which seems most plausible to you?"

"The smarter ones visualize some sort of universe-shaking new tech. I think that's the most likely possibility." Diamond Bob shifted, as though attempting to find a more comfortable position.

Ruiz resisted the temptation to loosen her bonds. "That's what I think, too," he said. "And then what happened?"

She went on with her story. After a period of relative calm, the battles had begun in earnest, and in the first three days, almost thirty percent of SeaStack's combatants had died, by the estimates of her unit's strategists. The weaker Lords had been destroyed, their stacks broken open and sterilized like so many termite mounds.

Then the violence had waned. Since then, the fighting had been periodic and intense, and another large portion of the city's population had gone to feed the margars.

"But there's no resolution, no matter how many die, which is why most of the merc units in the city sent representatives to this meeting. When you grabbed me, I was sure you were a Lord's man, come to shut my mouth." She grinned. "Are you sure you're not?"

"I'm not," Ruiz said. "Why do they want me so bad?"

She developed an incongruously coy expression. "I have a theory. Which was one reason I suggested my plan at the meeting."

"Tell me."

She hesitated. "Will you kill me if I guess true?"

"No . . . I just won't tell you if you're right." Ruiz smoothed all expression from his face.

"A good gambler mask you have, Ruiz Aw," Diamond Bob said, and then she smiled an oddly guileless smile. "All right. This is what I think: Because they associate you with this great treasure."

"Why so?" asked Ruiz.

"Because of your connection with Publius the monster maker. They know you hired fighters for Publius—and Publius is connected to the changeling Lords, the puppets whose discovery began the war. He made them, or so it seems." She shrugged. "And whatever job you did for Publius appears to have precipitated the first outbreak of fighting. Some unknown force destroyed his laboratories, and Publius disappeared. No one knows where he went, but his puppets were apparently equipped with some sort of deadman switch, so they lost any semblance of volition after he was gone—when he could no longer contact them with instructions. But none of this came out in the first days of the fighting."

She stopped and gave Ruiz a shrewd look. "Any of this useful to you?"

"Maybe," he answered.

"Well. So, Publius had some sort of vast scheme going, which may or may not have had anything to do with the Lords' treasure. I think it did. He apparently had an ally— hence the deadman switches in his puppets. Insurance against treachery."

Ruiz shook his head. "But why would they think I would know anything about Publius's scheme?"

"Mostly, I suppose, because you're the only loose end they can see in the fabric of the scheme. You might be this unknown ally."

"Oh," said Ruiz. "I take it you don't think so."

"No. I'm sorry to say, you just don't have the air of a kingpin, Ruiz Aw. You're more the cornered animal type. I think all you want to do is get away from Sook in one piece. I'm astonished to see you again, in fact."

Ruiz wanted to tell her that she was absolutely correct, but he didn't dare. "I was astonished to see you," he said.

"So you say. Anyway . . . remember when you came to me and asked about Remint y'Yubere? And you spoke of a woman, a slaver called Corean? Of the connection between Corean and Alonzo Yubere? Yes?"

"Yes," Ruiz said. He attempted to prevent any reaction from reaching his face.

"Well. No one but me knows of the connection between you and Yubere—and this is probably the reason no one has mounted a heavy assault on the Yubere stronghold. So I believe. If the Lords had found out what you told me, they'd have scoured the Yubere stack down to the magma. Right after they'd fought each other into extinction for the right to do so." She shook her head wearily. "They really have gone mad. But anyway, you should be grateful to me for my silence . . . even if I was only waiting for the most opportune moment to make use of my speculations."

"Why do you say that?" He had found out the crucial piece of information—Yubere's stronghold remained intact—but he was curious.

She looked at him, wearing a crooked half-smile. "You're no longer interested in Corean? In her whereabouts? In anything connected with Yubere's stronghold?"

He shook his head. "I long ago removed what I valued from Yubere's custody." He told this half-truth easily.

"Oh," she said. "Well, I had a bit of information about Corean . . . but I guess you wouldn't be interested."

"I might," he said cautiously.

She laughed. "You might? I work for Battalion Le-

Febvre; you know it? Good intelligence arm, right? Three days ago one of our agents, monitoring a long-range spybead, saw a woman return to the Yubere stronghold with several prisoners. The woman matched your description of the slaver Corean. She unloaded three prisoners and went in."

"So?" Ruiz strove for an air of casual curiosity.

"Our agent described the prisoners. The descriptions exactly matched those of three slaves you left with me, the ones Remint took." She shook her head, her eyes full of some odd amusement. "Have you noticed how full of coincidence life seems to be?"

"Not really," he answered. "In fact, I'm not sure I believe in coincidence anymore. Well, that's interesting, but irrelevant to my current purposes."

And then, for the next half-hour, Ruiz quizzed Diamond Bob on the military situation in SeaStack—troop strengths, dispositions, fortifications—all the things an ambitious warlord would need to know. As they spoke, he heard the shuffle and clatter of the returning mercenaries.

By the time he had drained her of all the news he could think to ask for, she had become uncertain again.

"Perhaps I underestimated you, Ruiz Aw," she said, biting her lip and shifting within her bonds. "Are you raising an army? I'd enlist, if so. The situation here is volatile, but exploitable, for a properly ruthless person."

Ruiz looked at her, expressionless. Perhaps he could make use of her suspicions. "I won't say. But when I'm gone, talk to the other delegates. Don't use my name, unless you'd trust that person with your life."

Diamond Bob nodded somberly. "All right. Will you release me?"

He shook his head. "No, but I'll leave the access open and someone will hear you."

Her thin mouth trembled. "I must rely on a kindly mercenary?"

"I'm sorry," he said. He smoothed the skinmask back into place, donned his helmet, and left. He didn't look back.

When he was halfway to the lift cages, he heard fighting break out in the resumed meeting—the sound of weapons and the screams of the wounded. He ran the rest of the way and was well above the sub-basement when the first survivors came from the hall.

CHAPTER 19

THE Roderigan destroyer crushed its way into the Spindinny's lagoon as the last of the escapees were fleeing down the adjacent waterways. Gejas stood in the navigation pod, watching the blips speed away.

"Something has happened here," he said to the destroyer's commander. "Decant a squad of cyborgs. I'll reconnoiter."

He hoped, as he waited for his squad to reach the deck, that he might find Ruiz Aw here. Where else would a man like Ruiz Aw go for sanctuary in SeaStack? And he could easily justify his lust to see Ruiz Aw again—who knew what the slayer might have learned in the virtual? Perhaps he was here in SeaStack to take the treasure for his own.

He took his squad through the Spindinny in a methodical manner, stunning everything that surrendered, for later interrogation—and killing everything that resisted.

When he reached the sub-basement and saw the charnel house that the meeting hall had become, he smiled in manic approval. "He's been here," said Gejas to no one in particular.

When his cyborgs found the woman bound in the maintenance niche, he went to see. "Hello," he said to her, instantly certain that this was a meeting ordained by fate. He called for a chair, and got out the black leather pouch that held his instruments of persuasion.

"You won't need those," she said, as he laid out the glittering hooks and knives in a neat little row.

"No?" he asked, in a soft attentive voice. But he used them anyway. Why take a chance?

When he was done, after he had learned so much more about Ruiz Aw than he had hoped to learn, he felt an abstract gratitude toward the lump of screaming bleeding meat that the woman had become.

"Put it out of its misery," he said to the cyborg as he left.

Ruiz returned to Deepheart's moorage without incident, to find his clone standing on the narrow deck of a small, heavily armored submarine.

"Hello, Dad," said Junior, raising a hand in sardonic greeting. "What do you think?"

Ruiz motored slowly along the flank of the sub, noting the rust weeping from the vents, the chipped anti-fouling paint along the waterline, the other small signs of neglect. He shook his head.

Junior, pacing along the deck, laughed. "She's in better shape than appearances would indicate, I think. Though I'm no expert. Tell me, were you provident enough to take a course in ship surveying since you made me?"

"No," said Ruiz regretfully.

"Too bad," said the clone. "I'm in better shape, too. I've finally settled into my new body. It feels good." He shrugged elaborately, as if enjoying the play of muscle and bone. "It almost seems to fit better than my old one. I can't help wondering who would win, if we wrestled."

Ruiz smiled. "Let's hope we never get a chance to find out, Junior."

He tied up his squirtboat to the quay and went ashore.

He took off his helmet and breathed deeply, grateful to have survived his trip into the Spindinny.

After a minute he went down the quay and vaulted aboard the sub. "Show me what we have," he said.

WHEN THEY WERE ready to go, a small group assembled just inside the blast doors, to see them off.

Ruiz, searched the unfamiliar faces, wondering if one of them hid the mind of Nisa. No one seemed at all familiar, except for Hemerthe, who had assumed the body of a beautiful elderly woman. Her dark skin stretched tight and polished over lovely bones, and her long white hair fell down her still-straight back in fanciful curls, gathered with a blue ribbon.

Hemerthe gave Ruiz a hug and a kiss, and then turned to the clone. "Come back to us," Hemerthe said earnestly to Junior.

The clone smiled but made no reply.

As they went out to the quay, the blast doors ground shut behind them. It seemed to Ruiz that there was a certain finality in the clang the doors made when they met their sills.

The two of them boarded the sub and spent a few minutes stowing weapons and other gear. When it was time to start the engines, Ruiz swung himself into the commander's chair without thinking.

Junior smiled wryly, but he buckled himself into the copilot seat with no other sign of resentment.

Immediately outside Deepheart's lagoon, Ruiz submerged and set the planes to force them into a steep dive. "The Lords will have their antennae out," he said. "We'll go as deep as we can and then switch to noiseless propulsion."

Junior nodded in somber agreement. He tapped the datascreen and called up a chart showing deep currents. "Design limit is seven hundred meters, Dad. Look." He pointed to a thin orange line that slid sinuously around the roots of the city, winding in the general direction of the Yubere stronghold. "Insert us into this current and we could drift at five fifty, and draw no attention at all. The last two kilometers we'd have to shift streams, but it's our best shot."

"You're right," said Ruiz. He had been about to call up the current chart. He was somewhat distressed that his clone had beaten him to it. What did it mean, if anything?

Junior was still thinking a bit faster. "All these currents are wind-driven," he said, and called up a weather module. "Strong southeast wind for the last two days—the current should be running strong."

When they reached the level of the current, Junior's prediction was borne out, and Ruiz shut down the engines.

An hour after they began their silent drift, they detected a large surface vessel, thrashing along their course at high speed.

Ruiz sank back in his chair, expecting the worst—but the vessel went on without pause.

WHEN THE RODERIGAN destroyer crashed through the sill of Yubere's lagoon and began shedding cyborgs, Corean's first incredulous thought was, *How did they find me so fast?*

She locked Yubere's remaining exterior weaponry on the destroyer, but before she could fire, tracer beams touched her emplacements, followed instantly by grasers that melted her weapons into useless slag.

A moment later, the destroyer hailed her on one of the trade frequencies. She shut down her transmitters so the Roderigans wouldn't be able to see her. But her screen displayed the mad face of Gejas the tongue, eyes bright with anticipation. "Ruiz?" called the Roderigan. "Are you there yet?"

She was abruptly furious. Her heart pounded and her vision went a little blurry with the power of her rage. Ruiz? He thought Ruiz was coming here? The Roderigans weren't even after *her*?

She slapped at a switch and opened the channel, so that he could see her. She had the satisfaction of seeing surprise on the Roderigan's narrow face. But an instant later the surprise was replaced by hideous gloating satisfaction.

"You too?" breathed the tongue in delight. "Oh, I *have* been very lucky today."

Corean cursed and shut down the channel, already regretting her foolish gesture. She turned to the Dirm bondguard who waited behind her and told it to withdraw her forces to the second line of defense.

Her mantraps on the first level killed only a handful of the cyborgs, and she began to be afraid.

WITH SOME DIFFICULTY, Ruiz and his clone found the air lock he had left welded to the ingress, 600 meters below the entrance to Yubere's stronghold. When he had mated the submarine to the ingress, Ruiz shut down the maneuvering jets. He sat back in the seat and tried to gather his thoughts, but he found himself distracted by the ominous creak of the sea's pressure.

"So," said Junior. "What are our chances?"

Ruiz sighed. "Pretty good, I think. As far as I know, everyone who knows about this ingress is dead. So I assume no one will be guarding the tunnel, unless Publius left someone to watch."

Junior shook his head. "If you'd asked me to guess who might reach out from the grave and do us under, the name of Publius would come to mind first."

"True," said Ruiz glumly. "Well, time to get ready, kid."

The clone gave him a strange twisted smile, and Ruiz felt an odd shock of recognition. He knew how that smile felt from the inside, but he'd had no idea what a bitter shape his mouth could make. One thought led to another: Why did that smile seem so strange to him now? Ruiz put on his helmet to cover his face, to hide it, lest it assume some shape even stranger than his clone's face had taken.

As they were buckling on the last of their weapons and surveillance gear, Ruiz turned to Junior and patted his clone on the armored shoulder. "I'm grateful to you, Ruiz Aw," said Ruiz to the clone.

The clone shrugged away the hand, and pulled his helmet on so that his face was hidden. "Think nothing of it," the clone said over the close-range comm.

Ruiz felt a cold sense of rejection. "Sorry," he mumbled, and latched down his own helmet.

"Don't be, Dad," said the clone. "You can't help it if you like me better than I like you."

Ruiz was still puzzling over the meaning of that, when the lock cycled open and filled the chamber with foulness. Ruiz smelled ordinary decay, but worse was the dead earthworm stink of the Gencha. Ruiz quickly toggled his armor's filtration system, and the worst of the odor gradually cleared from his nostrils, though it left a lingering taint in his mouth.

"High body count?" asked Junior, as he moved ahead with his sensors.

"I guess so," said Ruiz.

THEY REACHED THE great central pit of the stack without incident. The remnants of the acrophobic sisters still lay there, though stripped of their armor and looking as if animals had worried at their flesh. The vilest stink came from a small heap of Publius's monsters, who lay where Publius had apparently killed them in a fit of pique. In the reddish light that glimmered from the tunnel walls, the dead shapes formed a dreadful sculptural mass, black and hideous.

Ruiz ignored the corpses while he waited for Junior to report from the rim of the tunnel. He remembered the faces of those who had accompanied him on his last venture into the stack. Albany Euphrates, Huxley the Nomun clone, Durban the beaster, the sisters Chou and Moh, the nameless ex-gladiator . . . all dead and forgotten, except by Ruiz Aw. That train of thought afflicted him with a melancholy inertia, so he stopped it and began to check over his weapons, one more time. The ritual, so familiar, calmed him, and he finally felt ready for whatever was to come.

The clone came back at a trot. "I can't find any signs of surveillance in the pit—the spectra seem dead. It's weird. The tramway shows fairly steady use; the rail is bright, if that means anything."

"No movement in the pit?"

"Not that I could tell," said the clone. "Maybe some life back in the tunnels—the walls are like cheese, especially deeper in the pit. So, what do we do now?"

"Wait a moment," said Ruiz, and sat down, slinging his ruptor across his back. He took a deep breath, activated the camera, and switched on the link.

A small voice whispered in his ear. "Ruiz? I see you. Or is that my fellow clone?"

Ruiz felt tears come to his eyes, so that his vision blurred for a moment. For some reason, he hadn't expected Nisa's clone to speak with her own voice. "I'm here," he said, using the private channel. "I'm here."

GEJAS HAD SECURED Yubere's security rotunda with little difficulty, and now he set up his command center in the shattered remnants of the kiosk that had guarded the drop shafts. His cyborgs were fighting their way through the secondary defenses just above the stronghold, encountering better-organized resistance.

One of his monitors crackled and cleared to show the steel face of a squad commander, who stared calmly into its wrist camera. "Gejas Tongue," it said in its uninflected voice. "A report."

"Report, then," answered Gejas.

"A setback. Three of my fighters rendered dysfunctional by a Moc of high lineage and great ferocity. The creature irresistible in our present configuration. Ten fighters unable to lay down sufficiently comprehensive firing pattern."

Gejas cursed. A Moc! An unexpected obstacle, indeed. He was about to instruct the commander to amalgamate his squad with a nearby unit, when a blur crossed the screen and the viewpoint slammed sideways.

The image shuddered and grew still. The screen showed a twitching metal foot, kicking feebly at the plastic tile. The foot grew still, and a puddle of hydraulic fluid mingled with blood spread across the corridor floor.

Gejas turned away and issued instructions to his remaining squad commanders. The squads condensed into larger units and progress slowed. The Moc became more cautious and was able to make only an occasional kill.

Another monitor chimed at Gejas, but he ignored it. It was only Roderigo, trying to question his tactics, trying to find out why he was attacking the stronghold of Alonzo Yubere.

Gejas grinned. He knew what he was doing and he had no time for the hetmen and their complaints. It was as if The Yellowleaf's ghost dwelled in his mind's eye, the strong beautiful face still vital, still telling him what he must do. He watched her. He was almost content.

RUIZ AND THE clone laid out their climbing gear just inside the tunnel. "I'm afraid of heights," Nisa whispered in his ear.

"You can look away from the screen," Ruiz replied.

"No," she said. "If you can stand to be there, I can stand to watch."

She sounded so heartbreakingly like herself. So true, so strong. "Well, everyone's afraid of something," he said.

Ruiz fired a piton into a crevice at the edge of the pit and hooked his descender line to it. He thought of the last time he had stood here, waiting. That time he had ridden the tram upward, spiraling around the sides of the pit to the fortress of Alonzo Yubere high above. There Ruiz had killed Yubere in the slaver's beautiful bathtub. A simple piece of work, it seemed in retrospect—though it had failed to purchase Publius's willing assistance.

He wished he were going up again.

He stood for a long moment looking out into the haze that filled that great emptiness, and then looked down at the dull red glow below. It seemed to him the glow had dimmed perceptibly since the last time he had stood there. "Gencha heaven," he said out loud.

"What?" asked his clone.

"Nothing. Just nattering," said Ruiz, and, turning about, began to lower himself down the wall.

When he reached the rail, he set another piton and waited for his clone. Junior swayed down the face with a lithe grace that Ruiz had to admire, even though it was his own.

When his clone hung suspended above the rail, Ruiz got out the railrider and shackled the device to a recessed pad eye on the chestplate of his armor. Junior did the same.

"Well," said Ruiz. "Let's try it." He swung out and over the rail and dropped to the face just below it. He reached out and set the railrider over the polished alloy of the rail and, tightening a knurled knob, cranked the rider into a shape that conformed perfectly to the rail's cross-section. He locked the rider into that shape and gingerly slid it back and forth a few centimeters—the almost frictionless lining of the rider made no sound.

Junior had his antennae extended in all directions and an inductance sensor almost touching the rail. He examined the screens strapped to his left forearm, and after a moment said, "Nothing. Hard to believe, but no one's watching, as far as I can tell."

"All right," said Ruiz. "Get rigged, and we'll go."

Junior put away his sensors and lowered himself to Ruiz's level. In a moment his rider was attached.

Ruiz jerked a tab from his climbing gear, and the descending lines and pitons puffed into dust. He dropped with a jolt, to hang from the rider's tether, his hand on the brake lever at his chest. Junior destroyed the remaining evidence of their presence, and dangled from his own rider a few meters up the rail.

"This looks like fun," said Junior darkly. "It's going to be a lot easier getting to Genchaland than it will be to climb back up."

"Maybe we'll find a tram at the bottom," Ruiz said hopefully. "Besides, it's traditional—it's always been easier to go to Hell than to leave it."

Junior made a fretful sound. "I know now why people have so frequently criticized my sense of humor. I used to laugh at folk who bought therapeutic clones—I never thought I'd become one."

"You seem to be learning more from this than I am," said Ruiz. He released the brake and slid downward for ten meters before he reengaged it. "Give me a couple hundred meters head start—if I run into something lethal you might be able to stop. Remember not to shoot me, if you have to fire across the pit when I'm on the far side of the spiral."

"The same to you," said Junior.

Ruiz smiled and took a deep breath. To Nisa he said, "Here we go."

"Good luck," she whispered.

He pushed up on the lever and began to slide down the long spiral into the red-gleaming darkness.

ALONE IN HER war room, Corean took some satisfaction in having slowed the advance of the Roderigan cyborgs, but they were slowly pressing her deeper into the fortress. The Moc was her best weapon—it had accounted for more enemy casualties than all her other fighters combined. But it was insufficient.

Yubere had, in her opinion, somewhat neglected the defenses of his fortress. The Dirm bondguards were too slow and stupid to do much more than inconvenience the cyborgs.

She had decided to hold in reserve the half-squad of Deltan shock troops that Yubere had bequeathed her, as well as the Muramasa-Violencia killmechs.

The Roderigans had penetrated the cross-baffled elevator shafts and were slowly consolidating their position at the topmost level of the stronghold. She was starting to feel a little trapped. How was she going to get out, if she could not find a way to reverse the tide of the engagement? The only lane of retreat was downward, down the great pit that led to the Gencha enclave.

No, surely Gejas would eventually grow weary of his losses, or his superiors would recall him.

Still, there were some very odd things about Gejas's behavior, she thought. Why, for instance, was Gejas so sure that Ruiz Aw was here? Or did he intend to take the stronghold and then wait for Ruiz Aw to show up? She shook her head. Ruiz Aw was far too wary; he seemed to sense danger with inhuman sensitivity and accuracy.

Another unpleasant thought struck Corean. How long

would it be before the pirate Lords sensed that significant events were in the offing under Yubere's stack? She might soon be opposed by layers of enemies, pouring into the stack, pressing her deeper into the roots of the world.

"Well," she told herself sternly, "how bad can it be down in the enclave? Can it be any worse than Dobravit? If worse comes to worse, I'll take the Moc and hide. They'll never pry me out. Or better yet, I'll hold the Machine hostage."

She felt a little cold, and she put her arms around herself. She thought of Marmo and his slow cautious advice. She remembered again how much she had regretted having killed the old pirate. It was, she thought, another thing for which Ruiz Aw must pay—she would never have done it except for her hatred of the Dilvermoon slayer. Never.

But the thought lacked urgency. Was her hatred deserting her? She felt a thumping explosion, and a shiver ran through her. Without her hatred, she would be soft and helpless, nothing but a thing to be victimized.

So she sat in her war room and recalled all the things Ruiz Aw had done to her, starting with his arrival on Sook and ending with Gejas, whom Ruiz Aw had somehow called down upon her.

She finally began to feel a bitter heat, and soon she was strong again.

RUIZ WHIRLED AROUND the spiral, falling down the rail, the rider making only a whisper of sound as it slid. At intervals he heard a metallic snick as the rider passed one of the standoffs that supported the rail.

His body swung outward until he hung at a forty-five-degree angle to the perpendicular walls of the pit. His speed increased a bit more and his metal boots touched the wall, making a terrible screech, and trailing a rooster-tail of sparks. He spun violently on his tether. Recovering, he drew up his legs slightly and tugged lightly on the brake. He gripped the tether above the swivel in his gauntleted fist, and the friction slowed his spin.

When he had stabilized his position, he heard Junior's

low laughter in one ear and Nisa's whisper in the other. "Are you all right?" she asked. "It made me almost sick, just watching."

"I'm fine," he said, though in fact he was quite dizzy.

"Are you?" asked Junior, and Ruiz realized he had forgotten to switch channels. He felt a sudden confusion, and swiveled to watch the wall of the pit. Images almost too momentary for comprehension flickered past: the mouths of tunnels, the slagged-over scars of ancient battles, the scribble of incomprehensible graffiti—left by tram riders or perhaps by the devolved alien refugees that inhabited the deepest caverns of the stack. Once he saw the yellow flash of lamplight at a cavern mouth, and a moment later his passage startled a sticklike figure with too many limbs.

"Busy place," Junior commented. Then his voice changed, became metallic. "Something moving in the pit, dropping a little faster than we are."

Ruiz swiveled, tipped his head back. He could see nothing in the murk above. "Visual?"

"Not yet. Wait. Yes, I see it now. A bird, maybe, or a bat . . . but more likely an ornithopter drone."

Ruiz cursed and slowed his descent a bit. He unslung his ruptor, wrapped the sling around his upper arm so that he could use the weapon one-handed. He could see Junior above him and to the right; his clone had dropped quite a bit faster than Ruiz had. *Bolder than I am,* he thought.

"Slow down," Ruiz said, and he saw the clone's body jerk and swing as he applied his brake.

"It *is* a drone," said Junior. "I've got an uplink energy spill. The signal originates somewhere in the stronghold, I think."

Ruiz looked ahead, desperately seeking a tunnel mouth they might hide in. The pit was as smooth as glass for at least the next two hundred meters—as far as he could see through the thickening haze. "Of course," said Ruiz.

Now he could see the drone, a flash of silvery red glitter in the darkness above. At almost the same moment, whoever was flying it saw Junior; the drone plummeted with the speed of a raptor, metal wings folded against its meter-long body.

It slashed past the clone, snapping its wings open into bright knives—but Junior had applied his brakes strongly and the drone's operator misjudged the vector.

"Missed me," shouted Junior.

COREAN HELD THE inductor against the side of her head, seeing what the drone saw as it hovered in the pit. "How?" she breathed, watching the two armored men sliding down the rail. Her first reaction was bewilderment. How could the men have gotten below her, into the pit? Were they from her own forces, deserting the stronghold? No . . . deserters would have taken the tram, which was still locked to the top of the track. She made a mental note to post a reliable guard on the tram.

Then the uppermost man braked again, until his speed had dropped to a slow glide. He drew out a gyro-stabilized pinbeam, with a graceful purposefulness that she instantly identified.

"Ruiz Aw?" It was. It was.

RUIZ TRIED TO bring his ruptor to bear on the drone, which for some reason was hovering in the center of the pit, as if the operator had abandoned it.

But again Junior was quicker, and fired his pinbeam. The drone shattered into a cloud of glowing fragments, which drifted downward.

Ruiz released his brake and drew up his body, knees to chest. Now the need was to get down to the bottom as quickly as possible, before the person who controlled the stronghold sent someone, or something, after them.

He picked up speed with what seemed painful slowness . . . but soon he was falling down toward the Gencha at a speed close to terminal velocity, trying not to think about his destination.

Until the drone's arrival, he had truly believed that he might survive somehow. Might stand again in the sunlight.

CHAPTER 20

COREAN paced the war room in a frenzy of anger and indecision. Each time she passed the drone's dead monitor, she gave it a spiteful thump with her fist. Of course she had expected to find Ruiz Aw again. Of course. Over the past weeks their meetings had taken on a quality of inevitability. But she had never thought he would come to her so soon. And at such a terribly inconvenient time.

The shudder of Roderigan demolition charges had become heavier and more frequent. The Dirms had begun to fall apart under the relentless pressure of Gejas's cyborgs. Only the Moc's ferocity stood between Corean and disaster, and the longer it fought, the greater the risk that a lucky shot would kill or injure it, and then she would be in deep trouble. She shook her head. What to do?

Finally she reached a decision, though it was no great comfort to her. What could she do except fall back to a more defensible position? And if her situation deteriorated further, she could broadcast a message to the

Lords, offering to trade the enclave and its Machine for her life.

She called the Moc in and summoned the Deltan squad leader, a silent and watchful man named Kroone.

"Kroone," she said, "set up the killmechs for a harassing rearguard action—we need them to delay the Roderigans in the upper levels for as long as possible. Prepare your squad; infiltrators have penetrated the enclave below. We go to dig them out."

Kroone nodded. "How many? How armed?"

"Only two," Corean said. "A famous Dilvermoon slayer named Ruiz Aw, and his companion. Heavily armed, no doubt. He's a very competent man—but we'll have the Moc."

"As you say." Kroone bowed and would have left, but another thought occurred to Corean.

"Wait," she said. "Manacle the Pharaohan prisoners and we'll bring them along. Ruiz Aw values them and I'll take all the leverage I can get, with that man. And if we don't need them, I'll give them to the Gencha."

Kroone developed a skeptical expression, but went to organize their departure.

NISA FOUND HERSELF chained to the tram's platform, along with Dolmaero and the two Pharaohan conjurers. She ignored Molnekh, but gave Flomel a cold nod. "I hadn't expected to see you again, Master Flomel," she said. "Are you now a mechanism? Like Molnekh?"

Flomel was hunched over his own chains, examining the lock that fastened him to the platform. He ignored Nisa and probed at the lock with a bit of broomstraw.

Molnekh answered her. "No, I think not," he said in his customary cheery voice. "In fact, I think Flomel is at last coming around to the late Ruiz Aw's viewpoint."

Nisa felt a surge of revulsion. She could not see how Molnekh could act so much like himself, when he had changed so profoundly.

Flomel raised his eyes slowly, and gave Molnekh a look

of such deep hatred that Nisa was a little frightened.
"Monstrous thing," said Flomel hoarsely. "Abomination."

"See?" said Molnekh, and winked at her.

She turned away and looked at the Guildmaster
Dolmaero, who stared out over the airy emptiness of the
pit.

"And you, Guildmaster? How are you?" He didn't immediately respond, so she nudged him lightly with her
shoulder. "Guildmaster?"

He shook himself and turned his broad face toward her.
"Well enough, Noble Lady. But I'm afraid of what may
come. There is something of death in the air here, of assassinations and terror and final deeds. Do you smell it?"

Nisa sniffed. "It smells a bit like that creature we saw in
Deepheart. The Gench. Do you remember?"

"You're right," he said thoughtfully. "But there's ordinary decay as well."

A silence fell, and Nisa was left alone with her thoughts.
These seemed to center on Ruiz Aw and the time they had
been together. She wondered if he had somehow survived.

She hoped so.

After a long while, the doors above crashed open and
Corean came striding down the platform toward them, followed by her great insect and a squad of soldiers in black
armor.

Nisa looked at the slaver's perfect face, and saw that it
had begun to change, as if the skin had slipped away from
the bones just enough to destroy that marvelous symmetry.
Corean seemed inhumanly taut; she walked with a manic
bounce.

"Crazy as a dustbear in rut," whispered Dolmaero,
wide-eyed.

"Oh yes," agreed Nisa.

Molnekh's cadaverous head whipped around. "What?"
he said sharply.

Dolmaero shrugged and made no answer, but Nisa was
oddly reassured to see this evidence of Molnekh's changed
nature.

The men in black armor arranged themselves around
the perimeter of the tram's platform, and Corean took the

driver's chair; her Moc stood beside the other chair, unable to bend its six-legged insectile body into a shape that would fit the chair's contours.

Corean buckled her harness and strapped a big-bore ruptor to her left arm. She looked toward the blast doors that led to the stronghold; a Dirm stood there, the slump of its alien body betraying an almost human despair. "Hold fast; we'll be back soon," Corean called to it, and it waved slowly as the doors closed.

"So," said Corean. "We're off." Her lunatic gaze fell on Nisa, and seemed to grow hotter. "Ah," she said cheerfully. "The Pharaohan slut. Nisa, isn't it? Well, you'll be pleased to know that we're going to see your lover again."

At first Nisa didn't know what the slaver was talking about, but then it sank in and she understood.

Corean laughed, an ugly dirty sound. "Oh, don't look quite so bright-eyed. If I have my way, you won't see him until I'm done with him. And I'll have my way; of that you may be certain."

Corean released the tram's brake. They began to slide downward into the great pit.

Nisa shut her eyes, so that she wouldn't have to look down into that terrible gulf, but she was strangely happy. Perhaps Corean's words were simply a manifestation of her madness, but perhaps not. Perhaps Ruiz Aw was still alive, after all.

Even though she knew she was doing a dangerous thing, she couldn't keep a small smile from reaching her mouth.

WHEN THE SUMP at the bottom of the pit appeared through the steams that cloaked it, Ruiz gagged. The stench overwhelmed his suit filters, making his eyes water. He had to control an impulse to close his faceplate and go on internal atmosphere—but his supply of clean oxygen was limited, and prudence dictated that he save it until he was deeper in the hallucinatory caverns of the Gencha.

Apparently the current master of Yubere's stronghold was disposing of battle casualties by dumping them into the pit. Armored human forms lay half-dissolved in the sump's pink slime, and here and there the dark glistening purple of a decaying Dirm bondguard broke the surface.

When he was still a hundred meters above the sump, he noticed several moving figures along the far edge of the sump.

He slapped at the safety of his ruptor and began to slow his fall along the rail. He saw that he had left it too long, and that he was perilously close to the concrete platform above the sump, where the rail ended. He wrenched at the brake, so that deceleration tore at him, and his vision grayed. The rider whined, a sound that ran down the scale as he began to slow.

From the corner of his eye he saw the figures at the far end of the sump resolve into vaguely human forms, which began to run toward the platform, raising an odd thin ululation.

The platform was rushing up at him, and his eyes were drawn irresistibly toward the bumper at the end of the rail, which extended energy-absorbing arms designed to engage the edge of a runaway tram and then collapse slowly.

The arms would punch right through him if he hit them with enough speed.

He hauled desperately on the brake lever. It made a dreadful shrieking sound as the lining burned away.

But finally he stopped, halfway down the platform.

He hung there, swaying. It took a moment for his vision to clear, but then he slapped the rider's release and dropped to the platform with an echoing crash.

He glanced back and saw Junior gliding in behind him, under perfect control. He felt a stab of envy for his younger self, as he ran along the edge of the platform. He knelt behind a low parapet and heard the clatter of Junior's armored boots.

"You're a wild man," said his clone.

"Ah . . . it wasn't even close," Ruiz said, trying to catch his breath.

"If you say so," said Junior, clearly amused. He crouched beside Ruiz and looked at the creatures who ran toward them, waving an odd assortment of weapons.

"What are they?" said Junior.

"The Gencha keep human servants," Ruiz explained, though he found the creatures as amazing as Junior apparently did.

They seemed only marginally human. They trotted along a narrow causeway that spanned the sump, and as they came into clearer view, Ruiz felt his stomach twist. The creatures had once been ordinary men and women, perhaps—now their almost naked bodies were encrusted by exceedingly strange adornments. From every patch of skin, some piece of human anatomy sprouted. In the lead was a man whose hairless skull was decorated with a triple ridge of grafted-on noses. The useless nostrils flared in sympathy with the man's real ones as he pounded toward them, brandishing an antique punchgun. His arms were dotted with circular scalp grafts, each trailing a plume of different-colored hair.

Behind him ran a woman wearing a necklace of grafted fingers, which curled about her neck with a slow spasmodic movement. Tiny toes fringed each ear, and on her knees little mouths shouted silently. Her chest was covered from collarbones to navel with a number of breasts, all different shapes and sizes. She held some sort of obsolete energy weapon; it had a bell-shaped muzzle and an elaborate green plastic stock. Ruiz wondered if it even worked.

Behind the first two were another dozen horrors, all shrieking in thin piping voices. It struck Ruiz that the sounds they were making were somewhat reminiscent of the sounds that the Gencha made.

The voice of Nisa's clone whispered in his ear. "Oh. Oh, how awful. How can such things be?"

"What do you think they want?" asked Junior, whose air of detached confidence seemed to have frayed slightly.

"To kill us," said Ruiz impatiently. "And then they'll want to enhance their collections with our leftover parts, I suppose."

"Looks that way," said Junior. "Don't they know we're dangerous?"

"Probably not," said Ruiz. "They may associate the tram with legitimate visitors—those who have business with their masters. Everyone else they see has fallen into the sump . . . dead, or too severely injured to offer any resistance."

"Not very bright, then, are they?" The clone set his pinbeam on the parapet and sighted through its scope.

"Brightness hasn't much to do with it," Ruiz said. "They've lived with the mindfire—for generations."

"End of the line," said Junior, and fired his pinbeam.

It burned through the forehead of the lead man, and he went down, plowing through the viscous fluid at the side of the causeway, a loose bundle of limbs.

Junior shifted his aim, put the beam through the middle of the following woman's breast collection. She tumbled forward, rolling along the dusty path, but continued to shriek and writhe for a minute before dying, curled around her wound.

Junior shifted aim again and would have killed the next grotesque in the pack—but Ruiz put a hand on his arm. "Wait," Ruiz said. He found himself disturbed by his clone's callous efficiency—though of course there was no other reasonable course of action under the circumstances, no other way of reliably discouraging the sad creatures.

But now the surviving monsters had turned and were running away with as much alacrity as they had run to attack, still shrieking.

"Are you sure it's a good idea to let them get away?" Junior asked. "Won't they warn the Gencha?"

"Maybe," said Ruiz. "Though if I understand the mindfire, the Gencha already know about us. But you saw them. What could they do against us?"

Junior shrugged. "Who knows? I guess we'll find out. Do you think this will be easy?" His clone looked at Ruiz with a disturbing degree of speculation, as if wondering if Ruiz had lost all his violent judgment.

"I'm sure it won't be easy," said Ruiz. He looked up the tram rail and wondered if anyone was following them yet. He turned to tell his clone to check the rail, but Junior was already back at the rail, touching the metal with a slender probe.

"We've got activity, Dad," said the clone. "Someone coming down fast."

Ruiz looked across the sump at the low cavern mouths that gaped along the far side of the pit.

"Time to go," he said, to his clone and to Nisa's.

NISA SHIFTED, TRYING to find a comfortable way to sit as the tram spiraled downward into the murk. The manacles chafed her wrists, and the hot foul air blew past her face, like the breath of some decayed but not quite dead monster.

She glanced back at Corean, who wore a keen predatory smile on her lovely mouth.

Nisa's thoughts wandered, and after a while it occurred to her that there was a bond between Corean the slaver and Nisa the dirtworld princess. Both of them were looking forward to seeing Ruiz Aw, one more time.

The idea was tragically funny, and she laughed, too low to be heard by anyone.

RUIZ AND HIS clone ran along the causeway as fast as they could run, loaded as they were with heavy armor, weapons, and sensor gear. The nearest cavern mouth loomed before them, illuminated by the same dull red glow that lit the pit. But inside the entrance the light was a little brighter, which created an illusion of fires burning within.

Something stood up within the cavern and threw something, then ducked down.

The object spun toward them. Both Ruiz and his clone, assuming that it was a grenade, leaped off the causeway into the knee-deep slime, prepared to dive into it.

"Wait," said Junior. The object fell to the causeway, and Ruiz saw that it was a newly severed hand. On each finger, bound with a silver cord, was a different fetish: a bird's skull, a scrap of blue cloth, a rusty spring, a tiny vial of some opalescent fluid. To the thumb was tied a tiny plastic model of a man in black armor.

"They're trying magic," said Ruiz, feeling a sourceless pity. "Back on the path!"

The two of them charged onward, causing a chorus of

thin despairing shrieks from within the cavern, and then the patter of retreating bare feet.

At the edge of the sump were a row of pipes, which rose from the pink slime and ran to a pumping station just inside the cavern mouth. As they ran past the pumping station, Junior slapped a limpet mine on the casing. When they were fifty meters inside the rapidly narrowing cave, the charge detonated.

"Give the Gencha something to worry about besides us," said the clone when they paused to crouch behind a heap of broken stalagmites. "Besides, if they can't get their nutrient fluid piped to them, eventually they'll have to leave the caverns—either to fix the pump, or to feed directly in the sump."

"Good idea," said Ruiz.

"Your turn, now," said Junior.

"What?"

"To give us a good idea. How do we find this Orpheus Machine? It occurs to me that I should have asked more questions before I got involved in all this." But the clone's voice was easy and relaxed, not at all accusing. It struck Ruiz that he had spent his whole life leaping into dangerous situations and then relying on luck and ruthlessness to carry him through. He resolved that if by some miracle he survived, he would adopt a much more thoughtful style.

Ruiz looked about. The cave seemed to function as a trash pit and thoroughfare—the rubbish heaps along the walls left a clear path down the center of the tunnel. The rubbish consisted of the detritus of the sump—all those items of clothing and gear that the slime failed to digest, periodically raked from the sump and dumped here. An archaeologist could probably read the history of Sook in these remnants. Ruiz shook his head; his attention was wandering from the task at hand.

He got out the small dataslate into which he had transcribed his memories of Somnire's directions. He strapped it to his wrist and consulted the pattern of glowing lines.

"I think we're here," he said, with incomplete assurance. He pointed to a magenta squiggle. "Third cave from the north, right?"

"I think so," said the clone.

"All right," said Ruiz. "You go first. Take the second left-hand tunnel down. And keep your sensors twitching. According to Somnire, the defenses are mainly topological. We don't want to spend the rest of our lives wandering around in here, hallucinating our heads off."

Junior rose cautiously and peered over the barricade. "No. We don't. By the way—Somnire's information was very old, wasn't it?"

"Yes," said Ruiz.

THEY MET THE official welcoming party before they reached the first junction.

First Ruiz heard the shuffle of bare feet, and then the whisper of incomprehensible voices.

The two of them crouched behind a pile of rubble so ancient that it had lost its stink. "What now?" said Junior.

Ruiz shrugged and made sure his ruptor was charged.

A procession came around an angle in the tunnel—a dozen of the semi-human dwellers and three Gencha. The Gencha moved in the midst of the humans, a loose formation that had a ritually protective quality. The humans kept no particular order, seeming to circulate randomly around the Gencha. Ruiz watched for a moment before he realized that the humans were moving in a pattern similar to the movement of the eye spots on the Gencha's squashy skulls.

Ruiz sank down, trying to be invisible.

The leading human carried a staff, a long sharp-pointed bar of silvery metal, topped with a gilded carving of a Gench. He stopped and planted his staff before him. The procession straggled to a halt behind him.

"Unauthorized visitors!" he said sternly, and then giggled madly. His gaze twitched back and forth, unfocused. His forehead was shingled with eyelids, in three parallel horizontal rows. These opened, fluttering their lashes, but there were no eyes beneath, just shallow pits. "Unauthorized visitors," he said again. "Come out—you cannot hide from us! Your smell distends our nostrils; our nasal cavities ache with the pressure of your presence."

Junior gave a low laugh.

"Come out!" the spokesman demanded. When Ruiz and his clone stayed put, the spokesman turned toward the largest of the Gencha, a gesture so like that of a confused dog that Ruiz felt a pang of pitying anger.

The Gench made a low chirping sound at the man, who turned back with renewed confidence. "Come out; we will refrain from tearing your flesh from your bones and will even treat you as guests."

"Bighearted bunch," said Junior, and raised his pinbeam. Ruiz looked at his clone and thought, *Are my teeth really so long and sharp? Do I look quite so much like a rabid wolf?* He shook his head violently, trying to clear his vision.

"No, wait," said Ruiz. He considered the situation as carefully as the moment allowed and then said, "Stay down. If they attack me, then chop them up."

He stood slowly, holding his ruptor ready.

"Ah!" said the spokesman, looking at Ruiz as if surprised to see him. "You display the rudiments of mannerly behavior. Your companion is crippled in the legs, yes? So that he cannot stand? No matter. We ask you: Why are you here? Without the tram, without prisoners for the Soulstealer, without the scent of authorization?"

Ruiz considered the proper response to these questions. Guile was often of no use with a madman, unless one exactly understood the nature of his madness. But what could he do but try? "We come to see the Soulstealer, as it is accounted to be one of the wonders of the universe."

"Rude visitors!" shouted the man. "Tourists who kill the locals as their first act of admiration? I think not. No, no—it's plain now you're here to take the Soulstealer for your own. Plain, plain—Yubere warned us that men would come, in hard shells and bearing terrible weapons. To steal our glory, the means by which we will remake the universe. To steal our future—what crime is more terrible? But now we know you and your evil!" He raised his staff and threw it point first toward Ruiz.

Ruiz dodged to the side and the staff flew harmlessly past. Junior rose up and put beams through the spokesman and the largest Gench.

The rest of the procession wavered and then was gone, like switched-off lamps.

Only one body lay on the littered floor of the tunnel—the man with the eyelids on his forehead.

Ruiz and his clone approached the body carefully, but the man was dead.

Junior nudged him with a toe. "What's going on?"

"We're starting to see things. It'll get worse the deeper we go." He looked again at his clone's glittering ferocity and thought, *It's just an hallucination. I don't really look like that.*

"How long will we be here?"

Ruiz shrugged. "As long as it takes, I guess." He switched to Nisa's clone's channel. "Nisa? What did you see?"

"A deformed man harangued you, threw a stick at you. Then your clone killed him." Her voice had a muted, repulsed quality.

"I see." Ruiz had not expected the mindfire to begin so soon. He closed his faceplate and vents. He had to hope that they would find the Orpheus Machine before they ran out of oxygen and had to open their vents. Junior started to do the same, but Ruiz made a gesture of negation. "Wait," he said.

He came to a decision. "Nisa? Time to transmit this channel to SeaStack."

"Are you sure?" she said.

"Oh, yes." He turned to Junior. "You have the speech? Good. Take off your helmet."

GEJAS FELT A sweet warmth where his heart had once been, before the slayer Ruiz Aw had torn it out. The stronghold was all but his; in a few minutes the scattered resistance would be wiped clean.

At first he ignored the presence of the destroyer's commander, who stood at the door, waiting to be recognized.

Gejas sensed some unpleasant knowledge in the commander, knowledge which he was for the moment unwilling to accept.

But after a minute the commander stepped in uninvited and spoke. "Gejas Tongue: a development." The commander stepped to an auxiliary screen, tapped at its dataslate. "This was received in a general broadcast just a few minutes ago." He cued the screen.

Gejas saw Ruiz Aw, wearing armor, holding his helmet under his arm. It *was* Ruiz Aw, but somehow different, smooth-faced and confident, miraculously untouched by the pain Roderigo had given him. It was unnerving, as if the man was invulnerable, unstoppable. The slayer stood in a dark-walled tunnel, lit by a dim red light. At his feet was a grotesque corpse. "It surely must be him," whispered Gejas. "All the signs are there."

"Folk of SeaStack," said Ruiz Aw. "I'm making this broadcast from far beneath the fortress of the late Alonzo Yubere. Down here, their presence unsuspected by most of Sook, dwell a great number of Gencha and their formerly human servants. I'm here because of a treasure called the Orpheus Machine—a device for performing mass deconstructions, formerly under the control of Alonzo Yubere and Publius the monster maker. I, Ruiz Aw, intend to destroy it." Ruiz Aw paused and smiled a humorless smile. "I'll report my progress at appropriate intervals."

Ruiz Aw replaced his helmet and latched down the seals. Just before he closed the faceplate, he winked at Gejas.

He unslung a pinbeam and moved away down the tunnel, and the camera followed him for a moment before the transmission ended.

Gejas felt his mouth drop open. He had found the treasure Roderigo had sent him to find. He had found the creature who had slain The Yellowleaf. He opened his mouth wider, to laugh.

But before he could make the first joyful sound, he felt the lust of a million greedy souls, and realized that all over SeaStack fighters would be loading into assault craft, preparing to attack the stronghold he had just won.

"Oh," he groaned. "Oh, no."

"Exactly," said the commander. "Roderigo commands you to defend the fortress until they can get reinforcements to us. Prevent any other force from gaining control. No matter what it costs."

CHAPTER 21

Ruiz Aw was lost. He and Junior had wandered through the endless maze for an hour, meeting no one. Occasionally they'd heard the sounds of rapidly retreating feet, but always distant and distorted by the twisting tunnels. Sometimes the sounds seemed closer— the clank of machinery or high-pitched voices. The floors of the tunnel were slippery, the walls gave off the same dim red light. Uninteresting rubbish lined most of the tunnels.

Apart from those mysterious sounds, there was an air of long disuse about the areas they had passed through.

Ruiz paused at a wheel-spoke nexus, where there were seven possible choices of route. He looked at the dataslate and could find no correspondence with the map Somnire had given him. "I have the feeling that we really haven't gotten into the main enclave. I'd swear we were in an abandoned network."

"You're lost," said Junior sourly.

"Maybe so," said Ruiz. "How's your oxygen?"

"Down to sixty percent. You?"

"Worse than that." Ruiz felt a twinge of resentment,

that his clone excelled him even in so minor a thing as breathing—but then he reminded himself that breathing, after all, was not so insignificant an accomplishment.

"What should we do?" The clone leaned against the side wall.

"Let's rest and think," said Ruiz, and sat down on the nearest dry spot. He laid his ruptor across his knees and closed his eyes.

"You rest," said Junior. "I'll think. While I'm at it, I'll wander around a bit. Don't worry, I won't go so far I can't get back."

Junior went away down the corridor, his armored head twitching from side to side—a beast scenting its prey. Ruiz opened his mouth to protest, then closed it. Let his younger self try.

WHEN THEY ARRIVED at the bottom of the pit, Nisa was almost afraid to look, for fear that she would see Ruiz's body lying on the platform . . . or in the sump.

But if he were one of the huddled forms half-sunk in the pink slime, she couldn't tell. Corean seemed confident that Ruiz had survived. She unloaded her prisoners briskly and attached throat leads to each, linking them into a coffle. Nisa found herself staring at the thin dirty neck of Flomel; behind her was Dolmaero.

Molnekh held Flomel's lead in one bony hand and gave the conjuror his most cheerful smile. Muscles jumped in Flomel's shoulders; Nisa almost felt sorry for him, treacherous fool though he had been.

Corean finished conferring with her Deltan commander, a man called Kroone.

She came toward the prisoners, bouncing lightly on her feet, a look of ferocious happiness on her perfect mouth.

"Let's go, let's go," she said. "We have fish to fry, slayers to skin."

So they moved off, the coffle in the center of a formation of armored men. Nisa would have pinched her nose shut, had her hands been free. The stink at the bottom of the pit was so intense that she felt a bit dizzy. In fact she was beginning to get a strange wavery head-swimming sensation, as if the unpleasant reality about her had begun some subtle shift toward a new configuration. It reminded her a bit of the way she'd felt on the few occasions she had smoked snake oil.

She glanced back at Dolmaero. The usually stolid Guildmaster wore a faint nostalgic smile, and Nisa remembered that he had been an oil addict, back on Pharaoh.

She noticed that Corean and her escorts had all closed the faceplates of their armor.

ALREADY THE PIRATE Lords had brought force to bear on Gejas. The Roderigan destroyer had taken significant damage defending the Yubere lagoon, though it sank two pirate vessels in the lagoon's entrance. The pirates could easily have disabled the destroyer had they coordinated their attacks—but they were fighting each other at the same time they were trying to fight their way into the fortress. At the moment the pirates were busy outside. Gejas's forces had used the respite to improve the lagoon's defenses.

Gejas began to think that he might indeed be able to hold the fortress until reinforcements arrived. And then he would be free to follow Ruiz Aw, down to the place where he would begin the slayer's punishment.

He discounted the possibility that Ruiz Aw would actually carry out his threat and destroy the treasure; the man would have to be stupid as well as mad.

But the pirate forces gradually filled the channels outside, and then one of them put sappers to work on an angled tunnel, driving it into the far side of the stack, trying to bypass the fortress.

Gejas cursed violently and dispatched a squad of cyborgs to an upper level of the stack, with instructions to drop satchel charges on the tunnelers.

Most disquieting of all was a report from his observers topside. Two large Shard vessels hovered above the stack, apparently monitoring the battle for infringements of Shard law.

•   •   •

WHEN COREAN CALLED a halt, Nisa at first was unable to drag her attention away from her feet, on which she had concentrated all of her attention in an attempt to avoid seeing the frightening changes in the others. In the last few minutes, she had seen Corean and the other armored persons lose their humanity, become dire insectile creatures, stalking along on legs that moved too quickly. The Moc, ranging ahead, had become an even more demonic shape, as dreadful as Bhas the Dry God. Flomel's narrow back had become the back of a rodentlike creature, and Molnekh a walking corpse, dry bones covered by tatters of dried skin.

When finally she looked up, she saw, coming down the tunnel toward her, a great crowd of grotesquely disfigured humans, surrounding a trio of Gencha. The Gencha appeared to be the only solid objects in a sea of shimmering misperception—as though the drug that filled her head ceased to affect her when she looked at those ugly heaps of alienness. So she kept her eyes on the Gencha.

Corean went to the head of her group of fighters, pushing them out of her way in her eagerness. "Stop! Or I'll set the Moc on you," she shouted to the crowd of approaching grotesques, which did in fact stop, though they continued to mill about uneasily.

Eventually a woman came forward, a woman with ears set like feathers along the backs of her thin arms, and a tuft of red hair growing from the tip of her long nose. "What do you want here?" she called in a trembling voice.

"The cooperation you owe me, as Alonzo Yubere's heir." Corean took off her helmet and shook back her black hair. "Look at me; memorize my face," she said. "In every way Yubere protected you, I will protect you. In every way that you aided Yubere, you must aid me. Yubere is dead; only I can stand between you and the universe, which hates you."

The disfigured woman put her hands to her face; Nisa noticed that on the back of each hand was a large pink nipple. "How can we know the truth of this? Already this dayperiod, two men have come to kill and steal. And now you, with your monster and your shells."

Corean's nostrils flared. To Nisa's drug-dazzled eyes, she seemed some sort of hunting beast. "Yes," said Corean. "Those men are my enemies. Take me to them, and I will dispose of them for you."

The woman wailed, a thin sound of confusion, and looked around at the Gencha, as if begging for direction. "No, we must know the reality of this. Too important a decision, this, to risk on the currents of chance."

Corean shook her head impatiently. "Then listen: Send a Gench to me, that it may confirm my ownership of Yubere's fief."

"You would permit this?" asked the woman, eyes wide.

"Yes, yes—but hurry. Those men you describe are here to steal and destroy. Of *that* reality you should already be certain."

A Gench shuffled forward on its three short legs. Corean waited for it with her head high. When the Gench opened one of its mouths and extended a sensory filament, Corean stood still, and the only emotion Nisa could see on her perfect face was impatience. The filament sank into her forehead, and the slaver didn't twitch.

A moment later the Gench withdrew its sensor. "The situation is unclear," it whispered. "It seems uncertain that you will be able to protect us, as Yubere did for so long. Still, you appear to be telling the truth as you see it. I will recommend that we assist you, as long as you refrain from damaging our properties and servitors."

Corean nodded and replaced her helmet. "We'll be careful. But Ruiz Aw won't, so take us to him."

The Gench's eyespots ceased their endless circulation for a moment. "Yes. The men are currently wandering in the same parallel gallery that you have entered, where they can do little harm. But if they are at all clever, they will soon find a way to break into our Inner Spaces. I will give you a servitor to guide you."

The woman with the ear-covered arms came reluctantly forward. "This is called Soosen," the Gench whispered. "It will take you to your enemies."

Corean and her group followed Soosen through the crowd of grotesques, and Nisa returned her gaze to her feet, so that she wouldn't have to look at the terrible things these people had done to themselves.

But when they reached the turn of the tunnel, Nisa looked back, to see the three Gencha, facing each other and hooting softly but insistently. And then two of them disappeared into nothingness, along with their semi-human entourage. The remaining Gench turned toward her, though she couldn't tell if it was watching her.

It was almost as if they had been arguing, she thought, before she returned to her walking dream.

RUIZ SAT MOTIONLESSLY taking slow shallow breaths, willing his metabolism to gear down. He glanced again at his armor's readout slate—his oxygen was almost half-depleted. He manually retarded the rate of release. Surely he could do with a little less now.

He tried to think, to come up with a way to find the Gencha habitations and the Orpheus Machine. It was a maddening situation; the tunnels they had traversed bore a resemblance to the topography Somnire had described. But he had seen none of Somnire's landmarks, nor had they come across any other dwellers. What was going on?

His breathing slowed a bit more, and his eyelids grew heavy. He found himself nodding. His neck grew too supple and his head fell forward.

He dreamed. At first it was a dream of such stark simplicity that he was almost impatient with it. He was tending his flowers on the terrace. Behind him: the facade of his home. Before him: the great rift canyon with its jagged black cliffs, the airless black sky of his empty planet.

The sun beat through the protective field, warming his back as he bent over the beds. He loosened the black soil around each precious plant, dusted the soil with a handful of mineral supplements. Time passed, and impatience gave way to a sweet regretful nostalgia—though with the unruly time-slipped logic of dreams, he couldn't understand where that sense of loss and longing came from. When had he ever been happier than he was here, alone and safe?

He saw a clump of asters past its prime; the blossoms had gone brown and ragged. He reached out to pull off the dead flower heads, but when his hand closed around the soft flower, it hardened and twisted in his hand, like a small muscular animal.

It bit him with tiny sharp teeth and he jerked his hand away. The dead aster seemed unchanged. He looked at his hand, holding it palm up at his waist. The hand ached, as if the flower had injected some painful venom. Slowly blood collected in the cup of his hand, and he gazed down at it, unable to look away.

He saw his reflection in the shining pool of blood—the face of a terribly sad man, who cried silently, his mouth twisted with the effort of holding in the sobs.

HIS EYES SNAPPED open; his heart hammered. His vision blurred, and he pressed the chin switch that sent an emergency draft of oxygen into his lungs. How could he have fallen asleep, here in this place of death and deadly illusion? Was he completely mad? Had he lost all of the edge that had helped him to survive for so long?

He looked wildly from side to side, expecting to see Corean, or her Moc, or an army of monsters standing there, fingers on triggers, ready to laugh and kill.

He was still alone. How long had he slept? He selected the channel to Nisa's clone. "What's been happening? Why did you allow me to sleep?"

"I would have spoken if anyone had come. But you needed the rest, didn't you?" Her voice held a strong echo of that warmth that had captured his affection, back when he was still a slayer and she still a princess.

He was shaking. "Maybe, maybe. But it was an extremely foolish thing to do. I'll get plenty of rest when I'm dead. Meanwhile, keep me awake."

"If you say so," she answered. She sounded a little hurt.

He glanced at his chronometer. He had slept for only a few minutes. But still, he had dreamed. It suddenly occurred to him how strange this was, that he had dreamed. And he found that he could remember the details of the dream. He endured another shudder. Somehow he had always thought that if he ever began to dream again, his dreams would be more endurable. What did it mean?

He shook his head violently. "Have you seen Junior? My clone?"

"No," she whispered.

He got up, adjusting the oxygen flow to support moderate exertion. An idea had come to him along with the dream. Somnire's map had seemed to resemble the empty maze in several places. Suppose they were moving along the course of the occupied levels, separated from their goal only by a layer of meltstone and fused alloy? That surmise might explain the sounds they had heard at various points along the path they had taken.

How to find a way into these hypothetical parallel tunnels? Ruiz wondered where Junior had gone. The clone's sensors might make short work of the problem. Ruiz opened the short-range channel. "Junior?" he said tentatively.

There was no answer; his clone was out of range, at the least. Maybe Junior was thinking. Maybe he was dead. Maybe he had fallen asleep, too. No . . . he couldn't believe that of his younger self.

Ruiz sighed and tapped at the wall with the butt of his ruptor. It made a dull clunk. He moved a few meters down the corridor and tapped again. Was there a difference in the clunk?

He shook his head ruefully. The flaw in this approach was that if these tunnels did indeed parallel the inhabited tunnels, he would be constantly announcing his position to everyone on the other side. Though perhaps they already knew where he was.

He tried another spot and this time he heard a definite clink.

"Might as well be hung for a goat," he said to himself. He set one of his limpet mines against the wall and set it for a penetrating explosion. As he trotted off around the curve of the tunnel, he heard Nisa's clone ask, "What's a goat?"

The mine detonated, and an instant later Ruiz heard the shrieks of the wounded.

THE WORLD HAD grown very strange for Nisa by the time they reached the entrance to the enclave's habitations—a deep narrow shaft, down which a ladder descended into red darkness. She edged forward to look, but an armored man pushed her roughly back, as if fearing that she might fling herself down the hole, dragging the rest of the prisoners with her. She laughed; what a foolish idea. She had long ago passed that point. Now her overriding emotion was curiosity. What new weirdness would her life next serve up to her?

Another disfigured person scrambled from the pit and went up to their guide. The man, who wore intricate herringbone patterns of eyebrows on his otherwise hairless chest, spoke in an excited whisper to the guide. Nisa watched, repulsed and fascinated. The patterns seemed to move over the man's skin, as active as a swarm of hairy insects.

Corean took the guide by the arm. "Soosen," she said. "What's going on?"

The guide put her nippled hands to her face. "Uncomfortable events. The invaders have separated. We've lost contact with one of them, and the other has just broken into the Inner Spaces."

Corean gave the woman a little shake. "How close to the Machine is he?"

"Why? He would not really hurt the Machine, surely?"

Corean jerked her close, and spoke in a low intense voice. "Never ask me questions, Gencha garbage. Why else would he be down here? Of course he would hurt the Machine. How close is he?"

Soosen opened her mouth, as if to argue, but apparently her loss of humanity had not made her stupid. "He is relatively close to the Machine. If he knows the way, he can be there in a thousand heartbeats or less."

Corean cursed ripely. "How far are *we* from the Machine?"

"Much farther."

Corean turned away, shaking her head. To Nisa's drugged perceptions, she seemed as dangerous as a dustbear, as unpredictable, as horrifyingly strong. The slaver's armor shimmered with hallucinatory color, imaginary light sweeping over the polished metal.

Corean called Kroone to her. The squad leader trotted to her, holding his weapon high; his movements reminded Nisa of a dog's.

"We must travel fast now, Kroone; the coffle will slow us down and make us vulnerable. But I want to keep the Pharaohans in reserve . . . I'll never underestimate Ruiz Aw again. So. I'll leave you here with five of your men to guard the prisoners. The Moc and your two best men will go on with me. Pick them for me."

Kroone bobbed his helmeted head and gestured two of his men forward.

"Wait until I send for you, Kroone," said Corean. She turned to look toward Nisa, the red light shining on her armor. "I'll see him first, it seems. But I'll save a piece to show you, slut."

Then she turned to the pit and nodded at Soosen the guide. The woman with the ears on her arms made a sorrowful face and started down the ladder. The Moc followed, its insectile body moving with a flickering grace.

"Good-bye," Corean said to Nisa, and was gone.

RUIZ, PRESSED TO the wall beside the hole he had made, readied himself and then peeked into the jagged opening. Instantly he jerked his head back, but no fire came through the hole. He risked another look.

A half-dozen bodies lay on the other side of the wall. They had been monstrously grotesque before the explosion, but now they were only dead or dying people, returned to humanity by their blood and pain.

He darted through the opening, ready to defend himself, but nothing moved, except for the slow writhing of two of his victims. A line of dark spatters led away up the tunnel, as if the least badly hurt member of the group had run away.

Scattered among the bodies were the fragments of crude megaphonelike devices. It came to Ruiz that they had been following him, listening at the thin spots in the wall.

He ran along the trail of blood, hoping that human instinct would make the survivor flee toward home.

Somnire had said that the Orpheus Machine was kept at the core of the enclave, where the tunnels were most thickly inhabited—by the Gencha and their servants.

NISA SAT WITH the other prisoners on a bench cut from the wall. It reminded Nisa uncomfortably of the niches in the catacombs beneath her father's palace, where royal corpses were laid to rest. She shifted from one uncomfortable vision to another—each seen from the corner of her eye, tenuous and incomplete. She saw the faces of lost friends, the suffering victims of Expiations she had attended with her father, the gruesome illustrations in a book of dark fairy tales she had owned as a child. Once Flomel turned to her and she saw the mask he had worn for her Expiation— the dreadful countenance of Bhas. She jerked back; at the same moment he shrank away from her. She wondered what awful thing he had seen in her face.

She glanced at Dolmaero, whose broad face glistened with sweat, but who seemed remarkably unafraid. His features seemed somehow less distorted. He patted her hand and spoke in a voice of comfort. "This is only a new way of riding the snake, Noble Person. The visions can't hurt you. Give heed to their lessons. Try to learn from them—if nothing else, the attempt is calming."

"Thank you," she whispered. She looked at Molnekh, who retained his grinning-skull face. She squinted and thumped the side of her head with the heel of her hand. Just for an instant she saw his real features beneath the illusory bone. He seemed unmoved by the visions.

"Are you not at all frightened, Molnekh?" she asked.

His smile widened to show his long yellow teeth. "You forget. I've been here before."

Oh, yes, she thought. *So you have.* His reply reminded her of what in all likelihood awaited her. She wondered if it hurt to have one's soul removed.

She heard a low hiss—and somehow the sound conveyed some quality of mortality. One of Kroone's men staggered and fell.

The others dropped behind the various bits of cover Kroone had posted them by, but not before another hiss sounded and another man had gone down.

The cavern grew still. After a minute Kroone spoke in a strained voice. "Who's there? What do you want? We're here on the authority of Corean Heiclaro, proprietor of this place—and also with the permission of the Gencha."

No one replied.

"Don't trifle with us," Kroone shouted in a voice that cracked with fear.

One of his men crawled over to one of the fallen men. "Dead, Kroone," he reported in a low voice. "Pinbeamed through the bellows of his neck joint. Fancy shooting."

"I know the Deltan armor," someone said, though the source of the voice seemed oddly general, as though it issued from several speakers scattered around the perimeter of the cavern. "SeedCorp is so cheap. Besides, I have an acquaintance who occasionally wears the stuff."

Nisa felt hope begin to warm her heart. She recognized that voice. Ruiz Aw had apparently arrived to rescue her, with the same miraculous timing he had always displayed in the past. Nightmares still chased each other through the edges of her vision, but she felt a great deal better, suddenly.

"What do you want?" Kroone shouted again.

Ruiz allowed the silence to stretch out a bit. "I've a deal for you. I can kill all of you—but I'd rather get some use out of you."

"Really?" Kroone's voice had gone skeptical. "Who are you that you think you can best four of Castle Delt's finest, now that we're ready for you?"

"My name is Ruiz Aw. Have you heard the name?" Ruiz spoke gently, his voice falling low.

Nisa could almost feel the shock that the name produced. "Ruiz Aw? Yes, the name is familiar. You're the one the Lady Corean hunts. The slayer who has thwarted her for so long. A dangerous man, she calls you."

"Such is the rumor," said Ruiz Aw, very softly. "Tell me, how did you hope to survive this expedition?"

"Why shouldn't we survive?"

Ruiz laughed, a low pitying sound. "I take it Corean hasn't informed you of the situation topside? No? The fortress is in the hands of Roderigan cyborgs. But that's not the worst of it. All the pirates in SeaStack are gathering outside the fortress, and when they've finished killing each other and fought their way through the Roderigan maniples, they'll be coming down the shaft. Down here."

"Why should I believe you?" said Kroone, but his voice shook.

"Can your armor's transceivers access the SeaStack general datastream? Tune in. See what they're saying." Ruiz spoke in a voice of calm patient reason.

A minute passed. Then Kroone spoke in a weak frightened voice. "We're as good as dead."

"Not so!" Ruiz now sounded quite cheerful. "Not so at all. If we can come to an agreement, I'll take you to a secret egress from the stack, where a sub awaits to take us away from this unpleasant place. But time escapes us on swift feet, and you must decide. How intense are your loyalties to the slaver?"

Another short silence ensued. Finally Kroone spoke. "They do not extend past the line between life and death."

"A reasonable attitude! Let me make you aware of one more fact. In my helmet is a charge of explosive; wired to the charge is a neural deadman switch. Betray me and we all die, because you will not find the egress without me."

"Understood," said Kroone heavily. "But why do you need us? If you can kill us and get away, why not just do so?"

"Several good reasons," said Ruiz Aw. "One, I value these prisoners and would not wish them to be injured in the skirmish. Two, a crowd of monsters has recently assembled to cut me off from the pit; we must fight our way through them. Three, maybe I couldn't kill all of you. Who knows? Castle Delt manufactures efficient killers."

"At least you acknowledge this truth," said Kroone. "All right. We'll agree to your bargain. Come out; we'll arrange the details."

An armored man stepped cautiously from behind a curtain wall at the back of the cavern. To Nisa's drugged eyes, Ruiz Aw seemed no different from any of the other armored men who rose from their hiding places. No different at all—and this perception darkened, just a little, the hope that had taken root in her heart.

Abruptly Molnekh stood up. He stared hotly at Ruiz Aw, then at Kroone, who were slowly approaching each other in the center of the cavern.

In the next instant, the conjuror was running for the ladder shaft, his long legs moving much faster than Nisa would have thought possible. Ruiz Aw seemed oddly slow to react, as if he didn't remember that Molnekh was a traitor.

Nisa didn't have time to think it through. "Molnekh is Genched," she shouted. "He's going to warn Corean."

Ruiz raised his weapon, and a line of green sparkling light struck through Molnekh's narrow back. He tumbled along the ground, tried to crawl to the edge of the shaft, but his strength failed him and he died scrabbling toward his goal.

"I'd forgotten," Kroone said in a shaken voice.

"Once again I thank you, Noble Lady," said Ruiz. But his voice was oddly detached . . . and had a sadly formal undertone. "Treachery is no business for the bemused." He turned from Molnekh's corpse and began to confer in low tones with Kroone, and Nisa felt a great puzzlement. What was wrong with Ruiz Aw? What was he talking about?

She soon forgot to wonder, as the illusions clouded her mind again.

Before they left, Ruiz made Kroone unleash them from the coffle.

He even freed Flomel, to Nisa's astonishment—almost

as if he had forgotten all the dreadful things Flomel had done.

Flomel rubbed his neck and looked innocently grateful, and oddly enough, Nisa believed that he was showing his true face.

"Then anyone can change," she said to herself.

CHAPTER 22

COREAN ran behind the Moc, which followed close on the heels of the grotesque Soosen. The servitor was staggering a bit, gasping—obviously the pace was too quick for her. But Corean felt no fatigue at all, and the weight of the ruptor strapped to her arm was nothing, a deadly feather.

She called to Soosen. "Run, monster. If we fail to catch Ruiz Aw, I'll take you away from here, out into the cold universe alone, where you'll never smell another Gench as long as you live."

Soosen threw a terrified glance back over her shoulder, and Corean laughed aloud.

RUIZ AW FOLLOWED the blood trail, and with every step he drew closer to the wounded person he pursued. Now he began to catch glimpses of a thin woman, who limped around each new turning of the tunnel with a little more desperation, with an increasingly frightened face. She seemed at first glimpse to be as human as Ruiz—but when he got a little closer, he saw that chevrons of pink mucus membrane decorated her back, gleaming wetly in the red light. The design gave her back the look of some odd crustacean, its alien flesh bulging beneath a segmented carapace of human skin.

Her wound was bleeding less, he saw when he was almost on her, though her leg seemed to be stiffening. Her gait had become a lunging shuffle. He slung his ruptor and prepared to seize her. He felt a sickness in his stomach; would she tell him where to find the Orpheus Machine, or would he be forced to torment the information from her?

He wasn't sure he could do it. Despite his sealed armor, he suddenly smelled the ancient familiar scent of blood. A black memory of the Roderigo slaughterhouse slipped through his mind.

He was ten meters behind her when the Gench stepped out from a side passage, blocking his path.

"Stop, please," it said as Ruiz skidded to a halt, almost losing his balance on the slippery tunnel floor. He shifted his ruptor, ready to fire. It made no aggressive movement.

The respite had apparently given Ruiz's victim fresh energy; she vanished around the next corner with renewed speed.

He started to dodge past the Gench; their alien physiologies and psyches reportedly made Gencha difficult to torture—and how would one judge the truth of their admissions? But it spoke again. "Ruiz Aw. Wait. I would speak with you, to your advantage. Let the servitor go; it could provide no significant assistance to you in its present state of hysteria."

Ruiz was so startled by this remarkable speech that he forgot all about the escaping woman. "You know me?"

"Yes. You do not remember me? I feel no surprise. I was the young Gench you freed from Publius the monster maker. I have an opportunity to redress this imbalance of gratitudes now."

In his astonishment, Ruiz allowed the muzzle of his ruptor to drop for a moment, then jerked it up. "How? But more to the point, why? Gratitude is a human response."

"No matter. I have other reasons. So. I will lead you to

the thing the humans above call the Orpheus Machine. We must go quickly; the human Corean and her great warrior are close behind us. And two of her human killers." Its eyespots scurried around to the far side of its skull.

Ruiz hesitated, looking down the tunnel. "Give me a reason to believe you." He recalled an uncomfortable fact: he had once lectured this young Gench on the correspondence between sapience and the capacity for treachery.

A quiver ran through the Gench's sacklike body. "Above, they fight for control of this Machine. Not so?"

"Yes."

"And will they stop before they have it? Even if they must scour the stack down to bedrock, and slay everything that dwells within?"

"No," admitted Ruiz.

"Then it is not our treasure, but our doom." The Gench extruded a tentacle from one of its mouths; the tentacle lifted a small dataslate, apparently looted from the sump. "And did you mean what you said in your broadcast? That you will destroy the Machine?"

"I'll try," said Ruiz, who had passed beyond astonishment.

"Then if I wish to survive, I must aid you. As before. Though I must warn you, the Machine is persuasive and will argue forcefully for its life, so that you may lose your resolve."

"And do any of your fellow Gencha think as you do?"

It wriggled its torso in the Gencha approximation of a shrug. "Not all of them, or even most of them. The Old Ones' attention is fixed on Becoming. Nor can they believe in their own mortality; they believe they will live forever as gods. For too long they have hidden here from the human tide that fills the universe; they forget the danger that humans pose to our species. Thus in late years they thought to barter the use of the Machine for power."

The Gench paused, and its faint breath sighed through its spiracles. "I spent far too much time as the slave of Publius the monster maker; these foolish dreams are not for me, nor will I ever grow to godhood. Survival seems a sufficiently ambitious goal for such a corrupt creature as I.

And others find my limitations comfortable. We are a small faction, but determined. Hurry. A guide leads Corean and her bug to the Machine."

Ruiz toggled his short-range channel again. "Junior? Where are you?" he asked, aware that his voice had acquired a querulous undertone. He got no answer. He waited a few moments longer, then came to a decision. "Let's go," he said.

The Gench set off at its awkward-looking rippling gait. At the first branch, it departed from the blood trail.

It was much faster than it looked, and Ruiz was forced to increase his oxygen flow again, to keep up with the creature.

NISA STAGGERED ALONG, helped by Dolmaero, who seemed to have regained much of his strength down in this constricted Hell.

To either side of the passage were corpses—devolved humans who had tried to prevent them from returning to the tram. Ruiz and the others had gone ahead to do this damage, leaving one soldier to guard the three Pharaohans.

After a few minutes, Ruiz and the soldier called Kroone had returned alone. Kroone had limped and the black armor Ruiz wore was splashed with blood.

Ruiz still maintained his strange distance. *The visions, the madness,* she thought. *That's why he seems less than himself.*

They eventually emerged into the great pit and crossed the sump without incident. Ruiz began to act even more strangely, casting looks back over his shoulder—more looks, Nisa thought, than could be accounted for by caution.

"What is it?" she asked him. But he didn't reply, and the blank metal of his helmet gave her no clue to his thoughts.

They got onto the tram, and Nisa felt a sort of greedy eagerness to be away from this horrible place. She noticed that she was grinning. So wide was her smile that her face hurt.

Despite her anticipation, some formless misgiving had lodged painfully in her heart. She turned, saw that Ruiz Aw had not boarded the tram yet; his attention was fixed on the red-glowing mouths of the Gencha caverns.

"What is it?" she asked again.

Almost unwillingly, it seemed, his armored head turned toward her. Then he unlatched his faceplate and exposed his face. He was as dangerously beautiful as she remembered—the drug that possessed her only sharpened his beauty, made it both more predatory and more brilliant. He smiled at her with melancholy affection. Still, his black gaze was just a little colder, a little harder than she remembered. *Perhaps it's the drug,* she thought.

"Do you know how much I have valued you?" he said, so low that she could barely hear him.

"Yes," she answered.

"And have you noticed what a great fool I have always been?" He was smiling broadly now. She took no insult at the implication.

"Occasionally," she answered seriously.

He looked at her as if carving her face carefully in some gallery of the mind. "I will always be grateful for our time together, no matter what happens," he said, frightening her very badly. "Will you give me a kiss, soft and sweet, from your heart to mine?"

"Yes," she said.

RUIZ AND HIS guide moved rapidly. They began to pass an occasional semi-human person, who generally stood hastily aside and watched with open mouth as they passed. Down some of the side passages, Ruiz saw living areas, in which people had made pathetically ordinary little nests. In these dwellings, glowpoints gave a brighter light than the red bioluminescence that lighted the tunnels, so that Ruiz could see the few sticks of furniture the inhabitants had lashed together from the sump's rubbish. The walls were decorated by crude drawings in black and white paint—

stick figures with three legs and arms but human heads. Ruiz began to see children, and the youngest of these seemed entirely human. Their wide-eyed faces might have belonged to children anywhere in the pangalac worlds. He refused to think what their lives must be like, down here in the chemical madness of the Gencha enclave.

Abruptly the Gench veered into a side passage. Ruiz followed, to find the creature collapsed behind the concealment of a particularly high rubbish pile.

"What is it?" Ruiz hissed, looking back over his shoulder.

The Gench trembled. "Your enemy has reached the Machine first."

"How do you know?"

The eyespots regarded Ruiz with an approximation of astonishment. "This information inflames the pheromonic net. Which fills the habitations. How could I not know?"

"How is it that the other Gencha don't know what you're doing for me?" Ruiz felt an incipient panic.

"They do know," said the young Gench. "But what can they do? Our species does not act easily—only such corrupt ones as I can make any sort of individual decision. But now I have no information on which to act—my plan was based on the assumption that you would destroy the Machine before your enemy arrived to kill you."

"I see," said Ruiz dubiously. "So, do you also know what has become of my companion?"

"Yes, of course," said the Gench. "We lost track of him briefly; then he managed somehow to run down a servitor. He forced it to guide him to the place where Corean had left her prisoners and a detachment of her guards. He killed two guards, then negotiated a truce with the survivors. They took the prisoners back to the tramline, killing a large number of our servitors who had attempted to obstruct their escape."

"Prisoners?" A wild speculation filled Ruiz.

"A woman and two men, shackled into a coffle."

Nisa. Who else could it be? Junior had acted with Ruiz Aw's customary ruthless self-interest. Ruiz felt a sudden self-loathing—and a frantic disappointment. Why had he not thought to do the same? He had changed fatally, it seemed.

"Have they left?"

The Gench made its flaccid shrug. "I think not, but I speak with no assurance. The net grows tenuous in the relatively open air of the great pit, and convective currents fragment the data."

Ruiz felt an almost irresistible impulse to abandon this foolish crusade, to rush back to the pit in the faint hope that Junior had not yet gone, taking Nisa with him. He found himself drawing great shuddering breaths, trembling with anger and grief. *No!* he told himself. *It's too late.* Junior would start up the wall as quickly as he could load the tram, and soon he would reach the sub and be away. With Nisa.

No, only one significant act remained to Ruiz; he could keep faith with Somnire. He could spite Roderigo and all the other monsters of Sook who lusted for the Machine. That would be no small accomplishment, after all. He smiled crookedly.

He forced his attention back to the problem at hand. "Well, all might not be lost. Can you take me to a vantage point? Where I can see and not be seen?"

The Gench thought for a dozen heartbeats. "We can observe the approaches to the Machine, though not the Machine itself. Come. We go by old ways."

"What were these, then?" Ruiz muttered under his breath, looking at the ancient trash that half-blocked the tunnel. He checked his oxygen level. To his horror, he saw that his reserve was down to fifteen minutes. How had so much time passed? He switched off the flow, so that he would have one more chance to clear his head, should the visions overwhelm him at some crucial point. He took one last breath of clean air, and then opened his armor's vents.

The stench was too intense to be interpreted by the parameters of ordinary stenches. Ruiz gagged; then the impulse passed and he saw the universe slip sideways, twisted by the mindfire. There was a moment of terrible strain. Then reality tore into ragged scraps and blew away . . . to reveal the universe's new face.

The dull red walls of the tunnels now shimmered in a thousand subtle shifting luminescences, as beautiful as a fire opal. The darkness of the side tunnels seemed velvety, full of possibilities both good and ill—but all intriguing. He looked down at his armored hands and was amazed by the cold beauty of the machined metal. The ready-lights of his weapon twinkled like little gems. A lovely blue light hazed the barrel of the ruptor. The Gench alone seemed little altered, its squat ugliness a sour presence in the midst of the sudden beauty that filled the tunnel. Even the trash exhibited a compellingly rich texture, a tangle of meaningful shape and color.

"Are you able to go on?" said the Gench, and Ruiz woke to a sense of passing time. Urgency seized him.

"Yes," said Ruiz. He keyed the channel to Nisa's clone. "Are you there?" he asked.

"I'm here," she answered instantly. Her voice, always sweet, now seemed the most unendurably beautiful music Ruiz had ever heard. He felt his eyes filling.

He shook his head, shut his eyes, and forced his mind to cold purposefulness. "Listen. I've opened my armor; now I must depend on your eyes to show me what is true. If you observe me in erratic behavior, tell me what the camera shows you, since I'll probably be seeing something that isn't there—maybe my fear made visible, maybe the things the Gench believe about themselves and their servitors. Maybe events that have happened in this place—some of them long, long ago. Do you understand?"

"Yes."

"Good. Record everything, but broadcast nothing until I tell you to do so."

There was a pause, and Ruiz imagined her consulting with the Deepheart technicians to be sure she could do as he asked. "All right," she said.

Ruiz resisted the urge to take a deep breath, and moved off, following the Gench.

It led him away from the inhabited tunnels, down through rough twisting passages rich with antiquity and strangeness. The red bioluminescence was very low in these unused tunnels, as if perhaps the organisms that gave the light fed on the stink of the habitations and were here starved for sustenance.

The Gench seemed to move less surely in these places, as though the pheromonic network were less intact here, and Ruiz occasionally drew a breath of purer air, so that his head cleared a bit.

They came to a place where the roof lifted away, and the tunnel widened into an echoing cavern. Crumbling ledges rose to either side; Ruiz soon identified them as the risers of an amphitheater. The ledges were oriented toward the far side of the dark chamber, and Ruiz strained his eyes, trying to make out a huge ominous shape that loomed there.

Abruptly he became aware of activity to each side, of rustles and soft footfalls and the sighing sound of many people breathing. He glanced up into the risers and saw dim silhouettes moving there, hundreds of them. He stopped and crouched, weapon ready. "Who are they?" he asked in a quivering voice.

The Gench stopped and its eyespots floated around to focus on Ruiz. "No one is here, Ruiz Aw."

"I see no one either," said Nisa's clone.

Ruiz slowly straightened up . . . but the illusion persisted that he shared the cavern with a great crowd.

"What is this place?" he asked the Gench.

"This is the place where the Orpheus Machine was born," it answered.

Ruiz moved forward a step. At the far end of the cavern an unhealthy green light gathered into dripping clots. Gradually it illuminated a massive object.

The Orpheus Machine was as tall as four men, and ten meters wide. Its facade was in the semblance of a great face, but the features moved with an independent life, a pulsing crawling animation. At first Ruiz couldn't see why that should be so; he could only see the expression on the face, a sort of sly scheming lunacy.

He moved a little closer, and now he could see the source of the movement. The Machine's facade was a mixture of limbs and torsos, all knit together into those dread-

ful features. Here and there under that hideous crust of
flesh, a metal substrate glinted through.

What Ruiz had at first taken for wrinkles were the divi-
sions between the body parts. There was a certain symmetry and purposefulness to the design; it had none of the
casual stuck-together quality that marked the mutilations
the Gench servitors wore. As he approached, he began to
see the logic of the design. The cheekbones were a knotty
mass of arms, the muscles clenching nervously. The forehead was a horizontal striation of long smooth feminine
legs. The eyes were a pointillist design made up of thousands of real eyes—pale blue eyes for the sclera and black
for the pupils—and each blinking eyeball glowed with a
disorienting awareness. The lipless mouth gaped open in a
loose grin, and Ruiz saw that its teeth were the blond
shaggy heads of children, lolling in some ugly ecstasy.

Here and there on the face were patches of Gencha
skin, bristling with sensor tufts.

Ruiz felt terribly ill. To see the Orpheus Machine was to
want to destroy it, and he wondered how it had survived
for so many centuries. And then he wondered who had
made it.

He must have spoken aloud, because the Gench answered in its whispery voice. "A religious impulse—an aspect of human behavior I don't pretend to understand.
When we first divined that Sook would one day become a
human world and took humans from the surface to mold
into servitors, they fell prey to many madnesses. This was
one—an attempt to synthesize a cyborg containing both
human and Gencha elements. To make a god. They succeeded, to some extent. We theorize it was because they
didn't understand the impossibility of such a thing. . . .
Here they made the Machine, and here they first wor-
shiped it."

Ruiz's hands tightened on his ruptor. He told himself
over and over that he was looking at an illusion, a memory
of things long dead.

The Machine smiled even more widely and said, without
moving its lips, "Am I?" The voice would have been deep

and resonant had it not been so faint; Ruiz could feel it in his bones.

The tiny sound woke such a depth of loathing in Ruiz that his hands shook and he half-raised the ruptor.

"No!" warned the Gench. "Resist the illusions. The Machine's ghosts work to confuse you. If you lose control, you will alert the soldiers your enemy has placed in ambush at the entry to the real Machine's sanctum. Or your weapon may collapse the ceiling. The servitors refuse to maintain these passages—the ghosts afflict them also."

"Yes," said Ruiz, and lowered the ruptor. He moved toward the face, and with each step some hideous new monstrousness revealed itself. When he was very close, the face opened in a silent gloating scream, and the small heads that lined the jaws turned to look at him. They glared at him with mindless ferocity, their little sharp teeth snapping in an irregular rhythm.

"Too much," said Ruiz faintly. He purged the atmosphere of his armor with pure oxygen and closed his vents. He took deep breaths, trying to clear his lungs of the mindfire.

The Machine slowly faded, though not entirely, becoming a transparent, static image, dimly glowing, no longer threatening.

Ruiz thought about what the Gench had said and switched on his spotlight. He looked up at the roof of the cavern and discovered sagging slabs of meltstone and alloy, held up precariously by two central alloy pillars, which had corroded badly.

"Let's go," he said, and stepped through the ghost of the Machine, which broke around him into a tatter of pale streaming color.

The Gench led him through an arch at the cavern's far end, and then up a narrow staircase. Ruiz saw that his oxygen reserve was down to nine minutes; he shook his head and reluctantly opened his vents. He suffered an instant of vertigo, but no new horrors assailed him through the hallucinatory shimmer.

He didn't look back at the spot where the Machine had been.

At the top of the stairs, the Gench indicated a row of dark alcoves spaced along a narrow gallery. "Look carefully," it whispered.

Ruiz entered the nearest, moving cautiously. At the end of a short tunnel, a meter-wide opening glowed. He crept up to it and peeked through.

Below him a maze filled a vast cavern. The light was hotter and brighter—more orange, more energetic than the light of the tunnels. The thick meltstone walls, each a little higher than a tall man, rippled outward from a low central building. Corridors twisted and turned in confusing patterns, but from above, Ruiz could see that three paths led inward, from three separate arches in the perimeter of the cavern. Lying atop the walls at two of the entrances were armored men. Both men held weapons ready, all their attention concentrated on the arches. To Ruiz's drugged eyes, they seemed like icons of ambush, dire and monstrous. He wanted to laugh at their unknowing vulnerability.

Beside him the Gench whispered, "The slaver's mighty bug waits in a niche just inside the third way."

Ruiz considered. "Will we be interrupted by hordes of bloodthirsty Gencha? Or servitors?"

"No," answered the Gench. "We are not a physical race, and the servitors have all fled to the farthest holes of the enclave. They cannot understand this conflict among their gods."

"I see," said Ruiz. He forgot where he was and took a deep breath, attempting to calm himself, but the act charged his brain with distorted visions, and the armored men seemed to multiply, so that the maze was suddenly crowded with enemies.

Ruiz turned away and switched his oxygen back on. He fumbled with his weapons rack, then gathered the elements of a heavy pinbeam—identical to the one Junior had chosen to carry as a primary weapon. *An assassin's tool,* Ruiz thought, inexplicably contemptuous.

His mind cleared a little as he assembled the thing.

In the pinbeam's multiplier scope, the first soldier's image swelled until Ruiz could set the cross hairs on his neck bellows—the weakest area of the Deltan's armor. At first the man's hunched shoulder blocked the most vulnerable surface of the armor. Ruiz waited until the man shifted slightly, and then he drilled the beam through armor and vertebrae. The man slumped silently.

Ruiz shifted his aim to the other soldier and killed him with even less effort. He felt strongly the new sickness that filled him each time he committed an act of violence, the sickness that had taken root in his heart during his stay on Roderigo. He pulled the pinbeam from the opening, gasping. Slowly it penetrated his consciousness that an alarm was buzzing. He looked at the oxygen gauge. Empty. He opened his vents and let the mindfire back into his brain.

"It knows. She knows," said the Gench.

COREAN STOOD BEFORE the beautiful corrupt face of her Machine, listening to the wonderful things it was saying to her, breathing in the mindfire that filled the Machine's temple, glorying in her power. She had run out of oxygen some time before, but so far she felt no severe skewing of her perceptions.

The servitor Soosen had long since run away terrified, and Corean had seen no one since.

The Machine spoke in its own sonorous voice: "You will clone an army of Ruiz Aws and go forth to rule the worlds. Who could stand before you? Who?" It opened its mouth wide and the little skulls that lined its jaws sang a pure soprano refrain: "Who . . . ?"

But then the mouth snapped shut and all its eyes flared with hallucinatory terror. The eyes flickered from side to side, and the Machine began to turn away from her on its hundreds of feet.

"What is it?" She felt a panic as fierce as her exultation had been a moment before.

"He's here somewhere. Close," said the Machine, lumbering toward its innermost shrine, a hollow lump of monomol in the center of its temple. "Your enemy. He seeks my blood and yours."

"Where? Don't you know?" Corean backed away from

the arch that led into the temple, expecting to see Ruiz Aw, triumphant.

"No. But he's killed your two soldiers." The Machine scuttled into its shrine and crouched down. The shrine resembled a huge squat hat, and to Corean's drugged perceptions, the Machine now became the head of some gigantic monster, temporarily buried neck deep in the alloy floor of the temple. Its thousands of eyes glittered out at her from the darkness inside the shrine. She willed it to rise up and defend her.

"Protect me!" she demanded.

"I cannot," said the Machine. "My volition is a feeble thing. My great weakness is that I must obey the being who is physically closest to me. Is this not absurd? If you lose me to Ruiz Aw, he will be my master. Set your bug on him —quickly, before he can reach me."

She ran toward the shrine, shouting for her Moc. She stood for a moment outside the shrine, hesitating. Some remaining human part of her wanted very badly not to go inside. But that part of her died quite suddenly, and she went to crouch in the decaying embrace of her Machine. The Machine cycled the protective blast doors shut.

She looked down through the grating under the Machine, into the small sump that fed the Gencha elements of the Machine. Cilia dropped into the slime, roiling the bones and undissolved gobbets of flesh; somehow it seemed inappropriate that the Machine should be feeding, even as Ruiz Aw pursued her. "Stop that," she snarled, and the Machine retracted its cilia. It chuckled, oddly enough.

Then her Moc was outside, moving around the shrine in a flickering evasive pattern.

"Ruiz Aw is here," she shouted. "Kill him."

And the Moc was gone.

CHAPTER 23

"WHAT'S going on?" asked Ruiz. "Where's the Moc?"

The Gench shuddered, heaved its bulk forward, tentacles questing. Ruiz drew back from the glistening filaments; they made him terribly nervous, even though he believed in the Gench's sincerity.

"I cannot say for sure. The opposing faction sends confusing messages over the pheromonic net."

"Wonderful," said Ruiz sourly. "My life—not to say the future of the human race—hangs on the outcome of a Gencha farting contest. Why am I not more astonished?" He felt a wild laugh bubble up into his lungs; frightened, he choked it off.

"There." The Gench gestured and Ruiz looked.

The Moc flickered along the edge of the maze, its natural speed exaggerated by Ruiz's distorted vision. He hoped it couldn't see him in the darkness of the alcove above the maze, because in his present state he was absolutely certain to die in any direct confrontation with the uncanny thing. He jerked his head down and spoke to Nisa's clone. "What did you see?"

"Corean's giant bug, running along the edge of the maze. Why didn't you kill it?"

Ruiz groaned and felt a paralyzing fear—it seemed to suck all the strength from his legs. His imagination ran wild; he saw the Moc killing him in a dozen painful ways. He squeezed his eyes shut—which, he realized sluggishly, was a mistake. In the absence of competing vision, the hallucinations became a great deal more vivid.

He opened his eyes wide. "Is there another way in? To this old place?"

The Gench turned to him. "Yes. Below. At the end of the corridor that crosses the back of this place is a door, long frozen in its sill."

"Can you notify me of something at a distance? Send me a vision?"

"Yes—though not a powerful one. But something. All our faction's strength is devoted to repressing the madness the majority sends against you. They will not expect us to send you a small piece of insanity." Then the Gench drew its small transceiver from one of its mouths. "But why not use this?"

Ruiz repressed another gust of wild laughter. "Why not? Well, when the Moc is at least halfway to the far side of the maze, let me know. I'll give you a channel." He took the transceiver, keyed in a scrambled frequency, and fed in the proper decoding parameters. "And just so there'll be no mistake, send me a vision too. Something that has meaning for us alone; do you understand?"

"Possibly," said the Gench, accepting the transceiver.

RUIZ TROTTED DOWN the staircase, the mindfire burning him. The ghost of the Machine squatted at the foot of the steps, looking up hungrily. As Ruiz grew near, the Machine grinned and stuck out a tongue. Ruiz saw that the tongue was a mass of intertwined arms . . . and all the hands beckoned languidly.

Ruiz forced himself to run through the ghost, and he

kept his eyes half-closed, ready to ignore any horror that might appear in the interior of the ghost. As he passed through, he heard a faint resentful voice say: "Rude boy."

He went down the central aisle, to the first of the two pillars, to which he attached a limpet mine, set for remote detonation. When he had mined the other pillar, he went to the back of the amphitheater and found the corridor that led to the maze.

He stopped before the door, which was a mass of ancient corrosion. He checked the contents of his explosives pouch, found that he had a half-dozen mines left. He needed to save enough to destroy the Machine—if he ever got close to it. Reluctantly, he took one out and set it for a low-yield explosion, then locked it to the door. Would it open the door without bringing down the roof? He looked up, and his drugged senses showed him the roof in unsteady movement, as if it were already settling toward him. It was so real a perception that he huddled back against the door, cringing.

"Ruiz Aw," said the Gench's whispery voice through his helmet speaker.

"Yes?" He looked down at his feet, trying to focus on something other than the collapsing roof.

"The bug is checking the first of your kills. Is that far enough?"

Ruiz resisted the impulse to take a deep breath. "I hope so," he said. "Weren't you going to show me something?"

"If you say I must, then I will."

In the center of the amphitheater, a shape swirled into existence. It coalesced into a huge but familiar face. Ruiz recognized the vulpine features of Publius the monster maker, who smiled gently and horribly at him, and then looked down at the ghost of the Orpheus Machine with a great evil wistful longing.

"All right," said Ruiz. "All right." The face broke apart and dissipated in dim streamers. Ruiz set the mine's timer and ran away as fast as he could, willing himself not to look up at the roof, or to think of all that weight above him, the kilometers of meltstone and alloy.

When he was halfway back to the stairs, the mine at the

door detonated, and in the fading roar he listened for the grinding sound of collapse. It didn't come, but by the time he reached the foot of the stairs, another terrible sound came to him—the scrabble of the Moc's claws, as it forced its way through the demolished door. Even the ghost of the Machine turned to look, so that he didn't have to endure its regard as he ran through it.

He climbed up a few treads, then turned as the Moc broke through with a clattering crash. As he stabbed at the controller slate on his forearm, he caught sight of a blur moving away from the amphitheater's back.

The mines fired with a flat crack; the explosions blasted the bases of the pillars away, as though invisible hands had jerked them apart.

The Moc paused for an instant and then streaked forward. The roof fell toward it, so slowly that Ruiz was suddenly sure that the Moc would outrun gravity.

The great insectoid seemed to fill the world; Ruiz could see nothing else. He tried to get off a shot from his ruptor, but the Moc dodged so artfully that his shot went nowhere close.

He felt all the strength leave his legs. He was starting to sag toward the stairstep when a falling slab finally caught the Moc and took it down. Dust exploded upward, but not before Ruiz saw that the slab had crushed one of the Moc's lower legs, and that more stone was falling toward the creature, which jerked and mewled, trying to get loose.

When the dust parted briefly again, Ruiz saw that a layer of stone two meters deep covered the amphitheater's floor, and that nothing seemed to move beneath it.

THE MACHINE WAILED, as if from a hundred different throats. Corean held her hands over her ears. "What is it?" she cried. The ground trembled and a deep rumble rose and fell.

"He's killed your bug. Oh, he's too strong, too strong. I feel my mortality on me." It wailed again, a sound that sent shudders through Corean's body.

"Shut up," she said. It did. "He won't destroy you as long as I'm here."

It laughed hideously, until she shrieked at it to stop.

"WHAT NOW?" RUIZ asked himself. He looked down at the maze from the alcove. Nothing moved below, except for the walls, which swam in the slow hallucinatory dance of the mindfire.

"Your enemy cowers with the Machine, beneath its armored hat. You must extract her before you can set your charges."

"How?"

"You must devise a suitable scheme. Is this not your great skill?" The Gench spoke dispassionately.

"No," said Ruiz. "My great skill was less admirable; the schemes were only means to that end."

"Nonetheless," said the Gench. "Examine your past dealings with the slaver. What deceptions have worked with her before? Humans rarely live long enough to learn from their mistakes."

"I've lived a long time," said Ruiz, somewhat resentfully. He tried to concentrate, to shut out the shimmering illusions of the mindfire—though he dared not close his eyes.

To his surprise, an idea came to him. It was a dangerous idea, and it depended on Corean's foolishness, but it had one great advantage: If it failed, he would cease to suffer.

"Tell me," he said to the Gench. "Are you capable of lying to the Machine?"

The Gench failed to respond, for long moments. Ruiz had begun to search for new ideas, when it finally spoke. "Possibly. Can you believe the lie? Will you allow me to take your reason, for a time?"

Ruiz turned to look at the Gench, and considered what a monstrous alien thing it was. Its eyespots grew still, ceasing their endless circulation over the lumpy skull.

"Why not?" he said. He heard Nisa's clone take a sudden gasping breath.

•   •   •

COREAN LOOKED OUT through a slit in the Machine's inner shrine, clutching her splinter gun in sweaty hands. She had almost grown used to the loathsome bulk of the Machine nearly touching her back.

"Does he come, yet?" asked the Machine in a throaty whisper.

"No," she said, but as she spoke, she heard Ruiz shout in his cold deep voice. "Don't shoot," he said from some hiding spot just inside the maze. "I've been captured. I'm coming out, with my captor."

The Machine laughed fearfully. "Kill him the instant you get a clear shot."

"Yes," she said. She slung the splinter gun and armed the big ruptor strapped to her left arm—if Ruiz Aw stood still and allowed her a shot at a perpendicular surface, the ruptor would be powerful enough to penetrate his armor and turn his chest to slush.

"All right," she shouted, repressing glee.

He stepped from concealment, and for the first moment she could not react. It was like the culmination of a lovely dream. He stood in plain view, motionless, arms crossed over his head, apparently weaponless. The faceplate of his helmet was tipped up, exposing his dark features. A Gench sidled out from the maze, close behind Ruiz Aw. The mindfire threw Ruiz into a burning white glare, a light that showed him to her in all his predatory glory.

His face was full of an alien emptiness, she noticed, as she settled her ruptor's sights on his vulnerable beautiful head. Her finger was tightening on the trigger.

She was so full of a transcendent relief, so glad that she was going to survive, that she almost didn't notice the tendril that penetrated Ruiz Aw's temple. She almost killed him. Then she saw the tendril and jerked her finger out of the trigger guard.

The Gench had him. It was true. She laughed, triumph washing her fear away. She turned to the Machine, just to be sure. "Is it true? The Gench controls him?"

"Maybe. Yes, it seems so. But take no chances; kill him

while you can." The Machine's foul breath made her head swim.

She heard the words and took from them the sense she wanted, though there was in them an echo of another person's words, words which she had once bitterly regretted disregarding.

"Oh no," she said joyfully, and went out to claim him.

RUIZ STOOD DUMBLY, watching Corean Heiclaro emerge from the Machine's monomol shrine. He couldn't see her face—just the bright glitter of her eyes through the narrow armorglass slot of her helmet. He hadn't been so close to her since the day she had loaded him aboard the airboat, so long ago, in the Blacktear Pens.

He felt like a powerless insect, caught in some thick amber nightmare. How had this happened? How had he been so easily caught? He couldn't remember, and the mindfire pulsed through him, hot and thick, frustrating his attempts to think.

She stopped before him, her splinter gun raised cautiously. "How sweet," she said, in a voice that trembled with joy. She reached up and touched his cheek with a cold metal gauntlet.

He couldn't answer.

She spoke to the Gench who had apparently captured him. "Come, monster. We'll take him right to the Machine and make him safe." She looked at Ruiz again. "Strange that it should end exactly the way I had planned it to end—but after so much pain, so much frustration." She gestured sharply with her splinter gun. "Come, I said."

The Gench made a hissing sound of negation. "I must see your face. Thus am I instructed by those who Become. Much trickery is afoot. We must know that you are the same woman whose soul we touched before."

She took a step backward, then another. "You may not touch me again. Trickery *is* afoot." She paused for a moment. "But I will show you my face."

Slowly she unlatched her helmet and then pulled it off, cradling it in the crook of her elbow. She shook back her black hair. The splinter gun was for a moment directed elsewhere.

Ruiz felt a tiny cold sting as the tendril withdrew from his brain. Just before it broke free, he heard a voice speak with the power of a god. "Slay," it said, and the order boomed along his nerves and muscles.

At the same instant, the Machine shrieked, a high grinding sound of despair.

Corean's eyes grew wide as Ruiz launched himself toward her. He moved in a red merciless dream, his self still hidden away somewhere far from harm.

HE CAME TO himself, kneeling there in the Machine's throne room, his gauntlet twisted in Corean's silky hair, his knee against her back, forcing her down. Her arms beat against the floor as she tried to throw him off, and her sonic knife flared and buzzed, trying to reach him. In his hand he held a splinter gun, and it descended, as if it had a will of its own, to press against the back of her skull. But for some reason he could not pull the trigger.

He could hear the thin screams of Nisa's clone, like whispering terror in his ear. He wondered distantly what could be frightening her so, and he glanced up.

The Moc was driving toward him, dragging its injured leg, only slightly hampered by the damage.

Time slowed.

Ruiz opened his mouth to scream, though at the same instant he knew the Moc would kill him before he could make a sound.

A blur slid into his field of vision and passed across the Moc. The great insect pivoted violently, as the blur chopped through its good leg. With a whistling shriek the Moc fell on the blur, which slowed and revealed itself to be an armored man.

There was a flurry of struggle, and then the thumping report of a ruptor. The Moc heaved and broke apart at its segmented waist. The pieces flailed aimlessly for a moment, and then the Moc's torso finished ripping the arms off the armored man. The arms came away with a dreadful tearing pop, and there was suddenly a lot of blood on the floor.

This instantaneous sequence of events seemed to take a very long time, but finally Ruiz began to react.

His finger jerked against the splinter gun's trigger, but his hand twitched the muzzle aside, so that the spinning wires bounced off the floor in a flare of pink sparks. Corean screamed and convulsed. She almost bucked Ruiz off, but he struck down with the barrel of the gun, hitting her behind her ear, and she went limp. He ripped her ruptor loose, flung it across the floor, and leaped up.

By the time he reached the remnants of the Moc, it was trying to pull Junior's legs off, but its strength was failing and all it could do was twist at the joints. It had succeeded in turning one leg backward, but at Ruiz's approach its torso turned the clone loose and scrabbled around to face him. It started to crawl forward, but Ruiz fired the splinter gun, holding down the trigger, so that destruction sleeted through the insectoid.

The wires chewed the Moc's head off and blew the carcass across the floor, to fetch up against the wall with a crunch.

The legs continued to wave feebly, but the creature was no longer a threat.

Ruiz knelt by Junior's torn corpse, careful not to slip in the blood. He unlatched the helmet gently, though he was sure that Junior was far beyond pain. He was therefore shocked, when he exposed the white face, to see life still in the opaque black eyes, and a small smile on the blue-lipped mouth.

He jerked a medical limpet from his rack and started to activate it.

"Don't be a moron, Ruiz Aw," said his clone. "Even if you could keep me alive for a while, how would I climb out of here with no arms?" The clone tried to laugh, but the attempt came out a wheezy gasping sound.

Ruiz shook his head, denying the obvious truth of this.

"Just listen to me for a bit," said the clone, his chest heaving, his breath rasping.

It was the sound of a dying body, a sound Ruiz had

heard a thousand times before. He wondered, his thoughts moving slowly and painfully, why it was affecting him so, now. Then he remembered: *This dying body is mine . . . and I'm full of mindfire.* "Sure," he said, his useless hands knotted together. He refused to imagine what it must be like for his clone, the pain heightened and focused by the mindfire.

The clone's back arched, and he made a sound halfway between a sigh and a moan. "No, no, wait, wait a minute," he said.

He fixed pleading eyes on Ruiz. "Listen to me," he said. "You've sinned, you've been a great monster in your life, but you've died for your sins. See? See how it is? Like Nisa did, remember? You're clean now. Now."

Fluid bubbled in the clone's throat. "Now you're clean," said the clone in a gentle reflective voice. "And you can . . . you can . . ." Then he died.

The only sound Ruiz heard was the low sobbing sounds that Nisa's clone was making, a sorrowful music coming down the link.

He looked down at his dead self for a time, wondering. Why had Junior come back? Surely he must have understood the probabilities of the situation—that at best he would be saving his rival for Nisa's love, that at worst he would find an ugly death. Why?

After a while an explanation came to him. Junior had been duplicated in the uncomfortable cusp of Ruiz Aw's changed life, halfway between the cynical machine he had been for so long and the human being he was still becoming. His clone must have acted with only the dimmest understanding of the motives that now drove Ruiz Aw. But he *had* acted, and in an honorable and decent way. Ruiz felt a kind of twisted crippled pride . . . and a great sorrowing anger.

He got up and went back to Corean. He pulled a heat-sealer from his waist rack and temporarily melted the wrists of her armor together behind her back, just in case she was feigning unconsciousness.

He raised his eyes to the Orpheus Machine.

CHAPTER 24

A VERY strange sound came from the Machine's hiding place, a sound so strange that Ruiz at first could not identify it.

Then he understood that it was laughing, nervously and from a multitude of throats.

"Come out," Ruiz said. "Now!"

The laughter slid seamlessly into an eerie moan, but the armored door opened and the Machine came forth, edging into the light unsteadily.

Were it not so monstrous a thing, Ruiz might have been moved to pity. Its health had deteriorated; it was not the sleek horror it had once been. Wrinkled flesh sagged from its bones, and here and there meat had sloughed away from its metal chassis. Among the hundreds of feet that moved it, many were hanging dead and half-decayed, nothing but dragging bones and scraps of sinew. Even the metal was corroded, and only a few of the Gencha segments still showed active sensory tufts.

"What may I do for you, new master?" it asked in a voice that broke and bubbled.

A rustle behind him made Ruiz whirl—but it was only the Gench. Evidently the creature had survived the Moc's return, a fact which pleased Ruiz a little.

"Do not trust your eyes, Ruiz Aw," the Gench said. "The Machine is old, but still strong. Here in its lair, we cannot entirely suppress its power to project a semblance."

Ruiz shook his head. "What do you see?" he asked Nisa's clone.

"A hideous thing. I cannot begin to describe it . . . but it does not seem weak to me."

"Thank you." He stepped forward and slapped the first mine against the thing's chassis, triggered its lock-on barbs. They punched into the metal with a pneumatic clang, releasing a puff of vapor. The Machine screamed, a terrible many-voiced harmony.

Ruiz took out the next mine. "Don't move," he ordered.

"Oh, please, master," sobbed the Machine. "Don't do this foolish thing." Its tongue came out, and the hands patted entreatingly at Ruiz, leaving trails of slime on his armor.

"Please please," it said. "Don't take my poor miserable life, such as it is. I'm only a tool, like a gun or a mech; I can only do what I'm told. Monsters have ordered me to do monstrous work. Is that my fault? No! No!"

Ruiz fixed another mine to the Machine. The mindfire seemed to have thickened inside his skull, so that everything was too bright, too loud, too painful. "Is the mine attached to metal?" he asked Nisa's clone.

"Yes," she answered. "But the metal bleeds red. Does that matter?"

"No," said Ruiz.

"Oh please," said the Machine. "You're no monster; you could make a new universe with my help. Think! Think, please. What do you hate most? I see it written in your soul—you hate slavery. A monstrous institution, no question. I understand these things. Who is more enslaved than I?"

Ruiz felt a dizzy uncertainty, but he went on to another patch of bare alloy and set another mine. "You're wrong," he said through clenched teeth. "I'm as monstrous a person as you're ever likely to meet."

The Machine made a high squeal of terror. "Oh, stop," it implored. "No no no. You're missing the great opportunity of your life, throwing it away like so much garbage. You hate the Art League? Their commerce in humanity? We could crush it, set a thousand worlds free. Think!"

Ruiz raised his last mine, then lowered it. "It's too late, anyway," he said, thinking of the soldiers who fought far above.

"No, no. Not at all." The Machine's voice strengthened, became sure and sweet, swelled with confidence. "You're too tired to think straight; that's why you're trying to destroy humanity's best chance for happiness. Listen to me: I'm your hostage against those who will come; you've secured me against all your enemies. You'll have your finger on the trigger, you'll demand men to defend us, in exchange for my services. Whoever comes will be afraid to risk destroying me—they'll give us men. We'll make them safe forever; they'll be the beginning of our army. And you're clever, much brighter than the slaver Corean was. Such an idiot she was. Soon you'll best your enemies and we can get on with making the universe free."

"Roderigo first," said Ruiz slowly, staring at the last mine, but not seeing it. Instead he saw worlds throwing off their ancient chains, rising into the sunlight of a new age. The mindfire consumed him, and lovely visions filled his universe: the laughter of freed slaves, the smiles of children, humanity sailing the void between the stars, safe and certain. He saw the wounds of humanity heal, the lifeblood no longer draining from humanity's heart.

He saw Gejas the Tongue, begging for mercy, begging to keep his soul, and he saw Ruiz Aw laughing and tearing it from his enemy. He closed his eyes, so as to see this prophecy more clearly.

He felt bright laughter well up in his chest. "Beautiful," he said.

"Yes!" sang the Orpheus Machine. "And look! See who has come?"

Ruiz turned to the arch. His heart thumped. Nisa stood

there, looking lost. He remembered that he still wore his helmet; naturally she did not recognize him.

He reached up to unlatch the helmet. But a small voice spoke against the roaring joy that filled him.

He didn't want to listen, but the voice, though small and sorrowing, was insistent. "Ruiz?" it said. "Ruiz? What are you looking at? I don't see anything there. Ruiz?"

The joy turned cold and heavy within him, and Nisa's ghost wavered into a warm shimmer . . . and then was gone.

"You've gone much too far, Machine," Ruiz said grimly, and set his last mine.

The Orpheus Machine made a panicky gobbling sound, then broke into an unintelligible babble. The babble resolved gradually into desperate words. "An honest misstep. I was just trying to show you how we could bemuse your enemies, when they come. And what about *freedom*? Can you turn your back on the universe?"

"I think I must," said Ruiz.

"No! No, you can't!"

Ruiz stepped back from the Machine's despairing face and tuned the mines to the transmitter on his forearm, so that he could detonate them remotely. "I cannot be the Emperor of Everything," he said, regret filling his heart. "I'm much too much less than a god."

The Gench still waited patiently by the far arch. Ruiz beckoned, and it came slowly forward. "A favor; will you do me one?" he asked.

"If I can."

"You can." Ruiz went to Corean, who still seemed unconscious. He stripped off a gauntlet and put his hand to the pulse in her neck. It was slow and strong. He put the gauntlet back on, got a grip on the neck flange of her armor.

The Gench stood beside the Orpheus Machine, its tentacle already penetrating the Machine, just over its monstrous eye. The Machine was finally silent, great terrible face frozen in abject collapse.

Corean began to wake as Ruiz dragged her the last few meters to the Machine. She tried to struggle, but her welded wrists prevented any effective resistance. She looked up at Ruiz, and then at the Machine. He forced himself to look into her wide unbelieving eyes.

She said nothing, but her face shifted through a spectrum of disbelief, horror, and then silent white-hot rage.

Hardest of all for Ruiz to watch was her expression at the last, just before the Gench's tentacle slid into her brain. Between one heartbeat and the next, all her rage melted away, and most of her years, so that she looked very young. All her beauty came back to her, heightened unbearably by the mindfire.

She smiled, and it was clearly a smile of relief. She closed her eyes and her lips grew soft, as if for a kiss.

He turned away, sick.

GEJAS STILL HELD back the tide that rose outside Yubere's fortress. He had returned to the destroyer, where he was strongest, even though the destroyer's commander and a large portion of its crew had been killed in repelling a squad of Obelisk berserkers. The only thing that still kept the pirates out was the bitterness of the fighting between the various surviving factions. But during the last half hour the pirates had withdrawn, and Gejas worried that they were forming alliances against him.

The Roderigan reinforcements were approaching the city; that was the only bright spot in the picture. They would have already arrived, were it not for the Shard strictures against warships maneuvering in large groups.

In the lulls, Gejas spent most of his time by the screens, waiting for Ruiz Aw's next broadcast.

COREAN WAITED FOR him by the arch with the young Gench. Her face was mild and docile—though to Ruiz, still dazzled by the mindfire, she looked like a breathing corpse. She held her splinter gun carefully, and it took all of Ruiz's resolve to turn his back on her.

He spoke to Nisa's clone, slowly and carefully, so that she and the Deepheart techs would understand exactly what he required of them. "I'm going now, but I'll leave the camera. When I'm safely away, I'll blow the mines, so you can record the Machine's destruction. But I don't want you to broadcast the event for an hour . . . or until soldiers reach the bottom of the pit. The Gench will tell you if that happens. I'm hoping a delay will give us time to get away from the stack unnoticed. Do you understand?"

"Yes," she said, in a low shaky voice.

Ruiz remembered that this voice was Nisa's, whom he loved. He wanted to say something to ease her heart, but he seemed to have forgotten all the soft words he wanted to use. "Well," he said finally. "You're dear to me, now more than ever."

"And you to me," answered the clone, her voice breaking a little. She paused for a long moment. "I hope you find her. I hope you take her to a place where you can love each other well."

"Thank you," Ruiz said, inadequately. And finally: "Good-bye."

He took off his helmet and wedged it into a wall niche, where it could transmit a view of the Orpheus Machine's last moments—but at a vantage point from which his clone's torn body was not visible. He spoke a few words into the camera, then latched down the helmet he had taken from Junior's armor.

He gestured to Corean, who nodded and began to lead the way out of the maze.

As Ruiz passed the Gench, he looked at that alien creature and felt a cold gratitude. He glanced back at the Machine, and saw that it was touching the mines with its tongue, picking aimlessly and harmlessly at them, its voices merged into a low wordless drone.

At the far edge of the maze, he detonated the charges and felt the percussive thump of the explosion. The mindfire burned so bright for an instant that he was blinded and deafened. Then it faded, giving him back his senses.

Perhaps it was only the mindfire, but he felt a great and fatal emptiness beginning to spread through the enclave.

"Let's go," he said to Corean, his new machine.

• • •

COREAN LED HIM swiftly and silently back through the tunnels, and Ruiz was uninclined to speak to her, for fear that he would be even more horrified by the sensible but dreadful thing he had done. They met no living creature.

They passed the place where Junior had recaptured the Pharaohans, and Corean barely glanced aside at the corpses of her men.

Ruiz paused for a moment by the ugly remains of Molnekh, once a conjuror of the first rank on Pharaoh, but at the last only an organic machine belonging to a slaver. Ruiz wished the skinny mage had lived. Ruiz would have inherited Corean's property, and he would have tried the experiment suggested by Gunderd the Scholar . . . and ordered Molnekh to act as he might have acted on his own. To become himself, again.

"I'm sorry," he said. After a moment he went on.

When they reached the site of the battle between Junior and the servitors, Ruiz called a halt amid the pitiful bodies of the servitors.

They would shortly emerge into the central shaft of the stack, and if he was very lucky, he would find Nisa and the others waiting on the tram, guarded by the remnant of Corean's Deltan slayers. Presumably Junior had promised to take them to the sub in exchange for their assistance and loyalty.

He tried to weigh the situation, to follow where the tangled threads of betrayal led, to see where his best advantage lay.

He discarded an impulse to simply rely on the integrity of the Deltans and proceed with Junior's bargain. He laughed at himself for even thinking such a foolish thing. No, now was not a moment for trust.

"All right," he said to Corean. "This is what we'll do."

WHEN NISA FIRST caught sight of Ruiz Aw, she felt an incredulous joy. She had never expected to see him again—

she had been certain, somehow, that he was going to his death. His leave-taking had been so formal, so final.

When she saw who walked behind him, prodding him along with her gun, her joy turned sour, though it didn't entirely dissipate. At least he was alive.

But then she reconsidered. Perhaps Corean had taken his soul, as she had always meant to. No, Nisa decided, that was unlikely. Else why would the slaver be guarding him? And why would she have secured Ruiz's arms behind him, bent back at an uncomfortable angle?

The higher-ranking of the two armored soldiers stood. His tentative posture betrayed surprise. "Corean Heiclaro?" he asked tentatively, when Ruiz and Corean had reached the halfway point of the sump's causeway.

"Hello, Kroone," she answered. "I'm surprised to find you here, when I ordered you to stay in the enclave."

Kroone half-raised his weapon, then apparently thought better of his impulse. "An opportunity presented itself—the man you hold claims to know a way out. We intended to gain his confidence, disarm him, and wait for you."

"A good plan," Corean said dryly as she approached the tram. Nisa noticed that she prudently kept Ruiz between herself and the soldiers—apparently she was untrusting.

Kroone, shifting from foot to foot, looked as though he wanted to find some cover, too, but the tram offered nothing substantial. "Ah . . . what about the explosive in his helmet? What about the dead-man switch?"

"A bluff. He is clever." Corean's voice was weary, passionless. Nisa began to think that there was something wrong with the slaver.

Apparently Kroone reached the same conclusion, because in the next instant he snapped up his weapon and ignited a bright sparkling line of destruction. Nisa happened to be glancing toward him when he fired, and almost simultaneously Kroone flew backward as if struck by a fist. He smashed into the wall behind the tram and fell facedown, motionless.

The remaining soldier died just as swiftly.

Nisa was afraid to look at Ruiz, afraid that she would see him destroyed as thoroughly as the two soldiers had been. But when she finally turned back, he was rising from the ground, holding a huge weapon, which he had apparently concealed behind his back.

Corean holstered her weapon, from which vapor swirled, and then took off her helmet. Nisa saw the deadness in her face.

Ruiz came toward her slowly, as if he could not believe in Nisa's reality. "Are you really there?" he asked, voice muffled by his helmet and some wary potent emotion. But still . . . *his* voice.

"Yes," she said.

"Thank you," he said. He leaped aboard the tram and gestured at the slaver, a peremptory motion to which Corean instantly responded, boarding the tram and taking the other seat. Ruiz threw the lever and the tram gathered speed, sliding up the rail toward the darkness above.

NOT UNTIL THEY were all aboard the submarine, casting off from the air lock, did he finally remove his helmet. He was different again, she thought. His eyes were terribly weary, but somehow soft. His face seemed both older and more innocent.

"Hello," he whispered. "We must be very quiet." He pointed to the surface.

"Hello," she said. Her own eyes filled, so that his face was only a dark shimmer in the sub's red light. She smiled at him and touched his stubbled face. The smile spread from her mouth to her heart.

CHAPTER 25

Ruiz allowed the sub to drift with the deep cold currents, content to escape slowly and silently. From the sea above them came explosions and hissing jet drives and the metallic agony of sinking vessels as the sea crushed them.

Dolmaero had patted his back and squeezed his hand, broad face shining with the pleasure of their escape. Even Flomel, whose treachery and arrogance had given Ruiz so many difficulties, nodded and gave him a small but seemingly genuine smile.

He sent Corean to a dark corner, so that he wouldn't have to look at his handiwork. "She's harmless, now," he whispered to the Pharaohans.

While he waited for the sub to drift clear of the battle, he watched Nisa, who returned his regard with identical concentration. Occasionally he checked his chronometer, waiting for the time when the Machine's destruction would be broadcast.

Ten minutes before that moment, he judged it safe to start his engines. He pushed away from SeaStack with all the speed he could muster. Gradually he brought the sub closer to the surface, where he could further increase the speed with which they fled SeaStack.

When Ruiz Aw's face appeared on the screen, Gejas Tongue dropped what he was doing and gave all his attention to the slayer's cold dark face. He noted that the slayer's eyes shimmered with the mindfire's madness, and he thought, *Ruiz Aw isn't enjoying himself.*

The small pleasure of that perception evaporated as Ruiz Aw began to speak. "Listen, people of SeaStack. I promised to destroy the Orpheus Machine; I'm about to honor that promise." He stood aside slightly, so that Gejas could see something dreadful behind him.

The dreadful thing wailed and swayed, but Ruiz Aw's voice rose above that noise. "In a few moments the Orpheus Machine dies. You may not believe the evidence of this broadcast—but the Gencha will allow you to verify this event. So send observers, unarmed, and the Gencha will escort them to the remains of the Machine. There will be very little left, not enough for analysis, so abandon your dreams of domination. It's over."

Ruiz Aw stepped out of the picture, leaving Gejas to look at the Machine.

A minute or two passed, but Gejas failed to notice the passage of time. He was waiting for Ruiz Aw to return, to explain the *real* situation.

When the mines detonated, and he watched the Machine dissolve into scrap metal and shattered flesh, Gejas at first could not understand what he had seen.

A few minutes trailed by. The sounds of battle faded, until he was alone with his thoughts and his failure. His heart had turned into a small hard stone. He remembered The Yellowleaf. Her beauty and strength. The ugliness of her death.

His thoughts ran in shrinking circles, full of raging sorrow. Ruiz Aw had slain a god. No matter what else, Ruiz Aw must not be allowed to escape, to go unpunished. Gejas could not delay; Ruiz Aw was at this moment climb-

ing out of Hell. He must act, to preclude any possibility of
Ruiz Aw's survival.

Running as fast as he could, Gejas descended to the
destroyer's engine room, where the black gang maintained
the fusor that powered the ship. He approached the fusor's
control panel and began to nudge the fusor toward instability.

After the technician on duty tried to stop him, he killed
the man without really noticing the act.

He charmed away the safeguards one by one. When the
reaction trembled over the line into irretrievability and the
alarms rang continuously, he had time for one last smile.

AS THEY PASSED through SeaStack's abandoned perimeter,
Ruiz had released a tiny sensor buoy, which trailed on a
filament just under the surface. Occasionally Ruiz checked
the buoy for evidence of pursuit.

He happened to be watching when the image turned
white and then failed. A few moments later a shock passed
through the water they traveled through, a sensation somehow different from any other they had felt beneath the
battle. The hull rang, a pure bell-like sound.

"What was that?" Ruiz muttered, amazed. He released
another buoy and looked back to see a great white cloud
hovering over SeaStack. Several of the stacks had collapsed; as he watched, another leaned slowly into the boil-
ing base of the cloud.

He noticed a number of small aircraft swirling around
the cloud, a swarm of angry insects. Shards.

"Oh, they're going to be angry," whispered Ruiz. He
hastily cut the sensor buoy loose, hoping he hadn't been
noticed, and took the sub down to a safer depth.

Some hours later, he surfaced and the sub fled across
the ocean on its foils, making rainbows of spray.

TWO DAYS LATER they reached the mouth of the Soaam
River, where they found a safe harbor and a buyer for the
submarine. The small market town of Boca del'Infierno

was abuzz with the news from SeaStack—and of the subsequent events on Roderigo.

"Just a hole burning in the sea now, Roderigo," said the plump innkeeper in whose pleasant establishment they stayed while Ruiz bargained for an airboat. "The Shards punished the hetmen severely, they did. They say the spot will steam for a year."

Ruiz shook his head in theatrical disbelief. "You don't say," he said, wide-eyed.

"I do indeed say," said the innkeeper with obvious satisfaction. "High time, too, if you ask me."

Ruiz could afford separate rooms for them—though his room adjoined Nisa's. He put Corean in Flomel's room, since he didn't quite trust the conjuror. "She's perfectly harmless," he told Flomel, who accepted the slaver's strange presence without protest.

He left the door to Nisa's room unlocked, and waited in an uncomfortable chair. He felt no urge to sleep, though he was very tired. Remembrance possessed him, and he thought back over all the strange events that had led his life to this place.

She came through the door an hour after midnight, carrying a tiny oil lamp, not unlike the one that Dolmaero had given him so long ago, to light the empty House of the Alone.

The warm glow lit her face and glimmered in the sleek darkness of her hair. She held out her hand.

He took it gratefully.

IN THE MORNING, after breakfast, Ruiz and Nisa went out into the square, to find Flomel performing sleights for a small audience of amazed yokels, while Corean watched silently. After a while Dolmaero came out, picking his teeth. The Guildmaster assumed an approving expression and watched Flomel's technique closely.

Flomel presented his tricks with many an elaborate flourish, and in his expressions Ruiz saw nothing but the pleasure of this familiar work. When he was finished, he came over to them, mopping sweat from his brow with a new silk scarf. "Ah, they know quality when they see it, for all their unsophistication. Eh?"

"I'm sure," said Ruiz.

Flomel smiled and then looked a bit uncertain. "I would ask a favor of you, Ruiz Aw."

"What?"

"I'd stay here, if I could."

"Certainly," said Ruiz. "But I think I can return you—and Dolmaero—to Pharaoh, if that is your wish."

Flomel looked faintly regretful, but then he shook his head. "If that's your plan, only a fool would doubt that you can do as you say—and I've decided to retire from foolhood. No, I feel no great urge to see Pharaoh again. I crave a less exciting life. This seems a quiet and unremarkable place. Perfect for me."

Ruiz nodded. "All right."

Flomel smiled, his hard narrow face full of light.

RUIZ BOUGHT AN old but well-maintained airboat, which carried them uneventfully to the Blacktear Pens, where Ruiz appropriated Corean's fine little starboat, the *Sinverguenza.*

The slaver's household had fallen into disarray during her absence, so Ruiz allowed her to retake control of her enterprises. Unfortunately, the remaining members of Dolmaero's troupe had disappeared, sold away or otherwise lost. For a while Ruiz feared that they would lose Dolmaero, too, who was at first inconsolable. Ruiz eventually distracted him with stories about the Art League and its manipulations of Pharaohan society, so that Dolmaero's sorrow soon evolved into a cold determined rage.

When Dolmaero and Nisa were safely aboard the starboat, Ruiz gazed at his former enemy, who waited dead-faced on the blackened alloy of the launch ring.

"There will be no more slaving for you," he said to her gently. "Set your properties free. Be as kind as possible. And when you have a chance to free someone, do it, as long as you're not destroyed in the process. Avoid violence.

Coerce no one who has not attacked you. Never bother me or any of my friends again."

He looked at her for a long time. For some reason he could feel no hatred for her—it would be as pointless as hating the dead. "Otherwise, live your life as you choose."

She nodded her understanding.

The horror of what he had done to her had become less immediate, and now he felt only a sense of cloudy accomplishment, as if he had set a useful machine into motion.

"Good-bye, then," he said unnecessarily. He went aboard the starboat and lifted away from Sook.

They fell past the Shard orbital platforms and set course for Pharaoh.

EPILOGUE

T HE three of them stood on the Worldwall in the dawn chill, looking down into the mists of Hell. Nisa leaned lightly against Ruiz's shoulder, making a spot of delicious warmth between them.

In the nearby castle, all the Watchers slept at their posts, tranquilized by a sudden swarm of Corean's mechanical wasps.

Dolmaero retained his ponderous earnestness, though he was much thinner than when he had left Pharaoh. "I don't understand," he said slowly. "How can you hide anything down there? Besides, why don't you just take the slaver's starboat?"

Ruiz smiled at the Guildmaster. "I'm fond of my own little ship; I couldn't leave her to rot. As for the *Sinverguenza* . . . well, I give it to you. Perhaps you'll become a famous star pirate."

Dolmaero snorted; his jowls quivered, as if he were suppressing laughter with some difficulty. "What will I do with a starboat? I cannot pilot it, and if I could, I wouldn't know where to take it."

"No difficulty there," said Ruiz. "The boat has a Bansh revenant for a pilot. You say 'Take me to Dilvermoon' and it takes you. Or 'Take me to Stegatum.' Or 'Take me to the palace.' If you don't know where to go, say, 'Where can we go, that has green seas, coconuts, and friendly natives?' Or 'Where can we go to sell a conjuring act into a limited contract? Where can we find a reliable bank?' Or, when you're ready, 'Where do we go to apply for membership in the pangalac worlds?' The ship will tell you anything you ask of it. Though I wouldn't rely upon it for political guidance."

Dolmaero made a grumpy sound. "You make it sound so easy."

"I don't mean to, Dolmaero. It will be very dangerous for you. You know who owns Pharaoh and to what purpose. If you go around preaching in the town squares, you'll disappear or end up in the Place of Artful Anguish."

"So what do you suggest?"

"Be sneaky; what else? Remember, your responsibility now extends beyond your guild. You're the man who must drive the League from Pharaoh. Revive the Cult of Saed Corpashun—now you can *prove* that humans travel the stars. Keep in mind all I've told you—about the spies among you, the surveillance gear, the orbital cameras. Especially, remember to use the anti-snooping gear Corean so graciously bequeathed you. Keep the boat cloaked all the time."

Dolmaero shook his head doubtfully. "You should stay, Ruiz Aw. Who is sneakier than you?"

Ruiz laughed. "I'm sorry. I'm finished with the wars, at least for a while. Other things concern me now." He looked at Nisa.

She rewarded him with a slow smile and a gentle nudge.

"Foolishness," said Dolmaero. "How can you ignore the plight of a world for the transitory delights of infatuation?"

Ruiz shrugged and looked at Nisa. "Isn't it obvious?" he asked.

Dolmaero shook his head disapprovingly, but his eyes were soft, and he almost smiled.

AFTER A WHILE, Ruiz picked up a stone and tapped a rhythm against the face of the Worldwall.

"I hope she's still there," he said. "I was away much longer than I thought I'd be."

Long minutes passed. Ruiz began to fear that the corrosive atmosphere of Pharaoh's burning lowlands had destroyed *Vigia*.

But then the mists swirled and bulged and *Vigia* broke through. She rose up the cliff to hover before them. She was ugly; a thick green crust covered her once-shining hull.

When the lock opened, some of the corrosion flaked away, revealing the gleam of undamaged alloy. The corrosion seemed superficial.

A ramp extended and touched the wall at their feet.

Dolmaero embraced Ruiz awkwardly. "Well," he said in a muffled voice, patting Ruiz's back, "I will wish you the finest luck. You did your best for me."

He turned to Nisa, bowed his tattooed head. "And the finest luck to you, Noble Lady. Though I wish you were not so devoted to Ruiz Aw. A princess returned from the dead . . . what a wonderful miracle that would make, to rally a world."

"Thank you," she said, and kissed his cheek. "My ambitions have become a great deal more modest—or ambitious, I'm not sure which."

"I do not blame you," he said.

WHEN THEY LIFTED away, Dolmaero stood waving from the top of the Worldwall. His sturdy figure too quickly grew small and disappeared.

The Worldwall became a snake crawling along the edge of Pharaoh, and then Ruiz couldn't look any longer.

He turned to Nisa. She watched her native world diminish, a look of tender ambiguity lighting her lovely face. "Good-bye," she said finally, and shut off the screen.

She took a deep breath. "So," she said, "what now?"

"We'll live. We'll dream. We'll have flowers. Slow days and long nights," he said, and covered her hand with his. "Flowers and time."

"A fascinating mix of technology and humanity, soaring high into the mysteries of the universe and far into the depths of the soul."—*Chicago Tribune*

The *New York Times* bestseller by
Arthur C. Clarke and Gentry Lee

■ THE GARDEN
■ OF RAMA ■

"A genuine achievement...A novel that is not only the most satisfying of the 'Rama' series, but far beyond anything we might have ever expected from either author."—*Locus*

By the twenty-third century, Earth has had two encounters with the massive, mysterious robotic spacecraft from beyond our solar system—the obvious handiwork of a technology that far exceeds our own. The first time we greeted a Raman vessel, it was with wonder. The second time, it was with weapons. Now, with three cosmonauts trapped on board, Rama II hurtles toward an unknown destination. Traveling together for twelve years, Nicole des Jardins, Richard Wakefield and Michael O'Toole have faced the perils of an alien craft on a seemingly endless voyage. But now it's becoming increasingly clear that the ship does have a destination, and that they may ultimately be coming face to face with the alien creators of the universe's most challenging mystery.

The next chapter in the dazzling saga of alien contact
The Garden of Rama
is now available in paperback, wherever
Bantam Spectra books are sold.

AN 429 8/92

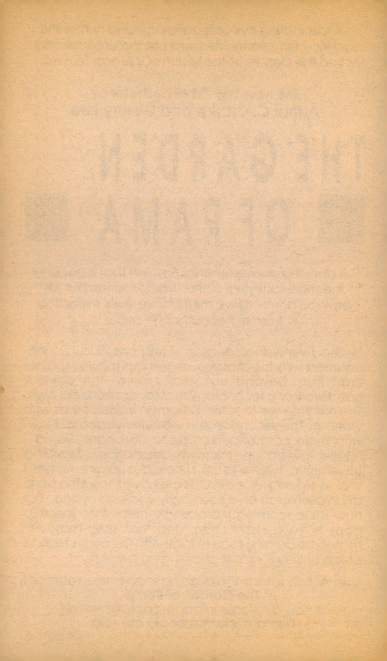

A dramatic new series of books at the cutting edge where science meets science fiction.

THE NEXT WAVE

Introduced by Isaac Asimov

Each volume of The Next Wave contains a complete novel and fascinating scientific essay about the same subject. And every volume carries an introduction by Isaac Asimov.

❑ **Vol. #1: Red Genesis** by S.C. Sykes
(28874-1 * $4.99/$5.99 in Canada)
The tale of a man who changed two worlds, with an essay by scientist Eugene F. Mallove on the problems of launching and maintaining a colony on Mars.

❑ **Vol. #2: Alien Tongue** by Stephen Leigh
(28875-X * $4.99/$5.99 in Canada)
The story of contact with a startling new world, with an essay by author/scientist Rudy Rucker on the latest developments in the search for extraterrestrial life.

❑ **Vol. #3: The Missing Matter** by Thomas R. McDonough
(29364-8 * $4.99/$5.99 in Canada)
An exciting adventure which explores the nature of "dark matter" beyond our solar system, with an essay by space scientist Wallace H. Tucker.

❑ **Vol. #4: The Modular Man** by Roger MacBride Allen
(29559-4 * $4.99/$5.99 in Canada)
Humanity tries to define what make something — or someone—human, with an essay by Isaac Asimov about the latest strides in robotics and artificial intelligence.

Available at your local bookstore or use this page to order.

Send to: Bantam Books, Dept. SF 160
2451 S. Wolf Road
Des Plaines, IL 60018

Please send me the items I have checked above. I am enclosing
$_____ (please add $2.50 to cover postage and handling). Send
check or money order, no cash or C.O.D.'s, please.

Mr./Ms._____

Address_____

City/State_____Zip_____

Please allow four to six weeks for delivery.
Prices and availability subject to change without notice.   SF 160 9/92